HARM

Kathy T. Kale

Harm

Published by
Pollux Press,
Fort Pierce, Florida

Library of Congress Control Number: 2014901640

ISBN 978-0-9836866-3-7

Disclaimer

This is a work of fiction. Names, characters, places, and incidents are either the product of the author's imagination or are used fictitiously. Any resemblance to actual persons living or dead, events, or locales is entirely coincidental.

Acknowledgements

Many excellent nonfiction books provided the factual background for the novel. In particular, G. Edward Griffin's *World Without Cancer: The Story of Vitamin B17* describes "how science has been subverted to protect entrenched commercial interests." Ellen Brown's *Forbidden Medicine* tells the shocking tale of the FDA's pursuit of a medical doctor who successfully treated cancer using alternative therapies. In an ongoing effort to "keep his clinic open, he faced raids and robberies, a near-fatal beating, a kidnapping, and a prison sentence many called justice gone wrong." Dr. Marcia Angell's book *The Truth About The Drug Companies* outlines in detail how the pharmaceutical industry has gained "nearly limitless influence over medical research, education and how doctors do their jobs." *Politics in Healing*, by legislator Daniel Haley, sheds light on the politicization of medicine and the effort to suppress promising anti-cancer drugs. *The $800 Million Pill* by Merrill Goozner and *On The Take* by Jerome P. Kassirer, MD, also expose a corrupt health care system whose costs far outweigh its benefits.

Many thanks to those who helped bring this book to fruition. I am especially grateful for the editorial efforts of Amber Barry, Jan Dawson, Ray Farrell, and Mark Springle, who examined the manuscript with a critical eye. Many thanks to my early readers: Ann Marie Montgomery, Mary Ferguson, Claudette Wingell, Ann Viljoen, Frances Kavanagh, and Ron Griffin. Thanks also to Mimi Alonso of Arista Graphics for the cover design.

This book would not be possible without the support of my husband, who read an early draft and offered much advice. I deeply appreciate my parents' endless enthusiasm for my projects. As always, my children, Will and Luc, inspire hope for a better future and a day when "health care" actually means what the words imply. In memory of Barb Swegles who died from accidental complications during preventative chemotherapy.

for Bill

First, do no harm.

– intent of the Hippocratic Oath

Chapter One

The thing that bugs me the most is that people think the FDA is protecting them—it isn't. What the FDA is doing and what the public thinks it is doing is as different as day and night.

—FDA Commissioner Herbert Ley

February 29

The upper-level suite in the upscale Prosperity Building said it all: Art Farber was finally on top. With the fall of his major competitor, Art's company was set to become the number one manufacturer of chemotherapy drugs in the country. He had to expand, think big, and a move was just the beginning.

Missy, the real-estate agent towering beside him, reeled off the selling features: twelve-foot-high ceilings, rare black marble floors, and teak trim imported from India. At twenty-nine, Missy was ambitious, both a digger and a climber, who reminded Art of his four ex-wives. Missy wanted the commission but flaunted the low interest rate. If Art assumed the terms of the current mortgage, he could lock in an excellent price.

He strode to the north-facing window and stared at a wall of skyscrapers on Broadway. He would be ramping up production and needed more space. Drug manufacturing could stay in the New Jersey warehouse, but top management would move. Production was set to double. Art made a four-drug cocktail that was used to combat a wide variety of cancers. It worked on leukemia, on tumors of the breast, pancreas, liver, skin, kidney, stomach, and colon; everything under the sun except brain cancer, thanks to the blood-brain barrier. The complete treatment involved thirty-two injections over an eight-week period and cost forty thousand dollars retail. With one out of four people dying from cancer every year, and with no end to the war in sight, he had a guaranteed market.

Missy stood at the doorway. "It won't last long," she said. "Not at this price. Not in this location."

He moved to the east-facing window and stared at his own reflection. He was sixty-two, soft in the middle, graying, and losing his hair. With lifts in his shoes he was five foot six, but he may have been shrinking. A life of stress, worry, and loss was taking its toll. He was lonely and alone, and Missy was keeping her distance.

"What about the top floor?" Art asked.

"The very top? That's pricey," she said, with a twinge of regret. She meant it was out of his stated price range.

"Show me." Art was a man who took risks, who bet on the future. He gambled on a deck stacked in his favor and trusted the power of money.

In the suite directly overhead, Art saw the same spacious rooms but also skylights and an outdoor terrace. There was no floor above him, no one stepping upon him, no one higher than him.

"There's nothing else like it in lower Manhattan," Missy said, eyes glittering. The short elevator ride had given her a new spark, bringing high color to her hollow cheeks.

They talked numbers. Wellspring Pharmaceutical was currently trading at $25.42, with analysts projecting $60 by year's end. Last year he made his investors nine billion. Company liability was low, and cash on hand was high. It would be tight, but he could swing it. With the recent IRS changes, Art had to either spend more money or pay more tax.

His financial disclosure made Missy giddy. "We'll negotiate hard, and I'll get you a good price." She moved closer, taking his arm.

Her long black hair smelled of vanilla. She was tall, over six feet, and he was eye level to her shoulder, which was rounded and milky white. Despite the damp February chill, she wore a beige sleeveless sheath and her long legs were bare. She didn't seem to feel the cold.

"The view makes a statement," she said, staring with him out the window. "You can see infinity. There's nothing in your way. You're on the top of the world." She turned and looked at him, raising one arched eyebrow. "What you see is yours for the taking."

He nodded, returning her eager smile. She was right; the building was impressive, the floor even more so. He could receive investors, government regulators, and important elected officials. He wouldn't have to show off balance statements or quarterly reports—the space spoke for itself. He caught her eye. "I'll take it."

She smiled broadly, revealing impossibly white, perfect teeth. "Then I say we have a drink to cinch the deal."

He glanced at his watch. It was six thirty. "Would you care to make it dinner?"

She reached for his belt. "Later. I'm hungry now."

Chapter Two

It was an hour earlier in Duane, on the dark side of dusk, and Cory Montclair was stuck in traffic. Stopped at a light, she glanced at her watch. Five forty. She was late already. Her eighteen-month-old daughter had to be picked up at day care by five thirty, and no tardiness was ever allowed. No unfortunate accident or unexpected trip to the hospital would warrant a pardon in the sitter's mind. Mrs. Pitt ran a tight ship and made no allowance for catastrophes. This was Cory's second late pickup this year, and she was on notice. She couldn't afford to lose the sitter. Mrs. Pitt was cheap—within the range of affordability of a single mother on a post-doctoral salary.

The light changed, and Cory shot forward. The college town in south-central Texas had a population of only sixty thousand, but the roads weren't designed for the state's recent growth. She inched her way north another block and reached the boundary of the bad side of town. The four-lane road turned to two, and the sidewalks disappeared. The asphalt was cracked and pitted, and traffic slowed further. Cory glanced at her watch. Five forty-five. Up ahead was an amber light. She gunned the accelerator, changed lanes, cut off a car, and ran the light, wincing as the bald tires on the old Volkswagen bug screeched.

She reached the sitter's just past six and zoomed into the driveway. She leapt out of the car, roared across the yard, and bounded up the steps. The inside door was closed, and she tried the handle—locked. She knocked. And waited.

Every day was like this. She had to leave work early and make a mad dash in traffic to be on time. It was a long day for Sophie too, and she screamed every morning when she was dropped off, crying inconsolably as Cory unwound the tiny hands from her neck and pried the legs from her hip. It was an agonizing but necessary arrangement for them both.

Finally, the hall light came on, the locks clicked, the chain banged, the door opened, and Mrs. Pitt stepped out. She was in her sixties, gray and heavy-set. She wiped her hands on a stained apron she wore over a polyester tracksuit. "You're late," she said coldly.

"I'm sorry. It won't happen again."

"That's what you said the last time. I told you, no more."

"There was an accident at work. A student was bitten by a rat and insisted on going to the emergency room. She wanted a tetanus—"

"I'm afraid our arrangement is no longer working," Mrs. Pitt said, interrupting.

"I had no choice. I would have sent the lab tech to the hospital, but she had to go to the hardware store and get a lock and a trap. The rat is loose. We can't let it escape. It's in a contamination lab. There was paperwork and—"

"The day ends at five thirty. Period. Seeing as you're a doctor, I'd think you'd get that simple fact."

"I'm not a medical doctor, and I do get it. I'm sorry."

"No one else is ever late."

But everyone else was married, and it was easier for one of two parents to make it on time. "It won't happen again."

"You're right; it won't. Sophie isn't coming back."

At the mention of her daughter's name, Cory noticed that Sophie was howling. Cory barged past the sitter and charged up the steps in the direction of the screams. The door to the room at the top of the stairs was closed, and she flung it open. Sophie stood in the crib in the dark room, crying. Dressed in her hat and winter coat, her face shone with tears. She was terrified of the dark. Cory vaulted across the room and swept Sophie up into her arms.

Sophie shuddered as heat radiated from her. Cory tore off her hat and unzipped the jacket. Sophie felt feverish. Her skin was clammy and hot, like it had been when she was dying. Cory hugged her tight, patting her back, wiping her face. "It's okay, it's okay, it's okay," she said, though it was not.

Behind her, from the doorway, the sitter cleared her throat. "I dressed her when the day ended. When she was supposed to leave."

Cory whirled around. "This is unacceptable."

"Precisely. Rules are rules, and a schedule is a schedule."

"I'm not talking about the time." Cory yelled so stridently that Sophie flinched.

Mrs. Pitt took a step back. "It doesn't hurt to cry. I raised five children, and I know what I'm doing more than you do."

"We won't be back."

"So I said. And there will be no refund."

Holding Sophie close, Cory swept past the grim-faced shrew and marched down the stuffy stairs. The air smelled foul, of burned grease. Cory stepped out into the clear night and took a breath of cold, fresh air. She smoothed Sophie's soft curls and kissed her warm skin.

The drive home was more relaxing. Cory cranked the radio and aimed the rearview mirror at the backseat so she could keep a close eye on Sophie. The music seemed to revive her. With her jacket off and Raffi singing, she sat contentedly in her car seat, chewing her fingers and happily staring out the window. She had olive skin and dark hair and looked like her Spanish father, euphemistically called The Count. Mother and daughter couldn't look more different. Cory had auburn hair, more copper than brown, with a few strands of gray, though she was only twenty-eight. She had pale blue eyes, and Sophie's were black and framed with long, thick lashes, another legacy of The Count.

Sophie had almost died at birth; there'd been trouble from the start. Though unexpected, she was not unwanted. She gave Cory three months of morning sickness, three more of heartburn, another three of exhaustion. Sophie was supposed to be born at home, but she was breech and ended up being cut out. A hospital physician thought she looked jaundiced and ordered full liver tests. At four hours old, she was injected with dye and given a scan to check her hepatic circulation. The nightmare set the stage for what was to come.

Cory hit another light and braked gently. At a full stop, she turned around and looked at Sophie. The baby reached out her hand and smiled a rare smile, showing tiny teeth. Her first set of molars were starting to come in. Cory blew her a kiss, and Sophie, who got it backwards, moved her hand to her mouth, catching the kiss.

The car behind honked. The light had changed, and Cory accelerated. She drove on, wondering what to do about day care. She needed two hundred dollars more a month to re-enroll Sophie in Campus Care. The co-op served Duane University and catered to working parents. The place was open daily from six to eight, and from nine to seven on weekends. Parents had to volunteer eight hours a month, and Cory enjoyed helping out. Sophie had spent five happy months there until she got sick.

It was just two hundred dollars. The day care was around the corner, so there would be less driving. They could change their diet. For six months, Sophie had been on a restricted food plan, and they weren't eating anything white—no flour, sugar, or salt. They ate mostly fruit and vegetables, all organic—nothing with additives and preservatives. If they lightened up on their diet and turned down the temperature in the house a few degrees, they could scrape by. It would only be for a few months. By August, if things went as planned, her boss, currently on sabbatical in Nigeria, would retire, and Cory would replace him. He was grooming her for his spot. As an assistant professor, her salary would double, and her financial worries would vanish. She just had to hang in there for another six months.

Chapter Three

Thirty minutes later, Cory was home. She lived on a dead-end street one block south of campus in a Victorian house that was built in 1875 by her great, great, great grandparents. There was a long, straight driveway, and Cory parked near the curb. She extracted Sophie from her seat, walked to the mailbox, and grabbed the mail. There were local flyers, election ads, and one regular-sized letter formally addressed to Dr. Cordelia Rose Montclair. It was from the legal department of Greenlee Hospital and marked confidential and urgent

The next-door neighbors were also just getting home, and Cory returned their waves. On a street where houses passed down through families, the neighbors were new blood. They had arrived in June when Sophie was at her worst. They were professors at the veterinary college and had an eight-year-old son called Frankie and an ancient terrier named Judy. Cory had learned this in the fall from the *Duane Tribune*, which ran a front-page spread about them.

She tucked the mail under her arm and headed down the driveway to the house. It looked welcoming, with the windows glowing in the darkness as if with ethereal light. The house was centered on an acre of prime real estate and surrounded by majestic trees. It was the family tradition to bury the placenta of newborn babies on the grounds. According to her grandmother, this nourished the land and kept it alive. It was easier when the baby was born in the house, as Cory had been, as had her mother, her grandmother, and on down the line. All except Sophie, whose afterbirth was mistakenly discarded.

Cory reached the house. It was two-stories high with big windows, a pitched roof, peaked gable, and decorative carved frieze. There were two front porches—one upstairs and one down. The master bedroom had a small balcony overtop the living room bay window, in which the dog stood, barking.

Pluto was a stray, approximately three, who had shown up a few months before Sophie was born. He looked like a black lab but was on the small side. He had sleek fur and a bit of a waddle. He liked to eat. The days were long for him too, and he was currently digging at a corner of the bay window. Adjusting Sophie on her hip, Cory climbed the cracked stoop, unlocked the front door, and let him out.

"Dada." Sophie said her only word. She was quiet and cautious, never babbled, seldom smiled. The pediatrician had warned that her development would likely be delayed because of the leukemia. She'd been diagnosed at nine months and endured one round of chemo that nearly killed her. She'd withered away, lost ten pounds—half her body weight. Now at twenty-two pounds, she was underweight but gaining ground. At thirty-one inches, she was of average height, but Cory thought she would be tall. She herself was five foot seven and The Count was at least six feet.

Pluto tore around the yard, peeing on his favorite trees. Cory sat down on the broken stoop with Sophie and waited. The house had fallen on hard times. Everything needed to be fixed. The roof had to be replaced, the white clapboards painted, and the plumbing redone. The trees were overgrown, and the walkway had more weeds than concrete. Cory had been saving for repairs when Sophie got sick. Now her savings were gone, and she was deep in debt. She was hanging by a thread, waiting for August.

Pluto loped to the house, and they went inside. Cory turned on lights as she headed for the kitchen. She slipped Sophie into the chair that hooked onto the table and poured her a cup of organic apple juice. Pluto got a dog biscuit, and Sophie got a homemade cookie made of ground oats, eggs, molasses, raisins, and chopped pecans. Cory looked at the letter. It wasn't a bill, which she would have tossed without opening. She had a box of them and paid bits and pieces every month, whatever she could afford. It would never be enough.

She tore open the envelope. The hospital had recently ceased all correspondence and sent a collection agency after her, which had been pestering her for weeks. Last month she disconnected the landline and blocked them from calling her cell phone. Now it was the hospital again. The letter was from their legal department and typed on heavy paper. She unfolded the page and scanned it quickly. It was short and to the point. Cordelia Rose Montclair was duly informed that a judge had garnished her wages to enforce the collection of her hospital bill. The withdrawal of five hundred dollars a month from her checking account would commence immediately and continue until the seventy-five-thousand-dollar debt was paid in full.

Cory buckled under the weight of the letter. She could barely breathe. She slumped into a chair, her heartbeat pounding in her ear. Sophie was looking at her with concern. Cory affected a smile, trying not to hyperventilate. *This wasn't possible. How could it happen?*

She got up, feeling weak, threw lentil stew in a pot, and turned on the stove. She chopped a banana, tossed it into the blender, added a splash of soymilk, and revved the machine, screaming inwardly along with the motor.

The hospital had made Sophie sick. During her first round of chemo, she got MRSA, the notorious hospital-based, antibiotic-resistant staph bacterium. She ended up in ICU for two weeks. Sophie had been pre-approved for chemotherapy but not ICU. Without pre-approval, health insurance refused to pay the bill. Cory appealed. The insurance company wouldn't budge. The hospital wanted their money, and it seemed they were going to get it. They would take it straight out of her account. It was too unfair. How could they do it?

True, they had warned her it was coming; they had called and sent letters. She thought if she ignored it, pretended it wasn't happening, that it wouldn't. Now she needed money. She had one credit card that was almost maxed out. She'd applied for others, but with outstanding medical debt, she'd been declined. She had tried to take a mortgage out on the house, but the banks weren't lending, especially not to someone with no "real" employment history. She could declare bankruptcy, but then she'd lose the house. That could never happen. Her grandmother said Cory was to defend it with her life. It had survived the 1900 hurricane, the 1918 Spanish flu that killed her great grandmother, the Depression, and the 1965 flood. Cory could not be the one to let it go.

She would have to borrow the money. She had a short list of friends but only one with money. Janie Bartlett was a third-grade teacher married to a Hollywood mogul. Cory had seen photos of their Bel Air mansion, their slew of servants, infinity swimming pool, tennis court, and sauna. Cory and Sophie had an open invitation to visit anytime. If Cory needed anything, "money, whatever," she was supposed to call.

She had met Janie at a Tijuana clinic in June. Against medical advice, Cory checked Sophie out of ICU and sought alternative treatment in Mexico. One shot of a wonder drug called Oxylace sent the cancer into remission. The drug cost a hundred dollars; a week-long stay at the clinic cost one thousand dollars. Janie was there with her six-year-old son, Brad, who was also suffering from acute lympho-blastic leukemia. He didn't make it. Eight weeks of chemotherapy had destroyed his body but not his cancer.

After dinner, when Sophie was bathed and in bed, Cory took her cell phone to the study and sat down at her mother's antique desk. She didn't need much money, just three thousand dollars—for just six months, until her post-doc was finished and she had her new position. It was enough money to cover Sophie's day care and the court-ordered payment. She could begin paying off the loan at the end of the summer. Crossing her fingers, Cory placed the call.

The phone rang and rang. She stared out the window at cold-look-ing trees and began to sweat. What if Janie had a new number? There was no one else Cory could ask. She had been raised to be self-sufficient. She wasn't supposed to ever ask anyone for anything, to never be in anyone's debt. She was to trust that everything would work out. According to her grandmother, the house was protected. Cory was to blindly rely on the help of unseen hands that would work behind the scenes to set things right. The hands, of course, belonged to the dead, for Anne Catherine Rose believed the house was haunted. The rooms were filled with ghosts: Cory's dead parents, who were mangled in an accident, and everyone else who came before them and refused to go. As a child, Cory was often told to be quiet, to listen for the sound of laughter, giggling, and the piano playing all by itself. Apparently the ghosts were boisterous, though she never heard anything. Her grandmother said the skill would come, but it hadn't come yet. So far, Cory had no evidence of ghosts. She heard pipes knocking and wood settling, but nothing untoward. If she discounted the owls.

She was about to hang up and close her phone when the call was answered. "Cory, is that you? It's been months. Everything all right?"

"Everything's fine," Cory said, sinking into the chair with relief. And compared to Janie, everything was fine. Janie's child was rotting in the ground, and Cory's was upstairs sleeping.

"Sophie okay?"

"She hates day care, still has nightmares, not talking." Cory was going out of her way to talk down her joy.

"It will get easier. You get that new position yet? Fixed up your house?"

"Hopefully in August. In the meantime, I'm working hard, nose to the grindstone."

"Any man to speak of?"

"Not remotely and not looking. Sophie is enough." As soon as the words were out, Cory winced. She had a habit of saying the wrong things. She changed the subject. "How's L.A.?"

Bad news. Janie was in D.C.—not on vacation but in the throes of a divorce. Cory said she was sorry, but Janie wasn't. She was happy being single. She was no longer teaching. She couldn't face healthy kids. She'd formed a new group she called END, which was an acronym for Enough Nasty Drugs. Her mission was to pass the Access to Medical Treatment Act, which would get the FDA out of health care and let doctors use whatever treatment they liked. "Have you heard of the bill?" Janie asked.

"No." Cory wasn't political. She didn't follow issues or get caught up in causes. She was taught to mind her own business.

"Did you read those books I gave you?"

Over the summer, Janie had sent Cory four books on alternative health. "I haven't had time."

"Read the books. In the meantime, you can join."

"What do I have to do?"

"Pay fifty dollars for a preferred yearly membership. You get a T-shirt. I'll send you an email with a link. You can pay with a credit card. Our start-up costs are high. We need pamphlets, a website, business cards, signs. We need money. I'm living hand to mouth."

There was no way Cory could ask for a loan. "Can I join later?"

"Sure. Tomorrow's fine. Will you do me a favor?"

It seemed so easy for Janie to ask. "Absolutely," Cory said. "Do you need a place to stay? I told you, you're welcome any time." A house was the one thing she had.

"I need you to write a letter."

"To whom?"

"A letter to the editor."

"Of my newspaper?"

"A journal."

"A scientific journal?"

"Yes. The Canadians are about to start an Oxylace trial to treat brucellosis in cows. Write to the *Canadian Journal of Cancer* and say that Oxylace works in people."

"There's no scientific study to support that."

"You've got the Mexican data."

"I can't use it." When the doctor from the clinic learned Cory was a biochemist, he gave her his recent case files and asked her to write a scientific paper about the merits of Oxylace. She would have helped him if she could, but it was not possible. "He had no controls. It wasn't a double-blind study. Anything I write would be anecdotal, not scientific."

"Fine," Janie said. "Get personal. Write about your own experience. Keep it short and to the point."

"Do I have to sign it? Can I be anonymous?"

"Be clear about your credentials," Janie said. "Don't worry, it's a small Canadian journal. No one reads it. It's not like it's going into the *Journal of the American Medical Association*. Not that JAMA would ever allow it."

Cory stared out the window at the skeletal trees that looked naked and exposed. The call wasn't going as planned. She wanted a loan and ended up with a request for fifty dollars and a letter. Typically she wouldn't get involved. But it was for a good cause. If it helped spread the word in the medical community of a good drug, it was the right thing to do. Besides, she'd never heard of the journal before, and it probably had few readers. "Okay."

"You're the best. Can you do it now? I'll stay up until I get it."

Cory had exams to grade and a statistical analysis to run on her latest research, but she wrote the letter:

While Oxylace has been used to treat brucellosis in cattle, it should be noted that the drug has been successfully used to treat a wide variety of human cancers. In Mexico, in the last *five years, 44 patients treated with the drug fully recovered. With the cost of the one-time injection at less than $100, the treatment is cheaper, more effective, and far less toxic than Wellspring Pharmaceutical's four-drug cocktail that costs $40,000 and is endorsed by the AMA and approved by the FDA. Anecdotal evidence certainly suggests there is sufficient clinical data to warrant, in addition to cattle, a thorough study in humans of a drug that may well cure cancer. Sincerely, Cordelia Montclair, PhD, Post-Doctoral Fellow, Department of Biochemistry, Duane University, Duane, Texas.*

She emailed the letter, got her book, and went to bed. She read Harlequin romances. Light reading took her mind off life and sometimes brought good dreams. Not tonight. Instead, she had a recurring nightmare. It was a dark night; there was no moon, no stars. She was in the backseat of a car with no one at the wheel. The car was airborne, flying down a mountainside, with the wind and snow-coated trees rushing by. She knew the car would crash and started screaming. It woke her up; it always did—the sound of impending doom.

Chapter Four

There is no alternative medicine. There is only medicine that works and medicine that doesn't work.

—Richard Dawkins

March 1

On Friday morning, Cory was heading back to the hospital. There was no way she could pay the court-appointed bill, and the hospital would have to amend it. She had Sophie with her. What else could she do? Cory had called the lab and left a message saying she'd be late and Sophie was coming in.

The hospital's business office was on the ground floor in the administration wing directly below ICU. To those in the office, it must have seemed like money was raining down from heaven. While Sophie slept in her arms, Cory sat in the packed waiting room waiting to speak to the insurance liaison officer with the unlikely but apt name of Terrance Killjoy. He was the interface between patients, the hospital, and insurance companies, but as his actions made clear, he worked for the latter two. She'd seen him at least a half dozen times in the last six months, and his story was always the same. Sophie may have picked up MRSA at the hospital but that didn't make them responsible. Nor did they have to tell the insurance company that Sophie was moved to ICU. Killjoy couldn't force the insurance company to pay, but he could force her. And she could forget the insurance negotiated rate, which was half the uninsured rate, because the hospital didn't bargain with individuals. They would discount her bill by twenty percent if she paid it in full, but she didn't have sixty thousand dollars.

After thirty minutes, he was ready to see her. She went into his office, took an uncomfortable seat across his desk, and adjusted Sophie on her lap. "You garnished my wages," she said softly, so as not to disturb the baby.

Killjoy tapped at a keyboard. He was overweight and laden with jewels. A diamond sparkled in his ear, a heavy watch dangled on his wrist, and gold rings shone on his fingers. So much gold seemed to weigh him down. He frowned at the computer screen, fat jowls hanging. "You left us no choice. You did not respond to our correspondence. You disconnected your phone."

"You wouldn't stop calling. I can't afford the bill."

"The judge thought otherwise."

Sophie woke up, looked around, and started to cry. Cory patted her back, soothing her to silence. "Did he look at my bank account? My monthly pay?"

"The judge went by your own figures."

"It's ridiculous. Can't we negotiate a reasonable amount?"

"The time for negotiation is over."

"What? There was a time for negotiation?"

"We provided a service. Your daughter appears healthy." He smiled at Sophie, who shrank away. She had been an outgoing baby until leukemia made her wary of strangers. Now she held herself back, clinging tightly.

"You made her sick," Cory said. "She got MRSA here."

"You are treated at your own risk. We are not liable for hospital-acquired infections or any wrongdoing on our part. If you would like to see your signed contract, I can oblige."

"So, I have to pay for what you did."

"That's the way it works."

"Aren't you nonprofit? Shouldn't you pay for your own mistakes?"

"Sorry, no." Killjoy spoke pleasantly and smiled on.

"What if I can't pay?"

"According to the judge, you can. You own a parcel of nice real estate. We could put you in contact with our agent. Try to reach an acceptable price."

Cory jumped up, gripping Sophie tightly. "You've got to be kidding." They would never get her house.

Killjoy continued to smile, never losing his cool. "Sorry we couldn't be more help," he said, not sounding sorry at all. "You know where we are if you change your mind and want that referral."

Outside, rain was threatening, and Sophie started to cry. Cory put her in the car seat, opened a box of organic juice, and she calmed down. If only Cory could be settled so easily. This happened every time. She was always the one who left angry and frustrated, never Terrance Killjoy. But what did he have to get upset about? All he had to say was no. That was his answer to every reasonable request: no, no, no.

Now she would have to try the bank. She used a credit union and had sought a loan when Sophie was first diagnosed. They turned Cory down because of the uncertainty of the situation and the possibility the bill could exceed the value of her house. Now the bill was final, and the uncertain situation had changed. If the loan was approved, Sophie could be back in Campus Care by lunchtime.

The manager was new—a Mrs. Helen Harper, who was middle-aged and matronly—and had a desk in the middle of the bank.

"I'd like a loan," Cory said quietly, after settling into another uncomfortable chair. "Short term. Just a small amount. Three thousand."

Helen smiled pleasantly. "Let's see what we can do." She waved to Sophie. "You've got a well-behaved daughter."

Sophie leaned against Cory, clutching her arm.

Helen pulled up the records, and the smile faded. "Five hundred a month garnishment. Ouch." She studied the monitor. "On a past-due debt of seventy-five thousand."

"It was for bad medical care."

Helen ran a finger down the screen. "You have one credit card, correct?"

"Yes, and I pay more than the minimum every month."

"Good for you. Interest is a killer." This brought hope, but Helen looked sad. She folded her hands together. "I'd like to help. Unfortunately, your financial circumstance would not support a loan at this juncture."

"It's only for six months. In August I'll be an assistant professor."

"Do you have a contract?"

"Not yet."

"I'm afraid it's not my decision. We have to follow strict guidelines."

"Can I take out a mortgage on my house?" If Cory's grandmother wasn't already dead, this would have killed her.

Helen clicked her teeth. "Normally we'd look at that, but not with your load of debt."

"My house is worth way more than seventy-five thousand. It's on Pecan Lane."

"I'm sorry. I really wish I could help."

"Can I get a new credit card? Say, with a limit of three thousand?"

"I'm afraid not."

"There's nothing you can do?"

"Unfortunately, no. I suggest you get a lawyer. Fight the garnishment of your wages. Get that reversed. It hardly seems fair."

But hiring a lawyer cost money that Cory didn't have.

***

Out of ideas and short on options, Cory drove to work. The biochemistry department resided in the Ellis Building in the heart of main campus, and by nine thirty the student parking lot was packed. Faculty got preferred parking, but since Cory was technically a post-doc, she didn't warrant the perk. A light rain began to fall and dashed at the windshield as she circled the remote lot. She found a space a half a mile away and jogged to the building, shielding Sophie's head from the rain with her arm. It was cold for the first of March, with a low of forty and a projected high of fifty-five. Spring was close but felt far away.

Cory snuck into the building and took the back stairs up to the second floor. Bringing a baby to work was against the rules, and it was imperative she keep Sophie out of sight. Cory had no clue what she was going to do with Sophie next week or the weeks after that, but for the moment, she had to keep her hidden.

She reached the lab without incident and slipped inside. The room was a large rectangle with a row of windows that flanked the south side and generally let in too much light and heat. But not today. In the overcast gloom, the windows had no light.

While technically Cory was a biochemist, the lab's focus was toxicology, which was where the money was. Her boss was in Nigeria, collecting oil-contaminated soil that he shipped back for analysis. He had three PhD students working for him who were trying different ways to measure and degrade oil hydrocarbons. There were two undergraduates. One worked on oil, and the other was dumped on her, thanks to the department head.

Cory was working on aflatoxin, on a project funded by the National Cancer Institute. Typically, post-docs were funded by a professor, but she had her own grant. She wrote the proposal during her pregnancy and got it the week Sophie was born. The two-year, two-hundred-thousand-dollar grant paid her salary and funded her research. Though there was six months to go, the research was already done.

The lab's one technician strode her way. Evonia Babinski worked for everyone. At twenty-five, she was going on fifty. Originally from Russia, she had come to Duane on a university scholarship when she was eighteen. She married during her junior year and got a green card and was counting the months before she could become a U.S. citizen. Stateside, she turned goth and wore only black. She had black, spiky hair and black fingernails. Her black leather boots came above her knees and clomped heavily as she crossed the lab. "You are not too late," she said in a heavy accent. "Were you successful?"

"Nope." Cory unlocked her office door. "Any news from the security officer?" She had to write an accident report about the rat bite.

"Not a peep." Evonia said.

Cory wasn't expecting any news. The officer was a lazy, uninterested, dull man who preferred to play video games than do his job. In this instance, she was happy the officer was disengaged, for she was loath to bring the accident to the attention of the department head. Dr. White didn't react well to surprises. He almost refused to allow her supervisor to take a last-minute sabbatical. White was a church-going man with traditional values and was visibly uncomfortable with Cory's pregnancy. But Sophie's illness mellowed him, and when Cory agreed to supervise Megan Carson's undergraduate project, she won his favor. He all but assured her that her effort would not go unrewarded. She took that to mean he'd support her bid to replace her supervisor when he retired. Dr. White would not take kindly to a missing rat and a bite that left his friend's daughter demanding a tetanus shot.

Evonia followed Cory into her office and closed the door. Like the lab, it had a row of south-facing windows. On the opposite wall, there was a tall, wide bookshelf stuffed with textbooks, reprints, and photos of Sophie. Three desks in the shape of a U faced the door. The middle desk, her writing desk, was clear, and Cory plopped Sophie on the top and dropped her briefcase.

"Dada," Sophie said as Evonia picked her up.

"When are you going to learn to talk?" Evonia said. She had been pregnant at the same time as Cory, but Evonia had lost her baby.

Sophie jammed her thumb into her mouth.

"And walk," Evonia said.

"She can walk," Cory said, though Sophie had started late and preferred to be carried. "Any sign of the rat?"

"I'm afraid, no," Evonia said.

"What did you use as bait?"

"Bread."

"Let's try peanut butter. If the electrical charge doesn't get him, the aflatoxin will."

Evonia patted Sophie's head. "What happened with the sitter?"

"I was late yesterday. She's not going back."

"Where is she going?"

"I don't know. But there's a problem." Cory showed Evonia the letter from the hospital.

Evonia read the letter quickly. "There is only one thing to do."

Cory waited. Evonia had unusual ideas. For someone who emerged from a communist country, she was a free thinker.

"Contact The Count. Demand child support."

Cory shook her head. The Count wanted nothing to do with his daughter. He wasn't listed on her birth certificate and legally wasn't bound to do a thing. She looked down at Sophie. "He's gone. I don't want him near her. I *won't* let him near her."

"Then you must get a roommate. Someone to help pay the bills. Perhaps baby-sit."

"Forget it. No way." Share her house? It was as unthinkable as asking The Count for child support. Cory was beginning to think the banker was right. "I'm going to get a lawyer." She would contest the bill, fight the hospital or the insurance company, possibly both. Get the bill thrown out.

"Yes. Go to legal aid. It is free for students and faculty. They have helped with my green card."

It was news to Cory that the university even had legal aid.

Online, she learned the department had opened in January. Apparently, the law school at the University of Texas in Austin couldn't keep up with the high demand for lawyers. Cory made an appointment, left Evonia to watch Sophie, and headed across campus on foot. The rain had stopped, but the wind had picked up and the temperature was dropping.

After passing through the old part of campus, replete with ornate Victorian houses built the same time as hers, Cory reached the law building. It was a new, square, three-story building on the south side. The young trees on the small front lawn were protected by cages. The concrete walkway was spotless, and the glass front doors were gleaming. Inside, she was immediately claustrophobic. The ceilings were seven feet tall, and the room reeked of paint and new carpet. It was fifty degrees outside, yet the air conditioner was blasting.

Her appointment was with a soon-to-graduate law student named Mathew Lang. He must have been good because two girls in the waiting room were trying to convince the receptionist they had to see him. Unfortunately for them, his day was booked.

Cory was directed to his office immediately. It was a tiny, cramped room the size of a closet with a low ceiling and one window with a built-in blind that likely couldn't be opened. The walls were stark white, and paint seemed to radiate off of them. The lawyer was behind a desk, surrounded by law books. He stood up. "You can close the door." He was tall and thin with prominent cheekbones. Good health and vitality emanated from him. He seemed old for a student, and she placed him in his early thirties. With a casual wave of a hand, he pointed to a chair. "What's going on?"

Cory sat down and gave him the letter from the hospital.

He glanced at it for all of ten seconds and passed it back. "It's a court order. You have to comply. As does the bank." He spoke with a northern accent; he was no native Texan.

"I'm not fighting the court order. I'm fighting the premise. My daughter was pre-approved for chemo and got MRSA during the first infusion. The doctor moved her to ICU. She should have told the insurance company. Instead, I'm stuck with a seventy-five-thousand-dollar hospital bill because ICU wasn't pre-approved. I think the hospital should pay."

"Do you have your health insurance contract?"

She didn't. "It's the university staff health insurance."

He opened a drawer and pulled out a folder bearing the logo of Universal Health Insurance, the company underwriting the university's policies. He leafed through the pages. He had large hands with very long fingers. He stopped reading and looked up. "It says here that all hospital stays must be pre-approved." He leaned across the desk, drawing her attention to the line with a tap of a finger. His nails looked polished, as if he'd just had a manicure.

"It was an emergency. How can you pre-approve an emergency?"

"You had twenty-four hours to inform them."

"I had a dying baby."

"I'm afraid it doesn't matter." The lawyer looked sincerely sad as he closed the folder. He brushed hair off his forehead. It was neatly cut around his ears, parted in the middle, bangs sticking up. He had sideburns and sunken brown eyes that were too close together. "Ignorance is no excuse."

"*Ignorance!* What about incompetence! Responsibility! The hospital made my daughter sick!" Cory's temper was rising along with her voice.

"Assigning blame is always difficult," the student lawyer said calmly.

"Where do you get MRSA?" Cory asked. "From a hospital. I'm a biochemist. I could prove it."

"That's not my point. Before admission, you would have signed a form absolving the hospital of any and all blame."

Terrance Killjoy had reminded Cory of that that morning. "Then I contest the bill. They charged me eighty-five dollars for baby aspirin. That's embezzlement."

"Not in the legal sense, though, technically it is. Tell the hospital."

"I did. They said they can charge whatever they like."

"They can."

"I want to sue."

He shook his head. "You won't win. You have no legal standing."

"There's got to be something I can do."

"I'm afraid the hospital knows how to protect itself from frivolous lawsuits."

"*Frivolous!* They make my daughter sick, they charge eighty-five dollars for an aspirin, they stick me with a seventy-five-thousand-dollar bill, which they deduct from my paycheck, and you call fighting it frivolous?"

The lawyer sat back. "I'm not saying it's frivolous," he said gently. "What I'm saying is, legally, there's nothing I can do."

"What if I don't pay? What if I close my bank account?"

"They'll come after you. Seize your assets. Do you have any?"

"A house."

"Is it worth more than seventy-five thousand?"

"Way more."

"Take out a second mortgage."

"I own the house. I've been to the bank. I can't get a loan, not without a job, not with this level of debt."

"You could sell the house."

Cory stood up and grabbed her briefcase. "I'm guessing you know an agent."

The lawyer stood up too. "As a matter of fact, no. I'm new in town. I wish I could help, but I can't. The system is rigged against you. You can pay the monthly bill, or sell the house and repay your debt, or the house will be sold for you." He was looming over her, his head dangerously close to the low ceiling. "I know how you feel. I'm in the same boat. I owe over a hundred thousand in student loans."

"Hmm, I'd say the situations are opposite. I paid for something I didn't want, and you paid for something you evidently didn't get."

For the first time, he smiled. Lights came on in the sunken eyes. "You could go back to the insurance company; try sweet-talking them."

"Right. Gee. Why didn't I think of that?" Cory smacked the side of her head and left the room.

Chapter Five

Sophie was asleep when Cory returned to the lab at noon. "Dr. White came down looking for you," Evonia said. "I told him you were at a meeting. He would like to see you the instant you return in regard to the safety incident."

"Did he see Sophie?"

"She was asleep. Then as now. I tried to block the view. He did not mention her. Nor did I. What did the lawyer say?"

"There's nothing I can do. Maybe I should pay a real lawyer."

"Pay how? You must look for a roommate." From the depths of a lab coat pocket, Evonia extracted a folded paper. "I wrote an ad for the online school classifieds."

Cory took the paper and read: *Roommate sought to share historic house on quiet dead-end street next to campus with off-road parking. Rent $500 per month. Available immediately.*

Cory laid the ad on the bench. Had it really come to this? Did she have to open her house to a stranger in order to keep it?

"Your house is very big," Evonia said. "She will get so lost you will never see her."

What other options were there? Cory needed money, and she couldn't bring Sophie to work every day.

"Perhaps a roommate can teach you to cook. Something more than fruits and vegetables."

Cory sighed loudly.

"It will not be for long. Only until the end of the summer. Then you will be the new boss and have money."

Cory's grandmother maintained that any unpleasant task could be endured for a day. Add the days together and the time would pass and the disagreeable trial would end, and it would make her strong. This had been in reference to summers without air-conditioning, but it worked for a roommate as well.

Cory plucked a pen from Evonia's breast pocket and amended the ad: *Professional roommate sought to rent furnished room. House close to campus. Must be clean and quiet, willing to babysit and walk dog. Rent $150 per week. No lease. References and good credit essential.*

Evonia didn't like it, but Cory was firm on the wording. Evonia agreed to post the ad anonymously under the name LabRat and generate a temporary email account to receive responses. Anyone who didn't look good would be deleted, though Evonia thought it unlikely that anyone would respond. Leaving her to the task, Cory headed upstairs.

The office of the department chair was in the southwest corner of the building on the third floor. There were two walls of windows, built-in bookshelves, and an oversized desk with an in-box and out-box, both empty. Rupert White was staring out of the window when she knocked on the open door. He beckoned her inside.

Dr. White was an African-American with caramel-colored skin. He was in his late sixties, wore wire-rimmed glasses, and was graying lightly at the temples. According to his university biography, he grew up in Duane and was a high school basketball star. He attended Duane University on scholarships, did a post-doc in California, and came back. He still worked out and was in good shape. A personal friend of the university president, Dr. White was a physical chemist and had been promoted to head the biochemistry department two years ago.

"Dr. Montclair, thank you for responding so promptly," he said as he waved her into a chair. He was always formal and respectful. They never shook hands; he kept his distance. "Miss Babinski said you were in a meeting?"

"Yes." Cory declined to elaborate. Her personal business was her personal business.

The sound of a ticking clock perched on one of the shelves filled the silence. Finally, he opened a desk drawer, pulled out a file, and passed it to her. It was a printout of the accident report she'd submitted the previous day. "Your report is weak in detail."

That had been deliberate. There was no mention of the missing rat, which added complexity to a fraught situation. He couldn't know about it. "It was nothing, really," Cory said lightly. Dr. White hated unexpected events. "We were just feeding rats. We do it every day."

"With aflatoxin, correct? A Class 1 toxin?"

"Well, technically it was peanut butter," Cory said, alarmed the physical chemist knew the classification system of toxins. That was way outside his field.

"And Miss Carson was bitten. What of gloves?"

"She wore them."

"What happened?"

Cory preferred to answer questions as opposed to opened-ended queries. "Megan is careless. I'm not sure why she's doing an honors thesis."

"We are discussing the bite."

"She's nervous around the animals. She grabbed a rat, and it turned around and bit her."

"Why didn't the gloves protect her?"

"She thought the bite went through them." Cory shrugged her shoulders. "I didn't see any bite marks."

"Yet you had the presence of mind to take her to the ER. Good thinking."

Cory thought it was a waste of time and refused to take credit for it. She said nothing.

"What treatment was the rat on?"

Cory explained the protocol. "Since Megan is awkward with the animals, she only has contact with the controls. She was feeding corn oil by oral lavage. It's just oil in a syringe. The rats love it. It wasn't a treatment group." That would have been a nightmare. Megan getting bit with an aflatoxin-laced rat that escaped would have been a disaster.

"So, we don't have to worry about accidental poisoning?" Dr. White said.

"No."

Dr. White exhaled slowly and removed his glasses. "Her father was worried. He will be relieved. He's Chandler Carson, in case you were wondering."

Not really. "I don't know the name."

"The CEO of Carson United Foods."

Cory shook her head.

"He's a dependable donor to the university and a personal friend. I recommended you to his daughter."

"I see." It explained the favor and how Cory came to be stuck with the most incompetent and incurious student ever.

"Have you seen Miss Carson since the incident?"

"She only comes in on Tuesdays and Thursdays."

"She wants to quit. Naturally, her father is perturbed."

"Maybe it's for the best. She doesn't seem fit for this line of work."

"A good teacher can teach anyone anything," Dr. White said sternly. "If she does not finish, she will not graduate with honors. Her father would be very disappointed."

Cory sighed loudly. "All right, I'll talk to her."

"Don't let her give up."

"I'll do my best."

"I appreciate that. I know your hands are tied, as are mine, but it will be worth it in the end." White nodded at the door as he repositioned his glasses on his face. "That's all for now."

Cory stood up and was on her way out when he called her back.

"Was that your daughter in the lab?"

Cory feigned ignorance. "What?"

"Authorized personal only are allowed in the building."

"Exactly," Cory said, and she hurried out.

She headed back to the lab. She'd wanted to tell Megan that if she didn't like her project, she should quit, but now it seemed everyone had to persevere. And Cory had to do something about Sophie. She'd been busted. Cory might have been able to squeeze by on one infraction, but Dr. White did things by the book. Another day would not be tolerated.

For that reason, when Evonia told her the unthinkable had transpired, that someone had responded to the ad, she was temporarily relieved. Cory scanned the email from JP quickly: *House sounds perfect. Love kids and dogs. Will 5:30 today work?*

"She sounds pleasant," Evonia said.

Cory had cold feet almost immediately. "It's a bad idea."

But Evonia was already typing a response and providing the address and agreeing to the time. "If you don't like her, just keep bringing Sophie to the lab."

Chapter Six

Sneaking Sophie out of the lab proved more difficult than sneaking her in, and having to wend her way to the car made Cory late for her appointment. At home, there was no sign of a potential roommate. Her next-door neighbor, striding up the sidewalk, waved her over. Leaving Sophie in her seat, Cory went to the curb and learned a man was skulking about the backyard. The neighbor raised her cell phone. "Want me to call the cops?"

Cory looked at the house. "I'm expecting someone." Not a man. "Let me go look."

"I'll wait here. Give me a sign."

Cory tentatively approached the house, heard Pluto's loud, frantic barking, and positioned the car keys in her fist as a weapon. She walked toward the east side of the house that bordered the neighbors'. A tall man turned the corner. It was Mathew Lang, the student lawyer from legal aid.

Cory stopped short. "What are you doing here?"

Mathew looked taken aback. "I came to look at a room."

Cory sighed loudly and waved at her neighbor who lowered her phone. Cory knew this was a bad idea. It was shortsighted to the extent that she never considered JP might be a man. "I thought you would be a woman."

"What gave you that idea?"

"I don't know. Love babies?"

Mathew pointed at the car. "Speaking of which, yours is crying."

Cory raced to the drive and pulled Sophie from her seat, hating the idea of a roommate anew. This was never going to work. She wasn't going to show him the house. She hoisted Sophie to her hip. Across the lawn, the neighbor was walking slowly up her front steps, watching everything.

Mathew came to the car. "So, this is the little lady that caused all the trouble. She looks healthy."

"She doesn't like strangers," Cory said as Mathew reached out and took her hand. Cory drew back, pulling Sophie away, as her daughter said her only word, "Dada."

Cory covered her daughter's mouth with her hand and sternly said, "Shhh."

"Dada."

"That's a nice-looking dog you've got," Mathew said, turning to the house. "I look forward to walking him. I could take him running."

"He hates strangers."

"Oh? He seemed friendly."

Mathew must have been joking. Pluto was protective, a watchdog. To prove her point, Cory went to the house and released the dog.

Pluto barged out, leapt off the porch, and charged down the path. Mathew bent down on one knee, opened his arms, and Pluto came to an abrupt halt. His tail began to wag madly. They greeted each other as if they were old friends.

"He looks like he could use a run," Mathew said as Pluto rolled on his back, exposing his round, plump belly. "I had to leave my dog. He was a lab too. Yellow. I miss him."

Mathew looked like he would cry, but Cory just glared at him. She could never live with anyone who would give away a dog.

"He's with my fiancé," Mathew added.

"Oh, you're getting married?"

"Not anymore." Mathew seemed choked up, close to tears.

Cory averted her eyes. Fifty yards away, through thinning trees, she saw her neighbors on their porch. They sat in matching rockers, drinking beer, unabashedly keeping watch. Mathew was still in a crouch, face buried in Pluto's fur. He was maudlin; she found it unbecoming in a man.

Mathew looked up. "You're not thrilled about the prospect of a roommate, are you?"

"Does it show?"

He stood up. Pluto got up too, shoving his nose into Mathew's hand, still wanting attention. "I don't know if it will work for me."

Did he mean her, them, the house? No one dissed her home. "It's in better shape than it looks."

He surveyed the estate, and she tried to see it from his eyes. Against a winter-gray sky, the world looked dirty and drab, and the Rose House was no exception. Winter was never its best time. The trees were nearly bare, and the sweet scent of honeysuckle was long gone. The grass was muddy, the squirrels were slow, and the birds didn't sing. Even so, the house seemed above it, indifferent to the season.

"You've got some great trees," Mathew said, facing the road. He could name them all: pecan, magnolia, dogwood, oak, and holly. He walked to the pecan tree, put his hand on the bark, and stroked the wood. "This is the biggest pecan tree I've ever seen."

Cory didn't bother to enlighten him on her family tradition. "Most of the trees are very old."

"Like the house." Mathew turned his gaze to it. "It's beautiful."

A girly word if there ever was one.

"A little work and it would look fantastic," he said.

"It already looks fantastic," Cory said.

"I'm talking cosmetic. A bit of paint. Fix the stoop. Replace the sconces. Cut down some of those dead limbs."

"I know what needs to be done," Cory said sharply. It was her house, and she didn't want him doing anything. Still, the branches did block the light, and a carpenter wanted a thousand dollars to fix the stoop.

"Since I'm here, I may as well take a look," Mathew said without enthusiasm.

"Since you're here," Cory said, equally bland. She walked up the steps, crossed the porch, and held the door for him. This caused an awkward moment for he wanted to hold it for her and wouldn't enter first. She gave up and went in. He kicked off his shoes and crossed the threshold, peering up at the doorway—which, at eight feet, was taller than the norm. In the foyer, he gazed at the ceiling, his jaw dropping.

"The ceiling's thirteen feet tall," Cory said. It was the Victorian standard, particularly in southern climes. "There's no air-conditioning." She wondered if that would turn him off.

"Great. I freeze at work. I was cold all day. The house feels warm."

It was like that—indifferent to the weather. It could rain all day, be damp and cold outside, but the walls held the heat. In the summer, strategically placed windows allowed a cross-breeze to blow.

Mathew ran his hand across the wainscot. "They knew how to build houses once upon a time." He patted the wall. "You're lucky to have this."

"It has me. It holds on and won't let go."

"Like it's alive."

Exactly, she thought.

She gave him a tour. There were four rooms downstairs, as well as a bathroom. The living room and study were on either side of the foyer facing the street, and the kitchen and dining room faced the back. There was a piano in the dining room, and he ran his fingers across the keys. "Needs to be tuned."

He seemed overly critical. "No one plays," she said.

He picked up her novel lying on the sideboard and read the title out loud. "*The Devil in Durban.*"

Feeling self-conscious, she teased the book from his hand. "It's actually a good story." Even if it was a Harlequin romance. She returned the book to the sideboard and headed for the stairs. "I'll show you the room. You came on short notice. It hasn't been cleaned."

"I don't mind cleaning."

"Well, it's clean. I meant dusty."

"Not a problem," he said, walking too close to her heels. "I should probably tell you, I like my privacy."

"Good to hear."

They climbed the grand staircase; he tread behind her like a shadow. There were eighteen steps, one landing. Originally there were six bedrooms, but that was before the days of indoor plumbing and electricity. Now, the top floor had four bedrooms and two bathrooms. She had the master bedroom on the north side, with Sophie's room at the back, facing the yard. Farther down the hall were two more rooms that shared a bathroom.

What she called the spare bedroom was her old room. It was of good size, with high ceilings and lots of light. There was solid chestnut furniture: a four-poster double bed, dresser, and desk. Two windows faced east, and French doors led to the upper balcony that looked north onto campus.

He stood in the doorway, taking in the room. "Do the windows open?"

"Sure."

He didn't take her word for it; he had to try them. The screens were in bad shape. He opened a door and went out onto the balcony and came back. He hit the switch for the ceiling fan, and the blades clicked as they hit the chain. "That will drive me crazy."

She felt like telling him to go find somewhere else to live. He was far too critical.

"I guess I could tighten the mount," he said, looking up at the fan. "That will stop the wobble." He went to the closet and opened the door. It was packed with her grandmother's cartons. "Is there somewhere you can store these?"

"I'll see," Cory said.

He looked at Sophie. "Does she cry a lot?"

That was it. He could just fuck off. "All the time."

"You shouldn't let her cry. It's not healthy."

Christ, was he blaming her for Sophie's leukemia? "Oh, you're an expert in parenting, are you?"

"Actually, I'm a certified therapist. A clinical psychologist."

"I didn't think you were a lawyer."

He laughed, and everything about him softened. His sunken eyes crinkled and lost their intensity. He played with his hair, fixing his bangs. "So, we go week to week? No lease? If it doesn't work out, that's it? No hard feelings?"

He was talking as if it might not work out for *him*. "It's a two-way street."

"I thought it was a dead end."

"You may be right about that."

He stared up at the ceiling, chewing one of his polished fingernails, as if considering his next move. Finally, he shrugged. "I'm willing, if you are."

"I'll need a week's rent and a month's security deposit." Campus Care had to be paid up front.

Mathew reached into his pocket and pulled out his wallet. Cory accepted his money, feeling as if she'd sold her soul.

***

Mathew drove a forest-green Mustang stuffed with his worldly posses-sions, and it took him five minutes to move his boxes upstairs. Cory, in the kitchen making dinner for Sophie, didn't offer to help. She kept a close eye on the clock. If he moved in fast, he could move out fast too.

At six thirty, he left for the grocery store. She didn't want any-thing, just the kitchen to herself. With Sophie in her chair munching a cookie, Cory stirred quinoa and black beans. . . and set boundaries. He wasn't a friend, and she didn't want to get to know him. She would stay out of his way, and he could stay out of hers. In a month, she would re-evaluate.

He returned when she was washing the dishes. He dumped his grocery bags in the corner and went upstairs. When she heard pipes knocking, she knew he was in the shower, and she waited until the water stopped running to take Sophie up for her bath.

An hour later, with Sophie in bed, she found him in the kitchen frying onions. His hair was wet, the bangs swept to one side. His hair was cut perfectly and angled back in layers like a model's. His skin shone as sleek as a seal's. He smelled of baby shampoo and tooth-paste—and he better not have cleaned up for her.

He stepped over Pluto and picked up a bottle of red wine. "Would you like a glass?"

"I have papers to grade."

"On Friday night?" He put the bottle down. "I bought a steak. I thought we could have dinner."

"I don't eat meat. Too many nitrosamines."

"I've got salmon, if you prefer." He had all sides covered. "It doesn't go with the wine, but I could open a bottle of white."

Jesus Christ, was he an alcoholic? "No, thank you."

She looked outside and saw smoke billowing and was about to yell fire when he said, "I lit the barbecue. I hope you don't mind."

He was making himself at home. She didn't like it at all.

"I fixed the porch swing."

It broke when she was pregnant after the hook holding the chain to the armrest rusted out. She missed it, but the swing was too heavy to rehang herself. She went outside to have a look and took Pluto with her.

The air was crisp and cold, in the high forties. There were no clouds, no moon, and the stars were shining bright. The smoker was billowing mightily. The scent of the burning coals made her stomach growl, and she wondered what Mathew would cook.

She sat down gingerly on the swing, testing the weight. She saw he'd removed the old hook and replaced it with a bolt. She began to sway back and forth and was soon swinging higher and higher, no longer feeling the cold.

Pluto didn't like it. He scratched at the door, and Mathew let him in as he came out. He poked at the fire, sending sparks up into the night. "You swing pretty high."

"Will it break?"

He promised it wouldn't. "I'm going to get my wine. Sure you don't want some?"

Maybe she would have a glass and then go grade. She got her jacket.

He dragged a wrought iron patio chair to the swing, and they sat facing the yard. The view was ugly this time of year. The live oaks had lost many leaves and looked as brown as the grass. The garage with its peeling paint was visible, as were neighboring houses. In the spring, thick foliage hid everything with verdant green, but that was weeks away.

Cory would have been content to look at the yard in silence, but Mathew found it necessary to talk. She learned that he'd transferred from the University of Texas in January. He didn't like big cities. He'd been commuting, in search of an apartment. Last week he found one he liked and sublet the one in Austin. He was set to move last weekend, but the Duane landlord rented the place out from under him. Since then he'd been sleeping on the floor at legal aid and showering at the gym. He needed a place immediately and had been watching the classifieds, which was why he answered her ad so quickly.

He was thirty-two, originally from Connecticut. He went to Harvard, where he studied psychology and got a Masters in family studies. He passed the state board exam and became a therapist in Watertown, population twenty thousand. Two years down the road, he changed fields and states.

"Why law? Why not continue with therapy?"

Undeclared personal reasons made him want a big change. He would graduate in May and take the bar exam. He already had a job lined up with Barrow and Craft, a local law firm. "Have you heard of them?"

She had not.

Besides his interest in law, he was a history buff, a self-professed student of the revolutionary war. When he learned she knew little about it, he felt compelled to teach her. He abhorred the corporate influence on government. In his view, so did the colonists, which was the basis for the war. Not all the tea went into the Boston Harbor, just that belonging to the Indian Trading Company. It was in dire financial trouble. Since most British MPs owned stock, to help the failing company, the Brits lowered the taxes on the company's tea. This gave it an unfair advantage through a lower price. The colonists saw this as another egregious example of government corruption and rebelled. In retaliation, the Brits closed the harbor, placed Boston under military rule, and absolved British officers from American prosecution.

"We've come full circle," Mathew said. "We're back where we were. A Congress owned by corporations. We're taxed and have no representation. We need to get money out of politics."

Cory listened half-heartedly to the history lesson. "I don't pay much attention to politics." She voted, but that was it.

Mathew leaned forward and passionately pounded his fist on his palm. "Everyone needs to pay attention. If you're not a part of the solution, you're a part of the problem. Corporations have taken over our government. Look at the health care industry. They pay more to lobbyists than they pay in tax. That's why you get to pay eighty-five dollars for a baby aspirin and have to pay the hospital that makes your baby sick. Given your seventy-five-thousand-dollar hospital bill, you should be mad."

"I am mad," Cory said, not sounding mad at all. She took a sip of wine. "But you can't fight the government."

"Of course you can. What do you think brings about change? One morning the drug companies wake up and decide they don't want to make an obscene profit any more?"

"What do you want me to do? Call my senator?"

"That's a start. Did you call?"

"No." She started swinging again, not liking the direction of the conversation. She didn't like politics, and she didn't like criticism.

"At least you'd feel better knowing you're not just taking it; you're doing something."

Cory planted her feet on the ground and stopped swinging. "I am doing something. I am looking after my daughter. I am doing my job. I am taking care of my house."

"It's because of people like you that this country is in the shape that it's in."

Cory leapt off the swing. She'd heard enough. "People like me who mind their own business?"

He smiled at her. "Now you're mad." He sat back in his chair, as if pleased. "I wondered what it would take."

"I'm going to grade papers."

He jumped up, laying a hand on her arm. "Don't go. I'm sorry."

She stared at his hand, and he lifted it. He grabbed a spatula and stabbed the fire. A spray of sparks jumped in the air. "The coals are ready. I've got good salmon. None of the GMO stuff. I think you're doing great. You're a good mother, and I know it can't be easy." He shrugged a shoulder and smiled a nice smile. "Please, have dinner. There's enough for two. I've got eggplant and squash, baby potatoes, garlic bread, and a Greek salad. I hate to eat alone." That said, he threw two salmon steaks on the grill and brushed them with oil. Smoke billowed and the coals flared, sending off a pungent plume. "Besides, you know everything about me, and I know nothing about you."

Well, she didn't know what had happened to his fiancé, or how he lost his dog and ended up with nothing, but she was charmed by his praise about being a good mother, which was something she often wondered about. "All right," she said. "I'll eat with you."

"I hope it won't be too tortuous."

They ate in the seldom-used formal dining room with the piano no one ever played. To the south spanned a wall of French doors leading to the backyard and the still-smoking barbecue. The furniture, a wedding gift to her great, great grandmother, consisted of a long mahogany table with twelve chairs, a sideboard, and a china cabinet. There was an ancient high chair, which Sophie hardly used. The large, red-rose-colored Persian rug had faded to pink and was threadbare. There was a gaudy chandelier, and, on the scratched table, tall candles in matching golden candelabras. Eight sconces threw yellow light on the walnut wainscot. Mathew wondered if they should light the candles, but the candelabras were too hard to clean. Besides, it sent the wrong message. Cory adjusted the chandelier to full bright.

The food brought temporary silence. The salmon was flaky with a hint of lemon, the eggplant was spicy, and the baby potatoes were dashed with parsley. The Greek salad had olives, feta cheese, and slices of avocado. The man could cook, and before long, she learned it was a chore he enjoyed.

"We could share the cooking," he said between bites. "I like to cook, but I hate to eat alone." He put down his knife, reached for his wine, and stared at her over the rim.

It was too much, too fast. "For me, it's the opposite."

He took a long guzzle of wine. "Is that a yes or a no?"

"Sophie's on a restricted diet." Cory had to explain it. "Nothing white, no red meat, no processed food."

"What about vitamins?"

Cory shook her head.

Mathew seemed surprised. "Why not?"

"The FDA doesn't recommend them. In fact, frowns upon them."

He put down his knife and took a sip of wine. "I wonder why?"

"They're not well absorbed," she said with undeserved confidence. She had read that somewhere, sometime.

Mathew lifted a dubious eyebrow. She learned he took a multi-vitamin, five supplements, and drank a protein shake every day.

She shrugged. It was a free world.

"Are you divorced?" He laid down his fork, then picked up his wine glass and swirled the contents.

"Never married." She took a bite of salmon, which dissolved in her mouth, leaving a taste of garlic and lemon.

"Where's Sophie's father?"

"In Spain." Cory offered her standard story of The Count. "He was a visiting professor of architecture."

"He doesn't want to see his daughter? Couldn't he get a job in the architectural department here?"

"He's happy where he is. And we're happy here without him."

"Where did you get the house?"

He was nosy, asking a lot of personal questions, which she usually saved for the bedroom, not the dinner table. But with the wine weakening her defenses, she told him the long, convoluted story about how she came to inherit it. The women in her family always did. It wasn't planned, it was just the way it happened. It wasn't to say there was no male blood, but when boys were born, they didn't last. She had been very glad that Sophie was a girl.

After some prodding, she told him the story. The great, great, great grandparents who built the house had one daughter. This was Cory's great, great grandmother, who had two girls, but only one married and had kids. That daughter, Cory's great grandmother, had five boys and one girl, but only the girl survived to adulthood. This was Cory's grandmother who had two children. Her son died in the Vietnam War, which left her mother. Cory was an only child, born when her mother was forty. Then there was Sophie. Cory ran through the names, Emma Mathilde, Beatrice Margrethe, Leticia Maria, Catherine Anne, and Mary Elizabeth; everyone named after European royalty—another family tradition—like burying placentas in the yard and scattering ashes on the grass.

Mathew listened with rapt attention. "Interesting names," he said. "But pardon me, Cory doesn't sound royal."

"It's short for Cordelia."

"Ah, the youngest daughter of King Lear and the mythical Queen of Britain. What of Sophie? Does she also have a grand name to aspire to?"

"Sophia Rose. Named after the Spanish crown in honor of The Count."

"Rose isn't a regal name," Mathew said.

Who was he? Some imperial expert? "It's the name of the house, my middle name, my mother's maiden name, and my grandmother's surname."

Mathew put down his wine glass and looked up at the ceiling. "Is Sophie crying?"

Cory didn't hear her. Usually she had a monitor but it was in the study. She threw down her utensils and raced upstairs. Sophie was in the crib, asleep but thrashing. Cory patted her back, made soothing sounds, and directed her thumb to her mouth, which settled her down. Ever since Sophie got sick, she got nightmares. When her breathing was slow and steady, Cory returned to the table.

"Everything okay?" Mathew asked as Cory sat down.

"She was asleep."

"I thought I heard noises."

"My grandmother said the house was haunted."

He picked up his fork. "Cool."

"Or, more realistically, it was Sophie. Her window's open. She was having a bad dream."

"Ah, unprocessed experience."

"Is that right, Dr. Freud?"

He smiled and resumed eating. "I prefer your grandmother's explanation. You ever see the ghosts?"

"No. I've seen owls, but I don't think there's a connection."

"Some Indian tribes believe that owls are the embodiment of the recently departed, that they carry the souls of the dead."

"I don't believe that."

"The disparity in the mythology is interesting. To the Greeks, owls were a sign of good fortune. To see one was a sign of victory. To the Romans, they warned of coming disaster, of defeat in war. The owl's hoot foretold certain death. In France, owls are said to help spinsters find husbands." He put down his fork and looked at her.

She looked back. "I'm not looking for a husband." She held his eye, his gaze was steady, sunken eyes unblinking, as he gawked over his hawkish nose with the intensity of a raptor. Was this how he was with his patients? Throwing out ridiculous comments and looking for a reaction? Cory took a sip of wine and decided to proceed cautiously. She was under a microscope. She dug into the salad, quaffed more wine.

Mathew reached across the table and topped her glass. The red bottle was finished, and they were on the white. Was the wine his version of truth serum? "Where are your parents?" he asked.

"Dead. They died in a car crash when I was three."

"How awful."

"I don't remember it."

That usually was enough to stop further questioning, but the ex-therapist wasn't beyond prying. "Who raised you?"

"My grandmother."

"Where is she?"

"She died when I was seventeen."

"And you've been alone—all this time?"

"I'm not alone. I've got Sophie."

"Just Sophie." Said like it wasn't enough. Cory had enough of his questions. "Are you like this with everyone?"

"Like what?"

"Intrusive."

He laughed again. "I call it conversation. Getting to know one another. You can ask me anything."

"Are you gay?"

He looked shocked. He dropped his fork. It clattered on the plate.

"Not that it matters to me," she added quickly.

"*No!*" he said sharply. "Why would you say that?"

She should have kept her mouth shut. "I wondered if that's why you didn't get married."

"That's not why." He took a slug of wine. "What makes you think I'm gay?"

"Your hair."

He blinked. High color came to his cheek as he blushed. "My hair? What's wrong with my hair?"

"That's something a girl would say."

He stared into her eyes. "A girl?"

"Never mind. You are who you are."

"Someone in touch with their anima, the inner feminine."

"Is that it," Cory said, going back to the food, wishing she had not broached the subject.

"Obviously you've never read Carl Jung," Mathew said.

"Obviously," Cory said, though she recognized the name.

"I had to take a year of analytic psychology before I could qualify as a certified therapist. It helps you get in touch with yourself, your feelings, and your purpose. I would recommend it for everyone. Especially you, given your—"

He paused. She glared at him. "My what?"

"Your early experience."

"I'm fine as I am, thank you."

"If you say so."

Her food was finished. She laid down her utensils and polished off her wine. Was she not fine? Of course she was. He didn't know her. Who was he to pass judgment? It was nonsense. He must be drunk. It was a long time since she'd drank so much, and she was feeling tipsy herself. Both bottles of wine were gone. Her brain seemed to be swimming, and she was exhausted. She looked at her watch and was surprised to see it was almost midnight. She looked at him. He was peering across the table with his too-close eagle eyes. "I'm going to bed," she said. "Thanks for dinner."

"If I upset you, I'm sorry."

He was overly sensitive. "I'm tired. It's been a long day."

"You can tell me to go to hell, to shut up."

She stood up and grabbed her plate. "I'll stick with good-night."

"Leave the dishes. I'll do them."

"Great." She picked her book up off the sideboard.

"I've read it," he said. "It's pretty good."

She looked at him curiously. What kind of man read a Harlequin romance?

He shrugged sheepishly. "What can I say? I'm a romantic at heart. Want to know how it ends?"

"I know." She left him at the table and went to bed, and for the first time in two years, broke her routine and fell asleep without reading a single page.

Chapter Seven

March 2nd

During the night, the wind changed; on Saturday morning, it was blowing up from the south, bringing humidity and heat and the promise of spring. Mathew was up early and made strong coffee. He said he would be out all day and was going out for dinner. He didn't say with whom, and Cory wondered if he had a girlfriend. They had spoken of her love life, not his, and she would never ask; she didn't care, and it was none of her business. She promised to clean out his closet. Her plan was to enroll Sophie in day care in the afternoon, which left the morning for the chore.

She watched an hour of cartoons with Sophie, who sat before the TV howling with laughter. Cartoons were the one thing that made her smile. Then they went to his room. He was neat. He made his bed, picked up his clothes, and put away his things. There was a shoebox on his dresser, and she peeked under the lid and saw photographs. She pulled out a stack. Mathew with a pretty blonde, both smiling. Picture after picture of them. Must have been the fiancé. She looked happy, not like someone plotting an escape. He looked happy too, more relaxed, laid-back, not as intense.

Cory felt guilty invading his privacy and returned the photos. She cleaned out the closet, ferrying cartons to the spare back room that was her grandmother's sewing room. She decided that if he was out a lot, the arrangement might work. It was a practical economic solution to a desperate financial situation. But from here on in, she would go light on the wine. Mathew was personable, good-looking, and smart, and it would be too easy to disregard her boundaries. She knew in advance that would be a disaster. According to her grandmother, some people were better off alone and not meant to marry. Apparently Cory was one of them. Maybe there was something off-putting about her, something she couldn't see that was obvious to others. Mathew would be the first man to spend more than one night in the house. She had to be careful and keep her distance or he'd bolt.

As Sophie played with cars on the floor of the sewing room, Cory went through her grandmother's boxes. She'd saved Cory's high school clothes, notes, and old books. In a carton, she found family photographs she'd never seen before. They had aged badly and were water damaged. Some were stuck together, others dotted red with mold. Still, it was like finding a piece of her past she never knew about.

They were pictures of her mother in her younger years, and Cory stared at her in wonder. Her grandmother had raised a hippie. Cory's mother wore bell-bottoms, tie-dyed shirts, and bare feet. She had long, straight, blond hair that came halfway to her waist. In one photo, she looked like she was on a picket line. Defiantly, she held a sign that said, END WAR NOW. Cory realized she must have been protesting the Vietnam War. She was born in 1945 and would have been twenty-four in the late sixties, which was how old she was when her younger brother died in Khe Sanh.

Cory found her mother's graduation pictures and her PhD diploma. Graduating long before she married, she'd kept her maiden name: Mary Elizabeth Rose. Cory got her red hair from her father, only his was more brown than copper. He wore it long, and it was gently curled, just like Sophie's.

They had a dog! It was a black lab that looked like Pluto, complete with a white diamond patch on its chest. Yet Cory's grandmother was supposedly allergic to dogs and said Cory could never get one. But evidently, at one point, her grandmother and her parents had had a dog.

The house didn't look much different now than it did back then, but the paint was fresh and the roof looked newly-shingled. In one picture, white Christmas lights were strung along the railings of the balcony and the porch. Only they couldn't have been Christmas lights because the trees and shrubs were in full leaf. It was a puzzle because her grandmother would never waste electricity and burn holiday lights in the summer. It occurred to Cory there was a lot about her parents that her grandmother had neglected to say. Perhaps, like some, her grandmother rewrote her daughter's history to her liking.

Cory finished going through the photos and repacked the boxes. There was no information on her parents' accident and no new photos of them with her. She had only three baby pictures, and they were framed and downstairs in the study: Cory coming home from the hospital, Cory at eight months in front of a Christmas tree, and Cory around two, in the backyard holding tight to the ropes of a plank swing.

She went to the bathroom. His. He had two thick, rose-colored towels neatly folded over the rods. Next to the sink, there was a container of baby powder, a pump bottle of liquid soap, and a nail-brush. The soap smelled of the forest. He used a triple-edged disposable razor and no shaving cream. There was Crest toothpaste and a toothbrush with flattened bristles that needed to be replaced. He used a brush, not a comb, and no hair gel. He had no blow dryer. He left the toilet seat up, but since this was his bathroom, she guessed it was okay.

She lowered the seat and sat down. On the edge of the bathtub was a bottle of baby shampoo. Given his demeanor, she wasn't surprised. Most men she knew used Brut deodorant and testosterone aftershave, and he favored baby products. She got up, flushed the toilet, and left the seat down. She used his soap to wash her hands, and she scrubbed her nails until they looked as polished as his.

She cleaned the sink with a paper towel and wondered about her boarder. The brief survey of Mathew's room and bathroom didn't tell her much. He was neat and clean, and for someone so girly, he had few toiletries. Pluto seemed to like him, and the dog had a good sense about these matters. There weren't many men that he liked. One may have abused him at one time, or maybe he was just a good judge of character. Unlike her. According to Evonia, Cory picked men badly. She made up her mind too fast—in an instant, really. She was to slow down, take her time. Evonia declared that when she found the right man, the relationship would last. Advice quite at odds with her grandmother's.

After lunch, it was time to enroll Sophie in Campus Care. The place was a five-minute walk away, and she took Sophie in her stroller. The day care was in a converted old bungalow set in the middle of a fenced, treed yard that sported a jungle gym, swing set, slide, and sandbox. Inside, the furniture was miniature, and the walls were plastered with artwork. There was an eating room, playroom, and a quiet room. The playroom had rows of toys and books. Reading was big here.

Ethyl, the gray-haired, middle-aged assistant director, had a Masters in child development and welcomed Sophie warmly. "She looks great." She reached her arms out, and Sophie shrank way.

Cory had to hold her while she filled out the paperwork, paid for the month, and signed up for eight volunteer hours. Then she spent the afternoon helping Sophie acclimate. Every day for the past six months Sophie had screamed whenever Cory left her, and she figured that was the legacy of the hospital, of having to endure strange nurses and doctors giving injections and spiriting her away for endless painful tests. When Sophie first came to day care she had never cried, but now Cory couldn't put her down without her fussing.

On the weekends, the classes were merged so that the three- and four-year-olds were with the babies. Today there were eight kids, and they watched *Sesame Street*, read five Dr. Zeus books, and finger-painted—all with Sophie sitting on Cory's lap. Outside, Sophie refused to go on the swing or down the slide. She sat with Cory in the sandbox, warily watching the other kids run races. There were kids younger than her playing, but she wouldn't join in. She was on her own until a little boy arrived and rolled her a ball. She rolled it back.

His name was Danny, and he was new too. He had blue eyes and brown hair cut in a pageboy with rounded bangs. He told Cory he was four, but it was almost his birthday. He had lived in Houston and moved at Christmastime. His father worked at the university, and his mother was a painter. He went to the big school in the morning and came to day care in the afternoon. He liked day care better. School had too many rules. "Why doesn't Sophie talk?" he asked as he rolled her the ball.

"She was sick," Cory told him. "She's better now."

"I was sick," Danny said.

"Did you go to the hospital?"

"To the bathroom. I had diarrhea and frow-up. At the same time."

Cory picked Sophie up, putting distance between them. One thing about day care—the kids shared germs. "When were you sick?"

"At my old house. In my old school. I was in Form One. Not the baby class. I can count to a hundred. Want to hear me? One, two, free, four . . ."

In the middle of the afternoon, it was snack time, taken in the eating room at a table that sat two feet off the floor and was surrounded by undersized chairs. The kids had apple juice, orange wedges, carrot sticks, and to Cory's dismay, small, white, powdered-sugar donuts. Sophie wanted one.

Ethyl gave her one of the organic cookies Cory had brought, but Sophie threw it on the floor. She pointed at the donuts, stamped her foot, and started screaming. Cory picked up the cookie, grabbed her daughter, and swept her outside.

Cory stood in the shade of a live oak and offered the cookie again. Sophie flung it on the ground and howled at the sky. Trying to hold the kicking feet and still the flailing arms, Cory wondered what to do. Going easy on their diet was one thing, but giving Sophie processed junk was another. The doctor in Mexico made it clear that in his opinion, processed food was poison. Cory's own diet during her pregnancy had been terrible. During the last three months of constant heartburn and constipation, she'd craved Oreo cookies, plain hot dogs, and peaches. Now, on sleepless nights, Cory worried if her diet had given Sophie cancer. Rather than cave-in and allow the donut, Cory bid Ethyl and Danny good-bye and took Sophie home, screaming all the way.

Up in New York, Art Farber, CEO of Wellspring Pharmaceutical, was on the phone with the FDA, and he was screaming too.

Chapter Eight

The dilemma facing a doctor, then, is this: Shall he follow his Hippocratic oath and his sense of moral obligation to do that which he honestly believes is best for his patient, or shall he abide by the rules laid down ... on behalf of vested commercial and political interest?

—G. Edward Griffin, World Without Cancer

March 4th

Art Farber called an emergency meeting first thing Monday morning. Standing in the new office suite surrounded by cartons, boxed artwork, and stacked furniture, he felt as discombobulated as the room. He'd felt this way since Saturday, ever since the FDA informed him of a letter to a Canadian journal that slandered his cocktail, insinuating that it was ineffective and toxic! No one disparaged Art's drugs and got away with it. No one.

At seven sharp, Hank, Art's right-hand man, filed in along with six of twelve board members. If the quorum voted unanimously, decisions could be made. Absent were the Wall Street reps, the secretary, and the lawyers. Art didn't want any leaks, he didn't want the minutes recorded, and most of all, he didn't want to hear about the law.

Hank got busy setting up the projector. Known as "The Fixer," Hank looked like a bulldog and behaved like one. He was the bully on the playground giving wedgies and making life tough for the small guy. Now he worked for Art. Whenever a threat arose, Hank moved in and made it disappear. In his fifties, with a vague military background, he had a square head and gray hair worn in a buzz cut. Weighing two hundred and fifty pounds and with arms the size of tree trunks, he could and would—one way or another—crush any foe. For the past forty-two hours he'd been hard at work sizing up the enemy.

It wasn't the first time Wellspring had encountered a charlatan. They were always dealing with communist kooks who believed in nature's pharmacy and free drugs. But Art had never seen anyone as credentialed as Cordelia Montclair, PhD. She was bold and foolish, with so little to gain—and as Art would ensure, much to lose. She would rue the day she wrote that letter. He would not only stop her, he would punish her. He would see to it personally.

As the quorum settled in their seats, Art took his place at the head of the table. He preferred to stand in meetings; he never sat. He felt more at ease with people looking up at him. He began by thanking everyone for coming on such short notice. The quorum may have thought they were here to discuss the move, but that was a done deal; there would be no discussion. It was Art's call, and he'd made it. "We've got a problem," he said, and he gave the floor to Hank.

The Fixer turned on the projector. There on the screen in high relief was the red-haired, blue-eyed bitch who'd slammed his cocktail. Art had seen the slideshow, but seeing it again did little to lessen his fury. Montclair was a hapless post-doctoral fellow, toiling away in a nameless university, in a nameless Texas town. She was twenty-eight, a single mother of no scientific distinction. To Art, it looked like she needed to be fucked. It would be arranged. No one messed with Art. Not anymore.

Hank moved to the next slide, and there was the offensive letter. Montclair had actually called Oxylace a cure for cancer. Art had never heard of the drug before now, but according to Hank, the FDA tested the drug in the fifties and found it ineffective. Now banned in the U.S., it was available in quack clinics in Mexico for a song. But it was no good, even if it was less damaging, less toxic, and less expensive than the Wellspring Pharmaceutical chemotherapy cocktail that was approved without reservation by both the American Medical Association and the FDA.

The CFO, Rick Vanguard, raised a finger. He was in his forties, blond and good-looking. As a closeted gay, he knew how to be discreet. "When will the letter be published?"

"The Internet version is going out tomorrow," Art said. "The print version on Friday. We spoke to the journal's legal department and raised our concern, but since it's only a letter stating an opinion, the editors couldn't understand our objection. We're supposed to make it clear in writing, and then they'll revisit their decision."

"Why'd she do it?" Rick asked.

"Revenge," Art said. "Her kid got leukemia, took the first round of the cocktail, got MRSA, and ended up in ICU. She got better and went to Mexico, took Oxylace, and recovered." Hardly surprising, he thought. Even partial treatments of the cocktail were effective. The full eight-week treatment of the four drugs taken together had a success rate of almost forty percent, which in terms of treating cancer, was a big fucking deal.

Hank ran through slides reinforcing the statistics that clearly demonstrated the cocktail's efficacy. Overwhelmingly, it enjoyed widespread doctor support. The only caveat was a minor and unfortunate side effect of one of the drugs. Valurex, the DNA synthesis inhibitor, caused allergic reactions, especially in young children. It was the primary treatment. The other three drugs in the cocktail complemented the inhibitor and served to either alleviate side effects or accentuate Valurex uptake and potency.

"Did the child react to Valurex?" Rick asked.

"No!" Art cried. "She got MRSA. Somehow that's our fault."

"She doesn't want to pay the hospital bill," Hank said. "A judge had to garnish her wages to enforce payment. Her response was the letter attacking us." He turned off the projector; the slideshow was done.

Art was ready for comments and suggestions. In his mind, two things had to happen. First, she had to be stopped. Second, they had to send a strong message and make her think twice before she pulled a stunt like this again. They would make her life hell. Wellspring was poised to be the largest chemotherapy manufacturer in the country, and the last thing Art needed was buzz that his drugs were no good. The market moved on rumors. They had to shut her down and keep her down.

Connor Loy, a former congressman from Wyoming who had recently retired after losing his last election, wanted the FDA on board. He was six years older than Art and sported a full head of hair that Art coveted. Connor was a fan of Botox and not one wrinkle creased his sixty-eight-year-old skin. "What this Montclair did is called false labeling. That's a crime. Doctors have been thrown in jail for less." He spoke barely moving his mouth.

"She's no doctor," Hank said. "She's a post-doc. She has no business talking outside her field."

"That's fraud, then," said Alistair Sasson, former president of the AMA. He was frail and over ninety. He thought the fifties' FDA study said it all. Oxylace had been tried and found wanting. "Send that to the Canadian journal, along with a stern warning," he wheezed.

Hank made a note.

Amet Patel, their retired FDA representative, thought the written response should come from the FDA. "We must have the agency respond in writing immediately following the letter. We will publicly assail her credibility."

Art liked it. Their current man at the FDA was Claude Smite. "Amet, do you think Claude should call her?"

"Excellent suggestion, sir. I will ask him to go in person. It is more effective. I will speak with Claude and let you know directly." Amet was originally from the Punjab and spoke formal English with a strong accent. He was seventy but looked far younger. He had worked at the FDA for forty years and knew the agency inside and out. He also knew who signed his paychecks and was always ready to help.

Martin Little, representing Universal Health Insurance, was perplexed why outside treatment was ever sought. Martin was the CEO of a top health insurance company in the nation. In fact, his company insured Cordelia Montclair and her daughter and all professional staff at Duane University. "We cover—without question—seventy-five percent of the Wellspring chemotherapy costs," Martin said. "Only a moron would reject that and head to a Third World country." He tapped the side of his head as if to indicate the post-doc was nuts.

Perhaps she was, Art thought, which would explain her inexplicable behavior. Why attack him? What did she want? If it was a question of payment, why not go after the hospital? Obviously, health insurance would have paid for the kid's chemo. And why not? Universal Health was one of their major investors. What the insurers shelled out for treatment, they got back in dividends and rising stock price.

Art thought it prudent to investigate Montclair more deeply. "Hank is going to Duane when we're done. See what he can learn." In Art's mind, "know thy enemy" was always the start of a good offense.

Everyone agreed they were lucky the letter was going to a small Canadian journal. The damage would likely be minimal. The quorum was unanimous in its desire to keep the story out of the mainstream news. Art would talk quietly to their PR director. If the letter leaked out, he wanted the story killed. It was in the best interest of everyone. Desperate, poor, sick people were always looking for miracle cures that simply weren't there. Someone had to protect the public.

"Should we peek at her email?" Connor asked. The former elected official was a devious man and considered himself above the law. "See what she's up to?"

Art looked at Hank. It was important to discern her motivation, to find out what she wanted, and how she planned to get it.

"I'll talk to the IT manager," Hank said.

"What about blocking the online version of the journal?" Connor added.

Hank looked at Art, and Art shrugged.

"I'll see if it's possible," Hank said.

"We will nip this in the bud," Amet said.

"Shut her down," Martin added.

"Crush her," Connor said.

Hank nodded. "Immediately."

The board concluded their meeting, and Art felt more at ease. The members were united and on the same page, willing and ready to launch a full-force attack. It would be done quietly; no one would speak of it, and no shareholder would be informed. The market was fickle, and if word of this got out, it could cause an ugly turn.

Art went to his office. He had a message from Missy, who missed him already. She wondered if he could get away for lunch. There was a condo overlooking Central Park she wished him to see. Maybe stop home first. It was code that she wanted to fuck. She was insatiable.

Chapter Nine

On Monday morning, Cory got to work early. She felt the tide had finally changed, and she was in the flow. For the first time in months, Sophie was left at day care without screaming. There was no long drive north fighting traffic, no more worries about a five-thirty deadline. Suddenly, life seemed easier. Cory was free to focus on her work, to do a good job, and advance her career.

It had been a good weekend. Spring was coming, and the weather was improving. Mathew had repaired the cracks in the front steps, cut down two huge limbs, and rewired the sconces on the front porch that died before her grandmother. He changed her oil and bled her brakes—he didn't want Sophie in an unsafe car. Cory still didn't know if he had a girlfriend, but she learned he'd gone out to dinner Saturday with two friends from back home. They were working on PhDs, one in astrophysics and the other in software engineering. No names were offered, and none were requested. They were keeping their personal lives separate.

A persistent blot in paradise was the missing rat. Cory assured herself that at least it was still confined. Hunger would eventually lure him to the golden glob of peanut butter waiting on the wired metal plate that would electrocute him to death. It was only a matter of time.

As was her routine, before starting work, she had a cup of coffee with Evonia. The lab tech demanded an update on the boarder. "How is JP? Does she babysit?"

"It's a he. The lawyer from legal aid. Mathew Lang."

Evonia frowned. "Does that not strike you as suspicious?"

"He needed a place to live, and I had one. He's a student and has access to the classified ads."

"You like him. You are making excuses for him. This not-real lawyer, as I believe you called him."

"He'll graduate next month."

"He makes you happy. Just look at yourself."

Cory tried to look serious. "He pays rent. I can afford Campus Care." She shrugged a shoulder. "Sophie likes him."

"What about Pluto?"

"Loves him." On Sunday, Mathew had taken him for a six-mile run and wore him out. During the week, Mathew planned to come home for lunch and let him out, so even Pluto would benefit from the arrangement.

Evonia took a sip of coffee. "I suppose it is good for Sophie to know a man. And you as well. For more than one night."

Cory ignored the slight. "He likes basketball. So does Sophie." They had watched a college game on Sunday afternoon. "She said her second word. Ball."

"Not mama?"

"No. She saves her words for what she wants and doesn't have."

"Dada," Evonia said.

Cory finished her coffee and went to her office and got to work. On Tuesdays and Thursdays she had official duties, but the remaining days belonged to her. Post-doctoral success depended on two things: research and publication. Her primary duty was to publish papers. Her current research was dedicated to improving the diagnostic testing of aflatoxin, a product of the mold *Aspergillis flavis*. The mold grew on corn, peanuts, grains, and cotton and was found in a variety of grain-based food, dairy products, peanut butter, and meat. The mold secreted a poison, aflatoxin, which was so toxic that undetectable amounts caused liver cancer. A safe level had never been found. Currently, for everything but milk, the level was twenty parts per billion. The only problem was, this level wasn't anywhere near safe. It was just a level that could be measured.

The current diagnostic test was time-consuming and expensive. HPLC, or high-pressure liquid chromatography, required a sample to undergo a lengthy and intensive cleaning procedure. It was then injected into a costly chromatograph machine for identification, which could take upwards of eight hours. The purpose of her research was to find a cheaper, quicker way.

In biochemistry, the state-of-the-art research used molecular biology techniques—primarily DNA analysis. Write a project that used DNA sequencing and the odds of getting a grant improved tremendously.

Cory used immunological techniques. It was old school, but for her purpose, it was the most effective and efficient method for detecting aflatoxin. Still, the research was not without critics. Using antibodies was likened to living in the age of dinosaurs. Yes, it was just like driving to the store in a car in the era of space shuttles. Why not fly? And that illuminated the problem; in some instances, the older techniques were more suitable than the new fancy ones.

Her research was a case in point. She used an ELISA, which stood for enzyme-linked-immuno-sorbant assay, to detect aflatoxin. The assay was fast and took only thirty minutes to run. She used a "capture" antibody, a monoclonal antibody she created in the lab. Antibodies were proteins that resembled a *Y* and were used in the body to fight disease. Nature had designed the upper arms for grabbing. She had engineered a monoclonal antibody that specifically grabbed aflatoxin. This involved generating numerous monoclonal antibodies and testing them for their affinity for the toxin. At no time was success ever guaranteed.

It took eight months to find an antibody. The rest was simple. To detect aflatoxin in food, a food sample was dissolved in buffer and added to an ELISA plate. There was a five-minute wait and the plate was washed. Add the monoclonal antibody, wait five more minutes, and wash again. If there was aflatoxin in the food sample, the antibodies would latch on and hold on tight. All unbound antibody was washed away. Add a color dye to detect remaining antibody, and positive samples turned blue. The intensity of the blue color was directly proportional to the amount of aflatoxin in the food sample. The exact level was determined using a spectrophotometer. When compared against the older method, there was no statistical difference between the two tests; HPLC or the ELISA, the accuracy of one test was as good as the other. Only hers was faster and cheaper—and therefore, better.

The test was optimized, and the research was about to be published. The paper was written and submitted to the *American Journal of Pharmacology and Toxicology*, one of the most prestigious journals in the field. It had been accepted with minor revisions. One reviewer wanted more information about how the monoclonal antibody was made, another wanted a different statistical analysis, and the third said the paper should be published as is. Cory had answered the questions,

ran the additional statistics, and resubmitted the paper. She was awaiting final acceptance and expected the paper to be published in June.

Publish or perish was a reality in her world. But scientists also
needed grants, and Cory was thinking ahead. What if she could optimize the test to use in the field? She envisioned a simple assay, like a
pregnancy test, which changed a color on a strip of paper. It could be
done by a farmer in a field, a cashier in a health food store, or a factory
worker in a peanut butter plant. The test would have good commercial
application, which was what the funding agencies liked.

She was already working on a field test. It was standard operating
procedure to write a grant proposal on research that was known in
advance to be doable. The only problem was that the monoclonal antibody was unstable. For optimal results, it had to be fresh and used
within three weeks. It couldn't be frozen without losing activity. Left
standing on the counter in the sun, it degraded within an hour. It was
a huge, unwieldy protein, and she thought if she could make it smaller,
it might keep its shape and still be active. She'd been trying different
enzymes to cut it down to size—so far without success.

Today she was going to use pepsin, a stomach enzyme. She added it
to the antibody and let it incubate for differing amounts of time: thirty
seconds, one minute, two minutes, four minutes, and eight minutes. Then
she ran the ELISA. During the pipetting steps, she concentrated hard, for
accuracy in pipetting determined the accuracy of the final result. She ran
all samples in duplicate, along with the positive and negative controls.

She had to get the field test to work. If she got a new grant, she would
have leverage—the university would want to keep her. Getting her boss's
job was no slam dunk, no matter how hard he pushed for her. The position would have to be advertised. People from all over the world could
apply, and the best candidate would win. It had to be her. Lose, and her
future at Duane University would be over. She'd have to go elsewhere.
The biggest problem with that was that her house was here.

She finished the assay. The accuracy was good, but the results were
terrible. Another failure. The modified monoclonal antibody didn't
work. Everything was negative except for the positive control that used
the native antibody. She cleaned up her mess and went to her office.
She had two lectures to prepare and didn't have more time to spend on
lab work that didn't seem to be going anywhere.

Chapter Ten

March 5th

Typically post-doctoral fellows didn't teach, but when her boss left suddenly on sabbatical, Cory assumed his two classes. Joe Carlisle said it was good experience, that it would make her a competitive candidate. Her teaching was reviewed, her performance on record; once each semester Dr. White sent an anonymous colleague to observe and critique. At the end of each course, students submitted mandatory evaluations. Good reviews on both fronts were necessary and would help determine who filled Joe's shoes.

Cory was currently teaching two classes: xenobiotic biochemistry and advanced pharmacology. The former class was no problem. It was a graduate-level class taken by PhD students who were attentive and engaged. The material was fascinating. The only drawback was there were only six students. In contrast, three hundred bored and fed-up undergraduates took pharmacology. It was a required class for both biology and biochemistry majors—and one most would elect not to take. Though taught at the respectable hour of eleven, some came dressed in pajamas ready to sleep. A few actually slept.

To catch their attention and wake them up, Joe suggested she ask questions. The technique was working, and she'd begun to get feedback. At times there was too much—a few students took over and veered off topic. So far it wasn't a problem because she was ahead of herself, but she was losing ground, and there wasn't much time left in the semester.

She had reached the mind-numbing section of the curriculum. Just preparing the lecture on drug testing and licensing put her to sleep. The drug-approval process was long and involved. Before the FDA sanctioned any drug, it had to be extensively studied. First, it was tested in animals. If that went well, there were three human trials. In Phase 1, the drug was given to healthy volunteers to assess side effects and dosage. The stage took a year and a half. If all went well, the testing progressed to Phase 2. Here, the drug was given to people afflicted with the condition the drug was supposed to treat. It was a double-blind test. Neither the patient nor the doctor knew whether a drug or a sugar-pill placebo was administered. This phase lasted two years and was designed to evaluate the drug's effectiveness. Phase 3 was a huge clinical trial involving thousands of patients and numerous doctors and hospitals throughout the country. This stage looked for contraindications and efficacy, and it lasted three and a half years.

At that point, seven years down the road, the FDA assessed the results. This typically took a year and a half. If the data looked good, the drug was approved. Approval was specific. A given drug was used for a specific condition. Doctors, however, had the latitude to prescribe any approved drug for any reason, in what was called off-label use.

The mandate of the FDA was to protect the public from bad drugs. It kept drug companies honest. They had to find effective, safe drugs and keep bad drugs off the market. If not for the FDA, thalidomide, the drug that was used in the fifties against morning sickness that caused skeletal deformities in developing fetuses, would have taken a much greater toll.

According to drug companies, the lengthy, time-consuming, high-risk venture to find drugs that won FDA approval was the reason drug prices were so high. Most drugs that were assessed went nowhere—at a great loss of time and money. When a drug did show promise, ten long years passed before any profit was realized. It was a money-losing prospect that drug companies endured in hopes of finding an approved, best-selling drug—a blockbuster. Built into the cost of any drug was ten years of clinical testing.

As she expected, the class slept as Cory relayed these facts. It was especially troubling because today seemed the day that Dr. White's anonymous colleague was auditing the class. He was in his fifties, with a big square head and a gray crew cut, sitting way in back. When Cory looked directly at him, he seemed to slide into his seat. When she thought about it, she remembered him in the hallway after her earlier class, bent down drinking from the water fountain. The door was open during the lecture, and he could have easily been listening in. When there were only six students in a room, you couldn't fade into the crowd;

but with three hundred, it was another matter—unless you were three times older. The man had to be the anonymous critic, which meant Cory had to do a good job. She had to wake up the class. She threw out a provocative question. "Do prescription drugs cost too much?"

Immediately Lyle Steele raised his hand. At thirty, he was older than she and had an undergraduate degree in political science. He'd been a government contractor in Washington and had worked with the FDA until he lost his job in the sequester and returned to school. Now he was doing a Masters in Business Administration and was taking pharmacology as a lark. He was one student eager to jump into any discussion about government regulation and the free market. "The American people are being screwed," he said. "The drug companies want us to believe they pour their profit into finding new drugs, which is why they're so expensive and why the company deserves a twenty-year patent, but that's not the case. Look at the facts. Last year, on average, drug companies spent three percent of their profit on research and development. Three percent!"

"That's not much," Cory said, amazed. She was coming from the scientific side, not the business side.

"Yes," Lyle said. "Drug companies spend nineteen times more on marketing than they do on research. What they call R&D is actually sales. Last year, we spent forty percent more on drugs than Canadians and seventy-five percent more than the Japanese. In the decade that ended in 2012, the top eleven drug companies made a total profit of seven hundred and eleven billion dollars. They made more money than five hundred businesses put together."

Frozen in the glare of the projector, Cory wondered how to respond. She didn't know if his numbers were right, and they sounded excessive. She looked at the class, wondering if she should try to rein him in or let him continue. It seemed he managed to achieve what she could not, and that was to win the attention of the snoozing seniors. They were paying attention, as was Dr. White's anonymous critic. She allowed him to proceed.

Lyle continued. "From 1998 to 2007, half the FDA-approved drugs came from taxpayer-funded research. The government pours money into basic research, looking for better drugs, better delivery systems, a better understanding of physiology and pharmacology. They put the results out for free, drug companies apply it, and then overcharge us for the final product. People on Medicare who paid taxes for fifty years can't afford the drugs they paid to research and could get in Canada for half the price."

Heads were shaking. "Health shouldn't be for profit," someone said. "It's not a commodity that can be traded."

"Exactly," Lyle said. "Look at the 'me too' drugs. They're chemical modifications of existing patented drugs. Change one atom in a block-buster, add some double bonds, or take out a few, and *voila*, here's a new drug that warrants a new patent. Is that right?"

Cory had no idea this was what they did. It certainly wasn't in any of her textbooks. "That's unbelievable."

"It's how we end up with worse drugs," Lyle said. "When a patent expires, the drug company needs a new drug, so they slightly modify the old one. They give it a different name and get a new twenty-year patent. Instead of testing the new drug against the old drug, they test it against a control. Often the new drug is worse than the old one, but so what? The new one's got a patent, and the old drug disappears. Then they send drug reps out *en masse* to convince unsuspecting doctors that the new drugs are fantastic and so much better than the drug that just lost its patent and anyone can make."

Cory stared at Lyle dumbfounded. "That's so wrong."

"It is, but it's legal. The pharmaceutical companies write the drug laws. It's the most profitable industry there is. They control Congress. They get large tax breaks and large subsidies. What do they do with their money? They hire lobbyists. They get whatever they want. Congress wouldn't dare cross them. When Bush passed the Medicare drug act, the law specifically forbade the government to negotiate with the drug companies over drug prices."

Cory was as surprised at this as the rest of the class. She kept up with the news and didn't know this.

"'That's right," Lyle said. "Negotiating drug price is something every private health insurer in this country does. When you have a big pool of people, you can negotiate. You're offering a sizeable clientele in return for a lower cost. But not our government. The drug companies said no. And so the government passed a law to allow drug companies to fleece the public. We get to pay whatever they decide to charge, and no one can stop them."

"It's outrageous," Cory said, adding her voice to the sentiment of the class.

"If you think *that's* outrageous, you should look at the clinical tests," Lyle said. "They don't use good science. Drug companies discard results they don't like. They take drugs meant for kids and test them in adults. They test drugs for men in women, and drugs meant for old people, in teens. We end up with expensive prescription drugs that are often ineffective."

"And sometimes cause harm," said a pajama-clad kid in the front. "Look at Vioxx. The anti-arthritis medicine increases the risk of heart attacks and strokes."

Lyle nodded his approval. "Or Sorcor. The drug was approved in the early nineties to treat depression, had a twenty-year patent, and made thirty billion in sales. The only problem was the drug was no better than a sugar pill. The drug-maker knew it and hid it. They paid doctors to promote it and ran glossy ads on television singing its praises. It became a blockbuster. Only it doesn't work. Now a patient is suing. She wants a refund for the money she spent buying a worthless drug. The drug manufacturer called the lawsuit frivolous. The president of the American Psychiatric Association said the lawsuit is ridiculous. The case is in court right now, but doctors are still writing twenty million prescriptions a year for a questionable drug."

Cory was dumbfounded, as were the students and the critic who was scowling deeply. This was the most responsive Cory had ever seen the class. She decided to let Lyle rant on.

"What about worthwhile drugs that will never turn a profit? What about them? Are they ever going to be tested?" Lyle didn't wait for an answer. "Of course not. Only potential moneymakers survive the FDA's ten-year testing period. Sure, the drug companies grumble about this, but they love it. It keeps out the small guy, eliminates competition."

"And natural products, like plants and seeds, they can never be patented, so they'll never be tested," offered a girl from a middle row.

Lyle nodded in agreement.

The girl went on. "What if there are promising new drugs that should be studied but no one will fund the studies because the drugs are too cheap to be profitable in the long run?"

"That's how effective and cheap drugs are kept out of the market," Lyle said.

Heads were shaking, and Cory gazed at a sea of frowns. The critic was bent over, taking notes. She decided to step in. "We call American medicine the envy of the world, but you can get better treatment for less money in a Third World country like Mexico. They use drugs we can't get here, and they have more success treating some conditions like cancer than we do."

"That's absolutely right," Lyle said, looking at her with admiration.

A voice cried out, "What can we do?"

"Learn more about it," Cory said.

"Then call your representatives and complain," Lyle said. "We need to change the system."

He went on and on, and the class went into overtime. No one noticed until a girl in front raised her hand and pointed to the clock. It was five past twelve. Though Cory hadn't given her planned lecture, she considered the class a success. She packed her briefcase, waiting for the gray-haired man. Typically an evaluator introduced himself after the fact, but when the room emptied, the critic was gone—hopefully hurrying off to submit a glowing review. In truth, this was the most engaging and informative hour the class had ever spent. At least Cory had learned a lot and would now have to investigate Lyle's extraordinary claims.

She turned on her phone, saw a missed call, and read a text message from Mathew: *Burst water pipe kitchen*. She called him immediately.

"I think it just happened," he said.

"How much water is there?"

"About an inch. I cleaned it up and turned off the main water line to the house. I need to open up the wall between the kitchen and the dining room. Is that okay?"

Cory pictured the wall with its old oak planks. "Rip out the whole wall?"

"A few planks. I'll be as careful as I can. I'll try to put them back."

"I'll be right home."

Chapter Eleven

Pluto was ecstatic to see her and nearly plowed her down when she opened the door. Mathew was in the kitchen, arm stuck in a narrow rectangle where two planks used to hang. There was a pile of dishtowels in one corner, an open toolbox in the other, and a crowbar on the floor. He was wearing an apron over a yellow polo shirt, which brought out his winter tan. His blazer hung on the back of a chair.

"I found the leak," he said. "I can't see it, but I can feel it. Do you want to see where it is?"

Standing beside him, she sunk her arm into the space, and he took her hand. His skin was warm and soft. He traced her fingers along a thin, cool copper pipe and stopped at a wet jagged edge that marked the boundary of a hole. She looked at him. He was so close she could smell his baby shampoo. She lifted her hand and stepped back. "So now what? Call a plumber?"

"What for? I'll solder it."

"I don't have solder."

He was down on his knees, rooting through his toolbox. "Lucky for you, I do."

While he went to work, she made tuna fish sandwiches. Chopping onions and celery as he fired up a blowtorch, she wondered what would have happened if he hadn't come home. What if he was as clueless as she when it came to fixing things? Apparently, she took after her father, because her mother and her grandmother could fix anything.

It took Mathew five minutes to seal the leak. He decided to wait until the end of the day to replace the planks, once he knew the problem was fixed. He went outside and turned on the main water line, then he turned on the kitchen faucet. No water leaked. He washed his hands using a new nailbrush, scrubbing like a surgeon.

Over lunch she told him of Lyle's bizarre claims about the drug industry. "I've never heard any of it before. It isn't in my textbooks. I know he worked for the FDA, and I let him speak. The students were more interested in what he had to say than anything I've ever said. Good thing too because an observer was monitoring the class."

"Why do you call it bizarre?" Mathew asked. "The drug companies are in it for the profit. They make money on their patents. They don't care if a drug works."

"That's why we have the FDA."

"The FDA doesn't work for the people. It works for the drug companies."

"No, it doesn't." Mathew may not believe in their government, but she did. "I'm going to look into it. I don't know much about it. I'll have to learn."

"Once you do, you'll be outraged."

She shrugged, chewed her sandwich carefully, and said nothing.

He stared at her across the table. "It's funny. You're a biochemist. You study poisons. You could have studied anything, but you studied the one thing that would help you make the right choice when Sophie got sick. It's like you arrived in advance of where you had to be."

Whoa. Cory concentrated on lunch. That was not her worldview. On a molecular level there might be no free will, but thinking people certainly had it. She swallowed, took a long sip of water.

He studied her as if she were an insect under a microscope or a patient on a couch. "So here you are. Where are you going? What are you going to do when you finish your post-doc?"

"Be a professor."

"Where?"

"Here. I can't leave the house. I'm going to fix it up. Save enough money so Sophie won't have to worry about losing it."

"And?"

"Live out my life and have my ashes spread under the trees."

"That's it?" He was shocked. "You don't want to live somewhere new? See the world? Have more kids?"

"No," she said with finality. Her plan was noble, beyond reproach. "If you had a house like this, you'd know."

"Where's the big picture?" he asked, genuinely taken aback. "A master plan that requires your participation in something great? It seems so small, pedestrian, shallow."

Cory put down her sandwich. Who was he to decide her plans were small? She took a large gulp of water.

He went on. "So you're just like a red blood cell, bouncing along, looking for oxygen, picking it up, releasing it, doing your thing, and for no bigger purpose?"

"I'm not like a red blood cell. I'm like a person with free will."

"Yes, everything you study is determined but yourself. And stick to those things that can be measured. Don't bother with the ninety percent of the universe that lies beyond the five senses. Pretend to know everything."

She didn't know if he was joking but laughed anyway. Then she turned around his question and directed it to him. "What are you going to do? Start a revolution? Write a new constitution? Is that big in your definition?"

He smiled and took a sip of water. "Maybe. Who knows? I follow my heart. Do what I feel passionate about. Right now, it's law." He put down his glass. "And I do know what the house means to you. I had one like it once."

"In Austin?"

"Up north. It was an old farmhouse, almost a hundred years old. This place reminds me of it."

"Did you own it?"

"Me and the bank."

"You sold it?"

"Not really. Got into a fight over it and lost."

Cory waited for him to continue, but his face blanched, and he seemed overwhelmed by the memory.

"I got screwed," he finally said. His voice broke, and he stopped talking and took a sip of water. "I paid the down payment and could prove it, but the judge was not impartial. Some laws suck. That's when I decided to go to law school."

"I gather your fiancé got the house?"

"Margaret. She got Shamus too. The dog. Her uncle is a judge, and he fixed everything."

"Oh." Cory tried to be comforting. "It must have been a long time ago." She meant, get a grip. Mathew was in his third year of law school; this didn't happen yesterday.

"Doesn't seem that long ago." He ran the back of his hand over his eyes. "Do you think I'm unmanly?"

She looked at her plate. "You are wearing an apron."

"I didn't want to get my clothes dirty."

"Then there's that."

"I know I'm too sensitive."

"But you can solder. Fix a leaking pipe. Chop wood. Change oil. Bleed brakes. They're my very definition of manliness."

Mathew didn't look convinced. "Anyone can do that."

"I can't." Cory's lunch was done, and she had to go. Outbursts of emotion like this made her uncomfortable. According to her grandmother, there were two types of people—the thinkers and the feelers. The latter were blubbering fools, out of rational control, unlike the Roses who were logical, reasonable, and deliberate. Anne Catherine Rose left no doubt as to which type was superior. Mathew would not be her type. Cory picked up her plate. "I'm late. My student's coming this afternoon, and I've got to convince her not to quit."

Mathew didn't move. "Just leave the dishes. I'll do them." He had a hand on his forehead, his eyes downcast.

Cory hurried out, not able to leave quickly enough.

Chapter Twelve

Cory was back at the lab at one thirty and found Megan Carson sitting atop a lab bench, staring intently into a compact mirror, carefully applying lipstick. She came from money, and it showed. Overly concerned with her looks, Megan spent an inordinate amount of time primping, pinching her cheeks, adjusting the line of her brow, and wetting her lips. She had big, flouncy blond hair that she was always adjusting; a flip here, a shake there. Her small blue eyes were outlined in an assortment of bright colors: pink, yellow, violet, purple, and green. She always wore the latest fashion and preferred tight, low-cut blouses, skinny jeans, and pointy-toed boots. Cory thought Megan would be more at home on a catwalk, but here she was in a lab, scowling deeply, which detracted from her pretty looks. At twenty-one she had the sour demeanor of an embittered shrew.

Cory couldn't understand why she was even doing a senior project. She didn't need to, she could still graduate, just not with honors. Maybe her rich father wanted her to have a career in science, or, as Evonia maintained, Dr. White wanted a spy. Either way, a high degree was hard work—at least in Cory's lab.

Megan had designed two projects. The first was to test the toxicity of store-bought peanut butter. She was feeding rats peanut butter diluted with varying amounts of corn oil. Because of the difference in size between a human and a rat, the rodents were getting a concentrated dose of peanut butter, and thus likely ingesting high levels of aflatoxin. Two months into the study, the rats in the high-dose group were already looking sick.

Megan's second project was to repeat a published study that compared the level of aflatoxin in peanut butter sold in health-food stores and big-chain supermarkets. The study showed that the level was lower in supermarket peanut butter. The offered explanation was that the jars didn't sit on the shelf as long as they did in the specialty shop.

The only problem was that the study had been funded by one of the leading food manufacturers, and Cory didn't trust the results. Megan was repeating the study.

Cory laid her briefcase on the bench and put on her game face. "Hi, Megan. It's good to see you. How's your finger?"

Megan held up her hand and showed a heavy bandage wrapped around her index finger. "The rat did break the skin," she said petulantly.

"Good thing you got a tetanus shot," Cory said with sarcasm she immediately regretted. "Shall we go feed the rats?" Said in a cheery, happier tone.

"Evonia can do it."

"They're your rats."

Megan tossed her lipstick into her purse and hopped off the bench. "I can't work with them."

Cory shook her head. "You wrote the project, and that's like a contract." She stared into Megan's sullen eyes. "You wanted to do it. You *can* do it."

"I can't." Megan bit her lip and scuffed a cowboy boot across the floor. "I won't."

"Why are you even doing a project?" Cory asked.

"You wouldn't understand," Megan said. "You have no idea what it's like to have a family legacy. There are expectations."

Cory knew exactly what it was like to have a family legacy, to have to live up to expectations, even when the holder of those expectations had moved on. "Maybe it's too late now, but when you graduate, you should try and find work you enjoy. It's hard to be good at something you hate. If you do what you love, at least you'll be happy."

"You don't get it. I can't do what I want. There is no happy."

There was no arguing with the girl. "You ordered the rats. What do you propose we do with them?"

"Evonia can kill them."

"How do we justify the money we spent to buy them?"

"I'll pay for them."

Cory exhaled quietly. In Megan's world, money was the answer to everything. She was entitled; she could pay others to do unpleasant jobs. She wasn't prepared to do anything she didn't want to do. She was spoiled and sulky and used to getting her way, and Cory had had enough. "Look, you designed this project. Do it or not, it's up to you, but the work is going to get done. Take off today if you want to think about it. If you're not ready to feed the animals on Thursday, don't bother coming in."

Megan bit her lip and folded her arms together, standing her ground. "My dad knows Dr. White. They're good friends."

"Dr. White's a good man. I don't know your father."

"Chandler Carson. He's the head of UFC."

"So I heard." The name still meant nothing to her. Cory looked at the door. "I've got to get to work."

Megan picked up her designer knapsack, her face one big pasty frown. "My father wants me to graduate with honors."

Cory looked at her. "That's up to you."

"I'm going to talk to my father."

Cory turned away from her. "You do that."

Megan left, and Cory went to her office, closed the door, and sat down at her desk. She'd handled it badly she knew, and she shouldn't have issued an ultimatum. She couldn't risk losing Dr. White's support. Professional positions at universities were hard to come by, and she not only needed a position, she needed it here.

Still, holding Megan accountable was the right thing to do. Giving in would have set a bad precedent. It sent the message that if you had money you could buy what someone else had to earn. Unlike Megan, Cory hadn't been brought up to expect any favors. You're all alone, her grandmother had said from the time she was a child. Don't bother crying about it. Get used to it. This same grandmother had said the house was the most important thing in the world, and Cory was to protect it with her life.

Chapter Thirteen

Doctors are particularly singled out for strong action ....
If many of them were allowed to use (alternative medicine)
without being chastised, it could result in opening the flood-
gates of medical acceptance. Each doctor that dares to resist,
therefore, must be publicly destroyed ...

—G. Edward Griffin

March 6th

Wednesday night, Art stayed late at the office, awaiting Hank's return
from Texas. It had been a good day, unseasonably warm, reminding Art
of spring. The financial headline news of the day was the fall of Merritt
Drugs, his primary competitor. While Merritt's drugs boasted a mar-
ginal five percent success rate higher than Art's, time had shown their
drugs were potent liver carcinogens. Patients lucky enough to survive
five years after the initial diagnosis and were thus considered cured,
came down years later with terminal liver cancer. Facing a class action
lawsuit, Merritt was about to voluntarily withdraw their drugs. With
Merritt out of the picture, Art's cocktail would soon be the most widely
prescribed anti-cancer treatment in the world. Futures for Wellspring
stock were already up five percent.

The FDA was rushing to approve the replacement of Wellspring's
blockbuster, Valurex. After a profitable twenty-year run, the patent
on Valurex would expire in the fall, and Xventra was set to replace it.
The new drug was closely related to the old drug, except four hydrogen
atoms had been removed. This compromised solubility and decreased
efficacy, but according to the FDA, the clinical data looked good, thus
ensuring two more decades of patent-protected profit. Any misgivings
about his rash purchase of the corporate headquarters and the Central

Park condo had evaporated. Now, if only the problem with the Texas quack could be solved so easily, Art could look forward to a stress-free night.

But Hank's news was not good. "Montclair's our worst nightmare," The Fixer said when he arrived an hour later, breathless and sweaty. "I don't know where she got her curriculum, but it wasn't out of any AMA-approved text."

Art leaned back in his chair and rubbed his forehead. "What did she say, specifically?"

Hank read from a small notepad. "We call American medicine the envy of the world, but you can get better treatment for less money in a Third World country like Mexico. They use drugs we can't get here, and they have more success treating some conditions like cancer than we do."

Art snapped forward. "She actually said that? To students?"

"Word for word. Said to over three hundred undergraduates. She thinks prescription drugs are too expensive. 'Me too' drugs don't deserve a patent. The government should negotiate drug prices. Sorcor is worthless, and the FDA protects bad drugs. Bottom line? We make too much money."

Art frowned deeply. It was unconscionable that hundreds of students had to listen to this dribble. Everyone knew drug costs were high because of the high cost of research and development. The country would be in the dark ages when it came to health if not for the investment drug companies poured into innovative research. "Did the students pay attention?"

"Up in arms. She wants them to call their elected officials and complain."

"Jesus Christ," Art said as his cell phone began to vibrate and nearly shook itself off the table. Missy was calling. He was late. "What the fuck does Montclair want?"

"It's obvious. She's on a crusade to limit pharmaceutical profit."

Art silenced his phone. He thumped his chest. "She's going after my profit. She made this personal. We stop her. Now. Didn't Claude talk to her?" Claude, currently at the FDA, would soon retire and join the Wellspring team.

"He will this week. In the meantime, he's crafting a rebuttal to the Canadian journal."

"When will it be published?"

"Shortly. It will appear directly below her letter. You won't see one without seeing the other. *If* you can see it at all." Hank pulled a sly smile. "The Canadian journal is having issues with its online version."

"Did IT hack her email?"

"Montclair uses a university address. They have a firewall, but it can be breached."

"Excellent. Any headway through legal avenues?"

"The lawyers are hard at work."

"Good," Art said as the desk phone began to ring. Missy was calling the landline. She was nothing if not persistent.

"What now, Boss?" Hank asked.

"Set up a meeting with Claude." Art reached for the phone. "Get him over here. As soon as he can make it. We're going to come down hard, Hank."

"She left you no choice," Hank said as he rose from his seat.

He left, and Art picked up the receiver. Missy whispered breathlessly into his ear, "I'm hot. Guess what I'm wearing."

Chapter Fourteen

March 7th

Typically, Cory and her boss communicated by email, speaking by Skype only during emergencies. For that reason, on Thursday morning when a ping on her laptop informed her of an incoming Skype call, she went on high alert. She wondered if Megan had complained to Dr. White, who complained to Joe Carlisle that Cory had antagonized his friend's daughter.

She answered the call, and Joe's picture filled the screen, showing a man who resembled Santa Claus. He had twinkly blue eyes, snow-white hair, and a full white beard that had sprouted during the sabbatical. The video feed was grainy, but the sound was clear. "What's up?" she asked cautiously.

"I was going to ask you that."

"Are you referring to Megan?"

"What happened now?"

"She won't work with the animals."

"I thought she designed her experiments."

"She got bit by a rat."

"Uh-oh." Joe stroked his beard. "Was it toxic?"

"No. A control rat. She went to the emergency room and got a tetanus shot. We had to write up an accident report for the security officer. Now she wants Evonia to kill the rats."

"Given Meagan's carelessness, you better test the rat. Make sure she didn't poison herself."

"It's not possible," Cory said. Everything in the rat room was color coded, including the rats' tails, which were brightly ringed with magic marker according to their treatment group.

"Test the blood," Joe said, pulling rank.

Which was a problem, of course, because the rat was still missing.

"You kept the rat, right?" he said.

Across the miles, Cory wondered how to reply. Since they hadn't dispensed of the rat, in theory they had kept it, and at the moment it was safely and securely locked in the animal room, even if its current whereabouts were unknown. She answered in the affirmative.

"Draw the blood, do an ELISA, and attach it to the accident report so there's no misunderstanding."

"Okay." Cory stared out the window. It was a bleak, overcast morning, with rain spitting at the glass. "I'm not sure Megan's coming back."

Joe groaned loudly. "What happened?"

"I told her to either do what she said she was going to do or don't bother coming back. I can't give her a pass and sign off on her research just because her father is friends with Dr. White."

"You could help her. Take her to the rat room, and let her watch you work. You took her on as a favor to Rupert. You need to see it through."

"Is that fair to Brian? He has to do his own work." Brian was Joe's undergraduate student.

"It's not always about fairness," Joe said. "Rupert wouldn't have asked you for a needless favor. You need him in your corner."

Cory sighed heavily. Joe had a point. If she wanted his job, she had to keep Dr. White happy.

"That's not why I'm calling," Joe said. "I saw your letter to the editor in the Canadian medical journal."

Cory was taken aback. She didn't know the letter had been published. She had a Google Alert set to notify her whenever her name appeared in the public domain, and she'd received no notification. "I haven't seen the journal."

"May I ask what that was about?"

"A favor for a friend," Cory said, wondering what he was getting at.

"You gave the impression you're a medical doctor."

"No, I didn't. I signed my letter the way I always do."

"You signed it Dr. Cordelia Montclair."

Cory turned to her laptop, pulled up her letter, and confirmed she had signed it Cordelia Montclair, PhD. She tried to view the online edition, but the link was broken. "Can you send me what you're seeing?"

Joe had to copy and paste the letter. He stood by, his face in a small rectangle in the corner of her screen, watching as she read.

Her letter was the same except her title had been changed. It was a minor alteration and not inaccurate as she was legally entitled to call herself doctor, which was short for doctor of philosophy. While physicians also used the term, on paper they typically appended MD for clarity. Still, she didn't like the change and wouldn't have made it herself. "Maybe the journal made a mistake."

From his tiny corner, Joe said, "I understand, after what happened with Sophie, where you're coming from, I'd just be careful picking a fight with the FDA. You don't want them coming after you for practicing medicine without a license."

Cory thought Joe was over-reacting. "I'm not picking a fight with the FDA."

"The thing is," Joe added, with what seemed like caution, "I don't know if Rupert has seen it, but you'd better bring the letter to his attention. He doesn't like surprises. Give him a heads up."

Was it that big a deal? Cory doubted if Dr. White would ever see it. The small, obscure foreign journal had a broken link. Still, she agreed to correct her title, and Joe suggested she do it immediately.

He signed off, and Cory shot an email to the editor of the journal requesting the correction. She couldn't go through the journal website as there was apparently some technical malfunction, and she was advised to check back later. Then she left the lab and went down to the animal room to look for the rat. Still no sign.

Chapter Fifteen

That afternoon, Megan didn't show. She didn't call, didn't email, just went awol. Spring break was the following week, and Cory hoped Megan left early and hadn't quit her thesis. Regretting the ultimatum and mindful of Joe's advice regarding her future, Cory gritted her teeth and picked up her phone. She called Megan, who didn't answer, and left a sickeningly sweet message. "I look forward to seeing you when classes resume." Cory paused and closed her eyes. "You don't have to handle the rats," she added, and she hated herself for it.

She hung up, and when her phone rang a few minutes later, she thought Megan was responding to the hollow groveling, but it was Ethyl from day care. Sophie was sick.

Cory grabbed her purse and left the lab, reeling with déjà vu and feeling sick herself. Her whole body was so tense she could barely breathe. She was running so fast she almost fell down the stairs. She reached her car out of breath, her heart on fire. Once again, she dealt with traffic and lights, and Cory was stuck, pounding on the steering wheel and wanting to cry. She couldn't do it. She couldn't go through it again. She couldn't deal with Sophie being sick.

At the day care, Sophie lay on a mat in the quiet room, radiating heat. Her fever was one hundred and four, and she was too sick to cry. Cory gathered her up, and she was limp, like a doll. Her hair was damp, her skin clammy.

Cory set her in the car seat, wanting to drive with her on her lap, in her arms, never to be separated again. Sophie seemed indifferent, eyes closed, looking comatose. Cory broke every traffic law racing to the doctor's office.

It was lunchtime, and the place was closed. Cory got Sophie out and sat on the front stoop, rocking her back and forth. It happened like this last spring, only Cory's reaction had been indifference. Ethyl had called at noon, and Cory wanted to wait until the end of the day. Ethyl insisted she come immediately. Cory had to leave work and ended up waiting at the doctor's office. All people with scheduled appointments were seen. The receptionist didn't think it was an emergency, and why would she when Cory was so blasé.

But when the doctor laid eyes on Sophie, he was immediately alarmed. Haygood Robinson was a tall black man from California with a kind and caring bedside manner and no poker face. He looked into Sophie's eyes and checked her throat in high distress. There was a bruise on her thigh that clearly upset him. He drew blood, and as he studied the slide under the light microscope, his jaw dropped. He let Cory look into the scope, and the reason for his dismay was obvious. A sludge of white blood cells. The signpost of leukemia. It was a cancer of the lymphocytes, the white blood cells that fight infection. Haygood went to the phone and called the oncologist at Greenlee Hospital. Cory left his office and went straight there. At nine months old, Sophie had Stage 4 leukemia. Three days and one round of chemo later, she was in ICU, fighting for her life.

Now, eight months later, Cory was back in that helpless, hopeless nightmare. Only now it was worse. She knew now what she didn't know then: the inadequacy of American medicine. It could diagnose but hardly cure. At least she knew about the Mexican clinic.

Another patient arrived and then the receptionist. Cory jumped up as the woman unlocked the door. "I need to see Haygood immediately."

The receptionist looked at Sophie. "I'll call him."

He rushed in five minutes later, ignored three scheduled waiting patients, and took Sophie right away. Cory lay her down on the examining table. She lay listlessly, unresisting, staring out of small, dull eyes as he listened to her heart and her breathing, and he then examined her skin, eyes, ears, and mouth.

Cory was shadowing him, heart pounding mercilessly as she waited for the verdict.

Haywood finally turned to look at her. "I'll take blood."

That revived Sophie and made her scream, no doubt summoning bad memories of ICU where she was tied down and endlessly pricked and poked. Haygood turned on the scope and read the slide. "It's not the same as before," he said. "Her blood looks fine."

Those magic words melted Cory's tension and made her shoulders slump. She bent down, peered into the scope, and saw textbook-looking blood. Her breathing reverted to normal, the squeezing of her heart eased. "What does she have?"

"There's a bad strain of the flu going around. It looks like that." Haywood gave Sophie five drops of prescription Tylenol. "Let me know if she gets any worse."

By the time they got home, the fever had broken. Cory put Sophie to bed, and she was asleep immediately, thumb in her mouth, breathing deep and slow. Cory sat in the rocker and watched her sleep. The worst thing for Cory about Sophie getting sick, besides her horrific pain, was crucifying guilt. How could a good mother not know something was wrong? Cory was so focused on work she hadn't paid close attention to Sophie's recurring colds. She'd blamed winter, the cold weather, day care; but she should have known. A good mother would know. Even worse was a darker question: What if she was to blame? Cory worked with poison. Toxicity was only a matter of dose. Too much water was deadly. It could be her fault. The only way Cory could handle the guilt was to block it out and not think about it. There was no coming to terms with it.

At least for now, Sophie was fine. But that was no guarantee she wouldn't get sick again. It could happen anytime. When Sophie was born, Cory's worst fear had been that, as a single mother, something would happen to her and Sophie would be left alone. But when Sophie got sick, Cory discovered a far worse fear. She could lose Sophie.

The odds were against life from the start. A human being was created from forty-six chromosomes, twenty thousand structural genes, tons of nonsense DNA, and two hundred thousand proteins. When you considered all the things that could go wrong, it was a miracle anyone was healthy at all. Life was precarious, health was a gift, and modern medicine was an abomination. Doctors didn't see it. They behaved like gods, acting as if they could defy death, when in reality they had no clue of what gave health. They viewed sickness like a broken car—treating symptoms and fixing parts.

Alternative medicine, like that offered at the *Clinica De Buena Salud*, addressed the whole system. Dr. Arrango was good, but he was working in the dark. With Oxylace, he went on trial and error; it might only be a temporary fix. There had been no dose-response study, no volunteers checking untoward side effects, and no long-term follow up that would show problems down the road. The drug needed to be rigorously studied.

Chapter Sixteen

May 8th

Friday came, and with it, spring break. Cory planned to leave early and pick up Sophie who was back at day care, fully recovered. Dr. White had already checked out for the week, as had the students in the lab. Though faculty, staff, and post-docs didn't get a holiday, with the undergrads fleeing the campus in droves, it felt like summer vacation. Cory was happily packing her briefcase when there was a knock on her door. She looked up to see two strange men.

"FDA," said the older one. He was bleary-eyed and pale with thin lips and a greasy comb-over. He was her height and overweight. A basketball-sized stomach strained the buttons of his plaid button-down shirt and hung over his baggy navy slacks.

She went to the door and took the offered business card. Dr. Claude Smite was an FDA agent working at the office of the commissioner in Silver Spring, Maryland. He introduced Mr. Tiggs, who had no card. Tiggs was younger, tall, skinny, and reeked of cigarette smoke. A package of Marlboros poked out his shirt pocket. Dr. Smite said, "We need to speak with you."

Cory invited them into her office and waved them into the visitor chairs. She walked around her desk and sat down. "How can I help you?"

With a loud click, Claude Smite unlatched his briefcase and withdrew a folder. He passed her a copy of her letter to the *Canadian Journal of Cancer*. "Did you write this?"

Was the FDA finally interested in doing a proper study on Oxylace? "I did write that. It's a fantastic drug. One shot and—"

Claude Smite interrupted her. "Where did you get your medical degree?"

She was taken aback by his tone. "I don't have one."

"Then you have misrepresented your credentials. You claim, fraudulently, to be a medical doctor, when you are not."

"I didn't write doctor on the letter," Cory said, aiming for a steady voice, despite growing unease. The man's tone was menacing. "I'm trying to get it corrected. The journal made a mistake."

"They printed what you gave them," Claude Smite almost shouted.

"I didn't write that, really. But everything in the article is true. The drug has been used in Mexico for years and is shown to cure cancer."

Claude Smite narrowed his eyes. "It is up to the FDA to define what is a cure for cancer. We looked into Oxylace in the fifties and found it ineffective. Period."

Cory leaned forward and ardently tried to make her case. "Science has come a long way since then. We could do a new study, use your rigorous method, run three clinical trials and test Oxylace—"

Claude Smite interrupted her with a shout. "The matter is concluded! Oxylace is useless."

Cory sat back. "Yet it works."

She said it nicely, but Claude Smite took grave offense. Glowering darkly, he pointed a finger at her. "You are making a false claim."

"Excuse me?" Cory heard what he said but needed time to think.

While Claude Smite repeated himself, her indignation grew, and when he was done, she said, "The letter wasn't published in the U.S. It's a Canadian journal. Isn't that outside your jurisdiction?"

"Obviously not." Claude Smite leaned forward. "You have misrepresented yourself as a doctor. Continue making your false claim and you will be arrested for fraud and charged with practicing medicine without a license."

Cory drew back, unnerved by the accusations. "How am I practicing medicine?"

"You offer false hope to people who would unduly suffer from an ill-advised, ineffectual treatment that has no promise. That is fraud. Let me be clear." Claude Smite held up a finger. "One, you refer in your letter to an FDA-approved chemotherapy cocktail as damaging, when in fact it is life-saving." He held up a second finger. "Two, you call a scientifically untested drug effective when the exact opposite has been shown." The third finger came up. "Three, you say it is a cure for cancer when that is not the case."

"But it—"

Claude Smite interrupted again. "Listen to me! Oxylace had its day in court and lost. In each instance just cited, you are are in violation of the law. Our mandate is to protect the public, and we will do our job."

"Oxylace is safe. It has no side effects. The public doesn't need to be protected from a drug that does no harm."

"You do not get to decide that. What constitutes harm is for the FDA and the FDA alone to determine."

"But you approve chemotherapy, and those chemicals cause harm."

"You have been warned." Claude Smite slammed his briefcase closed. "If you persist, you will be arrested and prosecuted for breaching the Safe Drug Act. Cease and desist this vendetta against Wellspring immediately."

Cory had been listening to the agent with mounting alarm, and now the reason for his visit was suddenly clear. "Are you here on behalf of Wellspring Pharmaceutical?"

"We are here on behalf of the American public. The U.S. Attorney will represent us and cost is of no concern. As for you, as a private citizen, you would bear the full financial cost of any and all lawsuits. As a danger to the public, the bail for charlatans who profit off the suffering of others is typically high. Beyond the range of affordability. I'll warn you that court cases like this tend to drag on and on. With unaffordable bail, you would of course be incarcerated during this time." With a click, the agent snapped his briefcase shut and was on his feet.

Cory hastily followed suit then felt faint as blood drained from her head. She couldn't believe what he was saying.

"This is a courtesy call," Claude Smite said. "In the future, I advise you keep your mouth shut and your pen idle. You have no idea what you're up against. There are repercussions you can't possibly imagine. Good day, *Dr.* Montclair."

The men swept from the room. Cory dropped to her chair. Her heart was knocking. She heard the whoosh of blood in her ear. Fraud! Misrepresentation! Court! Charlatan! Prosecution! Incarceration! One-word exclamation points screamed in her head.

Evonia came into the office. "Who were those guys?" She plunked herself down in the chair that Claude Smite had just vacated. She waved the air, as if dispersing phantom cigarette smoke.

"FDA."

"What did they want?"

Cory slid her letter to the editor across the table.

Evonia read slowly, her eyes widening. When she was done, she pushed it back. "Are you insane? Why would you write that?"

"I wanted someone to test Oxylace in people, to see how good it is."

"What did the FDA say?"

"Stop talking, stop writing letters. Otherwise they take me to court, throw me in jail."

Evonia shook her head in wonderment. "Did you think you could write this and no one would notice?"

"I was thinking that in a free country, you're free to tell the truth."

Evonia laughed sadly. "That is your problem. This is not a free country. Your government is not on your side. It is employed by the rich. You pay your government to pass laws that help companies hurt you."

Cory kicked the garbage can across the room. How could it be so clear to Evonia when Cory was just getting it now? "And you want to become a citizen?"

"It is still better here than in my country," Evonia said. "There, you would be imprisoned already. When it is worse here, I will go home. It may not be too long."

***

Ten minutes later, Cory was on the road, driving to day care in light traffic, her mind raging. Her government was using her tax dollars to block good drugs. The agency charged with protecting human health did nothing of the kind. The FDA had no interest in honestly evaluating Oxylace. Cory knew the primary concern of a drug company was profit, but she thought the FDA served in good faith. She was wrong. The last thing the drug industry wanted was a cheap anti-cancer drug that caused no side effects and actually worked. Through threats and intimidation and the authority of the U.S. government, the FDA was keeping cheap drugs off the market. They did it by threatening people like her. The warning was loud and clear. Stand down or go to jail.

At home, Mathew was in the kitchen making dinner. Looking unlawyerly in a red apron, he listened carefully to the story of the FDA's visit, examined Claude Smite's business card, and read the letter. He winced almost immediately. "You actually wrote Oxylace was a cure for cancer?"

"I wrote, *may well* cure cancer. It's not the same thing."

Mathew dried his hands on a towel and continued to scan the page. "Can you back up what you say? Are the four chemotherapy drugs provably damaging?"

"Absolutely. The incidence of allergic reactions to one of the drugs is through the roof. Especially in kids. The side effects are horrendous. Vomiting, muscle weakness, mouth sores, inability to swallow, loss of hair, loss of appetite, loss of weight, fatigue, diarrhea, sto—".

He held up his hand. "Okay, I get it. It's physically damaging."

"Versus Oxylace, which is cheap, effective, and without side effects. The injection doesn't hurt, there's no burning, no irritation, no pain, and no nausea. Eat a good diet and you're cured. One injection costs one hundred dollars. Sophie's whole treatment cost a thousand dollars. Yet that agent called *me* a charlatan and said *I* was trying to profit off suffering. What about drug companies?"

Mathew tapped the letter with a long finger. "What are you going to do?"

"Are you kidding? With a choice to shut up or go to jail? I shut up. Pray the FDA leaves me alone."

Mathew gave her back her letter, looking disappointed. What did he expect? That she would fight the FDA? She could never go to prison, would never willingly abandon Sophie or the house.

***

Later that evening, Cory called Janie. Her friend answered, laughing merrily. From the background noise, it sounded like she was at a party. "I'm still in D.C. I've met a great gang. We're gearing up to fight. Thanks for joining END. I'll get you your T-shirt. Can you like us on Facebook?"

Cory wasn't listening. "The FDA came to see me."

Over the manic brouhaha, Janie said, "Wait? What?"

"In the letter to the Canadian journal, did you change my title from PhD to doctor?"

"People at the clinic called you doctor. I thought it was okay."

Cory exhaled slowly and put a hand to her forehead. "It's not the same. The FDA can charge me with fraud. They say I'm practicing medicine without a license. They can throw me in prison without bail."

Janie's response was sobering. "That's what they do. The FDA loves taking the little guy to court. It sends a message to the big guy who has more money. Don't even think about speaking up."

"I can't afford to go to court," Cory almost screamed. "I can't go to prison."

"Calm down. If they wanted to take you to court, they'd have served you a summons, and you'd be locked up already. Cory, this is great news. You've got them scared."

"No, *I'm* scared. They definitely were not."

"Look, the FDA uses the power of government to enforce bad policy. Why do you think we have such ridiculous health care? Why do you think the mortality statistics haven't changed since Nixon declared the war on cancer? The U.S. has spent five hundred billion dollars in forty years and has nothing to show for it. Where did the money go? To the drug companies. They got exactly what they wanted. Expensive treatments that do more harm than good and spawn more expensive treatments. The industry spends a thousand times more on lobbyists and campaign donations than they spend on research. The drug companies write our laws. They decide what your doctor can and cannot use. It's lucky you're not a medical doctor or the American Medical Association would yank your license for sure."

"You knew this would happen?"

"Of course not. But I'm not surprised. And I'm not sorry. If you end up in court, that will make the news. We could use cheap advertising. Can you provoke them?"

"No," Cory cried, horrified. "I can't. I won't. I'm not doing anything more. I'm not fighting the FDA." Advice from Joe Carlisle that was recently given and about to be stringently followed.

Janie was silent for a moment. "We need you. You ruffled some feathers, something we haven't been able to do. You got the notice of the FDA. That's huge. Quit your job, and join our team. Help us out."

Cory closed her eyes and shook her head, banishing the thought. "I worked ten years to get where I am. I'm not throwing it away."

"Think about your daughter."

"I *am* thinking about her."

"Think about other kids. Health care won't change until people within the system stand up and fight."

"I'm not in the system."

'You're the closest one we've got. We need you. You got a little push, and you fell over. Get up. Put up your dukes. Start swinging."

Cory shook her head at nothing. "You're the fighter, not me."

"I'm coming to see you. We'll talk this through."

"I won't change my mind."

"I'm here until Wednesday," Janie said. "Then I'm going to L.A. I'll be stuck there a couple of weeks. Divorce shit. It probably won't be until the end of the month. I'll check my schedule and get back to you."

Cory stared at lightning flashing in the sky. Far off, there was the rumble of thunder.

"I'm still invited, right?" Janie said. "You told me I was welcome anytime."

"You are. Of course you are."

"I'll call you. See you soon."

Janie hung up, and Cory closed her phone. The study felt smaller, as if the walls were closing in on her—like a prison.

Chapter Seventeen

The American public does not have the knowledge to make wise health decisions... The FDA is the arbiter of truth ... Trust us ... We will tell you what's good for you.

—FDA Commissioner David Kessler

March 9th

During the night, a front moved in, bringing heavy rain, and Cory woke up to a flooded lawn. It was still pouring in the afternoon when the time came to volunteer at the day care. The kids were bouncing off the walls. There were twenty-five in attendance, when on a typical Saturday there would be eight to ten. Sandy, the retired social worker, had her hands full. They broke into groups and played Go Fish, and before long, the game became a card toss. Snack time came with fruit, juice, and powdered-sugar donuts of which Sophie had two. She licked her fingers and palms before she would wash her hands. The snack left the kids racing in circles. They tried bowling, and soon pegs were flying. Finally, Sandy put on a movie, and the kids calmed down and sprawled on mats to watch *Cinderella*.

Danny was sick with a fever. Sandy called his parents, but neither one answered their phone. Cory agreed with Sandy that it looked like the same flu Sophie had, which had lasted only an afternoon. Danny's parents had signed a drug consent form, and he was given a spoonful of pediatric Tylenol.

He sat in Cory's lap with Sophie and watched the movie. He cuddled close, nestling tight, burning with heat. Cory brushed his rounded bangs off his forehead. He was sweating, his pageboy-styled hair limp and damp. He fell asleep, and when he awoke thirty minutes later, his fever had broken. As rain fell, they watched the rest of the film.

Cinderella found her man, but the horses were about to turn into pumpkins, and time was running out.

Six o'clock came with the end of the movie—and the end of Cory's shift. She was leaving when Danny's father arrived. He had finally gotten his message. They walked to the street together, each carrying a child on their hip. The rain had turned to drizzle, and the air was wet and cold. The trees were dripping.

Daniel Weiss was a tall, thin, nervous type in his mid-thirties. He had the same hairstyle as Danny and the same type hair: straight and brown and worn long in the cut of a prince. As Cory learned previously, he had moved to Duane from Houston just before Christmas. He was an assistant professor of soil science, and his wife was a freelance painter. Danny was their only child. He had overheard the other parents talking about Sophie. "She had leukemia?"

Cory hated having this conversation with Sophie within earshot. "She's totally fine."

"That must have been terrible."

Cory smiled at her daughter. "It's over. She's okay."

"Danny was at the doctor last week for his annual checkup. He has enlarged lymph nodes in his neck. The doctor was concerned."

"It could be an infection. This flu."

"He took blood. Dr. Robinson. Do you know him?"

"He's Sophie's doctor." In the small town, there weren't many pediatricians.

"He sent the blood to the lab for testing. We haven't heard back yet. He looked at it in the microscope, and I could tell something was wrong. Did that happen to you?"

"No. He looked in the scope and called the oncologist. We went straight to the hospital. It was Stage 4."

Daniel looked relieved. "It's probably nothing, then."

"It's not Stage 4."

"Even if it *is* something, the treatment works, right?"

After the FDA's warning, this was a subject Cory was going to avoid. "Sophie is healthy" was all she would say.

"That's great news." Daniel clicked his keychain, and the lights on a minivan flashed and he said good-bye.

Cory got home and found a piece of paper taped to her door. The neighbors were having a party on Friday in honor of the Ides of March. It was a potluck. At the bottom, in a small scribble, was a note to bring a "plus one" and Sophie. Cory stuffed the invitation into her pocket, wondering whether to go. After Sophie was born she seldom went out, but she liked the new neighbors. It was just next door, she could bring Sophie, and maybe Mathew would want to go.

Bad idea. She reminded herself that that was a line she wasn't going to cross. Step over it and he'd be gone. And she wanted him to stay. He had become more than just a boarder—Sophie adored him. If past experience was anything to go by, when it came to having a relationship, Cory was a failure. Men weren't averse to leaving. It's what they did; they couldn't get away quickly enough. The Count left so fast he left behind a sock. Keeping a man in the house this long was a breakthrough, and Cory would do nothing to spoil the status quo.

Mathew was in the kitchen in his apron, broiling the crust of a casserole. He had the week off and had been home all day working on a legal case study that was due after the break.

Sophie ran to him. He picked her up, spun her around, and kissed her cheek. She threw her thin arms around his neck and hugged him.

Cory watched the display wordlessly and with wonder. Mathew flaunted his affection, while Sophie took it and returned it. He was much freer in his ability to express himself than Cory could ever be. He hoisted Sophie to his hip. "Do you like casserole?"

She looked at him with her dark eyes. "Mmmm."

"There's some wine, if you want," he said to Cory. He turned off the oven, removed the smoking dish. "I can't believe her father doesn't want to see her. I can't imagine that."

"Not every man is father material," Cory said.

"Why doesn't The Count have visitation?" Still holding Sophie, Mathew grabbed a big bowl of salad from the fridge.

"I told you. He lives in Spain."

"How long was he here?"

"Not long."

"So not a long relationship?"

She wasn't going to tell him the truth. "He left. He had to go back." She took Sophie from him, slipped her into her seat, and gave her a cookie.

Mathew grabbed wooden salad forks. "Did you feel abandoned?"

"Of course not." Cory grabbed a goblet and filled it with wine. At the time, she had been devastated.

"Even though you were pregnant?"

"I didn't know it at the time."

"Where did you meet?"

"At Stanley's Bistro, if you must know."

"You met in a bar?"

"It's also a restaurant." Though she'd been on the bar side. "Is there something wrong with that? It was Thanksgiving. They were showing a big game."

Mathew looked at Sophie, his long fingers moving as if he were playing an air piano. "She was born in August; you met at Thanksgiving. You couldn't have spent much time together."

"We didn't."

He turned his back and went to the stove to stir the beans. "One night? Then, what? You pushed him out?"

Mathew had it backwards. "No, I didn't push him out."

"Does he even know about Sophie?"

Cory sighed audibly. "Of course he knows." Though it was well after the fact.

"Aren't you lonely?"

Cory got out the silverware and shoved the drawer closed. "I have Sophie." And she'd had enough of the conversation. "What about you? You ask me about The Count, but I know nothing about your fiancé."

"You can ask me anything. I'll tell you. I don't have anything to hide. I'm not defensive."

"Let's eat." Cory picked Sophie up out of her seat and carried her to the dining room. She set the table.

For dinner, the menu was a cauliflower casserole with broccoli, beans, and a Greek salad. Cory filled Sophie a plate, cut up her food, and gave her a small silver fork, which she held in her left hand as she ate with the fingers of her right hand.

"When I had my practice, I saw many unhappy people," Mathew said as he sipped wine. "The reason in every case was the same. They had lost their own true self and were trying to be someone they weren't, and it just doesn't work. They were living a false life. Part of my job was to help them see who they really are."

"What's your point?"

"I don't think you're someone who's meant to be alone."

"You don't know me."

He wouldn't give up. "Or, you don't know you." He put down his glass of wine. "Look how you are with Sophie. You're an excellent mother. You're not a world unto yourself."

"Again, I fail to see your point."

"What about love?" he said, staring at the piano. "Of finding someone who took your breath away. Who you couldn't live without? Someone who enriched your life, expanded your world, challenged you, and pushed you to reach your potential? Someone who had your back, made things easier, and better? Someone who made you happy, magnified your good, and brought out the best in you?" He looked at her intensely across the table.

She took a large bite of the casserole and chewed carefully. She had met men like that in the past and lost them too quickly. It was too much to hope for. She was resigned to her fate and determined to make the best of it. She swallowed and took a sip of wine. "That's not real life. Is that what you told your patients? Weren't you supposed to ground them in reality?"

"I wasn't a shrink." Mathew said. "I guess you haven't read Plato's *Symposium*." He commenced telling a story of a race that existed before human beings, where the two sexes were joined together and lived as one. But this race defied Zeus, who in revenge cut the whole in half, creating men and women. Thereafter the separate parts were condemned to roam the globe searching for their missing half. Sometimes they succeeded, found their soul mate, and became whole.

Cory had never heard the story before, but then she hadn't studied philosophy, English, or psychology. She stuck to science. She liked numbers and empirical theories based on solid, observable facts. She didn't base her life on wild, fantastical tales.

"I thought I found her," Mathew said as he cut into a tomato. "Margaret, of course, apparently felt differently. She waited until the day before the wedding to call it off. We invited two hundred guests. The out-of-town folks were already there. I was getting ready for the rehearsal dinner. Everything was booked and paid for. Rings on hand, air tickets confirmed, a honeymoon in Cozumel all paid up."

"Maybe you should try to stop thinking about it," Cory said as Sophie stabbed broccoli with the fork.

"Shamus was going to be the ring bearer. Margaret made a pillow that she attached to a bow tie that went around his neck. It had a little depression in the middle with a clip so the rings wouldn't fall out. We planned the wedding for six months. I took dance lessons for a year."

Once again, he looked like he was going to cry. Even Sophie eyed him with concern. "I'm not sure talking about it helps," Cory said, wishing he would just eat.

"I like to process experience."

"By reliving it endlessly? It doesn't seem like it's working. Why not move on?"

"You take your baggage with you. You don't get to leave it behind."

"I don't see why not."

"That's not the way it works."

Cory ate on. It worked that way for her, and it worked well.

Chapter Eighteen

March 10th

Sunday brought daylight saving time and summer-like heat that dried up the rain. The time change wreaked havoc on Sophie's schedule, and by mid-afternoon she was wide-awake when she should have been napping. Cory was rocking her on the porch swing while Mathew dug up sod, turning the soil in the southeast corner. He was going to put in a garden to grow herbs and vegetables. Free food sounded great to Cory, and she was thinking about her favorite vegetables when the doorbell rang.

Pluto sprang up and began barking. Mathew stopped digging. Cory got up and went inside to get the door. Daniel Weiss was on the porch with a woman he introduced as his wife. Marie was in her early forties and pleasantly plump. Already gray, a long curtain of hair fell to her waist. She was braless and dressed in a tank top and an ankle-length denim skirt: a picture-perfect earth mother. She held the four-year-old Danny on her hip.

Danny said, "Hi, Sophie," in a sweet, high voice. He waved a small hand at her.

She said, "Dada," and waved back.

"Can we come in?" Daniel asked.

"We're sorry to disturb you," Marie said. "We need to talk to you."

Cory knew why they had come and wanted to close the door and set the chain. She didn't want to get involved; she wanted to stay out of it, even as she moved to the side and let them in.

They went to the backyard. Cory dragged chairs toward the porch swing and resumed her place as the guests sat down. Mathew threw down the shovel, mopped his forehead, and came their way. Daniel stood up and waited to shake his hand. Mathew didn't explain who he was, and Cory thought she should clarify his position, but the moment passed. He was offering drinks as if they were his guests.

But they didn't want anything, and he pulled over another chair and sat down. Sophie was wide-awake and reaching out for him. "Dada."

"He's not her father," Cory said, holding Sophie tight.

"We went to see Haygood Robinson this morning," Daniel said, ignoring her comment.

"I couldn't wait," Marie added. "I had to see him. I had this bad feeling. I knew something was wrong." She peered at Cory. "Did you feel that when Sophie was sick?"

Cory shook her head. That was her shame, neglect she could never forgive. Preoccupied, she'd missed the lethal warning signals.

"He got back the blood tests," Daniel said. "We have to take Danny for more tests."

"I'm so sorry," Cory said, passing the squirming Sophie to Mathew.

"We have an appointment with the oncologist at Greenlee Hospital tomorrow," Marie added. "Dr. Sullivan."

"She was Sophie's oncologist," Cory said. Like pediatricians, the small town had few specialists. Doctors were well-known and well-shared.

"But Sophie made it through okay," Marie said brightly. She was nodding as if to convince herself. "She got through chemo all right."

The conversation was almost too much for Cory to take. These strangers were about to relive her greatest nightmare, and she didn't want to get dragged into it. She wanted to forget. Forget how hard it was to find the right bore needle to fit into Sophie's thin vein. Forget her screaming as the chemo burned her skin as it coursed into her blood. Forget the diarrhea, vomiting, the sores in her mouth, the wasting of her body, and the dimming of her being as the light went out in her eyes. Cory didn't want to remember any of it.

Into the long silence, Mathew said, "Sophie took only one round of chemotherapy. She got an infection and went to ICU. Make sure you notify your health insurance company if it happens to Danny."

"The money isn't important," Daniel said.

Cory had thought the same, which was why the health care industry got away with highway robbery. At the time of diagnosis, money never mattered, only life.

"But Sophie recovered," Marie said, stubbornly holding on to the thought. "Dr. Robinson said she's in remission."

Cory said nothing; it was Mathew who said, "Sophie didn't finish the chemo. She went to a clinic in Tijuana." He shot Cory a bewildered look that silently said, *Why am I talking and not you?*

Because Cory was taking the FDA warning to heart. Medical doctor or not, she couldn't give medical advice without being guilty of practicing medicine without a license. She would watch every word she said.

Marie locked eyes with Cory. "Why didn't you finish the chemo?"

As Cory wondered what was safe to say, Mathew answered on her behalf. "After Sophie got MRSA, she was too weak. They went to Mexico for alternative treatment."

Marie was still staring at Cory. "What was it?"

Mathew was frowning. "Free speech is a right protected by the Constitution."

Cory sighed, relenting, and gave a measured answer. "Sophie took a drug called Oxylace. You can't get it here. She took one shot that cost a hundred dollars. A week in the clinic cost a thousand dollars. We changed her diet, and, so far, she's in remission."

Marie was on the edge of her chair. "Why didn't Dr. Robinson tell us about it? Why is he sending us to a cancer specialist? Why doesn't he just give us this shot?"

"It's not FDA approved. Doctors can't use it. If they do, they'll lose their license."

"The cancer specialist will know about it," Marie said. "She can prescribe it."

Cory shook her head. The town's sole pediatric oncologist did things by the book. When Cory checked Sophie out of ICU, Susie Sullivan threatened to send the Department of Child Services after her for endangering the life of her child. "She can only use FDA-approved treatments," Cory said.

"If your drug is so good, why won't the FDA approve it?" Daniel asked.

"They don't think it works."

"Do you think it does?" Marie said.

"It's what Sophie took," Cory said.

"Where's the clinic?" Marie asked.

Cory went inside and grabbed a brochure from the *Clinica de Buena Salud*. They could read up about the clinic, call them up, and make up their own minds. She had said too much already.

After they left, Mathew handed over the sleeping Sophie, and Cory took her upstairs and put her to bed. When she came down, Mathew was pacing in the foyer. "You could fight, you know," he said. "You don't have to stand down. A little boy's future may be at stake."

"So is a little girl's."

"The truth is on your side."

"I'm not fighting the FDA."

"Do you know why you can't get Oxylace here?"

"Yes," she said sharply. "It would have to go through rigorous FDA testing. That costs money, and the FDA has already decided the drug doesn't work."

"Because it's too cheap," Mathew said. "Drug companies don't want patients paying a hundred bucks for a cure when they can pay forty thousand."

"That's so cynical."

"Ever hear of Sorcor?"

"Of course," she said, disingenuously. She had learned about the drug the previous week in her class. "It's as effective in curing depression as a cube of sugar."

"This legal paper I'm writing is a brief on the class action suit. The drug is useless yet the FDA endorses it without reservation. From what I've read, their scientific studies are no good. They use statistics to get whatever results they want. The FDA works for the industry they're supposed to regulate."

"Why are you telling me?"

"You're a scientist. You could call them out on it."

"I don't know anything about it."

"You could educate yourself. I've got a book for you."

He ran upstairs quickly, taking the steps two at a time, as if he thought she'd try to abscond from her own house. Ten seconds later he was back with a book entitled *Political Ill-Health*. "There's a chapter on Oxylace," he said as he gave her the book.

She saw it was written by a former senator. "I'll take a look."

He nodded, smiling at her with his eyes, and she felt warmed, as if by the sun. "It will make you furious," he said.

He returned to the garden, and she went to the living room. She sat on the couch in the bay window in a bright swath of sunlight and opened the book. She turned to the chapter on Oxylace and began to read. She learned the drug was first used in the fifties by a physician called Dr. Ace, who used it to treat a wide variety of ailments, including cancer. In July 1951, he wrote about his experience in an article entitled, "Breakthrough in Cancer Treatment," which was published in the *Northeast Medical Journal.*

The paper caught the interest of the FDA, which decided to test Oxylace in five terminal patients. The five were already exposed to so much chemotherapy and so ridden with cancer they were almost dead. When they died, it proved that Oxylace didn't work. But people cried foul, and the hullabaloo was so loud the FDA had to run another study. This time, instead of using Dr. Ace's drug, the FDA made their own. It didn't work.

The FDA then arrested Dr. Ace. Not for using an unsafe drug but for fraudulent labeling. He had called what the FDA considered an ineffective drug a cure. The ostensible purpose of the lawsuit was to punish a rogue physician who was peddling false claims and to protect the public from a bad drug. The case made the news, but the only side that got coverage was the prosecution. Despite days of favorable testimony extolling the effectiveness of the drug, the prosecution lined up doctors to testify that "in theory" the drug "couldn't possibly" work. Back then, government witnesses were allowed to give "opinions" that the defense could not object to, nor cross examine. If a doctor had the opinion a drug *couldn't* work, that was it. No scientific evidence was needed to back up the belief. In the end, the jury was hung. The case was retried, and the new jury was hung as well. Asked later about the verdict, the jurors said they could not believe their government would launch a frivolous suit. Freed the second time, Dr. Ace fled the country to escape further prosecution. As for Oxylace, the FDA banned the drug in an act that was called "a heinous evil imposed upon the American public."

Sophie woke up and started crying, her sobs resounding over the baby monitor. Cory put the book down and hurried upstairs. She had known none of this. She didn't want to know. If Mathew thought this would get her to fight, it had the opposite effect. The FDA was more corrupt and more powerful than she could have imagined. No wonder the FDA agent was so confident he could throw her in jail for what she wrote. He obviously could! Her boss warned her not to pick a fight with the FDA, and it was a warning she would heed.

Chapter Nineteen

Treatment originates outside you; healing comes from within.

—Andrew Weil, MD

March 11th

At the end of an interminable day, Art Farber was staring up at the ceiling watching a janitor on the roof sweep snow off the skylight as he waited for the eight p.m. meeting. The sun had long set, and the junior staff had departed long ago. With the big city buried beneath two feet of snow, travel was difficult, hampering Claude Smite's travel from D.C. His flight had been canceled, and he'd been forced to take the train and was now walking from the station. In light of the whiteout, Art suggested rescheduling the meeting, but Claude was against it. So disturbing was his trip to Texas.

Art sighed tiredly to no one. The snow was crippling the city and trading was slow, even for Monday. His only solace was his rising stock price. Ordinarily he'd be dancing with joy. The proxy statement had just been released to stockholders in advance of the annual stockholders meeting, and the numbers had never looked better. The earnings per share had exceeded analysts' expectations, which had boosted stock price. Shares were now trading at $32.61 and set to go higher. At the upcoming annual meeting, shareholders would vote on his pay. The board had approved an increase in salary to $1.3 million, with an additional $2.7 million bonus, as well as $10.9 million in stock and stock options. Art could use the money. He'd cashed in $5.2 million of his vested shares to buy the Central Park condo that Missy called a steal. He was thinking about a boat. Decades of effort and hard work were finally paying off. This should be the best time of his life, and

Mont-fucking-clair had crashed his party. Instead of looking at yachts, he was worrying about her. She would pay dearly.

Claude arrived just after the hour, and the usual cast of characters was soon in place. Art gave Claude the floor. The agent wanted to stand, but Art pointed to a seat. He was the only one who stood in meetings.

"Montclair thinks we should retest Oxylace," Claude said as he pulled his chair to the table. "Run a full-scale clinical trial. To my face, she actually called Oxylace a cure for cancer. *Her words*. She said it was safe. She doesn't think the FDA needs to protect the public from a drug that does no harm."

Fucking lunatic! Art thought.

"For some reason she thinks Canada can flaunt American law," Claude added. "She thinks she can say whatever she likes, so long as it's true. I let her know in no uncertain terms that was not the case."

Art began to pace, something he did when he was worried. "How do we respond?"

"I warned her about a long, expensive lawsuit. Threatened her with prison. I made it clear we'd fight with the full resources and backing of the U.S. government—Which we will, if we must. That seemed to register."

Art stopped pacing and felt a measure of relief. Money spoke. Money was power. Money moved mountains. And money could silence Mont-fucking-clair.

Claude went on. "The problem is, you don't want a lawsuit."

Amet Patel, Claude's former colleague at the FDA, agreed completely. "It is never prudent to shine a spotlight on our business. We must strive to keep the clinical data private."

Claude nodded emphatically. "You don't want to go to court. That doesn't mean you can't go on the attack. Fire from all sides. You have friends in Washington, right?"

"Some," Art said.

"Call them," Claude said. "Explain the situation. She's raising false hope. The law was made to stop charlatans like her. We have a number of legal options. My personal favorite is the IRS."

Art looked at Connor Loy, the former congressman from Wisconsin. "You've donated millions to Congressman Harris," Connor said, smiling tightly, not showing a wrinkle. "He's looking at re-election in

November and sits on the Committee on Appropriations. He'll know someone at the IRS. He has influence."

Art looked at Hank. "Can you go to Austin and talk to him?"

"First thing tomorrow."

"Do you know anyone at Duane University?" Claude asked.

Art woefully shook his head.

"We have money," the CFO offered. "We could make a donation."

"Work out the details," Art said.

The FDA agent was done, and Hank took over. There was both good news and bad. He began on a high note and announced they'd hacked Montclair's email. They weren't into her computer yet, where they'd see every keystroke she hit, but they were close. Using information gleaned from email, public relations had written a news brief. He passed copies of it around the room.

Art scanned it quickly. It was good; he liked it. He would get PR to run it immediately in every newspaper in Texas. He couldn't believe a low-life trollop like Montclair could cause so much grief.

The bad news was Montclair had joined forces with a new group called END that wanted to water down the drug laws. "It stands for Enough Nasty Drugs," Hank said. "The group's founder is a dingbat called Jane E. Bartlett. She's tight with Montclair. Their aim is to pass the Access to Medical Treatment Act that will take power away from the FDA and the drug industry and give it to doctors."

"That's ridiculous," Art said. "How can something that ludicrous pass?"

Connor Loy shook his head. "It won't. Lobbyists have stopped it before and will stop it again. No one wants it. No one in the industry, that is."

"The public likes the FDA," Claude added. "We keep them safe, and they know it. We can't have doctors running around prescribing whatever they want."

"Bartlett's started a Facebook page," Hank said, sticking to his script. "She's collecting horror stories of chemotherapy."

"We're watching the page," Claude said. "If there's so much as a peep about the efficacy of Oxylace or any unapproved drug, we'll step in."

"Don't let them say anything negative about Wellspring," Art said.

"We're keeping a close eye," Claude said. "Who knows what they're capable of? They're a bunch of fringe fanatics. They're anti-corporation, anti-health, anti-medicine, anti-government, anti-everything. They're so extreme they undermine their own credibility. I can't see anyone taking them seriously."

At least that was good news, Art thought.

"There's one more thing," Hank said.

"Oh?" Art put a hand to his crown and a clump of hair came free. Too much stress was weakening the roots, and his hair was falling out by the handful.

"The Canadian journal is frantically trying to fix its online version. It believes it has been hacked."

"When's the next edition out?" Art asked.

"Tomorrow," Hank said. "We've got Claude's rebuttal below the letter, and they're merged for life. No one will read how good Oxylace is without reading how it doesn't work."

"Get the journal back online," Art said. "Let's not raise any suspicion. I want our hands clean. Our stock is on the move. We don't want untoward publicity." He jabbed a finger at Hank. "Stop her, but keep us out of it. We're a reputable company above reproach, and I won't be dragged through the mud."

"Don't worry, Boss." Hank smiled a grim smile. He wasn't called The Fixer for nothing.

The meeting adjourned, and Claude had to go. He needed to return to Washington that night and left with the comforting words, "When we're done, so is she."

Art bid his men good-night and returned to his office where Missy was waiting. She was wearing her new fur, and she opened it now. She was stark naked. "You work too late," she said as she kissed him fiercely. "Can we go?"

"Not dressed like that we can't."

He took her then and there on his new couch that still smelled of fresh leather. She took him in her mouth and carried him far away. Later, she said she had a friend who wished to join them.

Chapter Twenty

March 12th

On Tuesday morning, Hank was in the corporate jet flying to Austin. Normally Texas was warm this time of year, but the pilot informed him that Austin was as cold as New York, just without the snow. The flight was fast, helped by northern tailwinds. They landed at eight a.m. local time, twenty minutes before schedule. The stairs descended, and Hank hurried to the limo that was waiting to take him to the Sixth Street office of Republican Congressman Alexander Harris.

The congressman was currently in Washington taking care of the people's business, but Hank was to speak to his personal aide who could certainly help solve any Wellspring trouble. In return, Art had transferred six million dollars to the congressman's favorite super PAC.

The office occupied a former grocery store, and the front windows were covered with brown paper. The front door was unlocked, and Hank went in. The place was nearly empty. The checkout counter remained, and there were two fold-up tables bearing pictures of the congressman. The election was eight months away, and the campaign wouldn't kick into high gear until the summer. Still, from a look of the shop, campaign donations appeared in short supply. It was good to note. The candidate would be hungry.

Hank found Drake Mansfield at the rear of the store reclining in a plastic beach lounger with a venti Starbucks coffee cup and the *Austin Herald*. Drake didn't bother standing up but directed Hank to an adjacent lounger. Soon they were facing one another knee to knee.

The aide was thirty-five but looked younger. His bleached-blond hair was so light it was almost white. He had a winter tan that set off gleaming teeth. Drake looked like the surfer he was. A transplant from San Diego, he spent his free time chasing waves.

"We have a problem," Hank said, and he handed Drake a copy of the dossier on Cordelia Montclair.

Drake opened the folder and read the letter to the Canadian journal. He leafed through the file, reading bits and pieces. He picked up the eight-by-ten photo of Montclair that Hank had snapped on campus last week. "Not bad." Drake stared at it a while, then closed the file. "How can we help? My boss is anxious to do whatever it takes for your continued and much-appreciated support."

Hank passed Drake a press release. "We'd like this in newspapers across the state. Most importantly, on the front page of the *Duane Tribune.*"

Drake took the paper and read the article slowly. "Not a problem. Next?"

"When you search Montclair online, the news release should top the list. Possible?"

"Totally."

"We need to discredit her."

Drake lifted the press notice. "This isn't enough?"

"We're sending a stern message. Cease and desist this baseless attack on Wellspring Pharmaceutical. So far, she's not listening. Anything else we should consider?"

Drake listed a number of options that had been used in the past, and every one of them sounded good. Hank signed off on them all and ranked them in order of priority. "Start with the IRS."

"Anything in the press release accurate?" Drake asked.

"Marginally," Hank said.

"What set her off? Did her kid die?"

"No. She took the first round of the cocktail and recovered. You'd think Montclair would be happy, but she's not. She doesn't want to pay her hospital bill. Probably thinks the government should pay it for her. The week the hospital garnished her wages, she wrote to the Canadian journal."

"She's only a post-doc," Drake said. "Money works. Why not just pay her off? Why go to all this trouble?"

"She wants revenge. Art has taken the assault personally. Naturally, he needs to keep his distance. He doesn't want bad publicity. It would upset investors, not to mention our bank account during this important election season."

"Understood," Drake said. "I'll take care of it. Tell Mr. Farber not to worry."

"This can't come back to us."

"Not a problem. No one will know. My association with Congressman Harris is closely guarded."

"Excellent. We're monitoring her email," Hank said as he followed Drake's lead and stood up. "We can forward it, if you like."

Drake recoiled. "I'll pretend I didn't hear that. I'm afraid it's quite illegal." He walked Hank to the door. "We'll be in touch." He pushed on the handle and cold air rushed in.

"Sooner rather than later would be best," Hank said.

Chapter Twenty-one

Over the past two decades the pharmaceutical industry has moved very far from its original high purpose of discovering and producing useful new drugs. Now primarily a marketing machine to sell drugs of dubious benefit, this industry uses its wealth and power to co-opt every institution that might stand in its way, including the US Congress, the FDA, academic medical centers, and the medical profession itself.

–Marcia Angell, MD, former editor-in-chief,
The New England Journal of Medicine

March 13th

After a restless night, Cory was up early on Wednesday morning. Mathew was already up. He'd gotten the paper, and coffee was ready. As she rubbed sleep out of her eyes and grabbed a mug, he looked up from the paper and said, "You were screaming last night."

It was five thirty, still dark outside. "Sorry if I woke you." She went to the table and reached for the front section of the paper. It was his subscription, but he always started with the sports. "It's a bad dream. I have it a lot."

"Must be terrifying." He lowered his paper. "Tell me."

"Okay, Dr. Freud. It's very dark, and I'm in the backseat of a car that's going very fast. There's no one at the wheel, no one driving, and no one up front. The car's out of control. It's speeding down a steep hill, there's a curve in the road, and straight ahead there's a drop-off. I know I'm not going to make the turn, and there's nothing I can do. The car goes off-road, and I'm airborne, flying through the sky. I know I'm going to crash, and I start screaming."

"A common dream," Mathew declared. "Look at the car as a meta-phor for your life. What is it telling you?"

"You can't drive from the backseat."

"Or, your life is out of control. You need to make a correction."

"No, I don't."

"Next time, try to keep dreaming. See what happens."

Like that was remotely possible. She unfolded the paper. The weather was the headline. A cold front had blown in Monday, and now there was a warning of frost. It was a good thing they hadn't planted the garden. While Texas was getting the full blast of an Arctic wind, they missed the storm that had buried the northeast in snowdrifts. Cory stared at a photo of a whiteout and was about to turn the page when she saw *her* picture. It was her staff photo from the university website. The headline was "Disgraced Duane Post-Doc on Notice." With her heart in her mouth, she read the article:

> *The FDA last week reprimanded Duane University post-doc-toral fellow Cordelia Montclair for practicing medicine without a license. Misrepresenting herself as a physician, Montclair was promoting the use of a scientifically untested and poten-tially harmful drug. Preferring quackery to AMA-sanctioned medicine, the unwed mother recently cut short approved che-motherapy for her infant daughter. Following the infant's recovery after a two-week stay in the nationally acclaimed neonatal intensive care unit at Greenlee Hospital, Montclair made the unsubstantiated assertion that a drug currently on the American Medical Association blacklist and banned by the FDA saved her daughter's life. Rather than honor le-gitimate hospital expenses, Montclair has slandered the medical establishment that enabled her daughter's full recov-ery. The disgraced scientist is currently under investigation by the Department of Child Services for child endangerment. Recently cited by the university safety officer for hazardous lab practices, her laboratory is under investigation and will likely be shut down. She is currently under investigation for tax evasion.*

Cory dropped the paper, feeling dizzy. Her stomach shriveled to the size of a prune. Heat burned her cheeks like a fever. She stared out the window at black shadows.

Mathew said, "What is it? What's wrong?"

Unable to speak, she shoved the paper at him. Was the Department of Child Services investigating her? The DCS had the authority to take children from their homes.

Mathew read silently and quickly. "Wow." He whistled aloud, pushed the paper back.

"Can the DCS take Sophie?" she asked.

"You're a great mother," he said. "No one is taking Sophie anywhere."

Cory could have kissed him. She glanced at the offensive article. The content was from an anonymous "staff writer." No one signed it. "Nothing in it is true. Sophie wasn't an infant when she got sick. I was never cited by the safety officer. He's so lazy, I doubt he's ever cited anyone. And the FDA didn't reprimand me. They threatened me. This is bullshit."

"It seems both vague yet simultaneously rich with detail," Mathew said. "Whoever wrote it has a source. They know about your hospital bill. What was the hazardous lab practice?"

"A rat bit a student."

"Yikes."

"It was a control rat. It hardly broke the skin, if it broke it at all."

"I love how they call you an unwed mother. That was unnecessary. I wonder who they talked to."

Cory had no clue. "What can I do?"

"Call the DCS. Check with your security office. Is the IRS looking into you?"

"If they are, they haven't told me."

"If the allegations are unsubstantiated, contact the paper and demand a retraction. They'll have to do it. We'll make them."

She was grateful to have him on her side. She didn't know how she would handle this alone. Here were the repercussions, the fallout from the letter, courtesy of the FDA. She had been unjustly slandered, made to look irresponsible and incompetent—a disgraced harlot. How could she go out in public? Face her students? At least it was spring break, and Dr. White was out of town. Most of the lab was gone too. Still, it was no consolation.

***

It may have only been in her mind, but the other parents and staff at Campus Care seemed to regard her with pity. Keeping her head low and her sunglasses on despite the gray day, Cory dropped Sophie off and hurried to the lab, planning to hide out in her office.

Evonia was waiting for her. "You look worse than your mug shot. Who can you thank for those lies?"

Cory dropped her briefcase. "You saw it."

"Who could miss it? Right there on the front page of our one and only newspaper. It reminds me of home. Government-controlled news. Reporters writing what they wish. It is all crap, correct?"

"As far as I know."

"Did you cheat on your taxes?"

"Of course not. I haven't even done them. Did you tell anyone about the rat bite?"

"Only my husband. Magnus found it funny."

"I'm glad someone's laughing."

"Who would write such a thing?"

"I'm guessing the FDA."

"Yes. They could not take you to court. Instead, they did this. You must be careful. You have become a target. You must lose their sight. Stay low."

The question was, how had Cory become so visible in the first place? She wrote a short letter to a foreign journal she expected no one to read, and now this. The effect was so out of proportion to the cause. "I'm going to demand a retraction."

"Good luck. It will not be published. This is not news. It is propaganda. What we call in my country, a hatchet job."

"This is not your country, Evonia."

"It is not that different. In my country, the press writes what the government tells them to write. Everyone knows the news cannot be trusted. It is just lies. You may think what you like, but America is the same."

On that happy note, Evonia put down her coffee cup, and Cory went to her office. She called the DCS the minute they opened and confirmed there was no open investigation about her. She called the security office and learned the security officer was out of town for spring break. According to the secretary, he had not issued any safety violations before he left, although the FDA had recently called and she'd faxed them the accident report.

"Was that wrong?" the secretary asked. "They asked for it, the S.O. wasn't here, and I figured it was okay. What's this about?"

"Nothing." If the secretary didn't already know, Cory wasn't going to broadcast it. But how had the FDA found out about the rat bite?

Next, Cory called the *Duane Tribune* and got tossed around voice mail. She had to leave a message and asked someone to return her call immediately. No one did.

After lunch, a Google Alert notified her of the posting of her letter in the Canadian journal. The broken link was fixed, and Cory was able to read the letter that started it all. Only now, directly below it, the FDA had added a rebuke:

> *In the 1950s, the drug Oxylace was used by a handful of physicians as a potential treatment for cancer. It was, at that time, unequivocally proven by multiple FDA investigations to be ineffective as a treatment for cancer. No scientifically sound study ever conducted has demonstrated the drug's efficacy. For Dr. Montclair to laud it as a cure for cancer today is egregious at best and disgraceful quackery at worst. Oxylace is currently on the American Medical Association backlist and is banned by the FDA.*

Cory hung her head and closed her eyes. She wanted to disappear. Her heart raced as if she was having a myocardial infarction. She crossed her arms, holding herself together. The rebuttal in the journal was as professionally humiliating as the assault in the local paper was personally degrading. She wanted to scream as loud as in her dream.

She put her head down on her desk for an interminable length of time. When she could bear it, she read the rebuttal once more. This one wasn't anonymous. It was signed by Dr. Claude Smite, who gave his full title. In a twist of irony, listed beside her letter and the FDA's response was a large, colorful Wellspring Pharmaceutical ad showing smiling doctors and scientists happily contributing to the health of humans everywhere. "Wellspring = Wellbeing" was their message.

The day passed in an agonizing blur. For added punishment, Cory kept googling herself. The newspaper article was the top link of a long list. For over a year, her top stories had been multiple feeds of her NCI grant: "Duane Researcher Recipient of Coveted NCI Funds." Now it was "Disgraced Duane Post-Doc on Notice." The story had been reproduced in the Austin, Dallas, College Station, and Houston affiliate newspapers. It was all over the state, and people were reading it, which explained the high Google ranking.

At least the letter to the Canadian journal with the FDA's shaming rebuttal hadn't made the first Google page. It was on page twenty in the early afternoon and climbed five pages in an hour as the link got more traffic. It was on the bottom of the third page when the workday was up.

She was leaving when the newspaper finally responded. The caller could barely speak English, and despite numerous attempts to hear the name, Cory didn't catch it. Not that it mattered.

"I demand an immediate retraction," Cory yelled clearly and articulately into the phone.

"We check very carefully the facts of our stories," said a woman in a strong Hindi accent. She sounded far away, as if she was calling from New Delhi.

"You didn't check these facts," Cory said. "Who wrote the article?"

"I am not having that information. Often many sources contribute to a story."

"So no one is responsible? Who will correct it?"

"We will first have to check out your complaint. To what specifically do you object?"

Cory objected to it all and outlined her grievances, which were obviously lost on the caller. Acronyms like the S.O. and DCS escaped her, though the IRS she understood.

"The IRS is investigating you, but you are innocent, you say."

"No," Cory screamed into the mouthpiece. "They are not investigating me."

"I am sorry. We are having communication issue," said the caller, sounding sincere.

Quite the understatement. "I'll send it to you in writing."

"That would be very helpful."

"How long will it take you to correct?"

"We will first have to investigate very thoroughly."

"Unlike what you did when you published the story," Cory yelled, before slamming down the phone.

She sat down and typed out a correction: *Your libelous article of me in today's paper was wrong on so many fronts that I demand an immediate retraction. First, I was threatened, not reprimanded, by the FDA. You state they conducted multiple studies on Oxylace, when in reality, they did two. Their science was so shoddy, it would never pass scientific muster today. I also did not misrepresent the facts nor myself. First amendment rights guarantee me the protection of law to tell a personal story, which is what I did. Furthermore, the DCS is not investigating me. Since I am not a physician, I cannot be guilty of malpractice. Also, the university security officer has not cited my lab for hazardous lab practices. Nor has anyone at the IRS spoken to me. In conclusion, you have slandered my name, which is illegal. There is not one correct sentence in your article, and I demand a full correction immediately.*

She didn't bother to proofread the letter, she just sent it. Then she slunk out, skulking away as quickly and quietly as possible.

Chapter Twenty-two

March 15th

Ever since the newspaper article made the front page, Cory had laid low. Gradually she began to think other thoughts, but shame, disgrace, and fury still ruled her brain. She was relieved when the workweek finished, so she could hide in the safety of her home. At day care, she crouched in the car, waiting for a horde of parents to leave. With the time change, it was light late; the sun was still above the trees. The cold snap hadn't lasted. She had the windows down, and a warm south wind carried balmy air up from the gulf. The neighbors would have nice weather for their party. Cory wasn't going. She couldn't face anybody right now, especially not a houseful of successful faculty members. Hopefully Mathew would go out and leave her in peace.

When the coast was clear, Cory hurried out of the car and headed for the building. Sandy was on duty and was the third staff member to offer her condolences. "If you need a reference from us, we'll give it to you. This is so sad about the DCS."

"It's not true," Cory said again. "Nothing in the article is accurate. Nothing."

Sandy looked skeptical. "Well, we want you to know we're on your side."

Cory gave up. "Thank you." She got Sophie and left in a hurry. She was striding to her car and stopped short when she saw Daniel Weiss leaning against it. She walked slowly toward him. "How's Danny doing?"

"He's on chemo," Daniel snapped. "I saw the article in the paper about you. They're taking Sophie. To think we almost listened to you."

Cory shrunk back. "Everything in the article was false. The DCS isn't taking her."

"Dr. Sullivan said Oxylace didn't save her life. It doesn't work. Scientific tests proved that."

"The FDA didn't use the correct formulation. They used an ineffective drug on dying people."

She may as well have kept quiet. "Dr. Sullivan said the chemo worked for you, and that if we took your advice, Danny would die. She said quacks like you tout miracle cures just to get money. You push untested and unapproved drugs and take advantage of poor, sick people."

Cory's mouth opened as her jaw dropped. Did he really think she was that corrupt? "I just told you my personal experience. I'm not trying to get any money. What you do with the information is up to you. I didn't take advantage of anyone."

"You didn't tell us you were charged with malpractice."

"I'm not a doctor. I can't be charged with malpractice. I told you what happened with Sophie and what I did."

He stepped away from her car, pointing an accusing finger. "Don't talk to me again. Don't talk to Marie. We don't want to see you." He stalked down the sidewalk, hopped into his van, and screeched away.

Other parents were arriving and leaving—and staring with interest, and Cory got Sophie into her car seat as quickly as possible and sped home.

She couldn't fault Daniel. She'd been in his shoes. The calm authority of the medical establishment gave hope to hold on to. She knew; she'd held on to it fast. She had heard the sad statistics but thought they'd be lucky—one of the fortunate forty percent who would recover, or one of the happy twenty percent who wouldn't experience an allergic reaction. The Weisses had decided to listen to a medical authority and not a disgraced post-doc who by all published accounts was about to lose her child.

At home, Mathew was coming down the stairs, all dressed up and looking like he was heading out. He was freshly shaven, his hair was wet, and he smelled clean, like a baby. He wore a light-blue button-down shirt and pressed blue jeans. Sophie reached out her arms, and Cory handed her to him.

"You look glum," he said, fitting Sophie onto his hip.

She told him about her run-in with Daniel. "He thinks the DCS is taking Sophie because I refused chemotherapy."

"I'm trying to find out who wrote the article," Mathew said.

Cory looked at him with surprise. "How?"

"My friend from back home. The computer whiz who's doing a PhD in software engineering is actually a master hacker."

"Sounds illegal."

"It is. Don't say a word. He thinks you've been hacked."

Was someone reading her email? It would explain how someone knew about the safety report and the rat bite. "Can he find out?"

"As we speak."

"What's his name?"

"He wants anonymity. He doesn't want you to know who he is."

"Why not?"

Sophie was poking a finger at Mathew's mouth, and he took her hand. "It's best you don't know. He's hacked into things he shouldn't hack into. He could go to prison for what he's done."

"Why is he doing this for me?"

"He's doing it for me. He owes me a favor." Mathew shrugged a shoulder while Sophie tweaked his nose with her free hand. "I bailed him out of jail once. Let him crash at my place. He's repaid the favor many times over."

"Why are *you* doing it?"

Mathew looked flabbergasted. "Are you kidding? Because I can. You need help, and I'm here. I've got your back. You're not alone."

She needed him; she couldn't deny it. She didn't know how she would have handled the last two days without him—or the last few weeks. Stupidly and without thinking, she said, "I can't believe Margaret let you get away."

Mathew looked at the ceiling. "She found someone she liked better. Her soul mate. Bob. He got her, my house, and my dog. She met him days before the wedding."

"You called it off?"

"She did. I don't let go that easily. We'd been together since high school. I thought we could work things out. Put off the wedding, go to counseling. But no. She wanted Bob. He moved in and I moved out. He's a professional boxer. He beats people up for a living. Her idea of a real man. I had to explain to our wedding guests why there was going to be no wedding."

"Ouch," Cory said.

"That's when I closed my practice and moved to Texas."

He looked as if he might cry. Sophie looked uncomfortable, and Cory took the squirming child from his arms. "It's over. Close the door on it. Move on." That was how she handled disappointment. She changed the subject. "Looks like you're going out."

"I'm going next door to the party," he said, wiping his eyes. "Are you coming?"

"You're invited?"

He looked shocked that she was shocked. "Yes. I, too, know the neighbors."

"I'm not going. I can't face anybody right now."

"If you hide out, you let them win. That's what they want. For you to be as isolated and weak as possible. I've been there."

"You moved away."

"My case was worse. Yours is built on a lie. Face people. Tell them. Don't hide away and act guilty."

"I won't have any fun. I can't go." It was too mortifying. Especially after the *Duane Tribune's* glowing tribute to her neighbor who won the Teacher of the Year award in the fall, had a five-million-dollar Department of Defense grant, and at forty-six was promoted to full professor. She was an immunologist who worked at the veterinary college on the plague. Her husband was no slouch either and was an epidemiologist and the chairman of the department of veterinary immunology. Before they got married, he'd traveled the world studying rare and deadly infectious diseases. Cory couldn't face them.

"Have a drink, loosen up, forget about it," Mathew said.

"I'd rather spend the night with Sophie."

"You can bring her. Hold her like a crutch."

Cory loosened her grip on her daughter. Sophie had a small, sweaty hand on the back of her neck. "What's that supposed to mean?"

"You use her to keep your distance from people. It's not healthy for either of you. It's not just you and her against the world."

"You use your breakup to keep your distance. Is that healthy?"

He stared up at the ceiling as if considering it. Finally, he said, "Perhaps you're right."

She shook her head. "I'm not right. I don't know what the hell I'm talking about. If you're going to the party, you better go."

He faced her, looking into her eyes. "I told them you'd be there. I made a couscous salad to take, enough for both of us."

"That's presumptuous. I never said I'd go."

"I saw your invitation. I figured you would."

"I'm not."

"Okay. Stay home. Can Sophie go?"

"She's eighteen months old."

"Is that a no?"

And Sophie surprised her when she said, "Go." She raised her hands to Mathew.

He took her back, and it was decided. They'd all go. "I'm not staying long," Cory said.

Chapter Twenty-three

The party started at six. Though Cory and Mathew were late, they were among the first to arrive. From the backyard, smoke billowed from the barbecue, and music rocked the house. The front door was wide open, and a handful of strangers were huddled in the foyer. The floor plan of the house, at least the first floor, was the same as Cory's, with the living room in front and the kitchen in back. Cory headed there and found Dana Sparks at the sink, hands plunged deep in sudsy water. Mathew passed through the French doors and went outside.

"Ah, you made it," Dana said with a smile. Close-up she looked younger than the forty-six years the newspaper had given her. She had blond hair the color of corn and bright-blue eyes. She was dressed in sharp-toed cowboy boots, blue jeans, and a white T-shirt with a denim vest. Cory felt overdressed in a cotton sundress, though Mathew had said she looked fine.

Dana hugged Cory as if they were old friends. "I'm glad you came," Dana said, shaking Sophie's hand. "And you brought that skulking stranger I almost called the cops on. I hear he's moved in. Well done."

Cory didn't know why Mathew was always so hard to explain. "He just lives there."

"Uh-huh." Dana filled a goblet with red wine and poured Sophie a glass of apple juice. Cory gulped the wine. It was a Merlot, strong and fruity.

"I saw the article in the paper," Dana blurted out, as if she had to get that out of the way, clear the air.

Cory's face flushed as crimson as the wine. "All lies." She suddenly felt feverish.

"I didn't think the DCS would take Sophie. You must have pissed someone off."

Cory didn't want to get into it. "So it would appear."

"It'll blow over," Dana said. "You'll be amazed at how short the public's attention span can be."

A short, frizzy-haired woman came into the kitchen and said, "She knows what she's talking about. She speaks from experience."

Cory met Sheryl, Dana's lab tech and former college roommate. "Dana had her own scandal," Sheryl said.

"It was a long time ago," Dana said.

Sheryl poured herself a glass of wine, topped Cory's, and whispered, "It was a sexual scandal. It didn't go over too well in this conservative town."

"What happened?" Cory asked as she adjusted Sophie on her hip and gulped more wine.

The former roommates exchanged smiles. Dana lowered her voice further. "I was a student. I had an affair with my professor."

Cory raised her eyebrows. That was a violation of the professional code. "What happened?"

"I married him." Dana laughed and lifted her glass.

Sheryl took Cory's hand. "Come meet Penny. My daughter loves to babysit. She's certified, took a class."

They went through the dining room that had been cleared of furniture and was the source of the music. There was going to be dancing, and Cory made a mental note to leave before it began.

The front room, which was a study in Cory's house, was a family room here. A large-screen TV hung on the fireplace, and the over-sized couch was filled with kids. Cory recognized Frankie, holding his old dog, Judy, and was introduced to Penny and her brothers, Ricky and Paul. Penny was twelve, the epitome of health, with shining skin and long, silken hair. Sophie went to her willingly and snuggled beside her, fixating on the screen.

Back in the kitchen, Dana was stuffing mushrooms, and the room smelled of fried garlic and onions. Through the window, Cory saw Mathew at the barbecue, waving tongs, in deep conversation with Dana's husband. Nick wore a pink apron fringed with lace that was tied around his waist. He had a beer in one hand and a spatula in the other, which he used to disperse thick smoke. He was ruggedly handsome, with thick, dark hair and a rakish five-o'clock shadow. Sheryl joined her at the window. "You'd never know he had septicemic plague."

And that was how Cory learned about a terrorist attack that occurred the spring her grandmother died when she was a senior in high school. Nick had the plague, so did Frank, his dog, the namesake of their son. Penny had it too, and Dana, who was working on experimental plague vaccines, had saved the town.

"It's quite a story," Sheryl said. "Someone wrote a book about it."

"You do what you have to do," Dana said, dismissing Sheryl's words with a flip of her hand. She grabbed the tray of mushrooms. "TJ McCoy, my old boss, reminds me of yours. He has to control everything. At least I only had to deal with him for a few months. I'm guessing Rupert wasn't happy about the article."

"He's out of town," Cory said as she opened the oven door. "He took spring break off. He hasn't seen it. I'm worried about going to work on Monday."

"It'll be old news," Sheryl said. "He won't hear about it."

Dana shoved the tray in the oven. She didn't agree. "It's a small town. He'll hear. Be proactive. Face it head on. Don't wait for him to call you. Point it out to him. First thing Monday, go to his office. Let him know you have nothing to hide."

Given the two options, Cory preferred Sheryl's.

Dana wanted to know Cory's field of research, and she explained her aflatoxin assay and attempt to get the monoclonal stable enough to use in the field.

Dana was tossing a salad and put down the forks. "I had the same problem with the monoclonal against *Yersinia*, the plague bacterium. I used an enzyme that chopped the antibody in half."

"That's what I'm trying," Cory said, amazed they thought the same.

"It took me a year to get the right enzyme. Maybe I can help."

Cory was taken aback. "That would be great."

"Call me."

Cory smiled. "I'll do that."

Dinner was almost ready, and Cory checked on Sophie. She was in Penny's lap, enthralled with the movie. Kids grow up, Cory thought. They could encounter life-threatening disasters like the plague and leukemia and recover. She patted Sophie's head and returned to the kitchen. The party was picking up; people were arriving.

Dana put her to work making a pitcher of Bloody Caesars, which Cory learned was a variation of a Bloody Mary that involved mixing a large amount of vodka with clamato juice, pepper, Worcestershire, Tabasco, lime, and celery salt. "Keep adding hot sauce until you can't taste the vodka," Dana said.

Already a little looped, Cory switched from wine to the fiery vodka. She sliced celery lengthwise and arranged the sticks around the punch bowl to be used as drink-stirrers.

The kitchen door opened, and Mathew and Nick came in bearing trays of meat. There was some kind of roast and a rack of ribs. Hands free, Nick threw his arms around his Dana and kissed her neck. He kissed Sheryl's cheek and patted Cory's shoulder. His dark-blue eyes reminded Cory of the ocean. He sharpened a long knife that had a blade like a saber.

Mathew came over to Cory looking for Sophie and got a Bloody Caesar. He whispered into Cory's ear, "Nick's got a nice apron. Frilly *and* pink."

"Manly," Cory said quietly. "A wimp couldn't pull it off."

They watched Nick carve a roast and cut ribs. He wiped his hands on the apron, declared the food ready, and everyone filed outside.

The garden was alight with Chinese lanterns, and a fire blazed in the pit. The food filled three long tables, and the kids were first in line. Cory got Sophie a bowl, but all she wanted was bread. Cory let it go. It was a step above a powdered donut. The kids ate in five minutes and trooped back inside. Sophie took Penny's hand and left without looking back.

Mathew was socializing, flitting from one group to another. Besides him, the only guest Cory knew was Haygood Robinson, her pediatrician, who was also Frankie's doctor. Haygood's wife, Cory's obstetrician, was supposed to come, but one of her patients went into labor and she was called away. He said it always happened.

Cory filled a plate with ribs, chicken, black beans, macaroni, and three different types of salad and went to the family room where she sat on the floor, sharing her food with Sophie, Penny, and the old terrier.

Cory felt more at ease with the kids. She hadn't gone to many parties and wasn't good at making small talk. Still, she couldn't watch television all night, and when her food was done, she poured herself another Bloody Caesar and went outside.

After dinner, there were speeches. Dana talked about the Ides of March and the betrayal of Caesar, who had been stabbed twenty-three times by friends. It was a time known for madness, hence a murderous moon, which was not in view. The sky was either cloudy, foggy, or blurry.

After speeches, the dancing began. Cory helped clean up, deliberately staying away from the dining room, where at one point, Nick was dancing with Sheryl, and later Dana was dancing with Mathew. He was a good dancer; his year-long class had served him well. He moved in easy rhythm to a tune by a guitarist named Robin Wheeler whom Cory had never heard of before.

She returned to the family room and squeezed onto the couch between Penny and Frankie. They were watching a James Bond movie, and she settled back on the cushions. Sophie was asleep, sitting sideways on Penny's lap, head resting on her shoulder.

After midnight, when the movie was ending, Dana came in. "There you are. I need you."

Cory thought it was to help put away leftovers or make more Bloody Caesars, but instead of passing through the dining room packed with dancers, Dana led her by the hand to the corner where Mathew stood alone, iPod in hand, studying the playlist.

"Dance," Dana said.

And dance Cory did. A waltz or something; she let him lead. He was like a ballroom dancer, one hand on her back, the other around her waist, prudently keeping his distance as he twirled her around the floor, bringing her close, hurling her away, then sweeping her back without a beat. He had her breathless in seconds, her heart beating so loud she thought he could hear it. It seemed effortless to him. The only sign of exertion was his sweat that smelled of musk, adrenaline, and sex. He hummed in her ear, smiled in her eyes, flung out his arm, spun her away, and caught her before she could swoon. While Robin Wheeler sang:

You are what I fear, and I loathe it. I have what you need, and you know it.

By the time the song finished, she wanted him. She had to have him. When he finally stopped moving, she looked into his eyes, and he looked back. She said, "You can dance."

"Margaret wanted a show at the wedding."

"Her loss," Cory said.

A new tune started, and they danced on. Rock, country, jazz, the blues; slow dances, fast dances, cha-cha, jitterbug, salsa—he knew them all. He never forgot himself, never lost control, and never succumbed to her advances. He moved away when she moved against him, keeping his distance whenever she tried to close it.

Sometime in the early morning, the crowd began to thin. Guests were leaving, and Sheryl interrupted to say she was taking Penny. It was time to go.

Cory agreed. She unwound Sophie from Penny's arms and said good-bye to the hosts. With Mathew in the lead, they picked their way across the grass, already wet with dew. Cory took Sophie up to bed while Mathew let Pluto out.

Upstairs, Cory changed Sophie's diaper, slipped on her pajamas, and put her down without waking her up. She opened the window. The air was thick with humidity. She inhaled the aroma of honeysuckle that carried the hope of spring.

Out in the hallway she waited for Mathew, her heart racing. She could still hear the music in her head and swayed along with the beat. Not since The Count had she been with a man, and it had been too long.

Downstairs, the front door opened and closed. Mathew climbed the steps, coming toward her, swept up on a cloud of desire. She watched him come, her heart pounding as he caught her eye and smiled. He reached the top and stopped.

"You okay?" he said.

"Yeah." She looked deep into his eyes. "Okay." She meant, *okay, green light.* She lifted her hand, reaching for his.

"Well, good night." He swept past her, walked down the hallway to his bedroom, and closed his door.

Chapter Twenty-four

March 16th

Cory awoke in a bright room thinking of Mathew. He could have had her. She wanted him, she offered herself, and he turned his back. Another heaping of humiliation. This was the way things always turned out, only in this case, it ended before anything ever began. And now she had to face him. Later. With no sound from Sophie, Cory punched her pillow, rolled over, and pulled the covers up over her head. She wished she could blame the booze, but she'd been sober when they walked home. If she was drunk, it had been with desire.

Maybe he had been drunk! Maybe he hadn't noticed! She opened her eyes. The room brightened with a ray of hope. For him, maybe nothing was out of the ordinary. He had said good night and went to bed. She could pretend it never happened.

She listened for Sophie and heard the chirping of birds. *Birds?* Cory threw off the covers and saw sunlight dancing on the rug. According to the clock, it was almost nine. She leapt from bed and pulled on her robe. Sophie never slept past seven. Cory ran to her room. The door was closed, and she flung it open; the crib was empty. Heart pounding with thoughts of kidnapping, Cory raced downstairs.

Sophie was in the kitchen, strapped into her chair—Mathew didn't take any chances. She was dressed and wore a bow in her hair and a smile on her face. Mathew was feeding her oatmeal. "I heard her fuss," he said. "I thought I'd let you sleep. There's fresh coffee."

Cory poured herself a cup and stood behind him, inhaling caffeine fumes and listening to her heart beat.

"Dada," Sophie said, and added, "No."

It was the first time she had strung two words together. Cory smiled at her, glad she was here, in the room, in her life. The air in the bright sunshine felt thick, swooning. Cory went to the table and sat down.

"Fun party," Mathew said.

Loaded words, Cory thought. What was fun about it? Dancing? The dances he had before? Abandoning her on the landing? "I'm hungover," she said, disingenuously. She took a sip of coffee, but drank too much. It burned her lips and boiled her throat. She started coughing and put down the mug.

"Booboo," Sophie said, another first.

Mathew looked skeptical. "I didn't think you had that much to drink." He shot her a searing stare that went through her eyes and into her brain.

"Enough," she said and looked down at the table, brushing a crumb onto the floor.

"Do you want to talk about it?" he asked.

"Talk about what?"

"Last night."

"Is there something to talk about?"

Mathew stirred the oatmeal. "I guess not."

Cory picked up her cup, and blew on the coffee. What did he want her to say? She had offered herself to him, and he'd turned his back and walked away. She changed the topic of conversation. "What time did Sophie wake up?"

"An hour ago. I gave her a cookie, but she seemed hungry."

Cory nodded. "Thanks for getting her."

"My pleasure."

Sophie at least pleased him.

"I didn't know if I should wake you. If you had plans for the day."

"No."

"I'm going to the library. I have to finish my brief."

"We'll be here."

"Later my friend from New York is having a thing."

She looked at him. Was he asking her out on a date?

He looked away. "So I won't be home for dinner."

She strove to maintain nonchalance amidst a surge of overwhelming disappointment. He offered Sophie a spoonful of oatmeal, and she turned her head. He put the spoon down. "I should go."

He left, leaving her unsettled. She cleaned Sophie up, washing sticky hands and polishing a glowing face. If only the mess with

Mathew could be cleaned up so easily. The tone between them had changed. On the stairs last night, something was lost. He knew exactly what was offered and what he had declined. But why sing in her ear, dance so close, steal her breath away? He should never have opened a door and then not been there. He was just like all the other men who left. Only he was still here and she had to face him.

Chapter Twenty-five

Unless we put medical freedom into the Constitution the time will come when medicine will organize itself into an under-cover dictatorship.

— *Benjamin Rush*

March 18th

After debating it over the weekend, Cory took Dana's advice and first thing Monday morning went to see Dr. White. She rapped on his door, and he looked across three high stacks of mail. "Well, this is a pleasant surprise," he said, leaving her to wonder if that was an attempt at sarcasm.

She sat down on the chair opposite his desk. He removed his glasses and wiped his brow, as if anticipating trouble. She said, "There was a libelous article about me in the newspaper last week."

He laid his glasses down on his desk. "I was out of town. I did not see it."

She passed him a copy of the offending article, which still had not been corrected.

He repositioned his glasses on his face and took his time reading. Finally, he lowered the paper. "If we're shutting down your lab, it would be news to me."

"The DCS isn't taking Sophie."

"What's the hazardous lab practice?"

"We spoke of it earlier. The rat bite."

"So nothing new."

"That was more than enough," she said, and he agreed.

"And the hospital bill?" he asked.

"I owe them seventy-five thousand. The hospital garnished my wages and is taking five hundred from my paycheck every month."

"The IRS?"

"I haven't spoken to them. My returns are solid."

"I see."

"I think someone hacked into my computer. There's information in the article that could only have come from there. Can you ask IT to check it out?"

"As you wish. But I'm afraid you'll find that very little is private these days. What was the FDA reprimand?"

"FDA agents came to see me," she said.

That got his rapt attention.

"I wrote a letter to the editor of a Canadian journal about my experience with Sophie and Oxylace."

"Yes. The alternative treatment you sought in Mexico." He had been against it, had counseled it was likely a scam, but he hadn't held it against her that she ignored his advice. "What did the agents say?"

"They threatened to take me to court for misrepresenting the drug. But everything I wrote was true."

"Do you have the letter you wrote?"

She handed him a copy printed from her Word file that did not have the title doctor. It took him a long time to read. Finally, he lowered the paper. "It doesn't seem *that* provocative."

She nodded, relieved by his response. "I didn't think so either."

He handed back the paper. "If I were you, I would not write anything more on the subject."

"I won't."

"Good. The matter with Megan Carson. Is it settled?"

Christ, Cory had forgotten all about her. "Everything is fine."

"Excellent. I was hunting with her father last week. I assured him she would graduate with honors."

Cory bobbed her head in agreement.

"Is there anything else?"

Cory paused, wondering if she should mention the awol rat and decided against it. She would part on a good note and stood up. "That's it."

He looked at the door, his way of saying good-bye.

Cory went down to the basement. The padlock was still on the rat-room door, and she went in and turned on the light. The room was as she had left it. Though the remaining rats had been moved to a different room and the cages here were empty, the animal smell was strong. The room was cold, the temperature maintained at precisely sixty-five degrees. A ventilation fan never stopped running.

Down on her knees, she looked under the animal rack. Nothing. She opened the drawers in the cabinets. Nothing. The peanut butter in the rat zapper looked fresh, a golden glob on the end of the grill calling out to a starving rodent. Where the hell was he? How long could she wait before she had to let Dr. White know it was on the loose?

She locked the door, went to her office, and called Megan. No answer. She left another sickening message: "Megan, this is Cory. Hope you had a good break and you're ready to come back. We have a lot of assays and could use your help. Don't worry, I'll take care of the rats. You don't have much time left in the semester. See you tomorrow."

Cory smiled as she spoke and then scowled as she closed her phone. It was hard to compromise her principles, but given her precarious position, she had little choice but to suffer through.

She perked up remembering Dana's invitation to help optimize the monoclonal antibody and gave her a call. She thought she'd have to remind Dana who she was and why she was calling, but she didn't get a chance.

"Cory, it's great to hear from you. I've been thinking about your monoclonal."

"Thanks for a fun night."

"How's Mathew?"

"Fine."

Dana just laughed.

Cory said, "I know you're busy—"

"Do you want to do an assay?"

Cory was taken aback.

"I'd like to see your setup," Dana said. "I'll come over."

"Any time."

"I'm on my way. I don't know about you, but I don't like Mondays."

Fifteen minutes later Dana breezed in carrying an empty coffee cup, which she refilled from the pot. Cory offered a lab coat, but Dana refused it, and Cory felt overdressed in hers.

"The pockets get caught in the drawer handles and give me whip-lash," Dana said. She was wearing a version of her party clothes: cowboy boots, blue jeans, and a pink button-down shirt.

The grad students and Evonia seemed riveted, likely astonished to see Cory interacting with a colleague. Cory made introductions. "This is Dr. Sparks from the immunology department at the veterinary college."

The title alone sounded important, but Dana rolled her eyes. "Call me Dana." She shook hands with everyone and then surveyed the room, likely taking an inventory of the equipment.

Cory wanted to make a good impression. In the collaboration category on her annual professional evaluation, she always scored low. Joe had said she had to partner with other professors to show Dr. White she could get along with the faculty, but she wasn't gregarious or outgoing and had a hard time approaching people. No one had approached her until now. Cory could hardly believe it and was determined not to blow it.

They started the assay. Dana wanted to do it herself to get a feel for it, and Cory was supposed to watch, which made it hard to be impressive. She got the samples from the fridge and explained what they were. "We're repeating an undergrad's assay. These are peanut butter samples from the local supermarkets and the health-food store."

Dana grabbed a pipette and swiftly added samples to the plate. There were ninety-six wells, and with Cory uncapping the samples, the plate was done in just over a minute.

Cory put the plate on the shaker and set the timer for five minutes.

Dana washed her hands and said, "So, the goal is to run the test in the field?"

"I'm thinking it would be like a pregnancy test. A strip that changes color."

"Perfect," Dana said.

For no reason, Cory felt inanely proud.

"But for a field test, you need to decrease binding time," Dana added. "For a farmer, five minutes standing around doing nothing is five wasted minutes."

Cory felt deflated. She'd given no thought to the practical application of the test.

"Do you know any farmers?" Dana asked.

"No."

Dana knew some and thought a nearby farmer with a small corn field would be interested. "Jock Thorne had an aflatoxin problem last summer. He has a few cows, and some of them got sick. I didn't know we had an aflatoxin expert at the university."

And pride was welling once more. Cory hardly thought of herself as an expert and wondered what she was doing to come off looking like one. She knew she had to be more visible, get a more extensive biography up on the university website, but she hadn't gotten around to it. There'd been no point. Now here she was collaborating with a faculty member and possibly a farmer.

The timer dinged, and Dana removed the plate, emptied it over the sink, and slammed it onto a stack of folded paper towels. The students and Evonia had given up any pretense of work and were watching and listening intently.

Dana added buffer to wash the wells. "You're using Tris. Have you tried a citrate buffer?"

"No."

"Try it. It seems to work better."

Next came the antibody-addition step, and Cory got the monoclonal from the fridge.

"What enzymes have you used to chop the antibody?" Dana asked.

"Trypsin, pepsin, chymotripsin."

"Just random enzymes?" Dana asked.

Cory winced. "Yes."

"Hmm. I'd look for something specific. Have you gotten the RNA sequence for the monoclonal?"

It had never occurred to Cory. "No."

"I've got a company that can sequence in a week." Dana finished the pipetting and put the plate on the shaker. "I'll email you their website. From the RNA, we can get the amino acid sequence and target the cut."

It sounded good and was what Dana had done to optimize the plague assay. Back then, the sequencing took six months and she had to translate the sequence by hand. Now she had software that would do it. She ended up chopping the bottom third off the antibody, and it worked great. She paused and took a long gulp of coffee. "I've never heard of using an ELISA to test for aflatoxin."

"It's new," Cory said. "The research isn't published. I wrote a paper and submitted it to the *American Journal of Pharmacology and Toxicology.*"

"Great journal," Dana said.

And Cory felt proud again. "The paper's been accepted with revision. There wasn't much."

"There's always something," Dana said. "No one can approve a paper outright."

"One reviewer did," Cory said, and then wondered if she was bragging.

"Impressive," Dana said.

The timer rang, and the plate was slammed, washed, and slammed again, and a color reagent was added. Then there was another five minutes of waiting, which Dana thought could be reduced to one, once the assay was optimized.

After the timer buzzed, the plate went into the spectrophotometer. From an eyeball look of the plate and the matching colors in the duplicate wells, Cory knew the results would be good. The positive controls were an inky blue, and the negative controls were clear. It took about ten seconds for the machine to read the plate and another ten seconds for the printer to spit out the results. Dana ripped off the page.

Cory had never seen such accuracy. Most of the duplicate samples matched exactly, and where the numbers were off, they were off in the third decimal place. She matched the results to the samples. Dana had unequivocally disproved the published results. "You've just shown that when it comes to peanut butter and aflatoxin, the health-food brands are less contaminated than the big-store brands," Cory said. "That's not what the published paper showed."

"Was it a vetted paper in a reputable journal?" Dana asked. "Big corporations publish journals that *look* like scientific journals, only they're not. None of the articles are refereed, and anyone can write what they want. They're usually very preferential to corporations."

Cory had no idea who published the original paper, but she knew who had provided the funding. "The study was paid for by a leading food manufacturer."

"There you go." Dana picked up her empty coffee mug. She had to get back to her lab. "You've got a good assay. We'll get it better."

Cory walked her to the door. Dana would email the name of the sequencing company and check with Jock Thorne, the farmer, to see when he would be free for a site visit. They would go out and talk to him, collect samples, and gauge his interest.

"I'm busy Tuesdays and Thursdays," Cory said.

"I'll be in touch," Dana said. "This could work out for both of us."

"What do you mean?" Cory didn't see that Dana was getting anything out of it.

"In our profession, you can't work alone," Dana said. "Might as well find a collaborator you like." She gave Cory a smile and a thumbs-up and left the lab.

Chapter Twenty-six

March 19th

If Dana was a joy to work with, Megan was the polar opposite. At least she returned to the lab on Tuesday, which was a relief. "I'm glad you're back," Cory said when Megan came in. "You're almost finished. There's only another month left in the semester. It would be a shame to give up now."

Megan shrugged.

"I fed the rats for you. The rats in the high-dose group look sick."

Megan screwed her face up into a frown. "What can I do?"

"If they get any sicker, we should put them out of their misery."

"You said I don't have to work with them anymore."

"You won't have to do anything. On Thursday you can take notes." From the far side of the room, Evonia groaned and shot arrows of disapproval across the lab. Cory ignored her and continued. "You can watch, get used to them."

"That's not going to happen," Megan said.

Her comment was ambiguous, but Cory wasn't going to pursue it. "Let's do an assay." She wanted to retest the samples that Dana had run yesterday and show Megan what good results looked like. "Do you have your lab book?"

"It's at home," Megan said.

"It should stay in the lab."

"I'll bring it."

"Good. Let's start the assay. I'll help you."

"Is there a problem?"

"I just want to make sure you're on the right track."

"I don't want any help."

"Okay, fine. Suit yourself."

Cory spent an hour doing her own assay while she watched Megan do hers. The girl was sloppy with the pipette, drawing up various amounts in the tip and squirting reagent all over the place.

Unsurprisingly, the results were horrendous. None of the duplicate samples matched, and one of the negative controls was positive.

Cory got out Dana's results. "Here are the samples you just ran. Do you see a difference?"

Megan barely gave them a glance. "Are you checking up on me?"

"Of course not. I'm hoping you'll notice that when you run duplicate samples, the numbers should hopefully match. You could be more careful. Try to pipette the same amount into each well. That will really help."

"I have to go."

"Slow down. It's not a race. Watch what you're doing. Get closer to the plate. It won't bite you."

Megan turned and faced her squarely. "This is about the rat, isn't it? You think it was my fault. That I should have carried on and not gone to the hospital."

Cory was taken aback. Perhaps she'd used the wrong word. "It's over. Finished."

"I was sick over the weekend. I thought it was my period, but maybe I've got aflatoxin poisoning."

"Megan, it was a control rat. Surely you would know the difference between your period and liver failure."

"The rat could have rabies."

"It's a Fischer lab rat. It comes from a factory. It doesn't have rabies."

"You don't know that."

"Well, I do."

Megan ripped off her lab coat and tossed it on the bench. "I did my assay. I'm going." She grabbed her knapsack and flounced out.

Cory ignored Evonia's telling look and went to her office and closed the door. There was only a month left. Cory could put up with her for that long.

The door flung open, and Evonia marched in. "Will you really allow her to act like this?"

"It's only a few more weeks. She'll graduate and be gone."

Evonia leaned against the window ledge and picked at a black fingernail. "So, you will pass her?"

"If she does the work."

Evonia yanked at the heavy silver chain that hung around her neck. It was some kind of spiked dog collar. "But she is not doing the work. You are doing it. Feeding her animals that she should feed."

"I don't like it any more than you. We're doing this as a favor to Dr. White."

"I do not know what happened to you," Evonia said. "You once had a compass. You knew which way was right. Why not write A+ on her paper and be done with it?"

Cory was now being lectured by a twenty-five-year-old Russian lab tech wearing a dog collar. "We can make allowances."

"No, you make them. You accept bad science in order to keep safe. You do the very thing you hate. You are exactly like the drug companies. You sell your soul for the same purpose. You take the easy way out when the hard way is the right way."

Evonia left, and Cory stared out the window. Was she really the same? She didn't think so. She wasn't like the drug companies who suppressed good drugs and made bad drugs look better. There was a difference; she wasn't hurting anyone. But still, she knew what the drug companies were doing, and she did nothing.

She put Megan out of her mind and checked her email. There was one new message in her inbox. It was from the editor of the *American Journal of Pharmacology and Toxicology*. Only a few weeks had passed since she sent the revisions, and they were getting back to her early. They may have found the results so important they were pushing up the publication date. This was her tenth paper and a big one. She opened the message breathlessly. Hope fell instantly.

Dear Author(s), Upon further review, the lack of quantification of your paper poses a serious drawback and questions your assertion that the ELISA antibody capture really is an improved method of in situ aflatoxin testing. In addition, your paper falls short of the journal's focus on cutting-edge molecular biology technique. In light of these shortcomings, the editorial board has decided to rescind its prior acceptance of the paper. You are free to submit the research elsewhere.

Cory reread the email in disbelief. After provisionally accepting the paper in November, how could they reject it now? She picked up her empty coffee cup and hurled it at the wall. There was a loud crash, the cup broke, and coffee remains trickled down the wall. Cory glared at the monitor. This wasn't how things were done. Papers were rejected outright, not after revision.

She got up, grabbed a hard copy of the journal off the bookshelf, and scanned the article submission guidelines. She learned the acceptance of any paper could be pulled at any time for any reason.

She flung the journal at the window and rattled the glass. With references from last year, the article was already dated. She'd already stated on her year-end university update that the paper was accepted with revision. Now she would have to explain its rejection—not only to Dr. White but to the NCI. It called into question her competence and could impair the acquisition of new grants. She would have to tell Dana what happened. Thinking about it made her feel sick. It was a blow of unimaginable magnitude.

She'd been stunned they had accepted the paper in the first place. It was an outstanding journal; they took only the best articles. Joe pushed her to submit; she would never have been that reckless. He said it would look good on her resume. A great paper in an excellent journal could go far in raising her stature. Elevate her above the competition.

And now this. It was one thing to be rejected in the first place, another entirely to have acceptance withdrawn. No one would know if it wasn't accepted at all, and now everyone would know it was rejected. She would have to tell people. One more heaping of humiliation.

She retrieved the journal. The cover was open. On the inside page was a full-color ad featuring Wellspring Pharmaccutical. Scowling, she scanned the inside page with its list of editors, publication dates, and circulation numbers. The journal was endorsed by the AMA and FDA. Sponsors were listed in a sidebar in alphabetical order. No surprise, there near the bottom was Wellspring Pharmaceutical. Cory opened her mouth and let out a loud, silent scream. She ripped the journal in half and flung it at the garbage.

She sat down. She had to call Joe in Nigeria and tell him the bad news. His name was on the paper, and its rejection made him also look bad. She pulled up Skype and placed the call. There was no answer. He was away from his terminal. She copied him on the email and then crafted a rebuttal:

Hello, Ignoramuses, The whole point of the research, as clearly indicated by the title "A Qualitative vs. Quantitative Analysis of Aflatoxin," is the capacity to eyeball toxin contamination, not rigorously determine specific concentration. If you don't have a $250,000 HPLC or a $200,000 spectrophotometer, then reading a color on a strip of paper may well be a fucking improvement. In addition, while cutting-edge techniques are in some cases appropriate, go toast bread in your microwave, assholes.

She didn't send the letter. She saved the draft and would edit it later and forward it to Joe. Maybe he knew people at the journal; maybe he could get them to change their minds.

Joe got back to her later that night. It was morning where he was, and he was just getting up. On Skype, from thousands of miles away, he looked fresh and ready to attack the day. His white beard seemed bushier and a cup of coffee steamed in his hand. He had read her email and was as perplexed as she was as to why the journal had changed its mind.

"I wrote a letter of rebuttal," she said. "I'll send it to you in the morning."

"Send it now. Let's get on top of this."

She warned him it was rough but sent him the draft and watched him open it and chuckle. "I'll edit it," he said. "Ask them to explain. It's very strange. It's a good paper."

"Do you think they'll change their minds?"

"I don't know. I've never dealt with anything like this before. While we're waiting, let's reformat for the *Journal of Food Chemistry* in case they won't budge."

She wondered if it was worth the effort. The FDA probably endorsed the *Journal of Food Chemistry* too.

"What is it?" Joe asked.

She voiced her suspicion out loud. "This is payback for my letter to the Canadian journal. The FDA is behind it. They work for

Wellspring Pharmaceutical, who makes the chemotherapy cocktail that Sophie took."

Joe seemed taken aback. "That's quite a charge."

"The FDA came to see me. They threatened to take me to court, throw me in jail. Last week, a front-page article in the *Duane Tribune* completely trashed me. I asked for a correction almost a week ago, and the newspaper hasn't done anything."

Joe looked uneasy. He sighed audibly before saying, "Cory, you're getting off track. I know you've been through a lot with Sophie, but right now, focus on work. You've got a bright future. You don't need any roadblocks. What we do is important. It makes a difference. Don't screw it up. You can't fight the FDA. You won't win."

She nodded. He'd already given her that advice, and she'd taken it. The problem was, after writing the letter, she'd done nothing, and it didn't matter. She was in the crosshairs, and the guns were firing. Threats weren't enough. Her total humiliation seemed the goal.

Chapter Twenty-seven

March 23rd

The week passed slowly, and the weekend finally arrived. Cory hadn't told anybody but Joe about the rejection of the paper, and it weighed heavily on her mind. Claiming to be ill, Megan hadn't shown up for work on Thursday, and Cory was at a loss of what to do. Mathew didn't show up for most of the week, and Cory was at a loss there, too. She missed him. He came home late, got up early, and was out for dinner every day. And so she was surprised when he appeared at the kitchen table Saturday morning and said he was going to plant the garden.

"I'll help you," she said.

"You don't have to."

She hoped time spent together could erase what happened and reset the clock. They could rewind to easier times, before they danced, before she decided she had to have him, and before he decided to walk away. "I want to."

"It's your garden," he said without enthusiasm.

With the sun still behind the trees, they were hard at work. Sophie picked up a trowel and used it as a shovel to dig holes in the dirt. Pluto wanted to dig too, and he was banished to the house. They were planting eggplant, squash, tomatoes, cantaloupe, watermelon, green onions, lettuce, and green beans. Also herbs: mint, parsley, cilantro, sage, and oregano. According to the hacker's girlfriend, the day before a full moon was the best time to plant. Cory was skeptical, but Mathew had checked the *Farmers' Almanac* and confirmed the day was a good one.

It seemed unscientific, but what did Cory know, she'd never done any gardening. Now she was learning how deep to dig, how broad to make the holes, and how to remove the plants from the flats without damaging the roots. Sophie watched closely, listened to the instructions, and wanted to "Do self."

Cory liked being out in the fresh air with the sun on her face and hands in the dirt. Mathew wore gloves, protecting his immaculate nails. He thought the soil was excellent and that by May they'd have their first tomatoes. She was glad when he said that, for it meant he was thinking long term; he'd still be here in May.

After planting, they watered—carefully—without getting drops on the leaves. By now the sun was overhead and could burn the young foliage if they didn't take care. They needed to water again at night when the sun was on the other side of the house, and then twice a day until the plants showed new shoots, an indication the stress of transplanting was past and the roots were growing. Mathew was pedantic, explaining everything like a teacher.

They finished by noon, and Cory made lunch. They had almond-nut sandwiches on millet bread with fresh lemonade out on the patio. Mathew's normally carefully combed hair was messed up, and his nails were dirty despite the gloves. His shirt was soaked with sweat, and he smelled good. Even Sophie was damp from the heat. She was tired from the morning work and lolling sleepily in Cory's arms.

The usually talkative Mathew had nothing to say. He chewed his sandwich thoroughly, staring at the yard. Was he moping? Pouting? Giving her the silent treatment? She didn't like it. Finally, she said, "Is anything wrong?"

He swallowed hard, took a sip of lemonade. "Do you think there's something wrong?"

"That's what I was asking."

"I'd tell you if there was."

"Okay, then."

His phone rang, and he jumped up too eagerly. He went inside to take the call. She finished her lunch, Sophie fell asleep, and Mathew came back.

"That was my friend, the software engineer whose girlfriend told me when to plant." He sat down, tossed his phone on the table. "Your computer's been hacked."

It wasn't unexpected, but her mind reeled with the confirmation. She'd been violated. Who found her so threatening? Did the FDA have nothing better to do than read her correspondence? Or was it

Wellspring? The drug company probably had hackers on the payroll. She caught Mathew looking at her. "How does he know?"

Mathew looked uncomfortable. "Um, he had to hack into your computer."

Cory stiffened, and Sophie cried out in her sleep. "Who is he?"

"I told you, anonymous," Mathew said sternly, as if she had forgotten. "His father is an ex-senator. None of this can get out. He's a computer whiz—one of the good ones."

"Did he say how I was hacked?"

"Spyware. It's in both your laptop and desktop."

"Who sent it?"

"He's trying to find out. The spyware leaves a trail. Whoever hacked in knows what they're doing and covered their tracks. He told me to warn you that your security is compromised. They have your passwords."

"How did they get them?"

"When you log on, they can see what you're doing, keystroke for keystroke."

The scope of the hacking was mind-boggling. "What about Skype?"

"Everything."

She thought of her emails and conversations with Joe. Someone knew it all.

"They could crash your computers whenever they want."

"What can I do?"

"Wipe the hard drives clean."

Her jaw dropped. She had all her data from the last two years on her computers. Ten papers, not to mention hundreds of pictures of Sophie. "Can I copy the files?"

"You'll copy the spyware."

"I can't just delete my files."

"You have two computers, right? Clean one and reload all the programs from scratch. At least you'll have one secure computer. Maybe my friend can clean up the other one."

Cory looked at him. "I appreciate it. Everything. Not only this but the gardening, cooking, playing with Sophie. Thanks."

He nodded solemnly. "My pleasure." They stared at the yard in comfortable silence. Then he said, "There's an award ceremony this afternoon, followed by dinner."

She looked at Sophie, now breathing slowly. The day care was open late. She could go with him as long as she was back before they closed. Or maybe Penny could babysit. "What time will it end?"

He seemed surprised by the question. "It starts early. At five. So I suppose it will end early."

"The day care is open—"

He interrupted her. "I have a date. I wanted to let you know I'll be home late."

She smiled a fake smile, which she hoped hid her shock and choking disappointment. "Well, good," she managed to say. She felt her lips would split if she kept smiling, so she stood up. "I'm going to put Sophie to bed."

In the nursery, she rocked back and forth on the rocker like a maniac. *He had a date!* Cory couldn't believe it. Was that where he had been all week? Out chasing women? She was so stupid. How could her intuition be so off as to think he was asking *her* out? His rejection was explicit and complete.

She went to the study, closed the door, and prepared upcoming lectures while he watched basketball. At four, she took Pluto and Sophie for a long walk so she wouldn't have to be home to watch him leave.

He came looking for her, because later, when they were at the playground, he drove to the park. He got out of the Mustang and swaggered toward them. He was dressed in a tux, complete with a shocking white shirt with black buttons, a satin bow tie slightly askew, and shiny black shoes. His cheeks were red from the morning sun, and his eyes were bright. "I'm going, then."

"Have fun," Cory said cheerily. "You look nice."

His cheeks reddened further. "It's black tie."

"I can see that." She reached up and straightened his bow tie, trying all the while to smile and look happy for him.

"Come." Sophie reached out her arms to him.

Cory pulled her back.

"I wanted to remind you to water," he said.

"I remember. Sophie, you're not going."

Sophie started to scream, and he backed away. "Sorry, sorry." And then he was gone.

Chapter Twenty-eight

March 24th

Sleep was hard to come by. The traffic was loud, and the noises in the house were louder. Lying in bed, staring at shadows, Cory made new resolutions she was determined to keep. Mathew was once again at arm's length. He found someone he liked better, which was disturbing but fine. He could stay until August, then go. Cory would focus on work. Joe was right; that was the key. She needed to be competitive to advance her career. She couldn't antagonize Dr. White, which meant she had to tread lightly with Megan.

After watching the clock for hours and wondering if Mathew would bring his *date* home, he finally arrived at three a.m. There was only one set of footsteps on the stairs. Where was the mysterious woman? Who was she? Where did they meet? What did he see in her? Where did Cory fall short?

The questions carried her off to sleep and were waiting in the morning when Sophie woke up early. Cory got up tired and in a rare bad mood. In the Sunday paper, on the local gossip page, she learned Mathew had won the Duane University Law Student of the Year award. He got his picture in the paper, along with his date—a doctor, according to the caption: Winning recipient Mathew Lang, 32, with Dr. Nancy Rutherford. She was a short, cross-eyed frump who looked older than he did. She wore a suit, as if that was appropriate attire for a black-tie dinner. In the photograph, she possessively clutched Mathew's elbow as he looked away. But he looked happy; the camera caught the flush of his cheeks and the sparkle in his eye. Cory wondered if they had danced.

He got up in time to go out for brunch. She knew because he came to the study where she was reloading software on her laptop and told her. He picked Sophie up off the floor, gave her a hug, and twirled her around in a circle. He was off to a new pastry shop called Blé Sucré Patisserie. He didn't ask them to come but offered to bring something back, as if he was so clueless he'd forgotten Sophie shouldn't eat flour or *sucré*. "No, thank you," Cory said in a tone so cold it surprised her.

He was gone a few hours and came back when Sophie was sleeping and she was analyzing data. He felt it necessary to check in. "I'm home."

"I see that."

"Did you water this morning?"

She looked up from the laptop, which was now running fast, as good as new. She had wiped it clean and reloaded all her programs. "I watered last night. Am I doing it?"

"I'll do it."

Good.

He must have gone outside because the house was quiet for a while, and then he was back—and from the sound of it, in the living room watching basketball and making too much noise. There would be trouble if he woke Sophie up.

A car pulled up around three and parked behind the Mustang, partially blocking the drive. Cory got up to get a closer look, but no one got out. She went back to her data and forgot about the car until the doorbell rang.

Her mind raged. Had he invited Nancy over? To *her* house? Breathing hard, Cory listened on the monitor for Sophie's cry but heard nothing—until the front door opened, and there was muffled talking.

When she couldn't take it any more, she went to meet the cross-eyed hag. She couldn't be more surprised to see Marie Weiss, Danny's mother, weeping in Mathew's arms. He was patting her back, making soothing sounds. Why hadn't he come to get *her*? He didn't even know Marie! Cory waited, and finally they noticed she was there.

"Danny's in ICU," Marie said between sniffles. She was dressed in an over-sized track suit. Her waist-long hair was pulled back in an untidy ponytail. She looked as if she hadn't slept in a week.

"I'll make tea." Mathew extricated himself and went to the kitchen.

"Let's go to the living room." Cory pointed the way, seated Marie on the sofa, and turned off the TV. She went to a chair on the far side of the room and sat down. "What happened?"

"Danny had an allergic reaction to chemo," Marie said. "To the drug Valurex."

Mathew was back and sunk down on the couch beside Marie. He slung his arm around her shoulder. "There, there," he said consolingly as he offered a box of tissues.

"The drug's known to be allergenic," Cory said.

"I want to take him to Mexico." Marie dabbed her eyes with the tissue. "Daniel won't hear of it. Once he's made up his mind, it's made up, no matter how stupid it is."

The kettle was whistling, Mathew jumped up and left, and Marie went on.

"Dr. Sullivan told us that one of the drugs could cause an allergic reaction, but she never told us it would put him into shock. His blood pressure got so low his heart stopped. He was clinically dead. Now he's in ICU. They're trying to clear the drug from his body. He's hooked up to a ventilator. At least his heart is still beating, but he's unconscious. They have to stop the chemo."

"I'm so sorry," Cory said as Mathew returned and passed out tea that smelled of mint.

He resumed his place, offered Marie another tissue, which she immediately crumpled. "I want him out of the hospital."

"You have to wait until he gets out of ICU," Cory said. "Did Dr. Sullivan say when that would be?"

"She won't tell us anything. Just that he's in capable hands." Marie spoke in an artificially high voice. "*Trust us, we're doing everything we can.*" She lowered her voice. "I don't believe it. Not for one minute. She just feels wrong." Marie raised her eyes and stared at Cory from across the room. "*You* know what I mean."

Cory did not. She had no intuition, no instincts. Her grandmother said it was normal; brains were better and compensated for the loss, but Cory wasn't so sure. Balancing the teacup on her knee, she said, "I think Dr. Sullivan is trying her best."

Marie sniffled. "Don't say that. It's not true. You know Danny shouldn't be there. I know it too. Daniel won't listen. I'm just a painter. But you're a scientist. You could talk to him, tell him the facts. Why you chose Mexico over this."

"I tried to tell him," Cory said.

"He says if your drug was any good, the FDA would use it."

"He doesn't want me to talk to you," Cory said. "He made that crystal clear."

Mathew sighed loudly. "The FDA did a flawed study. Just follow the money. The standard chemotherapy treatment costs forty thousand dollars. The company that makes it makes over nine billion dollars a year. They don't want patients using a treatment that works and costs only a hundred bucks."

"That's disgusting," Marie said. "Why doesn't somebody do something?"

Mathew glared at Cory as if she was that somebody.

Mathew handed Marie another tissue. "Call the Mexico clinic," he said. "If Cory won't talk to Daniel, maybe the doctor there will talk to him."

"I did talk to Daniel," Cory said, coming to her own defense.

Marie wiped her nose back and forth with her tissue and warmed to Mathew's idea. She would do it, call the doctor, and get him to speak to Daniel.

That decided, Marie took a sip of tea, put down the cup, and got up to leave. She smothered Cory in a hug and held Mathew's arm as he walked her to her car. Cory cleared the teacups and went back to work.

After Marie drove off, Mathew came to the study and stood in the doorway. "She was looking for advice, ammunition to convince Daniel. You could have said something."

"I think what you said was enough."

"She didn't want my opinion. She wanted yours. You're the biochemist. The expert."

"What did you want me to say? Sorry, Marie, the FDA does bad science to protect a drug industry that doesn't want a cheap cure for cancer. They don't want you to pay a hundred dollars when you can pay forty thousand for chemotherapy. Never mind that the cheap cure has a success rate of almost a hundred percent and the expensive one is supposedly forty percent, you have to use the one that costs the most. Not that you have a choice. Your government outlawed the cheap, safe drug. It decided on your behalf that you should pay tens of thousands for toxic treatment that not only doesn't work but causes great harm."

"That sounds good."

"Right. I'll remember that when I'm on my way to prison."

"Or, maybe you talk and change happens. Maybe this is why Sophie got sick. To wake you up. To make you fight."

Cory jumped up. "That's crap. Sophie didn't get sick for a reason. Sometimes shit happens. You can say what you want, but the FDA's not coming after you."

"So, just do nothing? Don't get involved? Pretend all is well? Stay on the sidelines and hold fast to your small, short-term vision?"

"Thank you for granting me the freedom to live my life."

"Don't thank me. You could wake up, dream big, and be a part of something. Discard your misguided concept that you're in this all alone."

"You know what? I am. I go to jail, I go alone."

Mathew shook his head. "You're not going to jail."

"Easy for you to say."

He glanced at his watch. "I have to go."

Good.

He marched off, and she watched him leave. Heading to Nancy's, she guessed, when he should have been here making dinner for them. He drove off with his tires screeching. He was angry. Was she such a disappointment that she made him mad? Had she let him down, failed to measure up to his high expectations? He was right. She didn't get involved. She kept to herself. Had the great Nancy drawn a sharp comparison? Cory wondered what he saw in her. What attracted him to her? Cory didn't know, but it was obvious he was gone from her. He'd checked out, preferring to be elsewhere. She held his interest for almost a night, and she wasn't enough. Same old story.

Chapter Twenty-nine

[In 2003], the prescription drug industry spent $116 million lobbying for legislation to prevent Medicare from bargaining down drug prices — legislation that enabled drug companies to make an additional $90 billion annually. That amounts to an extraordinary 77,500 percent return on investment.

—Tom Edsall, Journalism Professor,
Columbia University

March 25th

Just past daybreak, Art Farber was flying to Houston. At five thousand feet, it seemed to him that things were looking up. He'd never had such a good month. Shares had jumped thirty percent in the last three weeks. Thrilled with analysts' forecasts, stockholders were overjoyed, and the annual meeting was a raving success. Art's raise and bonus were approved whole-heartedly.

There was good news on the scientific front as well. R&D had found an antidote to the troubling allergic effect of Valurex. The remedy was Alluron, Wellspring's over-the-counter allergy medicine. Sold as a capsule but soluble in water, it was possible to manufacture a liquid formulation that could be given by injection during chemo. Because it was already approved as an allergy medicine, oncologists were free to use it immediately as an off-label drug in cancer therapy. All they had to do was learn about it.

It had to be given before chemo ever started. As his researchers explained, Alluron selectively targeted an antibody class that triggered allergies. Inhibiting the production of the antibody reduced the allergic side effect of the cocktail by about twenty percent in kids and eighty percent in adults—not that it was ever that significant a problem in adults. Nonetheless, it was a stunning breakthrough, and sales reps would fan out across the country and spread the word. Armed with free samples, mugs, pens, and hats—all emblazoned with the Wellspring logo—they'd hit hospitals and doctors' offices, dispensing free samples of Alluron like candy. Glossy literature summarizing the latest data sent a stern message: Any oncologist who didn't use Alluron as a precaution was a fool.

The bottom line was that Wellspring profit was going to soar more than expected. The cost for the cocktail would go from forty to fifty thousand dollars. Art could charge whatever he wanted for a drug. When sold as a prescription, which all injected drugs were, the cost for an over-the-counter medicine increased a thousand percent. Since doctors got to set the price of shots, they loved injectables. Also, since a prescription drug had no business being sold over the counter, the capsule would now require a prescription. Which meant more profit on those sales too. At the closing bell on Friday, stock price was 56.27 and rising. It had never been so high.

Now, Art had money to burn. He was giving back to the community. Wellspring was making a number of charitable donations. They had assumed the financing of a bankrupt philanthropist and agreed to support a new cancer wing at Anderson Hospital, which was the reason for his trip. The wing, now renamed the Wellspring Cancer Treatment Center, was opening that afternoon at two, and Art would be on hand to crack open the champagne bottle.

Wellspring was also offering healthy university endowments. After Art made public noises about contributing to higher education, he got a call from the cash-strapped president of Duane University. Edwin Reed had accepted a last-minute invitation to attend the opening and was driving down. That evening they would fly together to Austin and dine with Congressman Harris, who was dropping not-so-subtle hints about another super PAC donation. Art leaned back in his seat and smiled out the window. This was what he had been working for, what he had strived so hard to achieve. Five years ago, no congressman or university president would talk to him, and now here they were calling him. Hardly a day passed when Art wasn't mentioned in *The New York Times*. People looked up to him and admired his vision and his steady hand. He'd come a long way from the playground where his small size made him an easy target, the butt of jokes, and left him in the sandbox with a mouthful of dirt, or worse. Let the bullies see him now. Living well was the best revenge.

He thought about his weekend. Missy had all but moved into the condo. She'd brought over a friend, and Art was worn out. He needed a break, time to catch his breath. Ahead, he saw clear skies, smooth sailing, sexual excitement. The only dark cloud on the horizon was the wretched post-doc, but they were making progress on that front too. IT had successfully hacked into her computer. They were watching her every move, seeing every keystroke, listening in on every Skype call. He knew her latest paper had been rejected. Art laughed inwardly at her response. Who was she to call the esteemed editors ignoramuses and assholes. What a hot head. Must go with her red hair. She'd had her fun; she'd defamed Wellspring and was about to bear the consequences. She wasn't down yet, but she would be. Art was just getting started. He took no prisoners. The noose was tightening around her neck, and the floor was about to fall.

Chapter Thirty

While Art was entering Texas airspace, Cory was preparing to go into the field. "I'm looking to collaborate with a farmer," she told an amused Evonia on her way out of the lab.

Evonia started to laugh. "Dressed like that?"

Cory wore a navy oxford dress with one-inch black pumps. It was near the end of March, the day would be hot, in the high seventies. She envisioned sitting around a coffee table in an old farmhouse drinking coffee with fresh cream and discussing the field test. She thought she was dressed entirely appropriately.

But when Dana picked her up in the parking lot, wearing her trademark jeans and button-down shirt, Cory wondered if she was over-dressed. She got in the Prius and saw gumboots in the backseat with a sinking heart. She wanted—no needed—this collaboration to go well. Her continued career in Duane could depend on it. A grant would compensate for the lost paper that Dana still didn't know about. Cory would have to find an opportunity to tell her.

If her clothes were all wrong, Dana didn't mention it. She was explaining the wrong car. Work only had a pickup, which Dana in good environmental conscience refused to drive. Whenever she drove any distance, she took her personal car. It was a Prius and the quietest car that Cory had ever been in. It didn't sound like the engine was turning. She decided if she ever had money for a new car, it would be a Prius.

They headed west as the sun climbed behind them on a glorious spring morning. Soon they left the city limits, and large fields of grass spread out on either side of an arrow-straight highway that headed to infinity under the wide Texas sky. Puffy white clouds hung in the air. Around her, scattered cows munched on greening grass. For the time being, Cory felt free. With the lab and all her problems behind her, a vista of possibility was opening up.

"I saw you and Mathew in the garden," Dana said with a twinkle in her eye as she sped north on Highway 6. "He's great with Sophie."

"He's seeing someone," Cory said as casually as she could.

Dana's eyebrows shot up. "Really? Wow. That's a shock. From the vantage point of my porch, you looked like a couple."

"Nope." Cory didn't want to get into it. If Dana couldn't see her flaw, Cory wasn't going to admit to it. Dana was married, she had her family, and here they shared no common ground.

"He'll come around."

"We're good," Cory said, hoping she sounded convincing.

"Speaking from experience, the brain can think what it likes, but the heart has a mind of its own. Sometimes it takes a while to get them both on the same page."

It certainly wasn't her grandmother's advice, which was that some people were meant to be alone.

"I married late, so I know how it is," Dana said. "If you follow your heart, it will show you the way. If you can't have the person you want, you'd rather have no one. And so you wait—for the right moment, the right time. The waiting is hard, but it's worth it. Don't give up hope."

"I'm good, really."

"Who is Sophie's father? What happened to him?"

Driving past dead fields of corn, Cory relayed the tale of The Count. Dana wanted to know why she didn't move to Spain.

"I can't sell my house."

"You could rent it out."

"No," Cory said. No way.

"Then you're stuck in Duane."

"I like it here. I hope to fill Joe's position when he retires in August." The appropriate moment arrived to mention the rejected paper, and Cory wondered how to say the words but couldn't find them. She decided to leave it for the way home.

"You'll get the position," Dana said. Based on nothing, she seemed to be an optimist.

They drove twenty minutes, chatting about nothing. Dana was easy to talk to. She drove quickly, way over the speed limit, and had to slam on the brakes when they reached a driveway with an overhanging sign with the name Thorne. Dana pulled into the drive and drove up to the house. The car made the same sound running as it did when the engine was turned off.

The front door opened, and a bow-legged man in his sixties emerged. He was dressed in pointy-toed boots, blue jeans, a flannel shirt, and a leather cowboy hat. He gave Dana a hug and tipped his hat to Cory.

They headed into the field. There was going to be no sitting around a farmhouse drinking fresh coffee. Using a random number generator, Dana had located ten sites to sample and the GPS told them where to go. They walked to the far east corner along the crest of a row of fallen corn. Wearing inappropriate pumps, Cory had trouble keeping up.

They reached the designated location, and Dana stopped and pulled off her backpack. She put on gloves, got out a plastic spoon, scooped up a sample of soil, tipped it into a test tube, and capped the top. In magic marker, she wrote the number one on the tube. Cory stood by stupidly and watched. She hadn't thought to make a random generator selection or bring test tubes for samples. Next to Dana, she felt totally inept.

As they moved on to the next site, Dana asked Jock if he'd be interested in a field test if one became available.

"Whatever works for you," he said.

"No," Dana said. "You would do the test."

"I don't think I'm up for doing tests."

"It's not that hard," Cory said, and Dana shot her a stern look.

"It would be like a doing a pregnancy test," Dana said.

"I've never done one of those," Jock said, and they all laughed.

"I could walk you through it," Dana said. "If you're interested. Once the test is available."

"That means I could monitor my field myself?"

"Exactly," Dana said. "Whenever you wanted. If you found anything, you could call me. Or Cory. She's the university expert in aflatoxin."

"I'm not really an expert," Cory said, and got another look from Dana.

They stopped to take the next sample, and Cory and Jock watched while Dana collected it. Then they were walking again, and Dana was asking Jock about his kids. It sounded like there were three of them. One was at the University of Texas and the other at Texas A&M, two big rivals.

"What? No one at Duane?" Cory said, and she got another look from Dana as sadness descended upon them all.

"My daughter was going there," Jock finally said.

"She died," Dana added quietly.

"I'm sorry. I didn't know." Cory decided to shut up.

They walked across the field, and she lagged behind. Dana and Jock walked shoulder to shoulder, easily shooting the breeze about the price of feed, GMOs, and fertilizer leaching into well water. Dana had a way with people that Cory didn't have. She couldn't make small talk. Maybe it was the way she was, or maybe it was the way she was brought up. Her grandmother didn't like company and didn't want strangers in the house. Cory had grown up alone. She wondered if she would have turned out differently if her parents had lived, but that was something she would never know. She was lost in thought when Dana stopped walking, and Cory tripped over her. Down in the corn stalks, dress flying up, one pump went airborne.

Dana offered her a hand and pulled her up, and Jock retrieved her shoe.

He said, "I was just asking how long it would take to test the samples."

Cory shoved on her shoe, brushed the grass off her hands and dress, and tried to catch her breath and remember her schedule.

Into the long silence, Dana said, "I can do it today."

"I'd much appreciate that," Jock said.

"I'll do it," Cory said belatedly.

Dana smiled at the farmer. "One way or another, you'll hear back by the end of the day."

They got their ten samples, and as an afterthought, Dana took two more from the barn. She didn't like the dank smell of the closed air or the black mold growing on the wall. "Does this look like *Aspergillus*?" Dana asked as she scraped a sample off the wall.

"I've never seen it *in situ*," Cory had to admit.

"If it is, what should I do?" Jock asked. "I hate to spray pesticide in here seeing as this is where we store the hay."

"You could clean the walls," Cory said stupidly, and she caught Dana's look of exasperation.

"I'd spray it down with a mix of bleach and water," Dana said. "About a one to ten dilution should do the trick. If you do have aflatoxin, I'll come out, we'll spray, and then retest."

"I can do it," Cory said, but no one took her up on her offer.

Jock walked them to the car. He was grateful to Dana for coming out. "Oh, and you, too," he said, looking at Cory as if he'd already forgotten her name. He opened Dana's door. "I appreciate all you're doing."

"My pleasure, Jock." She gave him a hug and sunk into the car.

Out on the highway, Dana looked over at Cory and said, "I think we can work on your people skills."

Cory had heard that before.

"Compared to him, we're the experts. He took time out of his day to see us, and we need to make him feel that we were worth his time."

"I didn't know his daughter died."

"She was driving. Drunk. Wrapped her car around a pole on Texas Ave. He doesn't like to talk about it."

"I'll stay clear of the topic." Cory slouched low into her seat, wishing she could disappear. She had never felt so incompetent in her life. Usually work was her strong point, where she excelled. Her bumbling was inexcusable. She could not mention the rejected paper, not now.

"Treat it like a game," Dana said, as if sensing her distress. "Put on a smile and go out there, even when you don't want to. In our line of work, we have no choice. Isolation is a killer. We need other people. Students, collaborators, donors, whoever. I try to go the extra mile and give people what they want. I know it sounds self-serving, but if I don't do it, someone else will. The end justifies the means."

"You don't come off as disingenuous," Cory said.

"Because I'm honest in my intent. Life is hard enough as it is. If I can spread some happiness, I will. Who was it who said, each minute you're happy is a gift to the world?"

Cory shrugged. *Someone actually said that?*

"Enough proselytizing," Dana said. "Have you thought about doing a collaborative project?"

"I thought first I'd make sure the capture antibody worked in the field."

"It'll work," Dana said with more groundless optimism. She tapped her fingers on the steering wheel. "I'm sure the USDA would fund the project. They like practical and applied research and collaborative work."

"You mean I would collaborate with Jock?"

"And, well, I was thinking, with me."

Cory looked at her. "You want to work with me?"

Dana laughed. "For someone your age, you're doing great." She put on a turn signal and passed a slow-going tractor. "I'll help you with the field test and find farmers."

Cory was so taken aback she was speechless and could only nod.

"Let me check out requests for proposals. We'll find an appropriate one and write it up."

Cory looked at her and smiled. "Sounds excellent."

Dana smiled back. "It will be fun. It's better to work with people than to be on your own. Expect synergy."

"What's that?"

"The whole is always greater than the sum of the parts. When you work with people, you get farther than you would on your own. It took me a long time to learn that."

Chapter Thirty-one

March 27th

Two days later Cory was heading to the vet school to discuss the collaborative project. It was almost April, the air was warm, and the bluebonnets were beginning to bloom. Within two weeks the flowers would turn the green grass of campus blue. Mowing was prohibited this time of year, and alumni came in droves to snap photos and remember happier days.

The veterinary college was on the north side of campus, and Cory walked quickly. Dana wanted the proposal submitted immediately, and the ball was rolling fast. Cory had done the assay for Jock and found the field clean, but the barn was infected. Dana had already gone out and helped him spray down the walls. He was organizing a meeting at the Farm Bureau to sign up participants in a field trial. There was only the small matter of developing the test and acquiring the funding. Swiftly, Cory felt swept up in events bigger than she could have ever imagined. Be professional, she kept telling herself, act like an expert, put on your game face, be a part of the team. Fess up about the rejection of the paper.

Dana had a big, bright office on the third floor of the veterinary administration wing. She had a massive desk cluttered with reprints. A long, low bookshelf stuffed with books spanned an entire wall. In a corner sat a green-flowered couch and a coffee table scattered with folders. A large picture window unencumbered by blinds or curtains overlooked the cow pasture. The office was nicer than Dr. White's, and Dana called it "a perk of marrying up." She offered coffee, which her secretary brought.

It was strong, like espresso, only instead of two ounces, there were eight. Cory got a caffeine rush as Dana went over the grant requirements. The next deadline to submit a proposal was a week from Friday. "Think you can do it that fast?"

"Absolutely," Cory said without hesitation.

"What kind of funding were you thinking about?" Dana picked up her mug and took a sip of coffee, eyeing Cory across the cup.

"I thought maybe three years, one million?" It was a huge step up from Cory's NCI grant.

"Too small," Dana said. "Let's go for ten."

"Years?"

"Million. We'll work with ranchers and farmers. Focus on corn, cotton, peanuts, and pecans. What do you think about going national?"

"Working with other states?"

"I have friends in California and Vermont who are interested."

"Sounds great."

"What about bigger? International." Dana put down her cup. "I know people in East Africa. Ever been to Kenya?"

Cory hadn't been out of the state. "No."

"Know anybody at USDA?"

Cory shook her head. So much for looking like the expert.

"I do. I'll give them a heads up to expect our proposal. It helps to know people on the inside."

They divided the work. Cory would focus on monoclonal development, optimization, and the field kit, while Dana would acquire collaborators, design the field trials, and help with the antibody. They needed to write extensive biographies. Every grant acquired, every paper published—as well as those pending—had to be listed.

Which meant the time for Cory to come clean had come. "You remember I mentioned the aflatoxin paper about to be published in the *American Journal of Pharmacology and Toxicology*?"

Dana remembered.

"It was rejected."

Dana sat up straight. "I thought it was accepted."

Cory felt her face burn with heat. She couldn't hold Dana's eye. "The editors changed their minds. They said, on second thought, because there were no numerical results and no molecular techniques, it wasn't really an improvement over the old method, and they wouldn't take it."

Dana took another hit of coffee. "I've never heard of that happening."

Cory put her coffee down. It felt like her whole body was on fire. "Joe Carlisle is appealing the decision. In the meantime, I'm rewriting the paper for the *Journal of Food Chemistry.*"

Dana frowned and stared into her cup. It wasn't nearly as prestigious a journal.

Cory could have explained it further, mentioned the trouble with the FDA and Wellspring, but that was another can of worms she preferred not to open. Unable to explain the reason for the rejection, she said, "I have nine papers published already."

Dana raised her eyes and smiled. "That's great for a post-doc. When do you finish?"

"August."

"When Joe retires. Good timing. Getting the grant will help. You can take the money anywhere. Trust me, Rupert White won't let you take it anywhere."

It was fantastic news. In an instant, the heat was gone, as if an air-conditioned breeze had swept it away and left Cory feeling cool. She picked up her coffee, took a long sip.

"I have to warn you, the funding is competitive," Dana said. "Even with contacts, we'll only have a ten percent chance of success. We'll likely be approved but with low priority. We'll keep revising and resubmitting, and at some point we'll get high priority and the money will come, but who knows when that will be. It could be years."

Cory was deflated again. Her newfound leverage was short-lived.

Chapter Thirty-two

Cory finished her coffee, returned to her office, and threw herself into the proposal. She was hard at work on the method section when Marie Weiss called at noon. At first there was only crying. Then, between sobs, Marie said, "I need your help. You've got to come. The doctor wants to give Danny some new drug. I don't trust her."

Cory saved the file on her laptop. "What drug?"

"An allergy medicine called Alluron. It's sold over the counter."

"It can't be too strong."

"This is an injection. It's new. Not FDA approved."

As if that meant anything. "What did Daniel say?"

"He's in a meeting. He just wants to do whatever the doctor says. Like she knows best. But if this is new, how does she know?"

There was no denying the logic, but Daniel had been clear. "He doesn't want me involved," Cory said.

"He's not here. I tried calling Mathew, but he's got office hours at legal aid. He said to call you. I'm begging you. Look at the drug, see what you think. Tell me if Danny's fit to fly."

Cory closed her eyes. She wasn't being asked for medical advice or to list the merits of Oxylace, just whether or not Danny should take a new drug or get on a plane. In the same situation, Cory had no one to ask; there was no one to concur that Sophie could survive outside ICU and endure a six-hour flight. She had been on her own, and it had been hell. "All right," she said. "I'll be right there."

Lunchtime traffic was heavy, and the drive took twenty minutes. Cory found Marie waiting in the lobby, huddled between tall plastic plants. Her eyes were puffy and red, and her long gray hair was falling out of an untidy bun. She dug her nails into Cory's arm. "Thank you for coming. Danny went for testing." She looked at her watch. "We can see him in fifteen minutes. Let's wait in the cafeteria."

It was not a request. Marie steered Cory down a quiet hallway to a small cafeteria where they stood in line, saying nothing, while elevator music played. They got coffee and sat down at a small, round, fluo-rescent-orange table. Marie opened her purse and extracted a shiny brochure extolling the magnificent Alluron. "This is what Dr. Sullivan wants to use."

Cory studied the pretty pictures. Children smiling, doctors deep in consultation, a white prescription bottle. She turned the paper over. More of the same. Cory read the text and learned Alluron was one of the most effective drugs on the market for treating allergies. This she found strange, given that in this day of drug advertising she'd never heard of it before. There were few side effects beyond a dry mouth and excessive urination. One pill was effective for twenty-four hours, and for those who couldn't take pills, the drug would soon be avail-able in liquid form and could be given via injection or IV infusion. Because it was already approved, physicians were free to prescribe it immediately. A graph showed that when the drug was used alongside chemotherapy, it decreased the allergic response in eighty percent of patients. Reading the small print, Cory saw that Alluron was made by Wellspring. She pointed that out to Marie.

"I know," Marie said. "And that's not all. Dr. Sullivan is a paid con-sultant for Wellspring Pharmaceutical."

Cory choked and put down her coffee before it could spill. "How do you know?"

"I looked her up. It's online. I came flat out and asked her, and she didn't deny it. She said it didn't matter; there was no conflict of inter-est, and it wouldn't cloud her judgment."

Cory sat in stunned silence. If she had known that six months ago, it would have made her own decision easier. Of course there was a con-flict of interest. "What did Daniel say?"

"He's on her side. He doesn't care that Wellspring pays her a hun-dred thousand dollars a year to promote their drugs. How could she prescribe anything for Danny that Wellspring doesn't make? I want to take him to Mexico."

"Did you call the clinic?"

"I tried. There's no answer. The phone rings and rings. There's no answering service, nothing."

Cory had encountered the same problem when she first tried to call. She later learned the phone lines at the clinic were always breaking down. There could be rain, or wind, or the phone company wanted a bribe and would disconnect the line. "Keep trying," Cory said.

"What's the clinic like? Who's the doctor?"

Cory told her about Marco Arrango, a Mexican national who attended medical school at UCLA. He became an American citizen and opened a booming practice. It didn't take long for him to become disillusioned with American medicine. He couldn't prescribe what he thought was best. His hands were tied by the insurance companies and the California State Board of Medicine who told him what he could and couldn't use. He finally closed his practice, moved to Tijuana, and opened the clinic. Everyone there loved him.

"I'll keep calling," Marie said. "What they're doing here isn't working."

"You don't need an appointment. If Danny is well enough to go, just go. He won't turn anyone away. If you don't have money, it doesn't matter."

For the first time, Cory saw Marie smile.

The door to the cafeteria opened, and a pack of interns streamed in. Bringing up the rear was a smart-looking young woman dressed in high heels and a skirt suit and carrying an expensive briefcase with gold clasps. Unlike the interns who wore scrubs with clipped ID cards, the woman had a gold lanyard with a tag that screamed drug rep.

"That's Cindy Fisher," Marie said, pointing. She reached into her purse and brought out a business card. "She said the new drug was perfectly safe."

Cory read the card. Cindy Fisher was a senior sales rep for Wellspring Pharmaceutical. "You talked to the rep?" Cory was shocked. An agent representing a drug company had no business talking to a patient. She tossed the card on the table.

"I talked to her *and* the doctor," Marie said. "They both said taking Alluron was the right thing to do."

Cory frowned as the rep opened her briefcase, removed a thick wallet, and paid for the interns' coffees and donuts before joining them at a big table. The drug rep was buying future influence.

"They said there was no reason not to use Alluron and every reason to use it," Marie added. "But that's what Dr. Sullivan said about chemo. And now Danny is in a coma. His blood pressure got so low he could have brain damage." A tear leaked out the corner of Marie's eye.

"Surely they've done a cat scan," Cory said. It would be at least ten thousand dollars for the hospital, likely more. They would never pass that up.

"They did one," Marie said. "It showed no bleeding, but it can't tell whether or how the brain is functioning." She sniffled and wiped her eyes. "I just want him out."

A voice came from behind Cory. "He's not going anywhere."

Cory turned around and saw Daniel, looking older, stiffer, and grimmer. His hair had grayed overnight and looked at odds with the young, pageboy-style cut.

"What are you doing here?" he said to Cory. He looked at his wife and repeated the question. "What is she doing here?"

"I called her," Marie said. "I'm not listening to a doctor who works for the chemo company anymore. I want to take Danny to Mexico."

Daniel sat down, pulling his chair close to his wife. "Marie, we trust the science," he said sternly.

"She didn't, and she's a scientist," Marie said.

"Read the clinic's brochure," Cory said, wanting to leave. "See what other patients have to say. It's not just me."

"Oh, now we go on what other people say." Daniel sighed loudly. "That's very scientific. How about we listen to what the doctor says? Dr. Sullivan made it quite clear that the medicine would stop the allergic reaction."

"Because in four-year-old boys that's been shown to be the case?" Cory said.

Daniel looked at Marie. "Why did you call her? Do you really think she's helping?"

"My point is, a few doctors noting something isn't a rigorous scientific study of a drug," Cory said.

"So now you're an expert pharmacist," Daniel said.

"I have never misrepresented myself," Cory said.

"We're taking him to Mexico," Marie said quietly.

"We're not." Daniel pounded his fist on the table, and the Styrofoam coffee cups jumped. "Dr. Sullivan said that would be like signing his death warrant. It's parental neglect. Something your friend here knows all about. It's just wrong."

"It wasn't wrong for Sophie," Marie said. "We did it your way, and look at Danny. Now we try my way." She stood up, dragging Cory up with her. "He should be back now. Come with me."

Over Daniel's strident objections and Cory's own reticence, they cleared their cups and headed upstairs to ICU.

The wing, as always, was spotless, with the tile floor shining and the windows gleaming. Machines hummed, and nurses and doctors moved with purpose. If you didn't know any better, you'd put your faith here, where the ambiance was professional, knowledgeable, and authoritative. In this place, for all outward purposes, in the war between medicine and disease, the winner was clear.

In limited respects, there were areas where American medicine excelled. Diagnostic capability was unmatched in the world. As was treatment for trauma and accidents. Surgery was generally successful too. Doctors were able to cut into people and get them back on their feet. Where they failed was in treating disease. They had no idea how to give health when it was gone. The propensity to over-prescribe drugs, which treated symptoms not causes, often did more harm in the long run than good. While there were new targeted drugs on the horizon, given Cory's experience with drug companies, she knew that when these became available they'd come at a price. Making a profit was a drug company's main concern. It was the goal of health care: Make as much money as possible. Getting and keeping people well was beside the point.

They walked down a wide, well-lit hallway, and Marie ushered Cory into Danny's room. It was a private room with a crib, though he was too old for it. He looked shrunken. His skin was yellow and his hair was thinning as if chemotherapy had already claimed it. He had a tube down his throat, his eyes were closed, and his small hands were folded together over his heart. He looked dead. Take out the tube and he could be lying in a coffin. There was no way he could take a commercial flight to Tijuana any time soon.

Marie gripped her arm. "What do you think?"

Cory chose her words carefully. "He doesn't look like he's suffering."

"No. Can he fly? Can he make it to Mexico?"

As Cory searched for the words to say kindly that he would have to get a bit better, an alarm on a machine began to screech. A flat line moved across a diagnostic screen. Blood pressure and heart rate fell to zero.

The alarm rang out in the nurses' station, and within seconds an emergency care team burst in, shoving Cory and the parents to the door. Dr. Sullivan, the young, ambitious oncologist and well-paid Wellspring consultant, took charge. Stethoscope in place, she bent over Danny, listening for a heartbeat. She yelled, "Paddles," as Marie began to shriek.

Sullivan ripped off the small smock, attached electrodes to the skinny ribbed chest, and shocked him. His body arced into the air and slammed down. There was no response. "Clear," Sullivan yelled, and she shocked him again.

She got his heart beating. The alarm stopped screaming. The nurses cheered. Daniel and Marie hugged one another. Cory left the building. She should never have come. It could have been Sophie lying in the crib. It still could be.

Chapter Thirty-three

Cory drove back to the lab and shut herself in her office. She did what she always did in response to a crisis—she worked. But death was following her. It took the squirrel she hit in the parking lot that ran under her tire when she left the hospital. It lurked in her office where she labored on the proposal. It filled the empty animal room with a foul, odiferous stink when she went to look for the rat.

Then she realized it was him. He wasn't in the trap, which was still empty and armed with peanut butter. He wasn't beneath the cage trolley, not under the sink, not in the drawers. She pulled them out one by one and stacked them on the floor. With the next to the last she found him, splayed and flattened, and trapped in the narrow space between two drawers. His body was decomposing, long past rigor mortis, now leaking brown fluid.

She pulled on gloves and scooped up the rotting remains. Using a pipette, she drew up the fluid. She dropped the animal in an animal bag and deposited it into the freezer. She went to the lab and did the assay.

Negative. Confirmation the biting rat was a control animal. Megan's fear of aflatoxin exposure was only in her mind. Cory photographed the ELISA result and uploaded it as an attachment to the accident report.

She was late getting to day care. Only a few children remained, which was fortunate, for the staff was bereft. Late that afternoon, Danny had died. In tears, Sandy told Cory he'd been shocked ten times, was dead five minutes, and then came back before dying again for good.

Cory didn't want to hear any more. She went to get Sophie. Danny had endured a different ending to life than Janie's son, Brad. When he died in the clinic, a harpist had played, soothing mint oil burned, and sage smoked to ward off bad spirits. He faded away in his mother's arms, his mind checking out long before his organs shut down. Cory had stayed up all night with them and was there when his heart stopped beating. He uttered a loud sneeze, and then it was over. There was no hard battle with death like there was in the hospital here. No heroic measures, just sad acceptance.

But Dr. Sullivan would have tried everything. She had to. She wasn't deliberately neglectful. She'd bought into the medical system and followed its authority without question. That was the difference between medical doctors and scientists. Cory was taught to question, to be skeptical, and to dig for the truth. Medical doctors created their own truth and didn't question it. How Sullivan could administer toxins that killed more patients than she saved day after day was a mystery Cory couldn't fathom. In the life and death battle, Sullivan had lost, and Danny had paid the price. Cory couldn't grasp what his parents were going through. In hindsight, they knew that, like Janie, they had made the wrong choice.

Cory grabbed Sophie and went home to a dark house and a hyper dog. The place felt empty and cold. There was no sign of Mathew, no inviting aroma, and no waiting dinner.

Later that night, when Sophie was in bed, Mathew was out somewhere, and Cory was working on her proposal, Janie called to remind Cory she was coming for the weekend. "I'm in L.A. Heading for divorce court in the morning. I'll be in Texas on Friday."

"Great," Cory said.

"Everything all right?" Janie asked.

"A four-year-old boy died of leukemia today."

Janie was silent for a moment. "Do you know his parents? Do you think they'd blog about it?"

"*No.*" Cory was horrified Janie would ask.

"It may be the best thing for them. Help them deal with what they're going through. Just ask them."

"He died six hours ago."

"You don't have to call them this minute. Tomorrow is fine."

Cory closed her eyes and shook her head.

"I'll arrive late Friday afternoon," Janie said, not pursuing it. She was flying to Austin where she hoped to speak with elected officials about the drug laws. If all went according to plan, she'd rent a car and arrive in Duane when Cory finished work.

"I'll make dinner," Cory said. She would sleep in the single bed in Sophie's room and give Janie her room.

"Plan on a busy weekend. Have you ever been to the Bluebonnet Festival?"

It was a street bazaar, and Cory had been exactly twice. "There are clowns, jugglers, and artisans. You want to go to that?"

"Enough Nasty Drugs is planning a protest. So far we've got two thousand signed up. We're joining another group, Move To Amend. Have you heard of it?"

"No."

"You will. I'll tell you about it when I see you. I've got to go."

Janie hung up, and Cory closed her phone. A protest? She wasn't going to a protest. She would take Sophie to see the clowns. When she was in the bull's-eye of the FDA and Wellspring Pharmaceutical, she had to be invisible. She sent Mathew a text message alerting him about a weekend guest.

He must have been close by because he came home ten minutes later and burst into the study. "It's your house. You can invite anyone you want." He went to the window and stared out into the night. "Who is it? A man?"

She wondered if he was jealous, if that was why he came so quickly. "She's a friend. Her name's Janie Bartlett." Cory gave a brief history of how they met. "She wants to go to a protest at the Bluebonnet Festival."

Mathew relaxed, his features softened. He turned around and sat down in the chair beside the desk. "I'm going. The protest is organized by Move To Amend. We're trying to fix the Supreme Court's ruling that corporations are people and money is free speech."

He went on and on, talking about bought elections and corporate influence running the country, but she stopped listening. She wondered where he had been. Did Nancy live close by? When he stopped talking, she said, "Where were you?"

He blushed and said, "Out with a friend."

"Nancy?"

"Did I mention her name?"

He had not, and Cory realized she was busted. She'd given herself away. Without trying, she knew all about his personal life. "I saw the name in the paper. Congratulations on your award."

"It's nothing."

"She's a doctor. I don't know whether to be happy for you or not."

"A chiropractor."

"Ah, not a real doctor," Cory said.

"If you say so." He looked into her eyes with the look that went straight to her brain and seemed to know everything. "What's wrong?" he said. "What is it?"

She averted her eyes, stared down at the desk that was scratched from years of use. Did he think she was upset about Nancy? She glanced at him askance. "Danny died."

Mathew closed his eyes, dropped his chin to his chest, looking stricken. "I talked to Marie this morning. I thought she was taking Danny to Mexico. I figured he got better."

Cory shook her head and swallowed hard. "It was too late. He couldn't go anywhere." Her eyes prickled, her nose started to run, and she sniffled loudly.

Mathew looked at her with unblinking intensity. "It's okay to cry."

She stared him down. "I don't cry."

His eyes glazed over with tears, and he wiped them away. "Never?"

"No."

"Why not?"

"What good does it do?"

"It releases sadness."

"Babies cry."

He pulled himself together and looked at her incredulously. "There's nothing immature about crying."

"According to you."

"What about when Sophie got sick?"

"I was worried."

"When she got better?"

"I was relieved."

He picked the baby monitor up off the desk and turned it over in his hands. "Worried? Relieved? Those are thoughts. What about emotions? Terrified? Overjoyed? You react intellectually."

"Like a scientist. That's not a bad thing."

"You know what I think?"

"I'm sure you'll tell me."

"There was some early trauma in your life that was so horrendous and so emotionally overwhelming that if you allowed yourself to feel it, you thought it would kill you, so you blocked it out. The problem is, by blocking it, you blocked your emotional being. You lost touch with your instincts and your intuition. You have no choice but to rely on your head."

"Is that right, Dr. Freud? Only I never experienced any childhood trauma."

"Your parents dying was nothing?"

"I don't remember it."

"That's the hallmark of trauma. The conscious mind blocks it. Your thinking brain ignores, it but the unconscious remembers." He tapped the side of his skull with a long index finger.

"If you say so."

"I gather you consider psychology a soft science."

"Not at all. I don't consider it a science."

He laughed. "So, for you, the world is only what you can know with the five senses."

"You got it."

"What about everything else?"

"What everything?"

"Everything not amenable to the five senses. Everything science leaves out. The emotions, the unconscious, the higher self."

"As I said, not real science."

"Just reality."

"Yours, not mine."

"Yes, study ten percent of something and convince yourself you know everything." He put his elbows on his knees and leaned toward her. "Emotions matter. They're not nothing just because you deny them and refuse to feel. Therapy would help. I recommend it. You'd be happier, more fulfilled, more in tune with yourself and the world. At least be a part of it."

Cory pushed back her chair. "Thank you, Dr. Freud, but I'm happy as I am. Why don't you go psychoanalyze Nancy."

"I'm sorry. You're right." Mathew raised his hands in surrender. "It's none of my business."

She was surprised he backed down. He didn't usually stop pushing. But at the mention of Nancy, he stepped back, detaching. He had Nancy, and his interest lay elsewhere.

He stood up. "There's a basketball game on. You want to watch? Have a glass of wine?"

It was a peace offering, and she accepted the invitation, glad for his company. They sat on either end of the couch watching the Duane Racers and Aggies tear across the court and fling the ball at the net. She couldn't stop thinking about what he'd said. Was she too rational? Did she intellectualize her emotions? Had she stopped feeling? Was that why she had no intuition? Was she a lost cause, beyond repair? Was that why he picked Nancy? She could weep and cry? Is that what he liked? Seeing his own reflection in her? Cory couldn't do it. She kept her wits about her. She didn't see it as a weakness but a strength. She made hard choices, and her daughter was alive. It was when she reacted without thinking that she got into trouble. She should never have sent a letter, never have danced with him.

Chapter Thirty-four

The pharmaceutical industry is so powerful that its interests take precedence over yours. It has essentially hired the government to do its bidding. In the words of Senator Richard J. Durban, the pharmaceutical lobby 'has a death grip on Congress.'

—Marcia Angell, MD, former editor-in-chief,
The New England Journal of Medicine

March 29th

Friday afternoon, Janie arrived in Duane before Cory got off work and was already at the house with Mathew when Cory got home. She was late. After picking up Sophie, she went to the grocery store to get food for dinner. In an act of defiance against the FDA, along with a baguette and tuna steaks, she picked up multivitamins—one bottle for Sophie and one for her. Mathew swore by them. He said despite their good diet, the soil lacked nutrients and supplements were necessary. The FDA disagreed wholeheartedly and called the practice "a waste of good money." Cory wanted to read the studies for herself and couldn't find them. She decided to take the vitamins and gauge for herself in a month's time whether she felt any better or not. She would be her own science experiment.

Mathew and Janie were sitting out back, drinking beer. Cory watched them through the window as she put away groceries. Pluto was with them, lying between them, luxuriating as Mathew rubbed his fur with his foot. They looked comfortable, chatting easily, as if old friends, laughing and smiling, and apparently in agreement on the matter under discussion. Cory guessed they shared a similar philosophy and easily found common ground. She reminded herself to watch out for their political agenda. They weren't the ones being threatened with a lawsuit and prison.

She poured drinks for herself and Sophie and went outside, interrupting boisterous hilarity. Janie was laughing so hard she was crying. For forty-four, she was looking good. In the summer when Brad died she looked older, but time had reversed the clock. Trim and in good shape, she was five foot two and weighed a hundred pounds. Her dark hair was cut short, which made her black eyes look huge and showed off high, sharp cheekbones. She wore a white T-shirt with AMTA written in large red letters. In shorts and sandals, her legs were crossed, the top foot swinging, and Mathew seemed hypnotized. Pluto wagged his tail at Cory but didn't bother getting up.

Sophie wouldn't go to Janie, but when Mathew raised his arms she leaned toward him. "Dada," she said, and by now, no one was correcting her.

They made humorless small talk that left no one in stitches. Janie liked the house, thought Sophie had grown, and looked healthy. Cory liked Janie's haircut and thought her life on the road wasn't taking a toll. They spoke of the weather, the grand trees, and the burgeoning bluebonnets. After a few minutes, the tenor changed.

"You didn't tell me you lived with a lawyer who supports Move To Amend," Janie said.

While Cory searched for an appropriate response, Mathew said, "I'm not a lawyer. Not yet."

"May is soon enough," Janie said approvingly. "We went to the funeral home."

Cory blinked. "Danny Weiss's funeral home?"

"To give our condolences. I talked to Daniel and Marie about the blog. They're going to do it."

Cory took a sip of beer and digested the news. She found it unfathomable that Janie would intrude on strangers at such a sad time. Yet they had agreed, apparently not affronted in the least. What did that say about Cory's read on people? They were mystifying to her.

"I know you'd never ask, and I see you don't approve," Janie said. "But they're happy to channel their anger productively into a needful cause."

Cory heard the rebuke and came to her own defense. "I'd be glad to do something too if the FDA and Wellspring left me alone. I wrote one letter and the FDA threatened me, the local newspaper shamed me, and the journal that accepted my research paper then rejected it. I'm the one they're coming after, not you."

Janie leaned forward. "Because I'm no one. You have a doctorate, and I'm just an ex-school teacher without a job. No one bothers with me. I can scream as loud as I want, and no one listens. You got their attention. You have clout. And you won't use it."

Cory sighed loudly. "There's nothing I can do."

"You could write a scientific paper on Oxylace."

"I already told you, no one would publish it."

"How do you know? You haven't written it."

"I can't write it. There's no clinical study."

"Dr. Arroyo gave you patient files."

"Yes, but for a rigorous scientific study, you have to run the trial double-blind with a control and do a comparison. I've got nothing to compare Oxylace to. Medical records here are private. I can't do anything without the data."

Mathew came to the rescue and agreed Cory had a point. "We have to focus on changing the law." He artfully changed the topic. "Janie visited our elected representatives in Austin."

But the trip had been a failure. "I met your two senators and a congressman," Janie said. "Not a one was willing to join END or support the Access to Medical Treatment Act. Congressman Harris was the worst. He called the police and had me thrown out of his town hall meeting. Too bad for him; he's down in the polls. But he's got money. His main super PAC just got a six-million-dollar donation."

"That's why we need Move To Amend," Mathew said as he adjusted Sophie on his lap. She was drinking mango juice, holding the cup with both handles and looking serious, as if following the conversation. "Money buys elections and our representatives."

Janie finished her beer and put the empty bottle down on the ground. "Which leaves us a government that serves the rich."

Cory wasn't interested in having a political discussion. "Do you want another beer?" she asked Janie. "A glass of wine? I got three tuna steaks for dinner. Mathew, are you going to stay?"

He looked at Janie. She looked at her watch. "This is my limit. The wake is tonight."

"Danny's wake?"

"It's starts at six. Are you coming?"

"I can't bring Sophie." It was the last place Cory wanted to go.

Janie smiled at Mathew. "I guess it's just you and me."

Cory looked at him. "You're going?"

He shrugged. "I'll pay my respects."

Cory felt guilty about staying home, but she wasn't willing to take Sophie, and it was too short notice to ask Penny to babysit. "I'll make dinner while you're gone. Have it ready when you get back."

"Don't bother," Janie said.

"Who knows when it will be over," Mathew added.

Cory nodded, disappointed. She had planned a nice meal, intended to be a great host, but she was being abandoned.

Chapter Thirty-five

March 30th

The pair returned home after two a.m., laughing and making too much noise about having to be quiet. Trying to get comfortable in the lumpy single bed in Sophie's room, Cory couldn't fall back asleep. It seemed as soon as she did, Sophie was awake and wanting out of her crib.

And so, on Saturday morning, they were up at dawn. Cory was feeding Sophie mashed bananas and oatmeal when Janie appeared. It had been a wild night apparently. They'd had dinner at Stanley's Bistro and then went to Nancy's to play Scrabble with another couple. "I hope we didn't wake you," Janie said as she sat down at the table with a cup of coffee.

Cory shoveled oatmeal into Sophie's open mouth. "I heard you," she said coldly, and instantly regretted it. She changed her tone. "What did you think of Nancy?"

"Loved her. Great sense of humor. Smart, funny, and nuts about alternative healing and willing to do something." Janie rolled her shoulders. "She gave me a neck rub. I can see what Mathew sees in her."

That was when he came in. "Never play Scrabble with a school teacher," he said as he poured himself coffee, sat down, opened the newspaper, and picked up the sports section. Janie grabbed the front section, leaving Cory the classifieds.

"How did it go at the funeral home?" Cory asked.

"Sad," Janie said. "There were lots of people. Parents and staff from his elementary school and the day care."

"They asked about you," Mathew said.

"Marie and Daniel?" Cory asked.

"No, Ethyl and Sandy from Campus Care. They hired outside help so the day care could stay open late and parents could attend."

"I didn't know," Cory said.

Mathew and Janie exchanged quick glances before hiding behind their newspapers. Mathew left as soon as his coffee was done. Nancy was making him breakfast, but he promised to be back before two, well in advance of the funeral at three.

"You're going?" Cory asked.

"Sure." He didn't ask if she was going.

But Janie did, in a circuitous way. "You don't have to go. I'm sure the parents won't mind. They may wonder why I would go and Mathew, and not you, but—"

She couldn't finish her sentence. Janie had no but because there was no but; there was no excuse. "I'll go," Cory said. "I'll take Sophie to day care."

"Good." Janie nodded her approval.

That settled, Cory made an omelet, and they had breakfast. She planned to show Janie the exciting sights of Duane, take her to the farmers market and the dog park, but at eight it started raining, and the clouds looked like they would last all day. In any case, Janie had plans of her own. She had to make signs for the protest.

"Don't mind me," Janie said. "Watch cartoons. Do whatever you normally do."

"You can use the study."

"Perfect. Can you help me carry in the boards? I've got like a thousand."

"You have time to make that many signs?"

"I'll do my best."

"All right, I'll help."

It took ten trips to carry in the boards. The plastic wrap around them got drenched in the rain. They stacked the boards against the desk, rolled back the rug, and sprawled on the oak floor with a box of colored magic markers. Sophie got her own board to scribble on. Janie had pages of slogans, and Cory was free to write whatever she wanted. Some slogans were funny: *If you don't like socialism, get off the highway; Believe in America, bank in the Caymans; Our Government: steal from the poor, give to the rich; You can't fix stupid, but you can vote it out.*

Cory decided to stick with the relevant subject: *Get Money out of Health Care; Health Care is a Human Right, No Profit from Sickness,* and *Down with Corporate-Ruled Health.*

As she worked, she thought Janie would try to convince her to go to the protest, but it was not mentioned. Janie lamented her divorce, her loneliness, her love for her husband, and the loss of her home. She still missed her son. Her husband had moved on and left his old life behind. He was a bachelor with a new twenty-three-year-old girlfriend who'd turned Brad's room into a clothes closet and thrown away his stuff. Cory listened without comment, concentrating on the signs as the gloom of the day seeped into her skin.

***

They left for the funeral at two thirty, driving in the rental with Sophie in the back, sitting on Cory's lap. At the day care, unfamiliar staff checked Sophie's name on a list and slapped a nametag on her shirt.

The funeral was held at the Catholic Church on Southwest Parkway. The place was packed. The trio sat in the back row with Mathew in the middle. Cory stared at the statues. She didn't want to be here. Janie and Mathew may not have said anything out loud, but she felt they blamed her for Danny's death. She should have fought harder to convince Marie and Daniel to go to Mexico.

The rain beat down, thrumming on the roof, at times drowning out the organ. Cory distracted herself, thought of other things. She'd been to one funeral before, and that was her parents', but she couldn't remember it. Her grandmother didn't have a funeral. She didn't want one, didn't want so much as an announcement in the newspaper. She wanted to be burned, have her ashes sprinkled in the yard, and remain close to the house for all of eternity. She said ashes and afterbirth were the real foundation of the house; they nourished the land and its people.

Sophie was the exception. Her placenta was missing. And she was the frail one. Though it was unscientific to consider, while sitting in church waiting for the service to start, Cory wondered whether her grandmother was right.

When her grandmother got sick and knew she would die, she told Cory to watch for her, that she would send a sign from "the other side." Cory expected bangs in the night, loud footsteps on the stairs, or the piano playing by itself, but there was none of that. What there was, was an owl. It came in the spring after her grandmother died and sat on the balcony railing outside Cory's bedroom window, hooting loudly through the night. It roosted in the trees out back and watched her swing. The owl came and went. Whether it was the same owl or different ones, Cory didn't know. One appeared the summer Sophie was born, and again when she was sick. Did Indians really believe a dead person became an owl? Were they harbingers of the future? But did they bear good news or bad? Her grandmother had never mentioned owls. She heard people. She said the ghosts liked to have parties.

The organ stopped playing. The organist flexed his fingers, and the service began. The congregation stood as the small, wet coffin came in. Pallbearers effortlessly carried it up to the front. The parents followed. Marie was sobbing. Daniel, stiff and stoic, was holding her up, though both seemed barely able to walk.

Janie was weeping, as was Mathew; they were clinging to each other. He was the only man Cory saw openly crying. At home, in church, out in public—he didn't mind outward displays of emotion. She liked that about him. He was strong enough to withstand looking weak.

The service was mercifully short. There were hymns, a short sermon, and communion. Then the coffin was carried out, and the congregation followed. Rain poured on, falling from the skies, like the tears of weeping gods. People quickly scattered. The headlights on the hearse blazed. Those going to the graveside got flags from the funeral home to display on their roofs.

The convoy left. Cory, Mathew, and Janie hurried to the car. They weren't going to the cemetery, which was for family members and close friends only. They picked up Sophie and went home. Cory thought she would make the dinner she had planned for Friday, only instead of barbecuing the tuna, she'd broil it, but when she broached the subject, Mathew and Janie had other plans.

"Nancy invited us for dinner," Mathew said.

They were both going? It took all Cory's concentration to hide her disappointment.

"I could call her," Mathew said. "See if you can come."

"That's okay. I wouldn't want to bring Sophie."

"That's what we thought," Janie said. "We'll get out of your hair."

That was how, after a funeral, when Cory needed a diversion to erase the sadness of the afternoon, she ended up alone.

Chapter Thirty-six

March 31st

Sunday morning, Cory and Sophie were the last to rise, even though Mathew and Janie had had another late night. They'd taken over the kitchen. Coffee was ready, biscuits were baking, and Mathew was frying bacon. Cory plunked Sophie in her chair and poured her a glass of apple juice. She got a cup of coffee and sat down. "I'm surprised you're up so early." She took a sip of coffee and made a face. It was too weak for her liking.

"We've got lots to do," Janie said. "Mathew helped me finish the signs and load the car. We've got to get to the festival early. Get a good site for the table. There's going to be a lot of people."

Cory drank more coffee. She would make a new pot when they left. She was glad they weren't trying to rope her into going. Later, she'd take Sophie to see the clowns.

"Over two thousand from Move To Amend are coming," Mathew said with his back to them. Bacon fat was spitting.

"We should have close to a thousand from END," Janie said. "Which reminds me." She reached behind her chair and passed Cory a T-shirt. "Complimentary with membership."

The T-shirt was fluorescent pink with the word "END" written on the front in bold black letters. Across the sleeve in smaller letters was the phrase: Enough Nasty Drugs. Janie was wearing a similar T-shirt only in yellow. Mathew wore a red T-shirt with MOVE TO AMEND on the front.

"I gather you're not going," Janie said.

Before Cory could respond, Mathew said, "You should stay home. There could be trouble. Move To Amend is expecting a police presence, and it could get rough. It's no picnic."

"It's a flower festival," Cory said. "They have a jumping castle. I'm taking Sophie."

"It's too dangerous," Mathew said. "There's a rumor undercover police will start a skirmish."

"Who told you that?" Janie asked.

Mathew raised his eyebrows, Janie nodded knowingly, and Cory figured he was referring to his anonymous friend who'd hacked her computer. She was beginning to feel like an outsider in her own home, and she didn't like it. "I gather your hacker buddy's going?"

"He might," Mathew said vaguely.

"And Nancy?" Cory asked.

Mathew and Janie answered simultaneously, saying opposite things. According to Janie, she wouldn't miss it for the world. Mathew said she was thinking about it.

"It could get ugly," he said. "Why put Sophie in danger? Just stay home."

He couldn't tell her what to do. Cory wanted to meet Nancy and the hacker. "I'm going," she said. "I'll take Sophie to day care."

Mathew and Janie smiled at each other. Intercepting the exchange, Cory wondered if she'd been set up. Were two master manipulators jerking her strings? When she awoke that morning she'd planned to go to a flower festival. Now she was heading for a protest and had the proper clothes to wear.

***

They left at ten, with Janie driving and Mathew riding shotgun. After dropping off Sophie, they went on to the university. Cory told herself she was just going to watch. She had never been to a protest before and was curious. She was going to stand on the sideline and be an observer.

The festival shut down Texas Avenue, the major artery that ran through town on the east side of campus. There was free parking in the student lot, and kiddie cops were out in force. They drove past the golf course on the southeast corner. The verge was cordoned off with orange police tape, as if a crime scene was already marked. Here were the serious policemen, wearing riot gear and holding Plexiglas shields and thick batons, guarding the grass.

"Keep off the course or go to jail," Janie said as she parked.

Under bright skies and a light southerly wind, they headed to the main drag. The street was already lined with vendors' tables and tents. It was primarily a craft fair if you ignored the expected three thousand protesters. Janie found a spot she liked between a stained-glass artisan and a candlestick maker, and Mathew unfolded the table. They made numerous trips ferrying the signs and brochures. When they were done, Mathew left to help Move To Amend.

Half the student parking lot was reserved for protesters, and Janie's plan was to hand out signs around the edges to make END seem bigger than it was. In her mind, *Down with the Supreme Court! Down with Corporations!* and *Down with Corporate Health!* meant the same thing. A protest was a protest, and if the powers that be thought three thousand had turned out to rail against the current health care industry, all the better for Enough Nasty Drugs.

Janie hung a six-foot-long banner along the front of the table and fanned out a row of colorful brochures. Cory picked one up and looked at disturbing photos of the sick. On the back were pictures of good-looking, healthy people smiling and having fun. There was a list of steps that could take you in that direction. There was nothing about exercise or eating well. You were supposed to write your representative, send a letter to your newspaper, join a protest, get involved, and let your voice be heard.

A news van rolled up. Janie grabbed a handful of brochures and ran to speak to the press, leaving Cory to staff the table. She stood behind it, watching the crowd. The air smelled of popcorn and cotton candy. With clowns juggling and mimes acting, it resembled a carnival. The sun was hot and bright, and Cory wished she had a hat. The crowd was growing thicker, and she knew her grandmother would be appalled if she could see her now. "Don't go along with the herd," she used to say, although whether this was going with the herd or against it was not entirely clear.

A tiny, dark-haired girl came to the table and grabbed a brochure. "These look good," she said in the deepest voice Cory had ever heard. "They turned out all right for a rush job, don't you think?"

"I agree," Cory said, wondering who she was.

"The polls say ninety percent of voters want doctors to have the freedom to use any treatment they want. Still, the Medical Access bill is never tabled because it doesn't have enough congressional support. That's our democracy. A government run by corporations that ignores the will of the people."

"It's about money," Cory said, quoting Mathew. She realized that she looked like she was in charge of the table and stepped back.

The girl extended her hand. "I'm Layla." She was young, in her early twenties, wearing sneakers, short shorts, and a bright-green Move To Amend T-shirt. She had warm skin and earrings that resembled lightning bolts. "There's going to be a crowd. Do you feel the excitement?"

Was that excitement? To Cory, it was anxiety. The crowd was closing in around her, and she didn't like it. She moved farther away from the table, and Layla moved with her.

"People are finally waking up," Layla said. "The planet is dying. Our government is screwing us. It sold us out so corporations can make a buck."

She sounded like Mathew. "Are you a lawyer?" Cory asked.

"Grad student. I'm doing a PhD in physics."

Cory was impressed. Biochemistry was easy, but physics, which her mother had studied, was something else.

Layla moved closer and whispered in Cory's ear. "Be careful. There's going to be trouble."

"So I heard."

A tall guy with long sandy hair wearing a black T-shirt with the words "FED UP" came by and laid a proprietary hand on Layla's shoulder. He towered over her and had to lean down to whisper in her ear. She had to go.

Cory watched them move into the crowd, and then Janie was back, radiating enthusiasm. She physically dragged Cory to the table. Janie had been asked to give a one o'clock television interview, and later that afternoon when the speeches began, she would have a chance to talk to the crowd. Now she wanted help handing out signs. "Remember, keep visible." She pushed a stack of signs into Cory's arms. "Keep to the front. We don't want to be buried."

Handing out signs wasn't exactly being an observer, but Cory did as instructed. When she was done, she stayed away from the END table, hoping to lose herself in the crowd. It was noon, and the lot was jammed with protestors. They were young, mostly college kids. Cory saw Brian, the good undergraduate student in her lab, walk by with Lyle Steele, the former consultant for the FDA who was auditing her class. They waved but didn't come over. Later, Evonia and her husband, Magnus, strolled down the street sharing pink cotton candy. She stopped walking abruptly, lowered her dark glasses, and peered at Cory. Evonia crammed the cone into her husband's hand and marched across the street.

"Are you crazy?" she asked. "Why have you no dark glasses? No hat?"

Cory looked up at the sun. "I forgot them."

"I am not speaking of sunburn," Evonia said. "You must remove that T-shirt. Bright pink? Really?"

Cory agreed. "I know. I like the blue ones."

"I am not talking about T-shirts." Evonia paused, looked to the right, then to the left. "Spies. They will be everywhere. You must disguise yourself."

"There's a crowd. I'm one of many."

Evonia shook her head. "There will be pictures; they will identify you." She raised her eyes and scanned the sky. "There will be drones. In the eyes of the law, protestors are low-level terrorists. Did you know that? You can be arrested. You think you are free, but you are not."

Cory looked up. The sky was clear. Was she being watched? No one was paying any attention to her. "It's fine," she said.

Evonia disagreed and stalked away, rejoining her husband. Still, when the cameraman from Channel 8 News came by and Janie jumped up and down and waved her sign, Cory turned her back.

She saw Mathew at the END table waving to her. He was with the pale, dark-haired woman from the awards ceremony. Cory went to the table and met Nancy. She was in her mid-thirties and dressed in the clothes of a teen. She wore a tight, white MOVE TO AMEND T-shirt, short red shorts, a fine anklet, and chunky high heels.

Janie pulled Mathew away, and Cory was left with Nancy.

It was excruciating. There was a long, strained silence while Cory evaluated the chiropractor. What about her caught Mathew's eye? Why didn't he bring her home? What did he see in her? How long had they known each other? So far, she didn't seem exceptionally funny or smart, all the things that Janie loved about her.

"Well, this is uncomfortable," Nancy finally said.

"I guess."

"Did you bring your daughter?" Nancy seemed relieved to find a topic of conversation. "I'd love to meet her. Is she here?" Nancy looked around expectantly.

"No."

"Probably for the best. The police have drawn a line in the sand. No one on the golf course." Nancy rolled down the waistband of her shorts and showed Cory a roll of cash. "I'm ready."

"For what?"

"Arrest."

"You'd get arrested?"

"Sure."

"Why?"

Nancy squinted at the sun, deepening the crow's feet around her eyes. "Because this is important. Don't you care about the world you're leaving for your daughter?"

"Of course I care. I'm here."

Nancy glanced down the length of the table, where Mathew had his back to them. Her next comment was so direct, it came as a shock. "You didn't come because of him? You don't mind me seeing him?"

Nancy was staring with hungry eyes, and Cory shrugged half-heartedly. "No." What was she supposed to say?

"I just wanted to make sure."

"Did he say something?"

"I just wondered, that's all. Seeing as he lives in your house."

Cory wanted to end the conversation, walk away, but she couldn't help herself. "How long have you known him?"

"Not long. We met on a blind date. He invited me to an awards ceremony. It was last minute. I thought maybe he'd been stood up."

Cory said nothing, but here was another surprise that left her stunned.

"Did he ask you?" Nancy asked outright.

Was she rubbing it in? Cory shook her head.

"Mathew's friend set us up."

"The computer whiz?"

"That's him." Nancy looked surprised. "You know Tyler?"

Cory lifted a shoulder.

"I wondered when I saw you talking to his girlfriend. Layla is amazing, isn't she?"

Ah, the anonymous hacker was no longer anonymous. He had a name. Tyler. He was proprietary, tall with sandy blond hair, and had a tiny girlfriend who studied physics.

"I didn't know you knew them," Nancy said, as if perplexed that Cory knew what was supposed to be a secret.

"They're friends of Mathew's from New York," Cory said with a disingenuous shrug.

"Yes. Tyler's sister died of leukemia, but he's here with Move To Amend. He was injured in a car accident a while back, and I've been treating his shoulder. He introduced me to Mathew, and the rest is history."

Cory wondered if she was supposed to say something. She had nothing to add.

Nancy pushed the conversation along. "I'd love to see your house some time."

"Sure."

"Mathew thought it might be awkward."

"Really."

"He thought it might send the wrong message." Nancy looked unhappy. "It's not like he's taking me home to meet his parents."

"No," Cory agreed.

"We're taking it slow."

Cory wondered what that meant. No consummation? Unlike her, did Mathew take his time, not rush into things? She looked into Nancy's sad eyes and thought she should say something. "He's been hurt. He's probably cautious."

"Hurt?"

"He was going to be married."

"Ah."

He hadn't told her. "Margaret left him at the altar. Well, the day before."

"That explains it." Nancy laughed as if relieved. "I knew he was hung up on someone. I thought it was you."

What gave her that impression, Cory wondered. She said, "It must have been a blow. It's taking him a long time to get over it. He wears his heart on his sleeve."

"You think so? He seems so controlled."

"Hardly," Cory said. Were they talking about the same man? Mathew couldn't hide his feelings, no matter how hard he tried.

"You don't think he's restrained?" Nancy asked.

"Wait until you get to know him," Cory said, hoping it didn't sound unkind. "Dance with him."

"Does he dance?"

"He does."

With that, Mathew disengaged himself from Janie and joined them. "My ears are prickling. Are you talking about me?"

They answered simultaneously. Cory said, "Yes," and Nancy said, "No."

Cory changed the subject. "Janie's giving a TV interview."

"I heard. The station wants a lawyer, and I guess I'm the closest thing they've got. To hear Janie speak, you'd think this was a protest for Enough Nasty Drugs and not Move To Amend." Mathew looked at his watch. "I should go." Janie, armed with a stack of brochures, was pointing at the news van. Thankfully, Nancy went with them.

Relieved, Cory hung at the table, watching the street and replaying the conversation. Mathew hadn't known Nancy forever. They'd just met. *After* the party. It was a flat-out rejection. Mathew hadn't set up the date with Nancy in advance; it was a last-minute invitation. When Cory moved closer, he moved farther away.

She didn't have time to think more about it. Her neighbors were approaching. Dana, Nick, and Frankie had crossed the street and were heading in her direction.

"So, this is what you do in your spare time," Dana said when they reached the table.

"Yes, change the world," Cory joked.

"Fantastic," Nick said. He was clean-shaven and had a cut on his chin that was spotted with dried blood. He was heartened to see progressive people in the conservative town and wanted to participate.

Dana explained he was an old protester at heart and a great supporter of the Access to Medical Treatment Act. "But that was years ago
when he was a medical doctor."

Cory looked at him, and he shrugged sheepishly. She knew he was
a professor of epidemiology, but she didn't know he was also a doctor.

"A veterinarian too," Dana said, as if reading her mind.

Nick nodded at Cory's sign. They had to go to a barbecue in an
hour, but he wanted to protest. "Got any extra signs?"

Cory found a small stack beneath the table, and the neighbors went
through them. Nick chose his: *When the power of love overcomes
the love of power, the world will know peace.* He picked one out for
Frankie: *Born-Again American.* Dana's sign said: *All is well. Please go
shopping.*

"You need to advertise these things," Dana said, jabbing her sign
at a cameraman. "I wish I had known. This is great what you're doing.
I'm blown away."

Finally, Cory had done something that impressed her. She waved
her sign at the camera as well. Hers read: *Down With Corporate-
Ruled Health.*

Suddenly, loud music began to play. Someone had set up a table
and a sound system in the far corner of the parking lot. Huge speakers
began to blast "Blowin' in the Wind." The crowd sang along. People
began to move. Nick shuffled his feet back and forth, moving an arm,
waving his sign. Dana grabbed Cory's hand and twirled her around in
a circle. Strangers joined in, and soon everyone was dancing. When the
song ended, people clapped, and a DJ welcomed them all and thanked
them for caring enough to come.

"Where Have All The Flowers Gone" began playing, and Cory felt
like she was in a time warp; it was the sixties again, and they were
protesting the war. Only the battle wasn't unfolding far away in some
foreign country; it was happening here, with a government waging a
war against the health and welfare of its own citizens.

The anxiety Cory felt had become exhilaration. She was dancing
in a crowd of people as if she were one of them. She was on their side,
they were in it together; everyone fighting for a common good. She
joined the polka, weaving in and out of the crowd, taking some stranger's arm and then another. She sang and danced and sweat broke out,

dampening her hair. She could picture her mother here, in a colorful tie-dyed shirt, blowing smoke rings and singing "The Times They Are A-Changin'."

The music played for an hour, and then the DJ took a small break. Dana, Nick, and Frankie couldn't stick around. "See you next week," Dana said.

Cory went to the table to get a bottle of water and found Layla, her arm wrapped around the waist of her boyfriend. Cory extended her hand. "You must be Tyler."

"Have we met?" asked the towering, blond-haired hacker.

"Online. I'm Cory Montclair."

Tyler's face brightened with recognition. Layla was amazed. "Oh, wow. You're that Cory? I, like, had no idea when I was talking to you."

They all shook hands, and Cory formally met Tyler Madison, the renowned anonymous software engineer. "I should warn you," he said in a low voice. "I've been watching your web traffic."

"Should I be worried?"

"I would delete your LabRat account."

Cory remembered the account Evonia had created when she placed the ad that found Mathew.

"It has your personal information on an unsecured site," Tyler said. "Your address, cell phone number, and place of employment. You don't seem to be using it."

Was he reading her email? Watching her web traffic? She felt open and exposed.

"I traced your hacker," he said. He leaned down closer and mouthed, "Wellspring Pharmaceutical."

That surprised her. She thought it would be the FDA. Not that it mattered. From her vantage point, they seemed one and the same.

"They left spyware on your hard drives that allowed us to trace them. They tried to cover their tracks, but they've got a security hole."

"What's that?"

Tyler shrugged nonchalantly. "When we traced them back, we gained access to their site."

"You hacked into them?"

"I prefer to call it taking advantage of a security hole. They're protecting something behind a secure firewall, but we don't know what. We figure that's where they keep their most valuable files."

"We?"

"I have support. I don't do this on my own."

"Will you give me the files if you get them?"

He leaned down farther and whispered, "I don't know if we will, but if we do, you can have them on one condition." He paused and looked into her eyes. "You can't tell anyone where they came from. Not in court, not even if a judge demands it."

"He could go to prison," Layla said.

"You would risk prison?" Cory asked.

Tyler shrugged. He was chewing a fingernail. All of them were bitten off. "Sometimes you just can't stand by and do nothing. At the end of the day, you have to live with yourself. When you can't stand what you see happening, you either kill yourself or do something."

There was a third option, Cory thought, feeling small. You could just ignore it. She had perfected the art of detachment.

Mathew, Nancy, and Janie emerged from the crowd, and Nancy was sweating. She grabbed Cory's arm and whispered excitedly in her ear, "We danced."

The music was starting up again; the DJ was back. The Rolling Stones's "Requiem For The Devil" began to play, and Nancy raised her hands and shook her body to the rhythm of the beat. She bumped her hip into Mathew, and soon he was dancing with her. Cory couldn't watch.

She turned around and saw Marie and Daniel heading her way. She turned back and was trapped by the dancers. She had no escape. She stood watching Nancy dance when a hand landed on her shoulder. She had no choice. She turned around.

"Thanks for coming yesterday," Marie said. She lowered her sign. It said: *Why Does Approved Medicine Kill?* Daniel's sign was the same.

"I was happy to," Cory said, and she then winced. "I mean, no, I wasn't happy. I'm so sorry."

"It's not your fault," Marie said. "As it turns out, there was no decision to make. We had no other options. We took the only possible course."

Cory must have looked confused, for Daniel explained. "The Tijuana clinic closed."

"We couldn't have gone even if we wanted to," Marie added.

"Why not?" Cory asked. "Is Dr. Arrango on vacation?"

"Not vacation," Marie said. "He's in jail. The whole place is shut down. That's why no one answered the phone. I called after you left the hospital. A nurse was packing up the place. It was raided three weeks ago. The doctor was kidnapped and taken across the border. He's in a jail cell in San Ysidro accused of wire fraud. Someone said on the phone that Oxylace cured cancer. His bail's been set at five million dollars."

Cory felt faint, uncapped her water bottle, and took a big gulp. The clinic was the ace up her sleeve, her insurance that if anything happened to Sophie they knew where to go to get affordable and effective treatment. Now the good doctor was in jail. If the *Clinica De Buena Salud* was shut down, Cory was back to square one. She was stuck with American medicine that was no good.

"That's why we're here," Marie said. "Janie is right. Doing something helps. We could sit home and cry or do everything we can to get that good drug here. Get it for every child like Danny who has to suffer and—"

From behind came a loud noise that sounded like gunfire. The music ended abruptly. There was screaming from the golf course and heads turned to the southeast. More shots rang out. People began to scatter. Mathew materialized from nowhere and grabbed Cory's arm. "Go home," he said breathlessly. "Take the street. Don't cut through campus."

Behind them, yelling rose to a crescendo. People were running away from campus, pouring into the street. Cory was swept along with them, while Mathew pushed his way against the tide and was swallowed by the crowd.

Chapter Thirty-seven

Safe at home, Cory watched the riot unfold online with Sophie on her lap and Pluto by her feet. It was too soon for the network or cable news to pick up the story, but someone was streaming the action live on YouTube. Video showed a group of men in Move To Amend T-shirts storming the cops who had responded in kind. Armed with shields and batons, they fought back, attacking protesters with clubs and pepper spray. Ambulances came, and from her living room, Cory heard the sirens. Overhead, a helicopter circled the sky. Video showed people being handcuffed and forced into a paddy wagon. She didn't see her friends, just a pushing, shoving, rowdy crowd before the video went black.

Cory turned the TV to the local station and listened to the weather. There was no breaking-news banner. After a commercial, a reporter came on, live from Duane at the Bluebonnet Festival. Cory sat forward.

The reporter was interviewing a clown. They were on the north side of campus, standing in the parking lot of a bank, as far away from the commotion as they could be. The clown gave the background of the event and commented on the remarkable turnout. On TV, Cory heard sirens and waited for the reporter to ask the clown about the protest. The question went unasked. Other attendees were interviewed. A painter talked about the bluebonnets, a four-year-old praised the jumping castle, and a potter showed off shoddy vases. No one from Move To Amend or END was interviewed. There was no shot of protesters in bright T-shirts waving signs or being handcuffed.

The clip ended, and the camera cut away to sports. There were final scores of a number of college basketball games to report. For all intents and purposes, it was just another quiet Sunday.

Cory hugged Sophie close. The reporter told half the story and omitted the most important part. It was beyond outrageous. How many people would watch the clip and think nothing had happened, that all was well. In Duane, kids liked the jumping castle and artists were inspired by bluebonnets.

Sophie wanted down, and Cory let her go. The hypocrisy wasn't lost on her. She was no better than the reporter. There was a big story, she knew it, and she was keeping quiet about it. If no word got out, it was as if it never happened. Her own silence made her complicit in the scam to protect expensive drugs. American health care depended not on making someone well, but on someone making a profit. Dr. Arrango was in jail, and his Mexican clinic was closed—all because he used a cheap drug that threatened a drug company's bank account. So the inexpensive drug was discredited and banned. Only drugs that cost a fortune were allowed—regardless of how well they worked or the degree of harm they caused. And people paid because they didn't know any better; they didn't know they had a choice. They blindly followed the unsubstantiated proclamations of a corrupt medical authority.

Cory's stomach burned with anger. Danny didn't have to die. Brad didn't have to. Countless other kids could be alive—and would be— if drug companies didn't use their profit to buy elected officials who passed bad laws to protect that profit. It was worse than wrong. She had to do something. She had to fight for Sophie and Dr. Arrango, for Danny and Brad, and for the millions like them who were denied good medicine for bad reasons.

Sophie wanted back up, and Cory lifted her to her lap and hugged her tight. She decided in that instant to write the paper. Let the FDA come. The truth was on her side. The case files from the clinic proved that what she wrote in the Canadian journal was true. She had a lawyer, a group of people on her side willing to fight, and she wasn't on her own. A scientific paper would show that Dr. Arrango was no charlatan and that he had used a drug more effective and less toxic than any-thing the FDA approved. A paper may help get him out of jail.

The front door opened, and Mathew and Nancy came in. Cory jumped up and ran to the foyer. "What happened?"

Mathew took Sophie and gave her a hug. Pluto was sniffing Nancy's feet but not barking. He must have approved. Cory didn't want to admit it, but she liked Nancy, who was willing to fight for Sophie's future.

"Someone provoked the cops," Mathew said as he put Sophie down. "They crossed the orange tape, and all hell broke loose."

"Where's Janie?"

He didn't know. They got separated. He tried calling her, but she hadn't answered. He was worried about Tyler. "The cops will use any excuse to lock him up. They find him a danger to society."

"When he's actually a danger to the establishment," Nancy said. She was looking around the foyer, eyeing the ancestors in the oil paintings.

"Come in," Cory said. "I was about to make dinner. We have three tuna steaks."

Mathew was starving, and they decided that the dinner Cory had planned for Janie on Friday Mathew would cook tonight. He put on an apron and shooed them out of the kitchen. Cory, Nancy, Sophie, and Pluto went out to the patio. After a day in the low eighties, the temperature was falling and falling fast. Mathew came out and lit the barbecue. With a whoosh, flames leapt into the sky.

"Fire," Sophie said. "Big fire."

Nancy thought she was adorable. "Can I hold her?"

Sophie reached out her arms, and Cory said, "I guess that's a yes."

Nancy had one ankle on her knee, and Sophie settled into her lap, playing with her anklet. "No dere." Sophie pointed to Nancy's wrist. Cory guessed Sophie had never seen an anklet before.

Nancy obliged and unclasped the chain and repositioned it on her wrist. "Better now?"

"Now right," Sophie said.

Headlights blazed in the drive. Cory left Sophie with Nancy and sprinted around to the front. Janie, Tyler, and Layla were back. Mathew, looking domestic in his red apron, came onto the porch. "Did you get arrested?"

"No," Janie said. "We went to the police station to help, but we weren't needed." She flung her arm around Tyler and hugged him hard. "Tyler got pictures of the instigators."

"The men who crossed the police line were FBI agents," Tyler said. "Face recognition software proved it. When the police saw it, they had no choice but to let everyone go."

"Well, come on in," Cory said. "Mathew's making dinner. We're all starving."

He took her aside and said in a whisper, "We only have three tuna steaks."

"Cut them in half," she said. "We've got a French loaf. We can have a big salad."

Half an hour later, dinner was ready, and Cory set the big table for seven. In her whole life, there'd never been that many people over to the house for dinner. She lit the candles, dimmed the chandelier, and closed the French doors to keep out the night chill. She put Sophie in her high chair and gave her a knife and fork. Sophie was entranced by the candles. "Fire," she said. "Little fire."

Sitting at the head of the table, Janie declared the day a grand success. She thought at some point the protest would make the headline news and give END much-needed publicity.

Tyler didn't agree. "They'll bury the story. It won't do to have the FBI posing as protestors charging the police."

"Someone went to a lot of trouble to stop us," Janie said. "They're getting scared." She smiled a big smile. "We're a threat."

"We have to be careful," Tyler said.

"Screw that," Janie said. "We're not going to buckle."

"We should sue the FBI," Nancy said. "Right, dear?" She put her hand on Mathew's arm.

He moved his hand and sliced broccoli. "You can't sue the government."

"What about Wellspring Pharmaceutical?" Cory asked, as she handed Sophie a piece of garlic bread. That's all she wanted. She wasn't interested in the tuna, corn on the cob, baby potatoes, broccoli, or salad.

"You won't win," Mathew said. "There's got to be willful harm."

"It wouldn't be about winning," Cory said. "It would be about publicity."

Janie liked it. Her big, luminous brown eyes grew brighter. "I'll sue the bastards. What is it? Wrongful death? Cory's right. We don't have to win, we just have to file. Imagine the headlines. 'Dead cancer victim's mother sues Wellspring over toxic cocktail.' We'll play up the publicity. Stir people up. Wake them up. Show them what's happening. It's the only thing that will stop it."

Mathew didn't like it. "A judge would throw the case out. You have no grounds for a suit. You could get sued yourself for filing a frivolous suit."

"I don't care," Janie said.

"I'm going to write a research paper on Oxylace," Cory said.

"So, you can write one after all," Janie said, not unkindly.

"It won't be a double-blind, placebo-controlled study, but I'll use statistics and compare Oxylace with Wellspring's cocktail. We know what's going to win and what's going to lose. The FDA's big lie is that Oxylace doesn't work. But no serious study has ever been done. If I can get the paper in a good journal, like the *Canadian Journal of Cancer*, the FDA will have to take another look."

"How will you do it?" Mathew asked.

"I'll go through Dr. Arrango's case files and compare his results with the results from official medicine. Say, he has ten patients with breast cancer and nine survive. That's a ninety percent success versus Wellspring's stated success of almost forty percent. I'll do it for every type of cancer Arrango treated. I'm limited by sample size, but I think I can write a statistical report that will pass scientific muster."

Janie jumped up, walked around the table, took Cory's head in her hands, and kissed her fully on the lips. "I love you. I absolutely love you."

Cory blushed. It was the first time anyone had ever said the words to her. She knew she was smiling stupidly, but she couldn't help it. It had been an exhilarating day. For the first time in her life, she was a part of the "in" crowd, a part of something big. Still, she felt she should clarify her motivation. "The clinic closed. Dr. Arrango is in jail for wire fraud. Maybe a paper will help get him out and the clinic reopened."

Janie raised her wine glass. "Here's to freedom for all and a good fight." Everyone tapped glasses. Sophie clinked her juice cup.

The party broke up after dinner. Tyler and Layla left, Janie went to the study to make a few calls, and Mathew and Nancy went outside. Sophie drove a toy car across the kitchen floor while Cory cleaned up, one eye on the window. She couldn't help herself. Mathew and Nancy were on the swing smooching. Nancy had a hand on the back of Mathew's neck and was massaging it deeply. Their lips were locked, she was pressing down on him, as if her tongue was deep down his throat. When they separated, he seemed short of breath. She massaged his shoulders; one side, then the other, and then both. He rolled his neck. And then her hand disappeared under his shirt, and she was on his mouth again. Cory stood there gawking, wondering how far they would go, when he looked at her. He stared straight into her eyes.

Mortified, she stepped back from the window. She swept Sophie up off the floor, rushed upstairs to the bathroom and locked the door. She ran a bath, wondering if tonight was the night they'd stop taking it slow, if Nancy would stay. But when Sophie was in bed and Cory went downstairs, they were gone.

Janie was going to bed. She was leaving first thing in the morning, flying to Washington. She kissed Cory good-bye, hugged her tight. "I knew you'd come around. You couldn't be indifferent forever."

Cory went to bed too. Sophie was sleeping easily. Mathew came home a few minutes later, alone. Soon his shower was running, and the pipes were knocking. Cory closed her eyes. The weekend hadn't gone as planned. She hadn't managed to stay out of the fray, but she was doing the right thing, and it felt good. She knew what had changed, what tipped the scale. Now the clinic was closed, and the risk of doing nothing had become far greater than the risk of doing something.

Chapter Thirty-eight

It is not our policy to jeopardize the financial interests of the pharmaceutical companies.

—*Dr. Charles. C. Edwards, FDA Commissioner*

April 1st

On Monday morning before sunrise, Art was at JFK International Airport on his way to Puerto Rico. He was in the jet, on the runway, awaiting takeoff. He was going for a week to check out future conference centers, and Hank was coming for the ride. Missy was coming for the duration. She sat up front while Art spoke privately with Hank in the rear. Rain was slamming down, delaying their departure.

A storm was raging, and Art was looking at her now: Mont-fucking-clair. She was openly defiant when she was supposed to be running scared. Know thy enemy was Art's motto, and he'd hired a PI to track her every move. He was going through a stack of photographs taken of her over the weekend. She'd been busy. She'd gone to a funeral, had a weekend guest, and attended a protest. It was on behalf of Enough Nasty Drugs. She wore a pink "Enough Nasty Drugs" T-shirt and had a sign: *Down with Corporate-Ruled Health.* She thrust it at the camera and was staring straight into it as if she were mocking him—goading him.

Art finished going through the photos and then slammed them down on Hank's drink tray. "I thought we took care of her. What the hell is this? Doesn't she learn?"

"She will," Hank said. "Imminently."

"I want her stopped. Yesterday. I thought I made myself clear. Why did we donate to Duane University if the president can't do anything?"

"He is doing something. It takes time."

"What happened with the IRS?"

"There was nothing they could do. Her tax returns check out."

"Can't they audit her anyway?"

"She's so stupid she does the returns herself. If the IRS did an audit, they'd end up owing her money. They won't do it."

They stopped talking as the stewardess came with coffee and a plate of steaming breakfast bread. Art had never seen her before, but he liked the looks of her. She was young, sexy, willing, and untroubled by Missy. With a pronounced sway of her hips, she sashayed forward, heading to the galley.

Art watched her go. "What's Harris doing?"

"Our congressman is working through his committee. It won't happen overnight, but he assures me he'll succeed."

"How's his campaign?"

"He's down in the polls. Running scared. He said to thank you for your check. Any additional support would help."

"Who's his opponent?"

"Kelly Mann. Only she's a woman. She's for gun control, women's rights, environmental protection, sweetening Medicare, and revisiting Medicare drug pricing."

"Jesus Christ," Art said appalled. "She's not one of us."

"No."

"Make a donation," Art said. "Go big. We'll play both ends. Hedge our bets."

"She might not take it. She's publicly against special interests."

Art ran his hand through his hair. It was thinning rapidly, showing his crown, and making him look older than he was. "The word is, publicly. Make it big enough and she can't refuse. Otherwise, it goes to Harris. She won't want that. She's running in Texas for God's sake."

The plane began to move, and Art stared out the rain-streaked window at low-lying clouds. The pilot came on over the loudspeaker and announced they had clearance for liftoff. Art and Hank buckled their seat belts as the plane picked up speed.

"Whose funeral?" Art nodded at the photos.

"A kid died from leukemia. His oncologist consults for us. Susie Sullivan. She said Montclair was interfering. The mother wanted to take the kid to Mexico."

"I thought that clinic closed."

"It did. The kid reacted to Valurex."

"Did Sullivan try Alluron?"

"She wanted to but the parents dragged their feet, and the kid went into shock."

"Jesus Christ. These activists are killers."

"The day after the funeral the parents were at the protest."

"What the hell is wrong with people?"

Hank rifled through the photos and pulled out one with a woman in a butch haircut. "That's Jane E. Bartlett. Her son died nine months ago. She's the force behind END and the Access Act that will crush the FDA's power."

"How big a force?"

"She's a third-grade teacher. A loud-mouthed heckler. Harris had her thrown out of a town hall. She was Montclair's weekend guest."

"The Access to Medical Treatment bill is an old one. It never goes anywhere, right?"

"Exactly. People support the FDA. They think it keeps them safe."

"Damn straight. How many in the crowd? A thousand?"

"Three."

"In that hick town?" Art put a hand on his heart. "Jesus."

"Bartlett's pretty crafty," Hank said. "It looks like there's huge support for Enough Nasty Drugs, but the majority of the crowd was Move To Amend."

Another freaking grassroots organization hell bent on reversing sound justice. Mitt had it right when he called corporations people. Of course they were. Lucky for Art, corporations got to vote—with money. He said, "I didn't see anything about the protest in the news."

"It wasn't deemed newsworthy. The networks don't give thugs free advertising."

"It was a peaceful protest?"

"Hell, no. There were fifty arrests. No targets. The FBI got involved and screwed up everything."

"What happened?"

"Details unclear. There were undercover agents. A setup that went badly. Best to forget. End of story."

"What now?"

"The congressman's aide Drake Mansfield is about to make his move."

Hank outlined the plan, and Art liked it. Mansfield had a free hand to do whatever had to be done.

The plane was in the air, so seat belts could come off. Hank stood up and headed to the fore. He wasn't staying. When the plane landed he would return to New York, keep up the pressure.

Missy came aft, tottering on impossibly high heels. She plopped herself down beside Art, sunk her hand into his crotch, and whispered in his ear, "Come on, things can't be that bad."

Nope. Already things were looking up.

Chapter Thirty-nine

April 2nd

Tuesday afternoon, after a two-week absence ostensibly blamed on the flu, Megan was back in the lab. With less than a month left in the semester, she had a lot of work to do, and Cory was waiting for her. "Ready to feed the animals?"

Megan laid her knapsack on the bench and grabbed a lab coat. "You said I didn't have to work with them."

"*I'll* handle them. You prepare the food. Load the syringes."

"Can't Evonia help you?"

Cory stared across the lab, met Evonia's cold stare, and looked back at Megan. It was a new day. "They're your rats; you ordered them. This is your study, your responsibility. Two of the rats in the high-dose group died yesterday. The other two are suffering, and we need to put them down."

Megan shrugged. "I'm going to start an ELISA."

"You'll let them suffer?"

"I don't have to work with them. It's not me making them suffer."

And that was it. Cory had heard enough. Megan stood on the side that represented everything Cory pledged to fight—people with money and influence doing whatever they wanted no matter who got hurt. She drew a line in the sand. "No more lab work until we take care of your animals."

Megan laid down her lab coat. "I'm going to talk to Dr. White. He said if I had any problems, I should go to him."

"That's your prerogative."

"I'm going," Megan said, unmoving.

"Fine." Did she expect Cory to cave?

Cory stared her down, and Megan slowly picked up her knapsack and flounced out.

Evonia crossed the lab and shook Cory's hand heartily. "I do not know what has happened to you, but I like it. It is time you stood up to that creature."

Fifteen minutes later, when Dr. White's secretary called and Cory was summoned upstairs, she wondered about the wisdom of her stance. Nonetheless, it was the right thing to do. She just had to convince Dr. White of that. There had to be standards. There was good science and bad. Megan had written her project, and it was up to her to follow through. A good teacher didn't do someone else's work for them. Surely Dr. White would see that. Megan was throwing her weight around because she thought she had influence. It was no different from Wellspring throwing *their* weight around because of their influence. What made one okay and the other not? There was no difference. They were both wrong.

She went upstairs to his office. Megan sat in a chair facing Dr. White across the desk. Not wanting to move the matching chair from the corner, which would give the false appearance of equality, Cory went to the window ledge and leaned against it, folding her arms together.

Dr. White said, "Ms. Carson is finding your lab a hostile environment."

"It's not the lab that's hostile." Cory stared at Megan. "We have gone out of our way to accommodate you."

Addressing Dr. White, Megan blurted out in a burst of emotion, "I got bit by a rat. I can't work with them. I have nightmares they'll bite my ankles the instant I step into the room."

"They're caged," Cory said.

"Not the rat that escaped."

The room went quiet. The ticking of the clock was very loud. Megan had one trump card, and she had played it. Dr. White frowned, removed his glasses, and tapped the stem in time with the clock. Cory expected him to ask about the outlandish claim, but he said, "From this moment on, Miss Carson will report to me."

"She hasn't finished her research."

"She will write up what she has."

"Her results are questionable. They have to be repeated."

"That is enough," Dr. White nodded at the door. "Miss Carson, you may go. Report to me on Thursday. Please close the door behind you."

Megan left quickly. Dr. White waved at the vacated chair, and Cory sat down. "The rat that escaped?" he asked, incredulously.

"Momentarily."

"Define momentarily."

"Technically it didn't escape because it was confined to the animal room. We locked it in and found it dead, trapped between two drawers. I tested the blood, confirmed it was a control rat, and attached the results to the accident report."

"Why didn't you tell me?"

"If we couldn't find it, you'd be the first to know."

Dr. White laid down his glasses and rubbed his eyes. "Edwin Reed came by this morning."

Cory sat up stiffly. She knew the university president was his personal friend. Dr. White handed her a paper. It was a reprint of the letter she had written to the Canadian journal. It had the uncorrected, adulterated signature, as well as the FDA's response.

"This is not what you showed me previously," Dr. White said. "As the FDA claimed, you misrepresented yourself as a physician."

"I didn't write the title. I tried to correct it." But a month had passed, and she'd stopped trying.

Dr. White pointed at the letter. "You're advocating a banned drug. No wonder the FDA was concerned."

"They banned a good drug. They prop up Wellspring Pharmaceutical's bad drugs."

"You have proof of this?"

Cory shook her head. *Not yet.*

Dr. White rummaged around his crowded desk, found a packet of stapled pages, and passed them to her. It was the staff evaluation package that she filled out every December. She had to state on paper her progress—the papers she published, grants she wrote, students she mentored, and research she ran. She had filled out the package four months ago. "What's this?"

"The president requested an update of your research."

"Why?"

Dr. White rubbed the bridge of his nose. "He can request whatever he likes. How is your research progressing?"

"It's on schedule. I'll be finished by August."

"In your last report, you stated you had a paper accepted to the *American Journal of Pharmacology and Toxicology*. What is the status of that paper?"

He asked as if he already knew the answer.

"It was accepted in November with revisions. Then, last month, for no reason, it was rejected."

"You didn't think I should know?"

"I told Joe, and he said he would talk to the editors. I'm reformatting the references for the *Journal of Food Chemistry*. Frankly, I'm not optimistic. The FDA endorses the journal, and Wellspring Pharmaceutical funds it. I think they got the paper pulled."

Dr. White frowned. "You make it seem like there's a vendetta against you. The FDA is an honorable agency. Wellspring is a reputable company. The president holds them in highest regard."

"Then why did they hack into my computer?"

The frown deepened. "Dr. Montclair, your computer is clean. You have not been hacked. IT looked into it, checked your email, and everything is fine."

Cory stared across the room and out the window at the sky. Tyler said whoever hacked into her computer was good and hard to trace. They were apparently better than the university specialists. Somehow she had to make Dr. White see the truth. "Someone did hack in. I know that for certain. My private information was made public. Look at the safety accident report. How did the FDA know about it? They called the office and requested a fax of the incident."

Dr. White sighed heavily. "We work at a public university. Our files are not confidential. Your work is made possible by soft money. Should you lose your grant, we would be unable to keep you."

"That is what Wellspring wants. This is what they do. They try to squash any dissent, exterminate any threat, and they get the FDA to help them."

Dr. White shook his head sadly. "I will not even comment on that. Congress is making steep budget cuts. Research is on the chopping block. Your grant can be rescinded at any time. Your position here depends on the National Cancer Institute's ability to pay you. This is about economics, nothing more."

"You're saying the U.S. government doesn't have fifty thousand dollars, which is all the money left in my grant," Cory said, pointing out the absurdity of Dr. White's argument.

"One more thing." It was as if he wasn't listening. He was polishing his glasses with the base of his tie. "The president was in Houston last month. He was invited to Anderson Hospital for the opening of a new cancer wing. The Wellspring Cancer Treatment Center."

Cory blinked.

"The drug company has offered the university a substantial endowment."

She narrowed her eyes. "We're taking research money from drug companies now? And you see no connection between that and what's happening here?"

"They're giving a sizeable endowment. Ten million dollars over five years. We're very lucky."

"That's unbelievable." She meant it was unbelievable that he couldn't put it together. It was laid out perfectly, all the pieces before him, and he refused to see it.

"I thought you should know." He looked at the door. "That's all. You may go."

So much for lining Dr. White up on the side of right. He didn't want to see what was going on. He refused to connect the dots. This unexpected review, the president's new association with Wellspring, their donation to the university, her losing the paper—it *was* a vendetta. He called it exactly and then dismissed it. He was doing what Wellspring and the FDA wanted him to do—he was getting rid of her. While it was nearly impossible to fire a state employee on hard money, but she was on soft money. She could be let go for any reason. Hence the re-evaluation. Her job was on the line. If Wellspring held sway over the FDA, what about the NCI? Did Wellspring pull their strings too? If her funding was cut, there was no money to pay her and no position. Poof. Never mind her future, there went her job. The dissenter would be silenced, and Wellspring could carry on without impedance.

***

Cory headed to her lab and found Evonia waiting. Cory put on her game face. She wasn't ready to tell any of this. It was her burden and hers alone. She'd taken a stand and had to deal with the consequences. "Megan's gone," she said.

"Good."

"Not good. She's now working for Dr. White."

"Her results are worthless," Evonia said. "You are lucky to be rid of her. Do you know who her father is?"

"Mr. Carson, I presume."

"He is the chairman and chief executive officer of United Foods. You will find him online. He owns two of the four biggest peanut butter companies in the nation. Do you think it is only by accident that she is here ruining everything she touches? Do you think she really wants to find aflatoxin in peanut butter?"

Cory just shook her head, appalled by the corporate connection to what was supposed to be impartial science.

"You must watch what she writes," Evonia said.

"I'll repeat what she's done."

"You were upstairs for some time. What else did White say?"

"The president called him. I need to update my progress."

"Lucky you are progressing so well."

"Indeed." Cory went to her office.

She began filling out the staff evaluation form. Not much had changed in four months. She left the status of the rejected paper as it was, for the possibility remained that Joe could get the editors to reconsider. On paper, at least, she looked good. She had a grant and nine papers in reputable, refereed journals. She taught two classes, which post-docs didn't normally do. They also didn't mentor undergrads, which made it easy to delete Megan from the record. Good riddance, Cory thought, as she did so.

Chapter Forty

April 3rd

First thing Wednesday morning, Cory was heading to Dana's to discuss the field test. The RNA sequence was back, and Dana's program would allow them to look at the antibody in three dimensions. At this point, getting a grant was her last hope at proving herself, and the deadline to submit was looming.

She arrived early and told the secretary she'd wait, but Dana called her in immediately. They sat down on the couch and reviewed the protest. Dana was sorry she'd had to leave, and Nick was even sorrier. As an MD and early supporter of the Access to Medical Treatment Act, he thought doctors should be left alone to practice medicine, and patients should have access to whatever treatment they wanted. But no, the FDA and AMA made the decisions. There was too much emphasis on prescription drugs that had too many side effects. Insurance companies meddled too much too. Nick had little patience for the bureaucracy and didn't practice long. He moved on to vet school but didn't like that either. When he started his PhD and went into research, he found what he liked. "That's the point, right?" Dana said. "Chances are, you enjoy what you're good at."

Cory agreed. She remembered saying something similar to Megan not long ago—not that she'd listened.

There was a small rap at the door, and Betty came in with coffee and passed out two mugs. Dana sipped hers, smiled with approval, and moved on. "I read your part of the proposal. It's excellent."

They were the first words of encouragement that Cory had heard in a long time.

"Did you bring the sequence data?" Dana asked.

Cory handed over a thumb drive with the RNA of the antibody. Dana got her laptop, and a few moments later they were gazing at a three-dimensional schematic diagram of an amino acid chain folded into a functional antibody. Dana pointed to the screen. "See these valine-leucine pairs?" She circled the antibody base with her finger. She had an enzyme that would cut the bond between the two amino acids.

"How long should I incubate?"

Cory was to try sixty seconds. Too short a time and the antibody wouldn't be cleaved. Leave it too long and it would be degraded. Dana passed Cory a small capped tube.

"Are we still on schedule with the proposal?" Cory asked. It had to be submitted by five o'clock on Friday.

Dana sighed heavily. "If our other collaborators get their shit together. We're still waiting on Vermont and Nairobi."

"What if we miss the deadline?" Cory hated the sound of desperation that tinged her tone.

"We'll have to wait until August to submit."

Cory tried not to look disappointed.

"What's wrong?"

Cory came clean. She finally admitted what was going on, how Wellspring hacked into her computer, were likely behind the hatchet job in the paper, and probably responsible for the journal rejecting the paper. Not only that, now they had gifted the university with ten million dollars. "They don't seem to stop. I'm worried what they'll do next. I could lose my job."

"What did you do to provoke them?" Dana asked.

"I wrote about a drug called Oxylace in a letter to the editor of a Canadian journal. You can only get the drug in Mexico. It's a good drug, much better than Wellspring's drugs, but it's banned here. It cures cancer. It saved Sophie's life. Only now the clinic is closed, the physician is in jail, and I'm under attack. The FDA came to visit. They threatened to take me to court and throw me in prison for practicing medicine without a license."

Dana shook her head as if with astonishment. "I know that big oil and the agricultural conglomerates run smear campaigns. They have a long history of silencing scientists who threaten their livelihood. Anyone with the guts to speak out is crushed. That's why people smoked for twenty more years than they should have and why we have climate change. I thought the health care industry was more compassionate, but apparently not. They're using the same playbook." Dana sat back and looked Cory in the eye. "Despite all this, you still had the courage to go to the protest. You're amazing."

Cory took the praise in stride. "I'm going to write a paper and statistically compare Oxylace with chemotherapy. Try to force the FDA to take another look."

"Wow."

"Wow, as in stupid?"

"Wow, as in stupendous. If you need anything, I'm on your side. I'm right here. You're not in this alone. You know what I've found?"

Cory shook her head.

"When you do the right thing, it works out," said the eternal optimist. "It may be hard, but help comes from unexpected quarters. You might think evil wins because it can break every rule in the book, but as if to compensate, good gets help."

"What if it doesn't?"

"That's what friends are for." Dana clinked Cory's coffee mug.

They finished their coffee, and Cory returned to her lab feeling energized. She had help, she had friends, and she was on the right side of good. She felt invincible, in a mood where everything would turn out and nothing could go wrong.

But no, it was false confidence. The enzyme didn't work. It completely degraded the antibody in seconds. If they couldn't get the monoclonal antibody stable, the grant proposal was a waste of time. There would be no field test, no grant, and no leverage. She stayed late, repeating the test, and got nowhere.

Chapter Forty-one

She was alone in the lab, packing her briefcase, when a text message came in. Mathew wouldn't be home for dinner. He wasn't keeping his end of the cooking bargain. She hadn't seen him since Sunday and guessed things with Nancy were heating up. Death would do that. It made you loath to be alone. At least that was the effect it had on her.

She grabbed her keys and was leaving when she stopped short. A good-looking tanned man with striking blond hair stood in the door-way. He was in his mid-thirties, stocky, not too tall. His shoulders were broad, and his stance was wide. He wore a baby-blue T-shirt under a navy blazer, good-fitting jeans, and boat shoes. He raised his knuckles as if to knock and then caught himself. "I was about to knock."

"I was about to hear you knock."

He stepped into her office. She had never seen hair that blond. It looked like it was bleached, only it seemed natural. He needed to shave, and even his facial hair was bright blond. His golden skin shone like it was scuffed with sand.

He stuck out his arm and stared into her eyes. His were big and blue and sparkled in a sea of brilliant white. They shook hands. His skin was pleasantly cool. He introduced himself, but she didn't quite catch what he said. "Jake?"

He smiled, showing white teeth as bright as his eyes. "No, it's Drake." He said something else, and she caught the word "paper."

"You're from the *Tribune?*"

He seemed taken aback she was able to guess. "I've come from Austin. You recently complained about an article that was incorrect on all fronts?"

"Have a seat." She waved at a chair. The newspaper was finally getting back to her. She'd been expecting an email or phone call, and they'd sent a reporter—and a fine-looking one at that. She'd have a chance to set the record straight, perhaps redeem herself in the eyes of Dr. White and the university president. She set her briefcase on the floor and sat down behind her desk.

He pulled a small notebook from inside his blazer. "Tell me everything."

"Let's see, I was born twenty-eight years ago."

He laughed at that. "Let's start with your daughter. What's the problem with the Department of Child Services?"

"There's no problem. That's just the point. Call DCS. They'll confirm it. They're not taking her. Sophie's a bright, happy, healthy little girl. Who wrote that article? Everything in it was wrong."

He made a note. "We'll correct the record. It was obviously written by someone with an ax to grind. Possibly the girl's father?"

"He's in Spain."

"What's his name?" Drake sat with his pen poised.

"Antonio Rios. Tony."

"Does he have visitation?"

"Good God, no. Not even remotely in the picture." She added, "I'm free."

He lifted an eyebrow. It was perfectly arched and may have been waxed. "And you went to Mexico. Where you—Sophie—received the drug Oxylace."

"You've heard of it."

He shrugged, letting her know she was dealing with a professional who did his homework.

"It was great. One shot, and that was it. The drug cost a hundred bucks."

"We need a drug like that."

"You're right, we do. Make sure you write that down."

He did so. "Now, your daughter had an allergic reaction to the chemo."

"No, she got MRSA."

"A resistant staphylococcus bacterial infection, correct?"

"Yes."

"So, the hospital gave her an infection, she ended up in ICU, and you got stuck with the bill."

"Because I wasn't pre-approved. And I didn't pre-approve. I don't, to any of it."

"What was the bill?"

"ICU cost seventy-five thousand, which insurance refused to pay. I guess they thought the eighty-five dollars the hospital charged for a baby aspirin was outrageous. As did I."

"And now you're in debt," Drake said, making a note.

He was a good listener, paid close attention, made the right comments, and asked the right questions. "They garnished my wages. They're taking five hundred a month."

"They wouldn't negotiate?"

"Wouldn't hear of it."

"That's infuriating. Did you talk to your insurance company?"

"Oh, I tried." She leaned across her desk. "The thing is, the three of them are thick as thieves. The drug companies, hospitals, and health insurance. The drug company makes the drugs and sells them for a thousand times what they're worth. The hospital marks up the cost and pushes the drugs, and health insurance pays because they own shares in the drug company."

"What about the hospital?"

"It's nonprofit and so no shares. They have to spend all the money they make. So they jack up their CEOs' salaries, build new hospitals, buy new equipment, and make people sick in order to fill their beds, make more money, and get bigger raises."

He laughed. "You sound cynical, but ain't it the truth."

"Every word. And what did the article say? I refused to 'honor legitimate hospital expenses'? I'd like to know the nature of these legitimate expenses."

He looked around her office. "It doesn't look like your lab was shut down."

"More fabrication."

"I shall make a note." He did so with a flourish." He closed his notebook. "I don't know about you, but I'm hungry. Care for dinner? On me."

Cory thought of Sophie. Dinner at the day care was served at six thirty for an additional three dollars. Cory wasn't a fan of the food, but it would only be one night. "We need to go somewhere close," she said. "I have to get Sophie from day care before eight."

"Ever been to Stanley's Bistro?"

He knew the campus. It was the place to go. The last time she'd been there, she'd met The Count.

Stanley's was on University Avenue, a ten-minute walk across campus. Touting the best barbecue in Texas, the restaurant was geared toward professionals rather than students. The ambiance was dark, the music was romantic but muted, and the food was expensive but good. One half was a bar and the other half a restaurant. After a five-minute wait, they got a good table by the window, thanks to the hostess who was flirting shamelessly with Drake.

They ordered margaritas and dinner. She got the barbecue chicken with broccoli and a salad, and Drake ordered steak with fries. They forged on with the interview.

"You work late," he said.

"Not really. I'm working on a new assay, writing a big grant."

"You work in the lab alone?"

"Not at all."

"You have students?"

"I had one. She just quit."

"Sorry."

"I don't know whether it's good or bad. She had no business being in a lab. She's careless. She dropped a rat, and it bit her."

"Wow. That must have caused some trouble."

"Mostly for her." Cory took a healthy gulp of the margarita. It was strong, and the glass was caked with salt. Outside the window, traffic was heavy, and Drake was checking his reflection in the glass.

"Did I read in the Author Citation Index you have ten papers?"

"Nine," she said. "There should be ten, but one was rejected. *After* it was accepted."

"What happened?"

"I suspect a drug company is behind it. Wellspring Pharmaceutical makes the chemo the hospital likes to push. They endorse and sponsor the journal that rejected the paper."

"The whole health industry has too much power."

"They buy our representatives who vote their way. So much for our democracy. You've got to go to a developing country for decent medical care. You can't get it here."

Drake agreed. He was agreeing with everything she said. She thought the interview was going well. Finally, something was working out. "When do you think your correction will be out?" she asked.

"Soon. The editors have to sign off on it, but that's never a problem." He shot her a winning smile.

"Front page, like the last?"

"I'll do my best."

The conversation turned to him. He was originally from L.A. and was born to surf. He was thirty-five, divorced, no kids, and no stranger to marital ugliness. He understood why she preferred to remain unmarried.

Another margarita came, and the booze was going to her head. Thoughts of Sophie were spaced farther and farther apart. It had been a long time since she'd been with a man. She was lonely. She knew it was rash; she didn't know him at all, but that was who she was—she made up her mind in an instant. Maybe his interest and intensity reminded her of Mathew, of how he once was. But Drake was also like The Count. The reporter was too good-looking, and he knew it. He glanced at the ladies going by, and they looked back. The Count had also been full of himself, entitled with royal blood she once thought, mistakenly.

Dinner came, and the chicken was caramelized to perfection. The broccoli was crunchy and the salad was generously topped with cherry tomatoes, onions, avocado, cucumbers, and chunks of blue cheese. They ate and spoke of surfing, of beaches in Malibu and Hawaii, where waves were fifty feet high. It was a dangerous sport, and he knew it and lived accordingly. "For the moment. Seize the day," he said with a long, lingering smile across the table.

He wanted dessert and ordered carrot cake, which they shared. When the bill came, she finished her drink and went to the bathroom. Coming back, she saw Tyler and Layla at a table. There were empty plates before them, and she wondered if they were coming or going. She stopped to say hello.

"I thought that was you," Tyler said. He looked furtively around the bar and then lowered his voice. "We got past the Wellspring firewall. Is there anything particular you're looking for?"

"Doctors' case files."

He nodded. "I'll see what's there. It will take a few days."

"Not a problem."

"Who's the guy?" Layla nodded in Drake's direction.

"A journalist from the newspaper."

"He doesn't look local," Layla said.

"He's from Austin, correcting an article in the *Tribune*." A waiter came, cleared the plates, and promised to be right back. Cory glanced at her table where the hostess was conversing with Drake. "I better go."

"Mathew is coming," Layla said. "Why don't you join us?"

So that's why he wasn't coming home. He was probably meeting Nancy for dinner; a happy foursome getting together. "I've got to get Sophie, but thanks for asking."

Cory and Drake left the bistro and headed back to campus. The sun was setting, and the sky to the south was a beautiful royal blue. "Are we calling it a night?" he asked as he bumped her shoulder.

"We could go to my place for a drink."

"I'll take you out. You have a sitter?"

"No."

"Your place it is."

He followed her, waited in his car at day care while she got Sophie. At home, the house was dark, and Pluto had peed on the floor. Holding Sophie, Cory cleaned it up while Pluto growled and snarled at Drake, who was pacing the foyer with seeming awe. "This your place?" he asked.

"It's been in my family for well over a hundred years."

Sophie didn't like Drake either and turned her head when he tried to talk to her. "She's tired," Cory said. "I'll put her to bed. Come on, Pluto."

Sophie fell asleep immediately, and Pluto lay between the crib and the door as if on sentry duty. Cory turned on the nightlight, left the room, and closed the door.

In the kitchen, Drake had found a bottle of Mathew's red wine, and she told him to open it. He filled two goblets to the brim, and they clinked glasses. She took a sip and smiled at him. He took her glass, put it on the counter, and they kissed. It had been so long.

They brought their wine to the living room, and he wanted a fire. They went out to the garage and brought in logs from the dead branches that Mathew had cut. She put on music, setting her iPod on random selection. She turned the lights on low, and they sat on the rug before the fireplace, sipping wine as the music played and flames danced. Before long, between kisses, she was telling him about her parents' car crash, her grandmother, and the long list of in-name-only matriarchal royalty that spanned the ages. At some point, they began to dance. The room seemed smoky, the music played slowly, and Drake moved clumsily, obviously aroused. It was clear he hadn't taken a year of dance lessons.

Then the front door slammed, the room flooded with light, and Mathew loomed darkly in the doorway. "Jesus Christ, look at the smoke." He waved his hand theatrically. "For God's sake, open the fucking flue."

He crossed the room and threw himself before the fire. The flue creaked as it came down. He jumped to his feet and glared at her before stomping across the room. He stopped at the doorway. "Where's Sophie?"

"Sleeping."

"Pluto?"

"In her room."

Mathew clomped upstairs and slammed his door so hard the walls shook. Drake made a face. "Who's that? The Count?"

"A boarder."

"Not an angry lover?"

"A housemate."

"You sure that's all?" Drake kissed her as he looked deep into her eyes.

The moment was over; the magic was gone. He was probably trying to see his reflection in her eyes. She pulled away from him. "I think we should call it a night."

There was a flare in his eyes, followed by a quick smile. "We don't have to let him ruin it." He moved into her space, put his arms around her waist, and pulled her to him.

She twisted out of his grasp. "I can't do this. I'm sorry."

"I can't drive like this." He tried to kiss her, but she turned her head. He stepped away from her. "Do you have a blanket? I'll sleep on the floor."

There was no way she could drive either. "You can sleep in my room."

"With you?"

"I'll sleep with Sophie."

Upstairs, he made a lot of noise, laughing too loud, running too much water, chortling at having to use Cory's toothbrush. He was in awe by the size of Sophie's toiletries, her tiny comb, and soft hairbrush. It was a relief when he was safely shut in her room and she was alone in Sophie's single bed listening to her breathe and Pluto snore. Mathew's toilet flushed and his door slammed. Dana had it right; she wanted Mathew, but he didn't want her. If she couldn't have him, she didn't want anyone.

Chapter Forty-two

April 4th

A bad night turned into a bad morning. Cory's head was throbbing, Sophie was fussy, and Mathew was furious. He wanted to speak to her privately, and she followed him to the living room, where the iPod still played, and the lights shone on dirty wine glasses and an empty bottle. "You left the fire going. You didn't replace the screen. You could have burned the whole house down." He was yelling so loud she was sure the neighbors could hear.

"Let it go," she said quietly. "Nothing happened."

"Down here, anyway."

He stormed out, marched to the door and left, slamming it behind him.

Upstairs, a toilet flushed, and Drake came down the stairs humming. "Morning, sunshine." He was unshaven, with messed-up hair and bad breath. He tried to kiss her, and she moved away. She had to get rid of him. She went to the kitchen and lifted Sophie out of her seat.

"Is she going back to day care?" Drake asked. "We could have breakfast. The two of us."

Under the kitchen table, Pluto began to growl. For once, a man wanted to stay. He had to go immediately. But it had to be done delicately, so as not to spoil his goodwill—or a good article. "I'm afraid Sophie's sick." A flat-out lie. "Diarrhea. Ever changed a diaper?"

Drake looked at his watch. "Shit! It's this late? I've got to go. I've got a story to write."

"When do you think it will be out?"

He smiled his charming smile. "I'll let you know." He stepped toward her.

She braced herself for another kiss, but Sophie started screaming. She kicked her legs and flailed her arms, and he stopped. Pluto came out from under the table, hair on his back raised, teeth bared.

"I'll be in touch," Drake said, backing away. He left quickly.

***

The day passed slowly. Cory spent long, futile hours trying to optimize the enzyme and slice the antibody without success. She was dried out, hungover, and tired. She tried to concentrate on the assay but couldn't stop thinking about the night. Drake had been a mistake. Cory would buy Mathew a new bottle of wine, apologize for the flue, and try to forget what happened. She knew now that any chance of anything transpiring between them was dead. She'd killed it. If Mathew had had second thoughts about his choice, his mind was at ease. He'd made the right one; he picked the right woman. Once again, it wasn't her.

The workday ended. Worried about a confrontation with Mathew, Cory was in no hurry to get home. She procrastinated so long she reached the day care when dinner was about to be served. Sophie grew irate when she was swept away from the miniature table laden with hot dogs and potato chips. She screamed all the way home to the empty house. She would have none of the creamed cauliflower and spinach Cory tried to get down her throat.

Sophie pursed her lips, shook her head, kicked her feet, and howled. Green puree sprayed everywhere. That was when Mathew materialized, caught Cory's wrist, and pried the spoon from her fingers.

"What are you doing?" He threw the spoon at the sink.

Hiccupping back tears, Sophie held up her hands, and he scooped her up.

"Trying to feed her."

"You set a bad example."

"I get it. You're pissed off. I should have opened the flue. I'm sorry."

"Is that what you think this is about?"

"Okay, I drank your wine. I'll replace it."

"You've got to be kidding."

"All right. Drake. What do you care? You've got Nancy."

"Do you ever stop and ask yourself what's wrong with this picture?"

"No," she said sharply and way too loud. She grabbed Sophie away from him.

"That's how bad it is," he said. "You don't even know you have a problem. Even your dreams are trying to tell you. You've got a car without a driver that's about to crash. Do you know who Drake is?"

"Nothing happened. He's gone."

"Yes, that's your style. What's his last name?"

"He's a reporter," she said, not liking his insinuation.

"You have no idea what his last name is. It's Mansfield. Drake Mansfield. He works for Congressman Harris."

"No, he works for the *Tribune*."

Mathew pulled a folded piece of paper from his jeans pocket and laid it on the counter. It was a black and white, grainy print of the congressman surrounded by well-wishers, toasting champagne. Next to him, unmistakably, stood Drake.

"He could be a volunteer," she said, grasping at straws and feeling more hungover than she had seconds previously.

"Well, he's not. Tyler's father was a U.S. Senator representing Texas, and Tyler recognized Drake. He's met him. He's Congressman Harris's aide."

"That doesn't mean he can't be a journalist."

"Did he write a correction?"

"Give him a chance."

"What does the congressman have to do with Wellspring?"

"I don't know."

"There's a lot you don't know. Wellspring donated six million to Congressman Harris's Super PAC."

Cory exhaled slowly and turned away, staring down at the floor.

"Yes, and Harris sent Drake. I hope he was worth it. Did you find him in the bar? He looked good, so you brought him home? What? You thought that was all he wanted?"

"Leave it," Cory said harshly.

Mathew's cell phone rang, cutting the conversation short. He wrenched it from his pocket, turned around and answered. He spoke cryptically in one-word answers, and then closed his phone. "I have to go."

He left, leaving Sophie in fresh tears, pounding her fists on the side window as he stalked to his car without looking back. Cory gave her a cookie, and they went to the living room, sat down on the couch, and turned on *Sesame Street*. If she could take back the night, she would. She should have listened to Sophie and Pluto. They knew. They hated Drake the moment they saw him. They weren't taken in by his good looks or feigned interest. He had lied from the beginning, and Cory offered what he hadn't asked, blathering on about the rat, The Count, Sophie's illness, and her theories about Wellspring and the FDA. And he was working with them! Elected officials were in on it too. The small corrupt circle was widening.

After Sophie was bathed and in bed, Cory went online and searched for Drake Mansfield. She couldn't find him. She pulled up Congressman Harris's website, and Drake wasn't on the staff list. It was as if he didn't exist. But she learned that the congressman was the chair of the Oversight and Appropriations Committee, which investigated the government and monitored its spending. It had jurisdiction over government departments like the Department of Health and Human Services and the National Cancer Institute, which funded her research. Not surprisingly, it had oversight of the FDA as well. The congressman, the FDA, and Wellspring were tightly connected. If Mathew was right, at Wellspring's behest, the congressman had sent his golden boy to seduce her. And she had jumped at the bait. How easy she was. Quaffing margaritas, she had spilled her life story. There was never going to be a retraction. He was no reporter. He wanted information, and he had gotten it. Now the question was, what would he do with it?

Chapter Forty-three

Dr. Bruce Halstead MD got a four-year sentence for recommending an herbal tea to cancer patients, in violation of a California law that forbids treating cancer with anything but surgery, radiation, or chemotherapy.

—Ellen Brown, author of Forbidden Medicine

April 8th

On Easter Monday, Art was back in New York. After a week of being in the warm Puerto Rico sun checking out conference centers and playing golf, he found the Big Apple exceptionally drab and cold. Winter lingered too long in the North. With the early time change, it got dark too late. He arrived at the office just after five. He sent Missy home in the limo, and she didn't want to go. Familiarity did breed contempt. He'd had too much of her. It was time to get his mind back on work. He'd called a board meeting; he had good news.

Once his team was assembled, Art shrugged off his blazer and loosened his tie. Standing tall at the head of the table, he said, "I'm happy to report that next week the FDA will provisionally approve Alluron as an adjunct to our standard chemotherapy drugs."

He was interrupted by loud applause, and he clapped as well. "According to Claude, the early clinical indications are too good to sit on. Sick people deserve better. We're to ramp up production. We need supply."

There was more applause, and Art felt compelled to give a small bow. He went on with more good news. "Alluron is set to make the Medicare list of approved medicine, which means other insurers will fall in line. The full treatment of the cocktail will retail for just under fifty thousand. No questions asked."

Now the applause was thunderous, and Hank pounded the table with his fist. Everyone could do the math. Sales would rocket twenty percent. When the din died out, Art said, "If you want to talk to the broker, now's the time. He's standing by." Although the market was closed to the general public, preferred trading didn't close until six. "We'll wrap this up, place our orders, and by the time the market opens tomorrow, we'll be upwards of five percent. Could be ten percent by the end of the day, twenty percent by the end of next month. Next quarter, analysts predict we'll be trading over a hundred. Gentlemen, Wellspring is on the rise."

The board clamored to their feet in a standing ovation, and Art tried half-heartedly to wave them down. When they finally sat, he let the CFO take over. Rick Vanguard showed a colorful PowerPoint presentation. Everyone stared at graphs of healthy sales with a parallel rise in stock price. They could expect an expanded market of Alluron from name recognition alone. Best of all, there were only two minor side effects of the drug: dry mouth and increased urination. Who couldn't love that?

When Rick was through, Art took questions. Connor Loy, always the worrier in the bunch, wanted to know if it was safe to trade. "What about insider trading?" It was something he'd been slammed for in the past, though it was legal in Congress.

"We can bet on our own stock," Art said. "Anyone could see this coming."

"What about the post-doc and the Canadian letter?" Loy asked. "Won't that hurt sales?"

Art looked to Hank. The Fixer shook his head. "That's history."

"What happened?" Loy asked.

Hank waved the question away. "Best not to say."

Art concluded the meeting with a description of the conference center he'd lined up in Puerto Rico. The beaches were magnificent, and the nightlife was stupendous. "We'll plan a shindig for doctors and other health care folks next month. They'll love it." He raised his hand in an imaginary toast. "Gentlemen, I salute you. Your country salutes you. Nay, the world. On behalf of everyone, I applaud your efforts to improve the health of mankind everywhere." Okay, he was a little over the top, but he couldn't help himself. He clapped Hank on the back and opened the bar. Before six, stock orders had been placed, and fortunes were set to rise.

Missy was buzzing him. Deep in his pants pocket, his phone didn't stop pulsing. Art didn't respond. Money was a drug. No, an aphrodisiac. He never looked so good to her than when he was counting billions. And she never looked so wanting.

Chapter Forty-four

In Texas, where the Baptists outnumbered the Catholics, Easter Monday was just another day. It had been a long one, coming on the tails of a long, lonely weekend, and Cory was tired. By the time Sophie was in bed and she was in her office staring at Dr. Arrango's case files, she was exhausted.

Mathew was gone all weekend. He didn't come home, not even at night, which meant he was staying with Nancy. Sophie missed him and kept asking about him. "Where Maffew is?" His rent was paid up for the month, but they were going week to week. He could give notice at any time, which meant he'd expect a refund. The money was already gone, day care was paid, and she would have a hard time reimbursing him if he left.

It had been a frustrating day. She was behind in her lectures and had to pick up the pace and pack in a lot of material to make up time. The assay was still not working, and despite following a number of Dana's suggestions, the enzyme made the assay worse, not better.

Over the weekend, she'd started the Oxylace paper. She would do it in her free time, working around Sophie's schedule. She was going through the case files, taking notes. The files were handwritten, and Dr. Arrango's handwriting was atrocious. The numbers were clear, but the words were nearly illegible and often mixed with Spanish. She had to use the online translator, and it was slow going. At this rate, it would take her a month to write the paper, maybe more.

She was building a spreadsheet to organize his cases. He treated all ages of patients, all kinds of cancers, in all types of stages. His survival rate was good. Patients who lived a month after taking Oxylace survived. Those who died earlier all had extensive pre-treatment—either radiation, surgery, or chemo. Cory's aim was to compare the success rate of Oxylace with traditional chemotherapy. That meant combing the National Cancer Institute's database for analogous cancer types. It was tedious work, made all the more difficult because the NCI was not forthcoming with the data.

Cory was searching the site when the doorbell rang. She went to the foyer and peered through the side window. Daniel and Marie Weiss. She opened the door.

"Can we come in?" Daniel said as he shouldered his way past her.

"We hate to disturb you," Marie said kindly, taking up the rear. "It's important."

Cory wondered if it was about Danny. He had been dead now two weeks. She pointed at the living room. "Please sit down."

She offered drinks, but they couldn't stay. "Is Mathew here?" Daniel asked.

"He's out."

"Can you call him?" Marie asked.

"What's this about?" Cory asked.

"Let's wait until he comes."

"I'm not sure when he's coming."

"We can wait." For someone in a hurry, Daniel settled back onto the couch as if he had all the time in the world.

"I'm not sure he'll be back tonight," Cory said.

"Everything all right?" Marie looked concerned. "You make such a cute couple."

"We're not a couple," Cory said.

The Weisses exchanged glances. Marie said, "He'll want to hear this. It may bring him home." She lifted her eyebrows.

Cory relented, but she wasn't going to call. She sent him a text: Weiss here with imp news.

Waiting for Mathew's response, they made small talk about the weather. Despite how difficult it must have been for them, they asked about Sophie. Finally, Marie blurted out, "Just call him. A text has what, one beep? Let it ring."

They didn't look like they were planning to leave before they talked to him, so Cory called. Listening to his phone ring and ring, she forgave herself for getting involved with the Weisses in the first place. With pressure like this, there was no way she could have escaped.

The phone went to voice mail, and Cory hung up.

"You didn't leave a message?" Marie asked. "Call back, and tell him we're waiting for him."

"No," Cory said firmly. "He's not answering. I don't know why." Perhaps she did. "He'll see I called and know I'm trying to reach him."

The Weisses looked at each other again. "Okay," Daniel said. "We want to ask him what he thinks about filing a class action lawsuit against Wellspring."

"I can answer that," Cory said. "There's no intentional harm. Without that, there's no wrongdoing and no case."

Marie and Daniel sunk back into the couch as if deflated. "Their drugs are so bad. How can they not be harmful?"

"It's intentional harm that counts," Cory said.

"Do you have any idea what a class action lawsuit can do to a company?" Daniel asked.

"Not a clue," Cory said.

"Merritt Drugs is going through one at the moment," he said. "They used to be the number one maker of chemotherapy in the country—until it came to light their anti-cancer drugs are themselves carcinogens. The lawsuit is making them bankrupt. I thought we could do that to Wellspring."

"Janie wants to sue," Cory said. "Mathew said she doesn't have a case."

"Maybe we have one," Daniel said.

"Talk to Mathew," Cory advised.

"That's why we're here," Daniel said. "When did you say he'll be back?"

"I don't know," Cory had to say again. The conversation was going in circles.

They had his number, and they decided to go home and try to reach him themselves, as if the futility of waiting had finally dawned.

Cory showed them to the door and returned to the study. If Janie couldn't sue successfully, there was no way that thousands could do it. She turned on more lights and sat back down at her desk. She'd been logged off the NCI site and logged back in. While she was waiting for admission, the doorbell rang again. Were the Weisses back?

It was Nancy—sporting new short bangs and looking ten years younger, but that may have been the sex. Cory opened the door and said hello, peering over Nancy's shoulder. "Is Mathew with you?" She figured he had seen she had phoned and had come home.

Nancy looked puzzled. "Why would you think he was with me?"

"I just assumed. Come in."

"Just for a second." Nancy stepped into the foyer. She held out a stack of file folders. "I have case files you may be able to use for your paper. Some of my clients took standard medicine. I deleted their names, but here are their files. Every one of them died. I was thinking you could compare the traditional and alternative treatments case by case."

Cory took the folders. It was an excellent idea. "How many case files do you have?"

"Seven."

It wasn't nearly enough. "Can you get more?"

"I'm asking all my patients to release their files. This is all I've got so far. If I get more, I'll get them to you."

Cory shoved the files under her arm. Nancy could have given the files to Mathew. She didn't have to come in person. Cory wondered why she had come.

Nancy was staring up the stairs. "Where's Mathew?"

Cory shrugged. "I don't know."

Nancy looked into her eyes. "He doesn't tell you where he goes?"

"Not always."

"Why did you think he'd be with me?"

"Just a guess."

"Did you think we were back together?"

Cory tried to look impassive as the floor fell.

"He didn't tell you we broke up, did he?" Nancy said.

"No." Cory should have left it at that, but she couldn't. "When?"

"Sunday."

"Yesterday?"

"A week ago Sunday."

Before Drake. On the day of the protest, the night Nancy ate dinner and made out with Mathew on the swing. "What happened?" Cory couldn't stop herself from asking.

Nancy looked pained. "He's not ready to commit. It's moving too fast. Do you think I'm pushy? Aggressive?"

Cory was taken aback. Nancy was seeking her advice about love? "Too fast? Hardly." Not by Cory's standards anyway. It was an eye-opener to see others as clueless about these things as she was. "It could be Margaret."

"His ex-fiancé? No, he said it was over, and I believe him. I think it's you."

"It's not."

"He adores Sophie. He loves the house."

Cory looked up at the ceiling, searching for the right words. She was not going to get into Drake. "We have a hard time."

Nancy's eyes brightened. "What do you mean?"

"We're two different people."

"How so?"

"He's emotional, I'm scientific. Can I ask you something?" Cory didn't wait for an answer. "Do you cry?"

"All the time. I bawled like an infant when we broke up. I think it almost changed his mind. But then he left."

"He didn't come here."

"When did you see him last?"

"It's been days. Almost a week."

Nancy smiled. "Since we broke up. He wants to be alone. That's what he said." She laughed at nothing. "He doesn't want to be with you. He just needs space." Nancy hugged Cory awkwardly. "Thank you. Thanks for seeing me. You're a good friend. I should go. I'll work on those files."

"If I see him, I'll tell him you stopped by."

"No!" Nancy said. "Don't. Please. I don't want him to know." She left quickly, hurrying down the path before zooming off in a blood-red convertible.

Cory returned to the study. She sat back down, unable to concentrate, rerunning the conversation in her head. Mathew was free, his affair had ended, and he'd never told her. Maybe he planned to do so the night he ran into Drake. Cory hung her head. And to think Drake had been her own reaction to Mathew's affair and her own loneliness. She stared out the window. A quarter moon was setting. She'd ruined everything.

She tried to focus on the spreadsheet. She was timed out of the NCI site again and logged back in. She tried to concentrate on cancer statistics but couldn't stop thinking about Mathew. Where was he? Why not tell her his relationship was over? Why not come home?

Midnight came, and she logged off, her eyes burning with fatigue. She hadn't accomplished much. Compiling the government's data was harder than she thought. It seemed scattered and confused, as if the government was deliberately trying to obscure how badly the war against cancer was progressing.

Chapter Forty-five

April 9th

At lunchtime on Tuesday, Cory returned to her office after her morning lectures to find Dr. White waiting in the lab with a look on his face that screamed bad news. He followed her into her office, and she offered a chair, but he preferred to stand. "I don't know how to say this, so I'll say it straight out. The NCI has cut your funding."

Cory tried to look stoic. It wasn't a huge surprise; he'd warned her it was coming, but still, her mind reeled.

"I realize there's not much money remaining—"

"Less than fifty thousand. It's—"

"We can't make up the shortfall. The department's discretionary funds have been spent for the fiscal year. This is a loss of money for us too." White laid a stack of papers on her desk. "These separation forms require your signature. You may check with the legal department, but you will find they are in order."

"I'm fired?"

"No. You have lost your funding. Please sign where indicated. You will need to leave your keys, your key card, and university ID. Your lab access is terminated after today. Your health insurance is paid up until the end of the month."

"What about my classes?"

"I'll cover for you."

"And the students?"

"I will step in until Dr. Carlisle returns. I have been unable to reach him. He will have to cut short his sabbatical and return as soon as possible. Believe me, I do not like this any more than you do."

Cory picked up the papers and looked Dr. White in the eye. "You know Wellspring Pharmaceutical is behind this. They just didn't give ten million to the university. They gave six million to Congressman

Harris's Super PAC. He's the chairman of the committee that has oversight over both the FDA and NCI."

White looked pained. "Do not take it personally. These are dire economic times."

Was there nothing she could say that would wake him up? To get him to see the scope of the injustice; to acknowledge the immense power of the drug companies and the FDA that supported them. Did he really expect her to believe the NCI had run out of money?

Dr. White removed his glasses and massaged the bridge of his nose. "I will give you a good recommendation. I wish I could do more."

And that was the end of it. She left without fanfare, with no going-away party, no hearty good-byes. She didn't even get a chance to see if she could get the enzyme to stabilize the antibody. She filled out the forms and took her copy. She got boxes from the chemistry store and packed her personal items. She didn't have much. She took her textbooks, reprints, coffee mug, and pictures of Sophie. Five binders stuffed with thirty months of research were proprietary and belonged to the university.

She said good-bye to the students, who were as dumbfounded as she. All except Evonia, who wasn't surprised at all. In her country, it happened all the time. People were fired for no reason. They caused trouble, they were out. The boss made up his mind and then found an excuse. But in this case, Cory knew the reason. One letter was all it took. It scared the shit out of the drug company, and they came out swinging and had stomped her into the ground. But science was on her side. Her ammunition was a paper that she now had time to write.

***

At two o'clock on a school day, Cory was home. At least the house was still standing—a foundation to hold on to when everything else was gone. Pluto was ecstatic, turning circles in euphoria. She tripped over him as she carried boxes to the study. She stacked them in a corner, then opened her laptop and called Joe. No answer. The timing was off. It was night there, and he would be home, soon packing boxes and preparing to bring his sabbatical to an early close. He was collateral damage, another sacrifice in Wellspring's growing pyre.

She wondered how hard it was for Congressman Harris to ax the aflatoxin project. Did he ask a friend at NCI for a favor in return for more NCI funding? For that, did Wellspring pay him six million? The irony was that she'd subsidized the corruption. The money she paid to the hospital and for health insurance paid Wellspring for its worthless drugs. They used her money to pay the congressman who cut her funding. Her taxes supported the FDA. She helped pay the salaries of corrupt FDA agents who destroyed her credibility.

Her computer pinged. Skype was calling, and Joe's picture popped up in the corner of her screen. She clicked an icon and magnified his congenial Santa Claus image. "We've got a power outage. The generator's almost out of gas, and the computer battery's dying. I'll make this short. What happened to your funding?"

"The NCI can't make the last installment of the grant."

Joe didn't look shocked. "It happens," he said as if it were standard practice. "What will you do?"

"I don't know."

"Rupert wants me back ASAP, but it will take a while to wind things down. I'm funded through UNEP and can't drop everything. Has he no discretionary funding?"

"Apparently not," Cory said.

"I'll talk to him," Joe said as his image got fuzzy and turned to snow as his computer died.

He was gone, and she closed Skype, wondering about her next step. For the first time in fourteen years, almost half her life, she was unemployed. She had started dog walking at fourteen, was a cashier at Piggly Wiggly at sixteen, an assistant manager of Dairy Queen at twenty, and a paid graduate student with a full scholarship at twenty-two. Now she needed gainful employment.

There was a community college in town, two other community colleges within commuting distance, and Texas A&M wasn't that far away. If worse came to worst, there were three high schools in town, and though the Piggly Wiggly had closed, a Safeway had opened in its place. One way or another she would find something.

She opened the file with her extended biography, recently revamped for the grant proposal. She knew she had to call Dana and tell her the bad news, but she couldn't face her. She'd do it later. She edited the bio down to size for a resume and went online to Duane Community College to look for job opportunities. They had no chemistry department, but they did have a biology department. She found the email address of the administrator and sent him her resume and an email offering him her services.

She started on her taxes, printed out the forms, and used her previous return as a guide. Not much had changed. She had no raise, no outside income, no increase in real estate tax, just ten thousand dollars paid for so-called medical care. She was adding numbers when Mathew drove up.

He had been unseen now for almost a week. He hadn't slept at the house since Drake slept here. He parked at the curb, got out of his car, and jogged to the house. He entered the study in a rush. "Why are you home? Is Sophie all right?"

"She's fine." Cory said. Was it only Sophie he cared about? "My grant was cut. I lost my job." She grabbed her separation papers. "Can I sue?"

He went through the papers but found nothing untoward. In her position, she could be let go for any reason. She couldn't sue the university just because they couldn't pay her. He laid the papers on her desk. "They didn't say you did anything wrong. Can you get another job at the university?"

"Yeah, right," Cory said. "Maybe when the president dies or retires."

"What are you going to do?"

"Look for a job. What happens if I have no wages to garnish?"

"You still have to pay. If you don't, the hospital can take your house."

Cory grabbed the separation papers and flung them across the room, missing the garbage pail by a mile.

Mathew leaned on the windowsill. "I've got some money."

She shook her head. She knew he had to start paying a hundred-thousand-dollar student loan as soon as he graduated. Still, she was touched that he'd offered.

He looked down at her tax forms and picked up a page. "You don't take the child tax credit?"

"What's that?"

"Seven hundred and fifty dollars the government pays you to help with child expenses."

Cory didn't know; she'd never taken the credit.

Mathew looked shocked. "They've had it for years. Amend last year's return. That's fifteen hundred bucks for you." He handed her the page.

Did he care, or was he on his way out? Was he finding her money so he could guiltlessly abscond? How could she not know where he stood? She was forced to come right out and ask. "I'm surprised to see you."

"I came to do laundry. I didn't think you'd be home."

He was avoiding her. "I called you last night."

"I know. I spoke to Daniel. He wants to start a class action suit. I told him it won't go anywhere. Not without proof of deliberate harm."

"Where have you been?" Cory's curiosity got the better of her.

He lifted a shoulder nonchalantly. "Around."

"How's Nancy?"

He folded his arms together, slunk lower on the window ledge. "I'm sure she's fine."

"You're sure? You don't know?"

He examined his fingernails. "She can look after herself."

He wouldn't come right out and say they'd broken up. The all-knowing psychological expert was showing some cracks. "Look after herself? You're not staying with her?"

"We broke up, okay?" he said with a wave of an arm and a burst of emotion that turned his cheeks crimson. "Is that what you want to hear?"

"Only if you want to tell me."

"I had to be alone."

"Are you gone then? Is this how Dr. Freud says good-bye?"

"I'm house-sitting for Tyler, if you must know."

"Where is he?"

"In Boston, helping his sister move."

"I thought she died of leukemia."

"He has an older sister in medical school. Why are you so interested in him?"

Mathew gave nothing away for free. He was guarded, well-defended, but protecting what, Cory couldn't say. "Tyler got past the Wellspring firewall. He was going to give me some files."

"He'll be back on Friday."

A school bus choked down the road and stopped in front of Dana's house. The doors opened, and Frankie came down the steps. Mathew waved to him, and he waved back. Cory waved too, but he disappeared from view.

"Why didn't you tell me you broke up with Nancy?"

"Would it make a difference?"

Were they talking about Drake? Of course it would have made a difference. "I don't know why you didn't. You break up with her and disappear. All this time I assumed you were with her."

"All this time? You know when we split up?"

Busted again. Cory stubbed her toe on the edge of the rug.

"You talked to her?" Mathew said.

"I promised not to say."

"So you knew. Why didn't you tell me?"

"Oh, it was up to me? You accuse me of being closed when you should look at yourself. You are what you accuse me of being."

Mathew pulled the chair over to the desk and folded himself into it. "I was going to tell you. And then there was Drake."

So, this was about him. "What does he have to do with anything? He's gone. Nothing happened. We had dinner. We had some wine. You came home. He was too drunk to drive. I gave him my room."

Mathew straightened, grew taller. "I didn't like him."

"I know. Sophie and Pluto didn't either."

At the sound of his name, Pluto wagged his tail and leaned against Mathew's knees. He patted his head.

"What now?" Cory asked. "Are you here? Are you gone?"

He stared at the floor. "I know you need the money."

"Don't stay out of pity. You just found fifteen hundred dollars for me."

"I guess someone has to look after the garden."

"You'll stay for the garden?"

"It looks neglected."

"More like dead."

"It needs water."

"It's been hot."

"It's just wilt. A little TLC will fix it." He stood up. "I'll take care of it."

And that was how he announced he was moving back in. He went out to the garden, watered and weeded, and staked up the tomato plants. Then he did his laundry, made dinner, and played with Sophie as if nothing was wrong.

She was happy to see him. "Maffew here," she kept repeating. "Ook Pooto, Maffew here."

For Cory, it was an uneasy truce. She didn't know where she stood, and she didn't know if he knew how she felt, if he'd run. At least for the time being he was here, ostensibly caring for the garden.

Chapter Forty-six

April 10th

The university endowment made the Wednesday morning headline: "D.U. Recipient of Generous Grant." Cory read the article at daybreak over coffee. Sophie was still sleeping and Mathew was out running, and she had the kitchen to herself. She read all about the new collaboration between the university and the drug-giant Wellspring Pharmaceutical. The company was going to pay for basic biological research that would facilitate the development of new drugs. A front-page photo showed the university president locked arm in arm with the Wellspring CEO, Art Farber. Cory studied the man closely. He was short, the top of his head barely reaching the president's armpit. Greedy eyes bulged out from a round, fat face. He was balding and trying to hide it with a comb-over. According to the article, his chemotherapy drugs saved millions of lives. The company had recently helped finance a cancer clinic at Anderson Hospital and generously donated to multiple charities. Cory tossed the paper aside. The article didn't mention how many people he'd killed with his drugs, or how much it cost to buy a congressman or an FDA agent, or fire a scientist.

The monitor squawked. Sophie was awake. For once, she got to wake up on her own, and they didn't have to rush out the door in the dark. Cory let Sophie pick out her own clothes. She'd become a fussy dresser and wanted to wear dresses but only if they had "potets."

Cory made eggs for breakfast, and they left the house at seven thirty with the dog. Sophie refused to take Cory's hand. She preferred to "walk self" with her hands in her "potets." They were in no hurry. Cory would submit her taxes, continue work on the Oxylace paper, and await the response from Duane Community College. She'd get a good refund, thanks to the tax credit she hadn't known about and the money she'd paid in medical bills. The university had paid her to the end of the month, and she had enough to keep going until July, especially if Mathew stayed put.

But she had to find a job. Networking was the key. She was supposed to tell everyone she knew that she was looking for work, but pride would not allow it. She would tell no one, keep her normal routine, and take Sophie to day care as if all was well.

Pluto found a tree whose smell intrigued him, and they stopped walking. Sophie turned her pockets inside out and began pulling out lint. A dark sedan rolled slowly down the street and veered over to the curb. A window lowered, and a man peered across the front seat.

Cory tugged on Pluto's leash and approached the car. She assumed the driver was lost, in need of directions. "Are you Cordelia Montclair?"

Without thinking, she said, "Yes."

He passed a brown envelope through the window. "You have been served."

The window went up, and the car shot away. Pluto found his place to pee. Overhead, a crow shrieked and a cold breeze blew. Goose bumps broke out on Cory's arms.

"What dat?" Sophie asked.

"I don't know." There was no sender and no return address on the envelope. Cory unwound the string, opened the flap, and pulled out a sheet of heavy paper. One page only. She scanned it quickly. In an instant, she felt weak and her heart hurt like it had been punched. She began hyperventilating, almost unable to breathe. The Count was suing for custody. He called her an unfit mother. There was a hearing before Judge Walker the following Friday.

She crammed the letter back into the envelope, picked up Sophie, tugged on Pluto's leash, and rushed home, her heart pounding. A moment earlier she'd been cold, and now she was sweating. Perspiration broke out under her arms. She could smell her own fear.

Inside, she put Sophie down and removed Pluto's leash. Sophie peered up at her. "What wrong?"

"Nothing." Cory knelt down and pulled her daughter close. "We're not going to school. We're going to stay home today and play."

Mathew was coming down the stars, toweling wet hair with his fingers. He stopped abruptly. "What is it?"

Cory put a finger to her lips, led Sophie to the living room, and turned on *Sesame Street*. Back in the foyer, she thrust the envelope into his hands.

He read the letter. Blood drained from his face. He exhaled deeply and looked at her. "I can't imagine a judge would give a Spaniard custody of an American child."

Cory stared at the floor. "The Count isn't a count. He's not from Spain. He's not actually a professor of architecture." She told him the truth. "His name is Antonio Rios. He's a roofer from El Paso. Originally from Juarez, Mexico."

Mathew shook his head.

"Look, when we met, he looked Spanish, he spoke with an accent, and he knew a lot about buildings and roofs. I wanted Sophie to have an exotic father, and I didn't think she'd ever meet him, so I gave him a good story."

"You don't think she deserves to know the truth?"

"*I* didn't know the truth. Not for a long time," Cory said, looking at the floor, kicking the rug.

"What else do you know about him?" Mathew asked.

"I had a P.I. track him down when Sophie got sick. A bone marrow transplant is another treatment for leukemia, and I wasn't a match. I thought maybe he would be, but he refused to be tested. He denied he even had a kid. He wanted nothing to do with her. I can't believe he'd fight for a kid he's never seen and wouldn't acknowledge."

"Is his name on the birth certificate?"

"No."

"And you're certain he's the father?"

"Come on."

"Did you have a DNA test done?"

"He refused."

Now that he'd examined her personal life, Mathew returned to legal matters. "Okay, the grounds are you're an unfit mother. That's a catchall phrase that can mean almost anything: abuse, abandonment, neglect. Your financial situation is another possibility. It's unfortunate you don't have a job. I guess there's no other money? No inheritance? No life insurance for Sophie in case something happens to you?"

Cory shook her head. She'd spent her savings on Sophie's medical care. Everything was supposed to change once she got a faculty position, which now was never going to happen.

"It could be the unorthodox treatment you sought for Sophie. Maybe your roofer read the newspaper article."

"He's not the type to read a newspaper."

"Maybe someone showed it to him. What were you accused of? Child endangerment? You didn't sleep with a rapist or molester did you?"

"Jesus Christ, no."

"Maybe you did and didn't know?"

"You're not helping."

"It could be blackmail," Mathew said. "Maybe he needs money. Does he know you own the house?"

"Probably." He'd spent the night, so no doubt she regaled him about her matriarchal history, as she normally did. She sighed deeply, finally able to catch her breath. Maybe it was just about money. The only problem was, she didn't have any. "What should I do?"

"This is just a hearing. The judge will decide whether there are enough grounds to warrant pursing the matter further." Mathew knew the judge. "Walker's a good one. He's not up for re-election. He's fair. He'll do what's in Sophie's best interest. From what you've said about the roofer, she's better off with you."

"Why is the hearing so soon? There's not much time."

"They did it on purpose. You're going to have to hurry. We need to get organized."

He was going to help, he was on her side, and he would represent her. They planned their attack. She would get her financial records together. Her house papers and tax returns showed a history of care and responsibility. She would need references from the day care. She volunteered at the place; people knew her character. She had to call her pediatrician and get her medical records and a reference. Then get her school records and slant her resume to impress the court. What judge would pick a roofer over a scientist?

And they would build a case against Rios. He had never seen his daughter. When she was sick, he refused to help. How would he care for a child who didn't know him? Cory was the only parent Sophie knew. Legally, Rios had no rights.

Put like that, Cory felt more at ease. What judge would agree to full custody—or even shared custody—under these circumstances? Since Rios lived in El Paso, that wasn't a possibility. He would never get her. In the light of day, the summons seemed as ridiculous as it was laughable.

But at night, in the dark, as she listened to the floors creak, fear and doubt crept in. She thought she knew what it felt like to be on death row awaiting execution and wondering about a last-minute pardon. The fate depended on someone else. Would a judge give Sophie away? It was too absurd to contemplate, too improbable to imagine. Yet the possibility remained. A judge could order it, and Cory would be unable to stop it.

That night the nightmare returned. Cory was in the backseat of a car accelerating in a steep decline, staring out the front windshield as trees blew past and the wind howled, not nearly loud enough to muffle the shrill screaming.

Chapter Forty-seven

April 19th

Time passed slowly, the semester ended, and D-Day came. Cory had kept Sophie out of day care for the duration to spend quality time with her. She was building a bond so strong it could never break. Mathew was on the backburner. He was busy with school and had to skip his last day of classes to attend the two o'clock hearing.

They left the house at one and were late leaving because Mathew didn't like her clothes. She had dressed in a black business suit that he thought sent the wrong message. He wanted her to appear matronly and chose a faded, flowery frock. They walked Sophie to day care as if nothing was amiss and then hurried home. He drove to the courthouse.

Cory had a file folder four inches thick. She had copies of her high school transcripts, a letter of notification of a full university scholarship, her undergraduate honors award, her graduate school scholarship, and her PhD course record showing a cumulative 4.0 grade point average. She had the deed to her house and three years of tax records—one recently amended. Both Ethyl and Sandy from the day care wrote testimonials lauding her fitness as a mother. Dr. Haygood Robinson wrote a glowing letter. He was sorry he could not endorse Oxylace as an alternative treatment to leukemia, but she wasn't expecting him to. She knew he could not; not without risking the wrath of the AMA and probable loss of his license.

They reached the courtroom only to find it had been changed, as had the judge. They were now expected in another building. The new judge was up for re-election and didn't rate high praise from Mathew. "Judge Tobin is the best-funded and most-corrupt judge in the county."

They arrived at his courtroom late, and the bailiff tried to exclude them. "Door locked at two sharp."

"You changed the venue," Mathew argued. "You never told us. This will invalidate any ruling."

The bailiff had a word with a judge, who agreed to admit them, though the proceeding would continue. They would not revisit covered ground.

The judge sat behind a raised bench, looking menacing and mean. He was in his late sixties and looked dour and gray; a hard man used to dealing with hard people.

There were two tables before him. One was empty, and three men sat at the other. Antonio Rios was flanked by two lawyers who exchanged business cards with Mathew. Rios would not look at him, nor would he look at Cory. He stared straight ahead at the judge.

Cory took her seat, unable to stop looking at the father of her child. He was gorgeous; well-built, tall, and muscular. He had a swarthy complexion, big brown eyes, and thick, dark, curly hair that crowned his face. He had a rakish stubble and tons of body hair. She only remembered that now. His flannel shirt was unbuttoned too low and revealed a too-hairy chest, which she recalled him stroking when he was about to be laid.

Mathew introduced himself to the judge. He had to disclose that he was not a state-certified lawyer but was representing Cory at her request. The judge nodded and told him to sit down.

The accuser's lawyers resumed outlining their case. They looked like twins and sported identical buzz cuts and similar three-piece suits. Both were pinstriped; one was navy, the other gray. Their case appeared to be built on the lie that Cory was under investigation by the Department of Child Services for child endangerment. One of the twins stood up, flung an arm in Cory's direction, and said, "Even the DCS is concerned she is an unfit mother."

Mathew shot up. "Objection. There is nothing to support that claim."

The judge waved him down. He could speak when it was his turn.

The twin approached the judge and passed him a paper. He gave Mathew a copy. It was the slanderous article in the *Duane Tribune*.

From his chair, Mathew said, "The information in this article is demonstrably false."

The judge raised a finger for silence and read the article. He moved it to the side and waved to the twin to continue.

"Ms. Montclair has refused visitation for my client. Mr. Rios has a right to see his child. He is requesting child support."

Mathew raised his hand. "Mr. Rios never requested visitation. He turned his back on the child when she was ill. He has contributed nothing toward her medical bills."

The other twin objected. "We are talking about the present, not the past."

"We don't know for sure he's the father," Mathew said, opening a can of worms.

But it appeared, somehow, some way, Rios had gotten Sophie's DNA tested. A twin gave the judge and Mathew a paper with proof beyond a ninety-nine-percent certainty that Antonio Rios was the father. Cory stared at the report with shock. How did Rios get Sophie's DNA?

One of the twins walked around his table and pointed to her. "This begs the question, your honor. Did she think there was another father? She has a long history of one-night stands."

Now, Cory was on her feet, objecting. The judge banged his gavel and warned her to sit down. Mathew alone would present the case.

"Objection," Mathew said from his seat. "Where is the proof of this allegation?"

"Withdrawn," said one of the twins, but the words were out, the damage was done.

Mathew didn't let it rest. "You don't have a one-night stand alone," he said. "Dr. Montclair is no more guilty than Mr. Rios, your honor."

A twin objected. "She is presenting herself as a role model, and she is no role model. She doesn't attend church, and Antonio is a devout Catholic. We have a letter from his priest."

The judge motioned for the letter, read it, and seemed satisfied. Cory and Mathew got a copy too. The bullshit was lathered on thick. Rios loved his mother and his priest. He attended church, ate fish on Friday, and went to confession once a month.

A twin continued. His client had a full-time job as a roofing supervisor and steady employment. As opposed to Ms. Montclair, who was unemployed when she wasn't agitating the public and trying to overthrow democracy with her anti-government activities. To back up the ludicrous statement, a twin showed the judge and Mathew a photocopy of Cory at the END protest holding the placard with the sign *Down with Corporate-Ruled Health.* The judge glowered at the photograph.

Moreover, Mr. Rios had an apartment and could offer a stable home life. His mother and sister lived nearby and could be relied upon for help. He had a right to get to know his daughter, which Ms. Montclair had denied.

Cory was on her feet. "That's a lie. When she was dying, he refused to help her."

The judge banged his gavel again. "Sit down."

Cory sat, and Mathew repeated what she'd said. "When Sophie was sick, he refused to help."

"Objection," cried a twin. "The mother refused standard medical treatment."

"When it was killing the child," Mathew said. "She paid ten thousand in medical bills and is currently repaying a seventy-five-thousand-dollar hospital bill. Before child support is settled, Mr. Rios should pay his share of these bills. For him that amounts to forty-eight thousand."

Rios whispered something behind his hand. A twin stood up. "Mr. Rios has waved his request for child support."

"So noted," said the judge.

Mathew stood up. "Your honor, we have letters from the university day care center and my client's pediatrician attesting to my client's character." Mathew picked up the file. "I would like to submit this testimony to the court."

"Overruled. I'm sure there's not a negative report amongst them."

Cory was on her feet. "How can you take a letter from a priest and not a pediatrician?"

The judge raised his gavel.

Cory sat down. "Sorry."

"The mother is a flight risk," said one of the twins. "She has no job and no reason to stay. The last two years have shown nothing but determination to keep the child from her father. We request the court approve co-parenting. The child can spend six months with the father and six with the mother, at least until she is of school age when other arrangements can be made. Until that time—"

Cory jumped up and faced Rios. "Six months? Forget it. No way. You don't even want her. You would have let her—"

Rios finally faced her and pulled a half-hearted shrug. The judge slammed his hammer. "Sit down! One more outburst like that and you're out."

Cory sat.

The twin resumed outlining his reasons for the immediate transfer of custody. "Ms. Montclair has shown obvious contempt for my client. In the likely event of an unfavorable ruling for her, she would be gone. Her house is currently valued at nine hundred and seventy-five thousand dollars. A real-estate agent can handle any transaction. She does not need to be present. With no job, no tie to the community, she can be gone in five minutes. My client is prepared to assume custody immediately. His mother and sister are on hand to assist. The child has a right to know her father, which the mother has denied."

"Your Honor—" Mathew was on his feet, but the judge banged his gavel.

He'd heard enough; he was ready to rule. Fair was fair. Cory had the child for twenty months, Rios could have her for six months, and then they would alternate every six months. There was no reason for him not to have her and every reason that he get her. They could revisit the agreement in six months, if necessary.

Another bang of the gavel and the decision was irrevocable.

Cory was on her feet, screaming. "You can't do this. You can't take her."

***

But it seemed that he could. The judge's ruling was law, and Cory no longer had full custody. The clerk outlined a procedure for the transfer. They would go immediately to the house and retrieve the child. At the plaintiff's lawyers' request, Cory would have no direct contact with the father. She was to stay at all times ten feet away from him.

Three vehicles left the courthouse in a convoy, with Mathew leading the way. Rios was in the middle driving an old white van with a rusted red hood. The court clerk, in a navy government-issued car, brought up the rear. Cory, frozen, stared out the windshield in shocked disbelief.

Mathew wiped his eyes as he drove. "We'll fight this. I knew we were in trouble when I saw the lawyers. They're from the top firm in Austin. Rios wasn't taking any chances. I wonder how much he paid them."

"Drop me on campus. They don't know where the day care is."

"You have to comply with the court order or they'll throw you in jail."

"I can't give up my daughter," Cory screamed. "I won't."

Mathew stared straight ahead, eyes on the road. "You have to. You have no choice. For now." He spoke calmly, in a slow, steady tone. "We'll file an appeal. You had poor legal representation. We had no time to prepare. I'm a law student. We start there. We'll get her back."

"When?"

"Not six months. We'll request a different judge. We couldn't have gotten a worse one. He's been investigated for corruption countless times. He's up for re-election, and he'll win. He's got more money than his opponents."

"You think someone bought him? Paid him off? Like Wellspring?" She punched the dash with her fist. She felt like she broke her hand. "Let's see what Tyler can dig up."

In no time at all they reached the day care, and the procession stopped. As prearranged, Cory got out, and Mathew and Rios went on to the house, leaving the clerk idling at the curb.

Sophie was fast asleep and had to be roused from her nap. Ethyl wanted Cory to wait, but that wasn't possible. "She has to go," Cory said as her voice broke.

Sophie was crying, and Cory tried to calm her down. "It's okay. Everything's okay." But everything was far from okay, and she was on the verge of crying too.

The clerk had overlooked the need for a car seat but was content to follow in the car while Cory walked home on foot. Before long, Sophie put her thumb in her mouth and stopped fussing. She fell back to sleep, her head resting on Cory's shoulder, the small arms clasped around her neck. Cory hugged her tight. How could she live without her? How could she let her go? It didn't seem possible.

At home, Rios had parked in the driveway and was leaning against the van. At the house, behind the bay window, Pluto was raging, hurtling himself at the glass. The clerk parked on the street and joined

Cory on the sidewalk. He placed himself between Rios and her, as if to preempt an attack.

She couldn't move. She clutched Sophie, feeling weighted down. The air was as thick as water, and she could barely breathe. Sophie, as if sensing the tension, woke up. She looked around, saw strangers, clenched her legs around Cory's hip and held on tight.

The front door opened, and Mathew appeared with her diaper bag. Shoving Pluto back with his knee, he closed the door, came down the steps, crossed the lawn, and handed the bag to Rios.

"It's time," said the clerk. He held out his hands for Sophie.

"No," Cory said. "Don't do this. Please don't do this."

He wrenched Sophie from her. Sophie kicked and screamed, flailing her arms as she tried to beat him off. He tried to still her lashing feet as he went down the drive to the van. Rios slid open the side door. "You don't have a car seat," the clerk said.

Cory found her legs and tore across the lawn. "Don't take her. I know you don't want her. Please, just leave her."

The clerk handed Sophie to Rios. He held up both his hands and headed for Cory. "Please proceed to the house. You are under court order to keep your distance. I have the authority to arrest you."

Mathew took her arm and pulled her back. "Give him your car seat."

"He can't take her. He can't do this. He's not prepared. He can't have her. He doesn't want her."

Mathew went to Cory's car, opened the door, and unlatched the car seat. The clerk took it from him, and together they secured it in the van while Sophie screamed and cried and squirmed, trying to escape.

The car seat was in. Sophie was reaching for Mathew, and he took her hand and kissed her cheek. The clerk helped Rios get Sophie in the seat. The van door slammed. The loud wailing stopped.

"*Gracias*," Rios said. He shook hands with the clerk, looked over at Cory and quickly looked away. Then he hopped in his van, started the engine, and backed up through a billow of black exhaust. The clerk waited until he was out of sight, then left as well.

Cory's knees gave out, and she sunk to the grass. She wanted to scream like Sophie, howl like Pluto. How could this happen? Mathew kneeled down beside her. "I'll order the transcripts. I'll go through the ruling. On Monday, we'll appeal."

"You said there was no way we could lose."

"I expected a different judge."

"You didn't say anything about me. About my credentials. My education."

"The judge never gave us a chance."

"You never said anything when Rios called me a slut."

"He didn't call you that. He said you had a habit of one-night stands. It's true."

"Fuck off."

"How did he get her DNA?"

"How should I know?"

"Drake?" Mathew asked. "Did you tell him about Rios?"

Cory put her hands to her head and yelled, "I want a real lawyer."

"Go ahead," Mathew shouted. "This isn't my fault. You did this."

Cory pushed his chest, shoved him away. "Go. Get out. Don't come back."

He lost his balance, fell backwards. Then he scrambled to his feet, jogged to his car, and roared off, tires squealing.

Chapter Forty-eight

If people let the government decide what foods they eat and what medicines they take, their bodies will soon be in as sorry a state as the souls who live under tyranny.

—Thomas Jefferson

Art heard the news at the end of the day. He was in his office, packing up, getting ready to leave early on a bright, warm, sunny Friday. Spring had finally come to New York, capping a perfect end to a perfect week. Art had made the newspapers every day. The numerous reports praising his tenacity, foresight, and business savvy were going to his head. He had built a great company. With his stock trading at 87.20, investors had their best quarter ever. Gifts, small tokens of gratitude, were pouring in: vintage wine, theatre tickets, and dinners at the best restaurants. He was going home to celebrate. Missy had invited a friend for the night, and he was supposed to pick up fresh lobster. Then Hank came in, and a fabulous day got even better.

"It's done," Hank said. "Montclair's lost it all. Her job and her kid."

Art plucked thousand-dollar sunglasses off his desk and put them on. "Do tell."

"NCI cut her funding."

"She's a quack. She should have lost her job long ago."

"Today she lost her kid. The father got her."

"Serves her right. She tried to take what was mine."

"She's finished," Hank said. "Her reputation's gone. Her grant's cut. She's got no way to pay back her debt. She'll lose her house." He wiped his hands together. "All gone."

"Good." Art paused. He wanted her broke, desperate, and begging. No one crossed him and got away with it. "Will she get another job?"

"Maybe at McDonald's, but not at the university. You gave them ten million, remember."

"Good for me." Art picked up his gold-plated briefcase and thumped Hank on the back. "There's a bonus for you, my friend. Don't think I don't appreciate all you've done."

Hank smiled. "Just doing my job."

Art bumped Hank's fist before heading out into the glorious sunshine, ready for a night of fun.

Chapter Forty-nine

Cory held it together until night fell, but when darkness came, she started screaming. It was the scream from the dream, the same dark night, the same sense of terror and approaching doom. By midnight, with her throat too raw to scream, she was crying. At first there were great gulps of air, bulging eyes, and a face about to burst. Then tears came, and once they did, they could not stop. A lifetime of stored emotion came pouring out.

By three a.m. her eyes were red and blurry and she couldn't see. She was so disoriented she was begging her dead grandmother for help. *Do something. Help me. Bring her back.*

Two hours went by and nothing. Cory knew it all along. She was alone. There were no ghosts, there was no help; it was all up to her. She dragged herself to the kitchen and washed her face. She filled a glass with water and found it hard to swallow.

She heard music. Someone was playing the piano. "The Death March." She threw open the dining room door. Silence. A curtain billowed through the open window. Silver moonlight fell across the yellowing keys. She was going crazy. She had to get it together.

She wasn't going to lose Sophie so easily. She had to do something. It was time to act. She wasn't waiting until Monday to file a complaint, and she wasn't waiting six months to revisit the judge. At first light, she would go to El Paso. Sophie had known immediately that Rios was bad news. Two and a half years ago, she and Pluto weren't around to sound a warning, and Cory had been duped. That was Evonia's word for it. She had disliked him on sight. "He is creature. Just good-looking creature." She tapped her heart. "Listen with this. The heart knows."

Yes, it did. It wanted Sophie. Somehow, Cory had to get her back. She needed money. It always came down to that. She had a couple of hundred dollars in her bank account, and that much could be put on her credit card. It wasn't enough. There was the house. Allegedly worth nearly one million dollars. She would sell. And just like that, for the first time, the possibility entered the equation. Her grandmother had said, *keep it, no matter what,* but she had never met Sophie, and the house meant nothing without her. Cory would put it on the market, take the best price, and use the money to buy Sophie back.

She put down her glass, headed for the study, and opened her laptop. For a sad moment, she heard crying, as if there really were ghosts who were lamenting the sale. Cory held her breath, straining to listen. The noise seemed to come from behind the walls. What sounded like sniffling. The room felt cold. Her arms broke out in goose bumps, and she shivered. She offered up a bargain and said aloud, "Help me get Sophie back, and I'll keep the house."

She was silent, waiting, listening. Of course, there was no answer. She was losing her mind. It was only the fan of the laptop.

Cory went online and researched how to sell a house. For the top price, it had to be in A1 shape. There was no time for that. She would sell "as is" and take a loss. Immediate money was the only concern. She'd take whatever she could get.

At five thirty, she heard an owl. She went out front with Pluto to look for it. If Mathew wanted to stay, he could watch Pluto, otherwise she would take him. She crossed the porch and went down the steps, the dog by her side. The yard was in shadow, the sky was black, and the stars were small and far away. She looked up in the black trees and saw nothing. She was hearing things. Perhaps having a nervous breakdown.

Then the owl came into view, gently flapping its wings. It soared across the lawn, curving away from the porch at the last minute. Cory looked into its dark eyes, and it looked back. She tried bargaining again: "*Help get Sophie, and I'll keep the house.*"

The owl kept going. It flew across the lawn and disappeared into the thick foliage of an oak. Cory sunk down on the steps and began sobbing. She had stooped so low she was bartering with birds. It was insane. The house was real money; she would sell. It wasn't the most important thing in the world anymore. She would do what had to be done.

Once more, from inside the house, she heard crying. It came from upstairs. Tripping over Pluto, she raced up to Sophie's room. Of course, the crib was empty, the bed tidily made, waiting for the baby who wasn't coming. Cory picked up the blanket, buried her face in the soft cloth, and started crying again.

There was a loud knock on the door. Cory pitched the blanket at the crib and raced downstairs. It was still dark outside. She flung open the door. Dana and Nick were on the porch. He had a baseball bat in his hand, resting on his shoulder, as if he was about to take a swing.

"We heard noises," Dana said as she stepped into the foyer. "We tried calling but there was no answer."

Nick came in and closed the door. The sad faces in the oil paintings stared out at them all. "Everything okay?"

"Sophie's gone," Cory said. "Her father took her." Just saying the words made her cry again.

"He kidnapped her?" Nick asked in alarm.

"A judge gave her to him."

Dana offered comfort with a tight hug and pats on the back. Nick lowered the bat. He gazed around awkwardly. He decided if there was no danger, he would go home. He said good-bye and left quickly.

Dana and Cory went to the kitchen where Dana made coffee. Wordlessly, they watched it drip, then hiss and spit. Dana poured two cups, and they sat down at the table. Cory stared into the cup at the rising spiral of smoke.

"What happened?" Dana asked.

"A corrupt judge decided Sophie was better off with a no-good fucking asshole. He got her for six months."

"Son of a bitch," Dana said. "Is this the pharmaceutical company?"

Cory nodded. It hurt too much to talk. Wellspring had taken everything. All the things she wanted and thought she couldn't live without. Sophie. Her job. Her house. So much for Dana's notion that evil could never win.

"I heard about your funding."

Cory lifted her eyes and looked at Dana. "I should have called you."

"I knew you would, when you were ready. I went to the lab and talked to Evonia. She told me what happened and let me look through your lab books. I hope it was okay."

"I couldn't get the enzyme to work."

"You didn't add EDTA. That stabilizes the monoclonal. I repeated it, and it works fine. We got it."

"Great," Cory said without enthusiasm.

"It is." Dana looked around the kitchen. "Where's Mathew?"

"Gone."

"He left you at a time like this?"

"I told him to go."

"He'll be back."

Tears welled up in Cory's eyes. "I'm leaving. I'm going after Sophie." She wiped her eyes with her fingers.

"He'll wait for you."

"I'm going to sell the house. I need the money."

"Don't do it; don't sell."

Speaking the words of her grandmother. "I have no choice."

"I've got money."

Cory looked at her. "I need lots."

"Give me a figure. Whatever you need."

Cory smiled and laughed softly. She couldn't believe it. Had the ghosts come through? The owl? A chill climbed her spine and made her shiver. She laughed louder. Asking for a loan had started it all. She'd called Janie looking for money and ended up writing a letter. If she had called Dana, none of this would have happened.

"Am I missing a joke?" Dana asked.

Cory shook her head. "What about five thousand?"

"That's all?"

Cory looked into Dana's bright eyes. "Just like that, you'd give it to me?"

"Of course. We're friends. Collaborators. Neighbors. We'll go to the bank when it opens. We'll get cash. Then you go. I'll watch Pluto until Mathew comes back."

Cory felt tears prickling her eyes. She could leave at nine and be in El Paso by nightfall. She was crying again, now with relief, her shoulders heaving, nose running, and eyes leaking buckets of tears.

While Dana drank coffee and stared out the window, dawn was breaking. The sun was rising, bringing white light and color to the world. Birds began to chirp, and Cory got a hold of herself. She wiped her face with her hand and swallowed hard. Once again, she heard a baby crying.

Dana said, "Do you hear that?"

"The baby crying?"

"That's what it sounds like."

"Ghosts. I've heard them all night." The whole household was weeping.

Dana put down her coffee, stood up, and walked to the doorway. She peered through the foyer. "It's your baby. Sophie's home."

Chapter Fifty

The old rusty van was at the curb. On the sidewalk, Rios wrestled with a screaming Sophie he held sideways under his arm. Cory flew across the porch, charged through the grass, and snatched Sophie away.

"Mama," Sophie cried.

Rios didn't try to keep her. "You're right, I'm not ready for a kid. I kept my end of the bargain, but I don't want her. You can have her."

Cory hugged her daughter, and Dana reached the sidewalk and extended her arm and shook Rios's hand. "You must be Sophie's father. She has your good looks."

Cory could have punched her. Rios stroked his chest.

"What bargain did you keep?" Dana asked, smiling sweetly.

"I got paid," Rios said as if he wasn't proud of it. "Seventy-five thousand to go to court. I never thought I'd win."

"You shouldn't have," Cory snapped.

Dana laid a restraining hand on her arm. "It was good of you to bring her back. A less-honorable man wouldn't do so."

Rios straightened, looking taller, sheepish almost with baseless pride.

"Who paid you?" Dana asked.

"Some surfer dude." Rios looked at Cory with eyes that looked too much like Sophie's. "I didn't believe it until I saw the money. Deposited straight into my account in advance. *Tonto del culo.*" Meaning, *idiot*.

"Can you wait just a minute?" Cory plopped Sophie into Dana's arms and ran to the house to search for the picture of Drake Mansfield. She tore through her office looking for it before she remembered it was in the scanner. She found it and rushed it outside.

Good God, Dana had given Sophie back to Rios and was showing him how to hold her on his hip as if she were a child. "There you go," Dana said. "You've got it."

"Mama," Sophie said, and Cory wrenched her away.

Cory gave Rios the photograph. "Do you recognize him?"

"Right there. The one with the bleached-blond hair. Dude can drink. He got me smashed. He was down about you. I guessed you were a lousy lay."

Cory opened her mouth, but Dana raised a finger, commanding silence. "Where did you meet him?"

"He came to my work. He had pictures of you. Asked if I knew you. He said we had a common problem. You. He wanted to take you to court, and I didn't have to do nothing but show up. He didn't say I'd win. He didn't say what to do if I did. I got money for filing the suit and going to court. My conscience is clear."

"You seem like a man of principle," Dana said.

Cory rolled her eyes. "You lied in court. You're an only child. Your mother's dead."

Rios made a quick sign of the cross over his heart. "Someone made it up. I don't know who. All I had to do was show up and shut up. That was the deal."

"Bringing her back was the right thing to do," Dana said and shot Cory a look. "Right?"

Cory could be magnanimous. Her heart was soaring. Her daughter was home. Sophie was safe. "Thank you for that."

"He shouldn't screw with you like that," Rios said in a stab at chivalry. "That was really mean."

"That's right," Dana said. "She *is* the mother of your child,"

"I think you looked after her real well," Rios said. "I should have helped. I felt bad that I didn't. Maybe our bones would have matched. Our blood is ninety-nine percent the same. That's close."

"You took a DNA test?" Cory asked.

"Dude yanked out my hair. He said I'd only get paid if I was a match. He must have gotten your hair too. That's how he knew yours didn't match."

Cory refrained from correcting his ignorance of genetics. "He'll come after you when he finds out you gave her back."

"He won't find me. The money's already in Mexico. I'm gone. *Adiós*."

"Maybe you could sign a statement saying you were paid and that you're willingly returning custody to her mother." Dana looked at Cory. "You have a pen?"

This time Cory took Sophie with her to the house. On the back of the page with Drake's picture, she wrote down Dana's words. Outside, Rios unhooked the car seat and laid it on the sidewalk. He signed the paper without reading it.

Then he had to go. He was heading for Juarez and had a long drive. Dana kissed him good-bye, and, God help her, Cory closed her eyes and did the same. Even Sophie gave him a kiss, putting her lips against his unshaven cheek.

He left, shooting off in a roar, and Cory was crying again. She buried her face into Sophie's shoulder and sobbed while Dana explained that mommy wasn't sad, she was really happy.

***

The house never looked as bright and the air never felt as fresh as it did with Sophie back home. Dana declined breakfast, and after she left, Cory made whole-wheat crepes rolled up with real maple syrup, which she and Sophie devoured as the sun shone down. To Cory, food never tasted so good, the oak trees never looked so green, and her heart never felt so full. "You're home," she kept saying. "You're home."

Sophie said it too. "Me home, Mama. Me home."

They took a bath after breakfast, sailing boats and blowing bubbles. Cory held the small, slippery body, understanding fully what her loss would mean. It was a loss Janie, Marie, and Daniel would carry every day of their lives. She had been spared. She lost Sophie for one night, and it was one night too many. She knew she had brought this on herself by blabbing to Drake, who had come for Sophie's DNA. He must have snuck hair from her brush, tracked down Rios, and paid him to seek custody. And Cory had brought Drake into the house. What did that say about her instincts? She had welcomed him warmly after nearly turning Mathew away. Sophie had known the right choice, and Pluto had known it too, while Cory, with all her so-called higher thought had no clue and chose badly.

The plumbing clanked, and Cory stared at the sepia-tinged photographs of the ancestors on the bathroom walls. Last night, she had finally heard the ghosts, bargained with them, and struck a deal. They didn't take any chances. First Dana came with money. Then, Rios brought Sophie back.

Overnight, Cory's worldview had changed. Reality had expanded into the realm of the unreal where deals were struck with the dead and owls came with messages. Disjointed events were tied together as if the future, not the past, tugged at the long string of causality. The current chain had started with Sophie's diagnosis, followed by a chance infection, treatment in Mexico, and an encounter with Janie. That led to a loan request and an infinitesimal yet consequential letter that changed everything. If Sophie hadn't gotten sick, if the hospital hadn't garnished Cory's wages, if she hadn't been so broke, she wouldn't have met Mathew. Perhaps that's what he meant when he said things happened for a reason. She had lived through hell to get where she was. She paid a high price for what she had. She was going to hold onto him.

When the water was cold, their skin was wrinkled, and Sophie was nearly asleep, Cory put her to bed. She rocked by the crib with Pluto stretched out by her feet. A gentle breeze blew, lifting and dropping the curtain. The air smelled sweet, of warmed sugar. The rough night was over, and they were safe, living in a protected house in a world infused with meaning and purpose. She was dozing off, thinking about a reality where cause and effect were reversed, when a noise startled her. Someone was on the stairs. Had Rios changed his mind? Had the courts learned Sophie was back?

Instantly awake, she leapt up and raced to the door. Pluto burst out and ran to the landing.

Mathew. He was dragging himself up the stairs, unshaven and looking as disheveled and defeated as she'd ever seen him. She ran to him, wrapped her arms around him, and hugged him tightly. He hugged her back. They said sorry, repeating themselves, until it dawned on her that he was talking about Sophie being taken.

She took his hand, drew him to the nursery, and pointed at the crib. "Rios brought her back. He didn't want her."

Mathew blinked. His eyes glazed over, and tears coursed down his cheeks. It choked her up to see him weep and made her cry too. Sniffling, he stared at her with disbelief.

In a day she'd become one of the wailers her grandmother distained. Cory steered him into the hall and eased the nursery door closed. "I know. I can't help it. I'm so glad you came back."

That was enough talking. She kissed him. She shut her eyes, found his mouth, locked her lips to his, and leaned into him, pressing herself against him. He kissed her back. Much time passed. She sensed his gaze, opened her eyes, and saw him staring. She disengaged herself from him.

"What's this?" he said.

"Here's the thing," she said. "We need you. Sophie does, and I do. You belong here. If this is not what you want, you have to leave."

She paused, waited, thought it was his turn to say something, and he did. "Go on."

"I didn't know if you'd come back. That's not what usually happens." She paused, took a deep breath, suddenly feeling the heat that came with the sunlight that spilled through the window, dappling the landing. "Men go, and they don't return. You think for me it's one long string of one-night stands, but it's not like that. They want to go; they can't wait to leave."

There, she had said it, for the first time, acknowledging a private secret hell. Her heart was pounding, like a drum roll, announcing her deficiency out loud to the world.

Mathew leaned against the banister, moving out of the light into the shadow. "You think there's something wrong with you that makes them want to go?"

She nodded, shrugged, and kicked the runner on the top of the landing.

"No," he said. "No one leaves willingly. You push them away. You shut down, you grow cold. You give nothing—no needed medical advice, no comfort to grieving parents, no hand to a friend. You expect people to go, so you push them away so that when they do, it doesn't destroy you. It's a vicious cycle. A self-fulfilling expectation. A way to protect yourself. You did it with Marie, Janie, me."

"Protect myself?" Cory stopped kicking the rug and wrung her hands. "Hardly. You started seeing Nancy, and I was devastated. Until Dana's party, I thought I'd be alone forever. When we danced, something changed. It did for me, and I think it did for you too. But you blew me off. Suddenly, there was Nancy, and you were gone." She looked into his eyes. She had to know. "What happened?"

He held her gaze, folded his arms across his heart. The angle of the sun had moved, and sunlight was slanting down across him. "You know how it was losing Sophie? It would be like that for me losing you once I had you. One night was never going to work. I'd rather have nothing." He lowered his hands. "Nancy was safe. I thought she would distract me."

Cory blinked. This was not what she'd expected to hear. She thought he'd chosen Nancy because she could express herself, cry like an infant, jump in and save the world, and get involved without regret. Instead, she had been a distraction.

"The night of the protest, on the swing, with one look from you, I knew it would never work with her. I finally understood how Margaret felt. Why she couldn't be with me when she wanted Bob. And then there was Drake." Mathew's hands were back, crossed over his chest. "It was déjà vu and having to face that nightmare all over again. Seeing someone else take what I wanted. A hulking brute just like Bob. A real man would have decked Drake out. What is he? A football player?"

"A surfer. When he's not a congressional aide. But nothing happened. When you came home that night I knew that if I couldn't have you, I didn't want anyone."

"I'm no boxer, and I'll never be one. I can't surf. I won't fight. I like to cook, I blush, I cry. If you can't take it, you have to tell me now."

Cory took his hand. "I can take it. It's a tough world, and you're not so tough, but that doesn't make you weak. I can learn something from you. I want to be more like you. You listen to your heart. I live too much in my head."

He put his arm around her back. "I can learn something from you, too. When it gets too hard, I run. You hunker down. You hold on and fight. Look what you've lived through. Having Sophie on your own, crushing debt, losing your job, holding on to your house. You never back down. You know what matters."

She leaned into him. "You matter." She threw her arms around him and kissed him while her heart swelled and felt like it would explode.

And that was when Sophie woke up.

They spent the rest of the day together as if they were a real family. They took Pluto to the dog park and went to the toy shop. She bought Sophie a tricycle, and Mathew bought her a basketball hoop. They built the toys while Sophie kicked the ball that Pluto chased. When the hoop was up, she dunked the ball. When she tired of that, she got on the bike. She couldn't work the pedals and used her feet to drag herself along. They tied the wagon to the back, and Pluto perched in it like a king. Mathew pushed them up and down the sidewalk while Cory waited for the night.

Later, Mathew opened a bottle of white wine and lit the barbecue. They had chicken for dinner, Sophie's new favorite. The free-range happy bird died of old age, which meant the meat had to be marinated, but by the time it was finished roasting on the fire, the meat fell off the bone, and Sophie loved it. "Meat good," she said. Her days as a vegetarian seemed to be coming to a close.

The sun sank behind rose-colored clouds, and dusk came slowly. It didn't get dark until eight, and they put Sophie down and stood by the crib, waiting until she fell asleep. It did not take long.

They went to Cory's room. She opened the windows, and the curtains fluttered in a warm night breeze that carried the sweet scent of honeysuckle. They went to bed. The sheets were cool. He was solid, muscular, and hard—and yet the opposite: tender, soft, and gentle. He trembled with excitement and was then controlled. Together they rocked in a pulsing rhythm that finally crested and must have left ripples reaching far into space. Out the window, an owl whooped and stars came out, close enough to touch.

Chapter Fifty-one

April 21st

Sunday brought unfamiliar territory. Mathew cooked breakfast, chopping onions like a chef and juggling eggs. He hummed along with Raffi, dancing with Sophie in his arms as he stirred the omelet. They spent the morning reading the newspaper, drinking too much coffee, and taking too much sun. Sophie rolled her basketball, Cory washed Pluto, and Mathew weeded the vegetable garden that was beginning to bear fruit. In the garage, looking for a spray nozzle, Cory found a box with the white globe Christmas lights from her parents' photograph and her childhood swing. It was a box made of wood. Mathew replaced the frayed rope and hung the swing on a maple branch. He pushed a happily shrieking Sophie as high as she could go. The sound reminded Cory of her happy childhood. Early memories were beginning to come back.

After lunch, while Sophie was napping, Cory finally got to look at the files hidden behind the Wellspring firewall. Tyler had given them to Mathew on Friday night. There were too many files for a flash drive, and Tyler had copied them onto a hard drive that held a terabyte of data.

Mathew plugged the drive into the laptop, and as they waited for it to load, he reviewed Rios's signed statement. Cory wanted to take it to the judge on Monday, but Mathew said it was best to do nothing. Tyler had hacked into Harris's computer and found the congressman had given Judge Tobin a check for one hundred thousand dollars. Unfortunately, as far as custody was concerned, she could do nothing with the information. Legally, in an appeal, no new information could be introduced. According to Mathew, the process of appeal was used to determine whether or not the law had been followed, period. Mathew thought she should lock the letter away in a safety deposit box in case Rios ever showed up again. What she definitely could not do was ever mention aloud that Congressman Harris had bought the judge. Information illicitly obtained was never admissible in court.

It was an atrocity, she thought, as the flash drive light turned green. The law helped hide criminal behavior.

She opened the disk, and a copyright protection seal appeared. It dissolved, leaving a screen of folders. One named "Correspondence" contained emails. With Mathew looking on, she opened random messages. The CFO had approved extra money for the IT department to hire additional software experts. The public relations director had a final draft of a news release entitled "Disgraced Duane Post-Doc on Notice."

"Now you know who wrote the article," Mathew said.

She closed the email. The *Tribune* had still not gotten back to her, and she guessed they had no desire to clear up the record. No doubt Wellspring paid them to print it, though there was no email evidence of this. She did see an email from Art Farber authorizing three million dollars more for A.H.

"Alexander Harris," Mathew said. "Wellspring's representative in Congress."

In another email, Cory read that Kelly Mann also got three million. "Do you know her?"

"She's running for the same seat," Mathew said. "Wellspring isn't taking any chances."

Cory saw an email from Hank requesting an appointment with Drake Mansfield, but with Mathew sitting so close, she'd wait to open it. She jumped down a page. There was an email from Art to the FDA, specifically to Claude Smite, thanking him for his help and asking when he'd be available to start at Wellspring.

"That's the FDA agent who came to see me," she said, pointing at the screen. "I knew he was working for Wellspring. I told him as much, and he tried to tell me he worked for the public good."

She closed the correspondence folder and read the labels on other folders. Most referenced clinical data. She opened a folder labeled "Phase 1" and learned that two decades back, fifty healthy prisoners in a Kansas penitentiary had "volunteered" to test Valurex for potential side effects. These were in evidence and included the standard response of hair loss, nausea, and depression. Over twenty percent also had a severe allergic reaction.

A few moments later, she found a questionnaire that indicated cancer doctors knew how badly the drugs performed. Out of one hundred and twenty-eight doctors asked, eighty percent would refuse the treatment they dispensed. Still, there was nothing illegal in Wellspring asking physicians to give out what they were not willing to take themselves.

She opened the folder labeled "Phase 2" and saw a long list of subfolders. She clicked on the first one and saw patient files from an Alabama doctor who had fifty patients on Valurex. Each patient was assigned a number, and for each there was a personal history, details of the initial cancer diagnosis, the blood work, treatment protocol, and outcome. She scrolled through the sick. They were aged six months to ninety and afflicted with different types of cancers, including: skin, leukemia, breast, pancreatic, esophagus, and stomach. Most had skin cancer.

She closed the file and opened the folder labeled "Phase 3." This was an Excel file with a spreadsheet summarizing clinical data over a five-year period. Scanning the footnotes, it didn't take Cory long to realize how selective Wellspring was with the data. When any control patient died, they were included in the final stats. If a treated patient died, they were dropped. That was just bad science. The groups should have been treated the same. Also dropped were patients who suffered from complications of chemo—pneumonia, heart attack, anaphylactic shock, and infections. They weren't included in the statistics either.

Most egregious was the *type* of cancer studied. Of five thousand patients, three thousand seven hundred and seventy-eight had basal cell carcinoma. It was the most common and least deadly form of skin cancer. This type of cancer often spontaneously stopped growing or disappeared without any treatment at all. But in this study, patients were treated. Not surprisingly, most survived. When Cory struck this group from the data and recalculated the results, she was left with one thousand one hundred and twenty-two patients. Of these, only seven percent lived at least five years. The *effective* success rate was way less than the forty percent that Wellspring claimed.

She told this to Mathew, and he frowned. "Then they're making a fraudulent claim."

"Yes, but it's the FDA making it, which is allowed. They can say whatever they want."

Cory began comparing the data in the Wellspring spreadsheet with the spreadsheet they submitted to the FDA. It was immediately obvious that Wellspring had not submitted all their data. The numbers didn't match. Wellspring had not included any patients under four years old—when they had given the cocktail to over four hundred kids. Wellspring had made it look like they never tested the drugs in the young. Incognizant of the danger, the FDA approved the drug across the board for patients of all ages.

Cory grabbed Mathew's hand. "Look at this. They deliberately dropped patients. The kids." She jabbed her finger at the screen. "The most common form of childhood cancer is leukemia. Wellspring wasn't going to miss out on that market. They knew how bad Valurex was in kids, and they didn't tell the FDA."

Mathew raised his eyebrows. A slow smile broke across his face. "Then we've got them. That's the basis for Janie's lawsuit. Deliberate harm."

Cory kissed him. For her, it was personal. She no longer just wanted to raise public awareness about Oxylace. She wanted to expose Wellspring Pharmaceutical. "If we could file one lawsuit, we could file many, couldn't we? A class action suit?"

Mathew leaned back in his chair. "There's only one problem. We got the data illegally. No judge will allow it in court."

"Can you ask a judge to order Wellspring to give us the data?"

"You mean subpoena it? That would work, but Wellspring will fight it to the death. Obviously they know there's a problem."

"We talk to the doctors who treated the kids," Cory said.

Mathew frowned. "They usually stick with the drug companies. Otherwise, they're liable for knowingly prescribing harmful drugs."

"So we file a Freedom of Information Act request with the FDA. Take that to the pediatric oncologists and prove to them that Wellspring didn't use any of the clinical data of the kids. It will let the doctors off the hook."

Mathew thought it was a good idea but was reluctant to proceed. "A FIOA request isn't anonymous. Wellspring will know where it came from. We've seen what they're capable of. They'll know you were responsible."

"I want them to know."

Over Mathew's objections, Cory pulled up the Freedom of Information website. She realized she could make a request to the FDA and send a demand directly to Claude Smite. She filled out the form, specifically asking for the Phase 3 data on Valurex submitted by Wellspring Pharmaceutical.

Mathew tried to stop her. He grabbed her hand. "When you push send, there's no going back. The FDA will come after you. They can tie you up in court for years. We know they put people in prison."

Cory paused and stared hard at the screen. With this data, she could prove Oxylace was better than chemotherapy. She knew Claude Smite was heading to Wellspring Pharmaceutical as soon as he retired from the FDA. Her crime was writing a letter, giving her opinion that Oxylace be tested, that it "may well cure cancer." Would a jury find her guilty for that? Or would they be disgusted to learn what the FDA was really up to? It was time to make a stand.

She turned and looked at Mathew. "I'm tired of doing nothing. I didn't do anything wrong. When they took Sophie, they made this personal. They block cures for cancer. They don't care how many people suffer and die. But I care, and I'm going to do something." With her free hand, she pushed send.

The action felt liberating. For so long she had been powerless, a victim backed into a corner with no good options. The freedom to finally act was exhilarating. "I'm going to call Janie and let her know."

Her phone was dead, so she plugged it in. She sent Janie an email: Found deliberate harm.

***

That night, Sophie went to bed at eight. Cory and Mathew finished the dishes and poured two glasses of wine, planning to turn in early. They were heading upstairs when the doorbell rang. They glanced at each other. "Should we get it?" Mathew asked.

The bell rang again and that seemed to settle it. He handed her his wine and clomped downstairs, turned on the outside light, and opened the door. Daniel and Marie Weiss stood on the porch.

"Janie asked us to come over," Marie said. She looked up the stairs where Cory waited with two glasses of wine. "Are we interrupting something?"

Cory didn't answer, and Mathew said, "What is it?"

"We'll just be a minute." Daniel of course had to come in.

"Janie has been trying to call you," Daniel said as Cory went downstairs and handed Mathew his wine. "She got your message. We have grounds for a lawsuit?"

Mathew offered wine, and the Weisses accepted. He went to get it, and Cory took the guests to the living room. They settled on the couch while she went to the study and checked her phone. It was off, and she powered it on and saw eight missed calls; two from Dana and six from Janie. She decided to call in the morning and returned to the living room.

The Weisses had their wine, and Mathew was on the loveseat. She sat down next to him, and he slung his arm around her. Marie said, "I knew you were a couple."

"The situation changed," Mathew said. "Since we last spoke. Why don't you tell them." He looked at Cory.

What did he want her to say? That they were on their way to bed when they were interrupted?

As she stammered and blushed, he jumped to her aid. "We have data from Wellspring that suggests they knew how harmful the cocktail was, especially in kids. They deliberately withheld the data from the FDA."

Cory smiled to herself. Oh, that was what she was supposed to tell them.

Daniel took a slurp of wine. "What does that mean?"

"Willful harm," Mathew said.

The Weisses jumped up and hugged each other. Marie came across the room, sunk down on the armrest, and patted Cory's shoulder. "We'll sue them. Take their money. Hit them where it hurts," Marie said.

Cory smiled at her, nodding in agreement.

Marie said she always knew there was intentional harm. The evidence was clear on Facebook. Danny's page had over three thousand fans. They were hearing from people from across the country whose kids had leukemia and took the cocktail and had allergic reactions. Not one kid had survived the treatment. The drugs were bad. The recovery rate was nothing like the doctors claimed.

"Maybe the parents whose kids survived didn't join your group," Cory said, reluctant to put much faith in Facebook evidence.

"We put out a call for survivors, but we haven't heard anything," Marie said.

"The stats are all wrong," Daniel said. "We've heard from adults, and there's no way forty percent of them survived either."

"Wellspring's own data shows about a seven percent success rate," Cory said. "They've misrepresented their stats. We just have to prove it in court."

"We've got lawyers who've joined our page," Daniel said. "They seem to think we can start a class action suit, no problem. They're begging to take it." He looked at Mathew. "We want you."

Mathew explained the problem. He had finals coming up, the bar exam in May, and he couldn't practice law until he passed. In his mind, it was too far off. If they were going to move, they had to move now—not give Wellspring and their investors a chance to dump stock. He offered to ask the lawyers in his new firm who were old hands at mass tort litigation if they were interested in the case. He couldn't see them turning it down.

The Weisses agreed. "How does a class action work?" Marie asked as she downed more wine.

Mathew explained the process. They'd file a suit and subpoena Wellspring's records. "We already know they didn't give the FDA everything. Their computer files will prove it, their doctors will confirm it. Maybe a disgruntled employee will turn on them. Cory's writing a paper that will show how bad the cocktail is and that there's a better drug out there. My guess is Wellspring will try to settle once they realize the strength of our hand. They won't want to defend a bad drug in court. We refuse, go to court, and expose the corrupt industry."

Marie put her empty glass down on the floor and clapped her hands.

"It won't be quick," Mathew said. "We're looking at two, three, or four years. It won't happen overnight. They won't wait quietly. They'll fight every step of the way."

"Will they go to jail?" Marie asked.

"It hasn't happened before," Mathew said.

"Will they go bankrupt" Daniel asked.

"It's possible," Mathew said. He advised them to restrict their Facebook page. "We don't want to give Wellspring a heads up. Keep this under the radar."

The Weisses agreed and got up to go. Marie suspected they had interrupted something, and Cory and Mathew didn't object. They walked the Weisses to the door and said goodnight.

Mathew closed the door, locked it, and they waved good-bye through the side window. "I thought they'd never leave."

Cory looked at her watch. "They were only here ten minutes."

With a sweep of his arm, Mathew pointed to the stairs. "Shall we?"

Halfway up the stairs, Cory's phone rang. Mathew stopped abruptly. "Don't answer."

"It's probably Janie. I won't be long." Cory ran to the study, saw Janie staring up out of the phone, and answered.

"I just spoke to Daniel," Janie said.

Cory walked to the window and saw their car in the driveway. "They're just leaving."

"Daniel said we have grounds for a class action lawsuit."

"Mathew thinks so, yes," Cory said as the car's headlights came on.

"Where's Mathew? Can I talk to him?"

"Um, he's busy. I'll get him to call you later. Tomorrow. I should go."

"Is it Sophie?"

"No."

"What's the rush?"

"Mathew is waiting."

"For what?"

"Me." Cory said good-bye and hung up. She turned off the phone.

Chapter Fifty-two

The FDA devotes a major portion of its resources and manpower to wiretapping, bugging, and following health lecturers in attempt to catch them making a claim that, even though it may be true, comes into conflict with an FDA ruling...

—G. Edward Griffin

April 22nd

At dawn, on a glorious spring morning with the trees in bud and about to burst, Art Farber was at the office staring at the price chart of his stock. Over the weekend, it was up ten percent, and he was waiting to see what it would trade at when the market opened in an hour. He marveled at how fast things could bloom. One day he was worrying about how he would pay for his upscale office, and the next day he was worrying about tax shelters. He had more money than he could have ever imagined. More women too.

Missy was a blot on his morning—as she had been on his weekend. The more money he made, the more possessive she became. She was dropping hints about tying the knot and was expecting a ring. Art was leaning against it. He liked her friend Ramone. He would have to make discreet inquiries, find out how much a breakup would cost him.

There was a knock on his door, and Hank came in looking grim. Art held up his hand as if to ward off evil. "I'm not hearing bad news today."

Hank threw himself into a chair. "I just got off the phone with Claude. The FDA got a FIOA request yesterday."

"What the fuck is that?"

"A request for information. Made possible by the Freedom of Information Act."

"What's it for?"

"Our Phase 3 data of Valurex."

"Tell Claude, no fucking way."

"By law he has to provide it."

"Who wants it?"

"That's the bad news. Montclair."

"Fucking hell!" Art sprang to his feet. "This is what you call shutting her down?"

Hank sighed, and Art could tell from the look on his face there was more bad news. "I know you're no computer expert, so I'll make this simple. When we hacked into her computer, we made ourselves vulnerable. We left a trail that led back to us. We've been hacked. She's not fishing with this FIOA request. She knows we didn't give the FDA everything."

Art was pacing. "She got through our firewall? I was told it was impenetrable."

"Well, someone uploaded a terabyte of data. Someone has the original Phase 3 data and confidential correspondence. I'm assuming it's her."

Art pounded his fist on his desk. "I thought we deleted what was too sensitive."

"We did. We kept one copy. In our most secure site."

"Goddamn it." Art pounded his desk again. He paced in a circle, pulling at his hair. How could things go so bad so quickly? "What does she want it for? Blackmail?"

"My guess? A lawsuit."

"A class action?" Art stopped pacing and put a hand on his heart. It was so tight, he thought it might seize. "She can't use what she stole."

"True. But what she stole told her where to look and what to look for. We could be in trouble."

Art walked to the wall and punched it. He made no dent, barely hurt his knuckles. He didn't fight with his fists. He shook out his hand and turned around. "Can Claude do anything? Didn't she violate labeling laws? She called Oxylace a cure. I thought she could go to prison for that."

"She should. I'll talk to Claude."

"Let me talk to him. He can talk to the attorney general and get the nation's top lawyer on her case. That should slow her down."

"It could take a while. Nothing in Washington moves fast. We need to nip this in the bud. Maybe we should try talking to her."

Art went to his window and stared out. As much as he hated Montclair, he had begrudging respect. She fought. When the knife was in her back, the sand in her throat, the dick in her mouth, she bit down hard. Art took the easy way out. He knew when to say uncle. He did what it took to stay alive. He would grovel if he had to. A class action suit could end everything.

"She's in debt," Hank said. "She needs money. We strike a deal. Give her what she wants. We can make her life easy or hard. I could go to Duane tomorrow. Have a friendly chat."

"No." Art smoothed down the remnants of his hair. "I'll go."

Hank nodded. "You do have a way with the ladies."

Chapter Fifty-three

Monday morning, Cory and Mathew slept in late. When Sophie woke up, they brought her to bed, put her between them, and everyone fell back asleep. Classes were over, exams were about to begin, and this was Mathew's last chance for sleep. During the next two weeks, he planned to put in long hours at the library.

When they finally got up, she made coffee, and he made crepes. As he cooked, he worried aloud about her being home alone and urged her to keep the doors locked. He didn't know what Art would do next, but Mathew was sure Art would do something.

Cory drank coffee and argued that she wasn't alone; she had Pluto. "I'll be careful."

Over breakfast, she told him about her revised plan for the paper. Per Nancy's suggestion, she would do a case-by-case comparison, only she would use the FDA's data.

"Try and get it in a good journal," Mathew said as he sliced into a crepe. "It will help us and Dr. Arrango. What are your chances of publication?"

"In this country, likely zilch. I'll try Canada. They were going to do a study on Oxylace in cows."

"When can you submit?"

"This week. Then it takes four to six weeks to hear back from the journal, and another two to three months before the paper is published."

He thought the timing would work. Once they obtained the FDA's data through official channels, it was in the public domain and she could use it in the paper. If they managed to introduce the paper as evidence in court, it would legitimize the value of Oxylace. "Wellspring will argue that while their cocktail's toxic, there's nothing better. Your paper will show that's not the case."

After breakfast, Mathew left, and Cory dropped Sophie at day care. Back home, she got to work. Her goal was to match two patients from the two treatment groups as closely as possible—by age, cancer type, and stage. She would match the forty-four patients treated with Oxylace with forty-four Wellspring patients. It wasn't a double-blind study, and there were no placebo controls, but she could run a statistical analysis and compare the two treatments.

Going through Wellspring's data, it was obvious the outlawed drug outperformed the approved drugs on every measure. It shrunk tumors, lowered white blood cell counts, stopped weight loss, and most importantly, gave life. In Mexico, five patients under four—Sophie included—were treated with Oxylace, and all survived. From Wellspring, four hundred and twenty-seven kids out of five thousand were under four, and of these, nine outlived their regimen by a year. That was a success rate of two percent. It explained why Wellspring never gave the data to the FDA. With a track record that bad, the cocktail never would have been approved for that age group. When it came to young kids, it was best to do nothing. Let them stay home and live out their last days in peace—unless they were one of the lucky two percent. That was the kicker. Chemo didn't fail completely. It left room for hope.

Unfortunately, since Wellspring hadn't given the FDA the data for young kids, Cory couldn't use it in the paper. It would have to come out in court—if a judge agreed to subpoena the Wellspring files.

By the end of the day, Cory had matched patients and was running the statistics for a paper she tentatively called "A Comparison Between the FDA-Approved Wellspring Chemotherapy Cocktail and the Banned Oxylace." She used an analysis of variance, or ANOVA, to compare the two groups. Mathematically, she proved with a ninety-nine point nine percent certainty there was a difference between the two groups. Basically, the statistics showed the outcome with the cocktail was different than the outcome with Oxylace. One drug killed, the other gave life. The one that killed was endorsed, while the one that saved was banned. If they were lucky, it would all come out in court.

The next day she began writing the article, now soberly entitled "A Statistical Comparison of Chemotherapeutic Drugs." She wrote in the standard scientific tone, which was bland, neutral, and objectively detached. She gave no opinion and allowed readers to draw their own conclusions. These were crystal clear: The drug industry was suppressing a cheap cancer treatment, and the FDA was helping them do it.

She worked on the paper all day and finished it to her satisfaction. It was short, only four pages long, with three tables, a graph, and thirty references. She followed the online submission process and uploaded the paper to the *Canadian Journal of Cancer*. The Canadians had published her letter to the editor, and she was optimistic they would publish the paper.

It was six by the time she called Pluto and went to get Sophie. She grabbed the mail from the box on the way home and found three letters. She took Sophie to the kitchen and opened her mail. Duane Community College was getting back to her. Unfortunately, they were in a hiring freeze and unable to employ any new personnel. They suggested she try the university. Cory threw down the letter. It was a blow. She needed work, but it had to be local. Moving was not a possibility.

The other two letters also had bad news. Human resources was notifying her that her health insurance would expire in May. She was welcome to continue her family plan as a self-pay for a mere nine hundred dollars a month. That wasn't happening. She either had to decrease her coverage or forego it completely, even though it was now the law of the land. She figured it might be cheaper just to pay the penalty.

And, her house insurance company was doubling her premium, starting in June. She only needed four hundred dollars more a month to cover that. There was no way. She'd have to cancel her coverage at the start of hurricane season.

She tossed the letters into the garbage and began making dinner. She smiled at her chattering daughter, wanting to cry. She was one letter away from financial ruin. She needed a job.

After Sophie was in bed, she was back in her office looking for work. The next-closest community college was in Brenham, sixty miles away. She was perusing their website when Pluto began to bark.

She was in no mood for company. Whoever it was had to go. Cory yelled at Pluto to be quiet and got up. In the foyer, through the side window, she saw a man on the front stoop. She gasped sharply. Art Farber, CEO of Wellspring Pharmaceutical, was at the door. She opened it a crack. Behind her, Pluto barked ferociously.

Art Farber, looking like his photo in the newspaper with the university president, offered a small bow. "You probably don't know me."

She stepped outside and closed the door, shutting Pluto inside. The sun was going down, but it was still behind the trees and the sky was not yet dark. A long black car idled at the curb. "I know who you are."

"I wondered if I could have a minute of your time." Art was a pudgy, pigeon-toed man wearing shiny shoes and an expensive three-piece suit. He was shorter than she was. He had a shiny scalp that was covered with a hank of gray hair, swept sideways across the dome. He had small facial features: a narrow mouth, thin lips, and small, watery eyes.

"You have one minute," she said. If he threatened her, she would scream. She would open the door and release her dog. Dana and Nick were home; their house was ablaze with light, and their Prius was in the drive.

"You can call me Art." He smiled like a lizard. "I'm afraid we got off on the wrong foot." He held up a bag. "A peace offering." He pulled out a bottle. "It's a Chablis. A thousand dollars a pop. Made from the chardonnay grape grown in the top vineyard in the world."

Cory looked at the wine and folded her arms together. "I'm busy."

Art went on. "All you probably know about me is what you read in the gossip columns and the financial pages. I can assure you—"

She interrupted him. "I don't read either."

"Of course not. You're a scientist. I have an MBA. There was a time I wanted to be a doctor, but organic killed me. Now I'm a financial mogul, philanthropist, ladies' man." He shrugged apologetically at the labels.

Was the creep coming on to her? "What do you want?"

"We each have something that belongs to the other. I was hoping we could make a trade."

"I don't know what you're talking about."

He smiled a little smile. "Your daughter, my files."

He didn't know she had Sophie back. She stared at him, refusing to respond.

"You are proving to be a formidable opponent, and I am no fighting man." He swept phantom hair off his forehead. "I'm a lover, not a fighter." He raised his bottle. "I propose a drink to discuss our future."

She looked at the bottle and shook her head. Was he flirting with her?

He lowered the bottle, smiling broadly. "Look, I know your situation. Single mother, unemployed, weak and sickly child, high hospital bills. That must be tough. I could talk to the judge, get your daughter back. Have a word with the hospital, help out with your bill. Get back your job. Whatever you want."

"You could do something?"

"It would take one call."

"To whom?"

The little smile widened farther. "My contacts." He shrugged. "I have money." He laughed at his understatement. "I could solve all your financial woes. I could have your child back here tomorrow. I'll write you a check. Name your price." He stepped back as if to take in a panoramic view of the house. "A home this old must be expensive to maintain. Say one million?"

"You'd write me a check for one million?"

"Okay, two. Invest wisely and you'd never have to work again. Think of your daughter. She wouldn't have to work. Or her daughter's daughter."

"You gave Congressman Harris three million."

"I don't think that's general knowledge—and it's actually nine, but who's counting? Would you take three?"

The amount of money was mind-blowing. It would solve everything. Her life would be as it was before she ever heard the words Wellspring Pharmaceutical or the name Art Farber. Only now, she'd have money.

As if sensing her indecision, he reached out and touched her wrist. "The funds could be in your account tomorrow."

A shiver shot up her arm. She shook off his hand. She could not forget what she knew. There was no return to ignorance. "You should go."

He opened his hands. "Tell me. Seriously. What do you want?"

"Good health care."

He laughed. "Not only pleasing to the eye but smart and funny. Can we stick to the realm of possibility? At least try to be reasonable?"

"I want to publish a paper in the *Journal of the American Medicine Association* comparing your cocktail to Oxylace."

"Ha, ha," he said without mirth as his face turned to ice and his small eyes froze. "To you, forty percent of dying people getting a new lease on life may be nothing, but I call it success. I'm sorry your child got sick. She's alive yet you attack my drugs. I don't know what you're up to, why you filed the FIOA request, but I came, in person, to let you know I will not allow you to harm the company I have poured my life into. You will not write such a paper."

"I would."

He lifted the bottle, wielding it as a weapon. "You think you can fight me? You have no idea who you're up against. I know you stole my files. If you think you can use them, you can think again. You have no idea how things work. One way or another, I'll stop you. You are nothing. You have nothing. You could have had money, but you blew it. The FDA will haul your ass to court. I'll see to it. Bail will be set so high you'll go to prison. You can kiss your daughter goodbye. You had a choice and you made it and fuck you."

"I've got her." Cory stepped toward him, though she was already telling herself to shut up, go inside, and lock the door. "She's upstairs, safe and sound, fast asleep. And I'm not going to write the paper, I wrote it. I don't need your files. I'll see *you* in court. See how you feel facing parents of one dead child after another. Let's see how a jury feels. Maybe the judge will make an example of you and send *you* to prison. How would that be? Bankrupt and all your money gone and bail so high *you* won't make it. You'll be the one left with nothing."

He stepped toward her. "No one threatens me." He hefted the bottle, hurled it at the tree, and missed his mark. It fell to the grass with a thud.

He whirled around, marched off the porch, and crossed the walk, elbows pumping. The driver of the car jumped out, and Art Farber stood on the sidewalk and waited for the door to be opened. Then he got in, the door slammed, and the car roared off into the night.

***

Art sank back into the limo as Hank pressed a button that closed the dividing window between the front and backseats. "No deal?" Hank asked when the glass was fully closed.

"God-damned cunt," Art spat.

"What did she say?" Hank looked alarmed.

"She'll see me in court."

"Relax, boss. She can't use what she stole. If she tries, she goes away for hacking. Our representatives are cracking down. They've had it with cyber attacks and leaked secrets. There's no mercy for hackers. Did you mention her kid?"

"She says she got her back. Tell me she's lying."

"She is. I talked to the judge myself. The kid's gone for six months."

"Cold fucking bitch. She couldn't care less about her kid." She reminded Art of his mother, may she rest in peace.

"Did you offer money?" Hank asked.

"Three million. She turned up her nose. She's fucking nuts. She said she wrote a paper comparing Oxylace to the cocktail. She said *I'll end up bankrupt and in prison.*"

Hank cracked his knuckles, one after the other. "That was disrespectful. We need to teach her a lesson."

Art turned to the window. "We go all out."

"Agreed."

"I never want to deal with her again."

"Got it. Why don't you go home? I'll stay and take care of it."

"Don't let it come back to us."

"It won't, Boss."

Out the window, Art saw the sign to the airport exit on the left-hand side of the road. He couldn't wait to get out of this back-ass-ward hellhole of a town.

Chapter Fifty-four

April 24th

Mathew didn't come home until two a.m., and Cory was waiting for him, pacing and sweltering. She'd closed all the windows, chained and locked all the doors. She ran outside to greet him.

He looked tired and haggard. "What are you doing up? Why is every light on?"

"Art Farber was here."

Mathew stopped walking. "Why didn't you call me?"

"I didn't want to disturb you."

"That's not disturbing me. If you're upset, call me."

They went to the kitchen, with Mathew turning off lights as they went. He opened a bottle of wine and poured two glasses. She sat down at the table and confessed her foolish outburst. She'd just lost it. Art Farber tried to buy her off, offered to get back her job and her daughter, which made her furious. He didn't know Sophie was back, and she had told him. She hadn't mentioned the class action lawsuit directly, but she talked of court and him facing the parents of dead children. She told him she hoped he'd go bankrupt and go to prison, and he hoped the same for her. She took a sip of wine, then put down her glass. "I knew I shouldn't have said anything, but I couldn't stop myself. I told him about the paper. He was slinging all these threats, and it just came out." She began to cry. She was completely out of control.

Mathew's explanation brought no solace. "You've had a lifetime of burying feeling. You have no practice containing your emotions, so out they come. You'll learn how to handle them."

She wasn't so sure.

"Art's a dangerous man. Did he say how he'd get back your job?"

"I gather Congressman Harris."

Mathew formulated a plan while Cory guzzled wine. They had to protect themselves. Strike a deal with the congressman. They knew Wellspring contributed millions to Harris's Super PAC. In exchange, Harris sent his aide to Duane and paid off the judge who swung the custody hearing. They were serious charges that could topple the congressman and the judge. Cory would agree to keep quiet if the congressman told Art Farber to leave her alone.

It sounded like a good plan, and the more she drank, the more she liked it.

"We'll go to Austin when I finish exams," Mathew said. "Next Saturday."

Cory shook her head. "I'm going tomorrow."

"You can't go alone."

But she could.

***

The next morning, she was driving to Austin. She had no plans to see the congressman. She was going to see his right-hand man—the two-faced, duplicitous Drake Mansfield who stole Sophie's DNA and bought off Rios. She found Drake's address on Sixth Street from Art's confidential email. A Google search showed it was one of Congressman Harris's local offices.

She dropped Sophie at day care and sped west, driving just under ten miles over the speed limit. Her stomach was grumbling and she was hungry, but she was too on edge to eat. If she was going to get her life back and live without fear, she had to strike a deal. Somehow convince Drake to get Art to stand down. It would be like bartering with the devil.

She rolled down her window and blasted country music in an attempt to distract her thoughts. It was a bright day. The sun was climbing in a cloudless sky, and she regretted leaving her sunglasses at home. She drove and tried to name her emotions. It was a technique Mathew said would help her get in touch with them. He claimed emotions were powerful—energy in motion. She came up with anger mixed with fear, outrage aligned with righteousness, and futility mired in determination. She knew she was in a heightened emotional state and, one way or another, had to keep control. It would be hard going. Overnight, her rational state of being had vanished. She had changed. She was more emotional, but she also felt more alive.

She arrived in the state capital just after eleven. The office on Sixth Street looked like a convenience store. The door was unlocked, and she went in. The room was packed with cartons marked with the Apple logo stacked floor to ceiling. There was a sound of an electric drill, and she walked down a narrow aisle between the cartons. Near the back, she found Drake assembling computer desks. He looked up, his jaw dropped, and he turned off what turned out to be an electric screwdriver. "Uh . . . uh . . . uh . . ." he said as she approached.

"Cory Montclair. I'd like to make a donation. How much will it cost me to buy a judge? Oh, wait. I know. A hundred thousand."

He pulled his stunning smile. "Is this a joke?"

"I was waiting for the newspaper to write a retraction, and then I learned you weren't a journalist but a political hack for Congressman Harris. How nice to meet you."

Drake looked around hesitantly. "Who told you that?"

Cory dropped her briefcase on a table and pulled out the photograph of Drake and his congressman. The surfer stared at it, mouth agape. Cory said, "Back to the judge."

"What judge?" Drake blinked stupidly.

"The judge who ruled in my custody hearing. The one who awarded my child's father full custody for six months. Somehow he ended up with two fancy Austin lawyers and my daughter's DNA." Cory heard her voice rising and couldn't stop herself. "DNA that you took from her hairbrush in my bathroom."

"You can't prove that," he said.

She took a deep breath, backed up, and turned her back, willing herself to calm down. Maybe if she didn't look at him she could speak calmly. Staring at brown paper that covered a window, she said, "A corrupt judge ruled Sophie would be better off without me."

"I'm sorry to hear that."

"I'm sure you are." Cory whirled around, pointing an accusing finger. "Too bad for you, the father identified you as the jerk who paid him seventy-five thousand to fight for custody." She turned over the paper with his picture and jabbed her finger at Rios's signed statement.

"You met with him, you drank with him, and you gave him money. You left a trail."

Drake's tanned face blanched. He seemed smaller, less confident. He opened his mouth and then closed it. He had no defense.

She strove for an even, steady tone and found it. "You know what I think? You did it for your boss."

"No."

"Yes. And why? Because your boss preferred to keep his hands clean and gave you the dirty job. Only, you botched it." She shook her head sadly. "Rios has his money, and I know all about it. I'm sure the Federal Election Committee and the Office of Judicial Ethics would be interested to hear how your boss gave Judge Tobin a hundred thousand dollars to fix this case."

"Where are you getting this information?"

She didn't answer. "I wonder how many cases the judge has fixed for your boss. With them both up for re-election, I'm guessing this wouldn't be a good time for this to get out."

"I understand you're upset about your daughter. I'll give you money. You can get her back."

He hadn't talked to Art Farber; he didn't know she had Sophie. She wasn't going to tell him. "I lost my job. And my NCI grant."

"I'm sorry to hear that."

"I'm sure you are. How convenient your boss sits on the Oversight and Appropriations Committee that oversees funding for the National Cancer Institute. For no reason, they cut my grant. How hard is it for the government to find fifty thousand dollars?"

"I know nothing about it."

"Talk to your boss. He knows. What is the committee that investigates government malfeasance?"

Drake held out his hands. "Look, we can settle this. All of it. What do you want? Would a hundred thousand dollars help?"

"So, I'm worth as much as a judge and more than a no-good father."

Drake pulled his winning smile. "I think we can say that." He sidled toward her.

"I want my job back and my funding."

"Absolutely. I'll make it happen. Just to be clear, in return for a check, your job, and your grant, you will be quiet. You will not mention Congressman Harris or Art Farber under any circumstance."

"Oh no, you're not cutting a deal on Art's behalf. You tell him to leave me alone."

"Look," Drake said, raising his hands and looking helpless. "No one tells Art Farber anything. I can only speak for myself and Congressman Harris." Drake checked his watch. "I'll talk to him. Run it by him. It's almost noon. What say we do lunch? Wait for his answer. I live nearby; we could pop in. Finish what we started." He flicked his eyebrows. "Seal the deal."

He was coming on to her. After everything he had done. How could she ever have found him attractive? She picked up her briefcase. "I have to go. Talk to your boss. If you don't keep your end of the bargain, I go public."

He laid a hand on her arm. "We'll work it out. Don't take this personally. I was just doing my job."

He had taken her daughter's hair and used everything she told him against her. He had made it personal.

His phone rang. He checked the screen, hit a button, and raised the phone to his ear. He listened intently as he stared at her. She mouthed good-bye and left the building.

***

She lunched alone at the Pecan Street Café, one of Austin's old restaurants. She ordered a cheese croissant and a beer for lunch, and she ate thinking about the money. She could fix up her house and pay her bills. Had she really struck a deal? Would she really get a check for a hundred thousand dollars? It seemed too easy.

She finished lunch feeling sleepy and ordered a tall espresso for the road. She drove back to Duane as if in a dream, spending the money in her mind. She was tired and caught herself nodding off. She had almost reached Duane when she was blinded by a bright light. She lowered the visor, blinked away stars, and tried to focus on the road. Through the rearview mirror, she saw a white sedan driving too close.

She was instantly awake. She hadn't been paying attention. She sped up, the sedan fell back, and her vision cleared. She fixed her eyes on the road, blinking away the light. The sun was at the zenith, shining vertically, not horizontally. She pressed down on the accelerator and checked the mirror. The white sedan lost ground. There were no other cars behind it. Only a slow-moving tractor coming her way.

The sun must have reflected on something inside the car. She slid her seat backwards—which was why when the light came again, she wasn't blinded but saw the stripe of blue light fall sideways on the lap belt. There was a flash in the rearview mirror, and the light was gone. A glance at the mirror showed the white sedan gaining ground as the tractor choked by, spewing black smoke.

She was on a quiet stretch of highway with no major turnoff before Duane. The road was surrounded by fields, no nearby houses. There was a jolt, and the Beetle shot forward. She'd been hit from behind. The white sedan was on her bumper. Then came another bright flash, bringing blindness.

She gunned the accelerator, blinking hard and seeing a black field of vision. The road was straight. She kept the wheel fixed, heard a horn, and veered sharply to the right. Too far. She hit the shoulder and bumped along the gravel verge as her vision cleared.

The white sedan kept up, holding steady and matching her speed. She took one hand off the wheel and twisted the rearview mirror hard to the right. Pebbles flew at the windshield. The car was shaking violently. She couldn't maintain her speed. She began to brake and steered back onto the blacktop. Down to fifty. She could slam on the brakes and cause an accident. But that could be the goal—to have her stranded and the car disabled. This was Texas, where everyone had guns.

A stream of cars came at her and passed as if nothing was amiss. A look over her shoulder showed the white sedan still at her bumper, refusing to pass, despite her slow speed. She accelerated again, soon going eighty, far too fast for an old Volkswagen Beetle that smelled of burning oil. The bright light came again, now bouncing off the wing mirror. She swung her arm out the window and punched the mirror to the side.

Railroad tracks appeared ahead, and she bounced across them, hoping not to blow a tire. She reached for her purse, searching for her phone. Crap in her purse got stuck. At a sharp curve up ahead, she left her purse and gripped the wheel as the white sedan slammed her again, this time shooting her into the middle of the road.

A horn blared. A semi had rounded the corner, lights flashing. The white sedan passed on the right, pushing her to the center. The truck advanced, slowing, arcing in the road, brakes screeching. Foot off the brake, she spun the wheel to the right, over correcting. She hit the back of the white sedan, and then the right barricade. Her car spun out. Time slowed. The horn of the semi blasted. She heard the scream from the recurring dream as the out-of-control car went airborne.

Chapter Fifty-five

Later, pitch darkness, loud hammering. In the distance, people mumbling. It took Cory a moment to recognize the pounding was coming from inside her skull. An eye was pried open. A blinding light brought an involuntary cry. Someone said, "She's awake."

Cory slowly opened her other eye. An African-American man she didn't know loomed above her with a pen light. "Pupils reflective." He squeezed her shoulder. "That's good."

"Where am I? Who are you?"

"Is she all right?" Mathew's voice sounded far away. Someone took her hand. She knew from the feel of it that it was his.

"What happened?" she asked as he slowly swam into focus.

The first man had questions. She had to say her name, where she lived, follow his finger, and she guessed she got everything right for he faded away, and Mathew grew close.

"You hit a semi," he said. "You were going over ninety."

"Where was I?"

"You don't remember? You were fifteen miles outside of town. Speeding. The police may charge you with reckless driving. They're waiting for the drug screen. You had a blood alcohol level of 0.06."

"I was drinking?"

"Apparently." Mathew sunk down on the bed. It made a noise. He lowered his voice. "You went to see Congressman Harris."

"I did?"

An authoritative voice in the background announced that trouble with short-term memory was to be expected in the case of a head injury, such as a concussion. It wasn't necessarily a sign of brain damage. Her memory of the accident might come back. Then again, it might not.

Brain damage? Cory lifted her head, trying to get her bearings. She was tangled in a thin tube. An IV. She ripped it out before anyone could stop her. An alarm shrieked. Both in the room and in her mind. She was in a hospital. "I want to go home."

"They have to do a cat scan," Mathew said. "To make sure your brain's not bleeding. If it is, you need surgery."

She squinted at him. "Where's Sophie?"

"With Dana. I'll get her on my way home. You've been out eight hours. How do you feel?"

"Like shit."

Cory closed her eyes. She must have fallen back to sleep for when she awoke, Mathew was gone, and the IV was back and two orderlies were transferring her to a gurney. Time for the scan. It was dark outside, and she looked at her watch but the face was shattered. She asked the time and learned it was one a.m.

She was back in her room at three and couldn't fall back to sleep. A nurse urged a sleeping pill. Her scan was fine; there was no bleeding, and she could have pain medication. Cory didn't want any.

Morning came early at the hospital. Nurses and doctors changed shifts, and students lined up to check her eyes. A bland breakfast appeared, and that was the final straw. Cory checked herself out. She was starving. She didn't want this food or the IV that could be given in its place, if she preferred. She didn't want to wait for the main doctor, and she didn't want any more tests. The sooner she got out, the safer she'd be. She put on bloodied clothes and combed her hair with her fingers. She had a row of stitches on her forehead, two bruised knees, and a swollen left hand. She grabbed her purse, called a cab, and went home.

***

It looked welcoming in the early-morning sunshine. She paid the cabbie and walked to the house, limping slightly. She heard the piano, stopped by an old oak and rested against it, listening to the melody. Were the ghosts looking out for her? She could have been killed in the crash. Had the house brought her home? She patted the tree and went inside. The music grew louder.

She went to the dining room. Mathew was playing the piano! Sophie sat on his lap, and Pluto lay by his feet while he worked the pedal. His fingers flew across the keyboard. He looked up, finishing with a flour-ish. "Well, look who it is. We were just about to come get you."

Sophie raised her arms. "Mama."

Cory bent down slowly and hugged her close. She kissed Mathew hello, rubbed Pluto's head, and sat down on the bench beside them. Her head was throbbing. "I couldn't stay." She took Sophie from him. "I didn't know you played. Why didn't you play before?"

"I didn't feel like it. Now I do." He played another ditty, fingers nimble and light as they skipped across the keys. He had rhythm; small wonder he could dance.

"I thought the piano was out of tune."

"That may have been me. How do you feel?"

"Like I was in a car wreck. Where's my car?"

"In the police yard. It needs body work."

"I want to see it." She hoped it would jog her memory.

They dropped Sophie at day care and went to the station. Cory told Mathew to go on to school; he still had exams, but he didn't want her to be alone. Besides, she had no car. As Mathew claimed, hers had to go to the shop.

It was out in the police yard. Two of the tires were blown. The front passenger side was crushed. There was blood on the driver headrest and on the seat. She limped around the car, her knees hurt-ing. There were scratches and white-pitted dents at the rear, a gash along the right side, and a dent in the front left. She flaked white paint chips into her palm. She noticed a surveillance camera on a lamp post and swiveled her palm, holding up her hand to record on film what she had.

Mathew was squinting and sweating in the bright sun. "What are you doing?"

She showed him the paint flakes. Her memory was coming back. Drake was going to give her a hundred thousand dollars to keep quiet. "Did the police mention a white car? A sedan?"

"All I know is that a red Honda Accord and a blue Toyota Corolla stopped. The semi was black."

She tried to open the driver-side door. It was inoperable. The passenger door worked, and she got into the car and sat down. The rearview mirror was twisted to the right almost as far as it would go.

The driver's wing mirror was broken and facing outward. The passenger wing mirror was in place. There was a receipt and an empty coffee cup in the holder, and she picked them up. She got out of the car sweating; it was as hot as an oven.

She walked to the rear of the car, got out her cell phone, and snapped a picture. She ran her finger along a deep gouge, collected more white paint, and took another photo. "There was a white car. It had a laser. It blinded me."

"There were witnesses," Mathew said. "They didn't mention a white car."

She opened her purse, got out her wallet, unsnapped the change compartment, and brushed in the paint. She pointed to the mirrors and took more pictures. "What did the police say about the mirrors?"

"Nothing. They must have figured they were twisted in the crash."

"Two out of three? The two I could reach?" She raised her bruised left hand. "I punched the mirror to block the laser. Can Tyler access the Department of Motor Vehicles' database?"

"We'll ask him."

"I want to know what kind of car Drake drives." She had seen his car the night they met when he followed her home after dinner. It was a coupe of some kind—could have been a sedan, definitely not a pickup—but she had no recollection of the color. Her mind had been on other things.

"You think Drake did this?"

"I saw him. He offered money. He got a phone call when I was there. Likely an order to run me down."

Mathew shook his head sadly.

She didn't know if it was in response to her seeing Drake, or what Drake had done. "Should we tell the police?"

"They ruled it an accident, and you've got no proof."

"The police just have to look at the car."

"You've got pictures. We'll call the mechanic. See what he says."

She had to call a tow truck. That was seventy-five dollars. The cost to keep the car in police lockup over night was a hundred and fifty dollars. Who knew how much the mechanic would charge to replace the tires, fix the driver's door, and do the body work. She had a high deductible.

The tow truck came and would deliver the car to the mechanic. Mathew had to get back to school. He drove her home and left her his car. He would bike to school. "Lock the doors," he said. "Keep your phone in your pocket. Stay home; don't go out alone. Call me if anything goes wrong."

Chapter Fifty-six

May 1st

Operating on high alert, Cory kept Pluto, pepper spray, and her cell phone within reach. She kept the doors locked but the windows open to let in the breeze. She took a week off. Mathew was still writing finals, and she kept Sophie home. They built Lego houses, swung on the swing, and went for long walks. Eventually Cory's head stopped hurting, the stitches came out, the swelling went down in her hand, and she stopped limping. Not until she got a letter from Brenham Community College informing her they had no open positions did she return Sophie to day care and focus anew on finding a job. Hospital bills were coming in, her health insurance had just ended, and her mechanic's bill was fourteen hundred dollars.

On her first morning back in the study, she checked a week's worth of email. Buried in a long list was a message from the *Canadian Journal of Cancer*. They were responding too quickly. The news had to be bad, and it was. They would not publish the comparison paper. The editor could not even consider it for evaluation, let alone publication. In fact, the veterinary trial with Oxylace had been suspended. The Canadians were unaware that the FDA had long ago closed the book on the drug.

Cory felt deflated but not surprised. She had only herself to blame. She had told Art about the paper, and he had taken care of it. Unfortunately for Wellspring, there were many other reputable refereed journals in the world.

After an hour-long search, she decided to submit to the *German Journal of Cancer Research*. According to Janie, Germany was way ahead on health care and had no qualms prescribing and using what the FDA deemed "unsafe." Instead of heart surgery, the Germans used chelation therapy on the evidence that EDTA unblocked blood vessels. They used the banned DMSO as a carrier for drug delivery. Best of all, the article didn't have to be translated. If accepted, the article would be published in both English and German. Cory checked the turnaround time and was stunned to see the efficient German response time was one to two weeks.

Only minor changes in format had to be made to adapt the Canadian paper to the German style, and most of these were in the references. Cory was making the changes when a dark car with black-tinted windows pulled into the drive. She called Pluto, grabbed her phone, and pulled the pepper spray out of her pocket.

A well-dressed man in a three-piece suit came up the walk. Pluto began to bark. She pulled up Mathew's number, put her thumb over the send button, and went to the door. She kept the chain engaged and stared through the crack.

The man passed her a business card. John Murphy, J.D., worked in the same Austin law firm as the twins. He removed his sunglasses. "I am here at the behest of Congressman Harris."

Cory undid the chain, opened the door, and let Pluto out. Murphy backed up, hands up guarding his face. Pluto growled and sniffed his feet. "Will he bite?" Murphy asked.

"If I tell him to."

Murphy put a letter-sized envelope down on the railing and backed down the steps. "This is for you."

She picked it up. The flap was unsealed. Inside was a check. It was made out to her for the sum of one hundred thousand dollars. She gulped with difficulty. Was Drake keeping his end of the bargain? "What is this?"

"The congressman heard about your sick daughter and your medical bills and was touched and wished to help."

Was it a trick? Was she being set up? Would she be arrested as soon as she tried to cash the check? "Is it certified?"

"Naturally. It's as good as cash."

"How did the congressman hear about my daughter?"

"He's engaged in the community. Known throughout the region for his generosity. It was further brought to his attention that a university grant you had was rescinded, and I am happy to report, it has been restored. Please understand it was an incompetent mistake." Murphy pulled a heavy letter out of the inner breast pocket of his black blazer.

"I have a document that certifies this concludes your business with the congressman."

She walked to the edge of the porch and took the paper, wishing Mathew was home so she could show it to him. She checked her watch. He was about to start an exam, and this wasn't an emergency. She read the document. She was agreeing not to take the congressman to court for any perceived or actual transgression that might have or may take place. She looked at the lawyer. "The congressman is absolving himself from any mistakes he may make in the future?"

"That is correct. Absolution from anything that may or may not occur at any time."

"Does that include murder?"

Murphy must have thought she was joking because he laughed, and said, "No."

Cory stared at the letter. "I agree to forget the past, not the future. The congressman is not off the hook for anything he may decide to do down the road."

"Scratch it out." Murphy did it for her. "Sign at the arrows, in three places."

She did so and gave him the letter. He studied it for a moment, folded it, and shoved it into his pocket. He gave her an unsigned copy. "Enjoy your day, Ms. Montclair."

Yes, it was looking up. She stood on the porch and watched Murphy drive away, wanting to turn cartwheels across the lawn. She stared at the check. Was this the end of it? The lawyer said it was as good as cash. There was only one way to find out. She grabbed her keys, hopped into her newly repaired VW bug and drove to the credit union.

She filled out a deposit slip, eyeing a security guard warily. As soon as she cashed the check, would an alarm go off? She went to a teller, heart thudding.

The teller took the check and examined it closely. She turned it over, frowned, then handed it back.

The hammering of Cory's heart escalated. The check was no good.

"You have to sign it."

That was it? Cory grabbed the pen on a chain and scribbled her name.

"Would you like a receipt?"

"Okay," Cory said.

The teller confirmed the funds were available immediately. "Would you like to make a cash withdrawal?"

Cory would. She withdrew five hundred dollars just to see what would happen.

The teller counted out the cash. "Is there anything else I can help you with?"

"Yes." Cory rented the smallest safety deposit box possible and placed within it the steel box, chips of paint, Rios's letter, and the mechanic's testimony that her car was likely in an altercation with a white vehicle.

She pocketed the key and walked out into bright sunshine, unable to stop smiling. When killing her didn't work, the congressman had coughed up cash. But what of Art? Who ordered the hit? Was she safe now or not?

At least she had money. She drove to the hospital and went to the business office where she had to wait forty-five minutes to see the be-jeweled Terrance Killjoy.

"You're back," he said, wearily. She obviously bored him. Today he was sporting a bright ruby earring, a thick gold bracelet, and a heavy silver watch.

"Last summer you mentioned a reduction in my bill if I paid it in full."

He tapped at his computer, bringing up her file. "You said that wasn't possible."

"If it is?"

"Your bill is what it is."

"I spoke to the insurance company." This was no lie, although she had spoken to them in September. "They agreed to pay forty-five thousand for your services."

"Yes, but they didn't pay."

"And if they changed their mind?"

"It would be news to me."

Of course, the insurance company hadn't changed their mind. They'd washed their hands of her long ago. "I am willing to offer you fifty thousand to settle the bill."

"Is this the insurance company?"

"Does it matter? Money is money." She was suddenly furious. "Why should I pay eighty-five dollars for a baby aspirin and they only pay forty?"

He rolled away from his computer and folded his arms over his chest, and she knew she had blown it.

"I'm sorry, that's not what I meant. I'm a single mom. I'd like to pay off my bill, honor my debt." She choked over the next words, though they were, in fact, true. "The hospital did save my daughter's life." It had made Sophie sick, she had to stop chemo, and that had saved her life.

"I saw the article in the paper about you. Did DCS take your daughter?"

"Of course not."

"May I ask the source of the funds?"

"Congressman Harris. He heard my story and was touched."

Killjoy scooted his rolling chair closer to his desk. "Why didn't you say so?" He pushed a button on his phone. "We can settle this right now. Fifty thousand, you say?"

She walked out of the hospital thirty minutes later—fifty thousand dollars poorer but with fifty thousand still in the bank. She could buy life insurance, start a college fund, fix up the house, and pay off her credit card. Inwardly dancing, she skipped to the car. Then she called Mathew and shared her good news. He brought her back to earth.

"Don't let your guard down. Not for one second. This might be the end of Drake, but we haven't heard the last from Art. He doesn't give up."

Chapter Fifty-seven

May 2nd

Thursday afternoon, Cory was strolling the grounds with a contractor, discussing replacing the roof, painting the house, and refinishing the floors, when a university car pulled up to the curb, and Dr. White stepped out. She left the contractor and met him on the path.

Under the glare of the sun, Dr. White looked like he was roasting. "I've been trying to call you," he said. He moved under the shade of an oak, removed his sunglasses, and gazed at the house. "I didn't know you lived here."

She shrugged.

"Great news," he said. "I have spoken with the NCI director personally. She's quite embarrassed. It seems there was a mix-up. She rectified the mistake, and your grant has been reinstated." Dr. White reached into his pocket and pulled out her university ID card. "I would personally like to invite you back."

Cory didn't move. Drake may have gotten his boss to restore her funding, but that wasn't the only problem. "What did the president say?"

Dr. White lowered his arm. "He has not been notified. There was no wrongdoing. You lost your funding. It has been returned."

"What about my progress report?"

"I forwarded it to him as he requested. You have your funding. That is all that matters." He pulled out a hanky and dabbed his forehead. "We have missed you. After covering your classes and your lab, I think you have been underappreciated. I have managed to procure a faculty parking sticker for you."

She folded her arms together. Would she get her job back, only to lose it again? It would be like getting a paper accepted, only to have it rejected. Had Art figured out that after Sophie, her work was her soft spot? She loved her job, and she missed it. "What about Megan's thesis?"

"I'm afraid she quit."

"School?"

"Her thesis. She will not graduate with honors. Her father had hoped she would go on for a Masters, but that is not possible now. At least not at a top school. He is disappointed, naturally."

"You didn't tell me he ran the two biggest peanut butter companies in the country."

"I hoped it would not be a problem." The sun went beyond a cloud, and Dr. White lowered his hanky. "Will you return? You could start tomorrow. We have the funds."

She wasn't going to make it easy for him. "I'm looking at other options."

"I am not surprised. Full disclosure, I have spoken with Nick Biget. He mentioned you and his wife submitted a joint grant proposal."

"We probably won't get it."

"I wouldn't bet against either of you." Dr. White stared across the lawn at the house. The contractor positioned a tall ladder against the side and began climbing. From the window of the study, Pluto was staring but not barking. "I've been here before," Dr. White said. "Many times. I knew your mother."

Cory looked at him quizzically.

"I didn't realize it until now. Your mother did not take your father's name. To me, she was Mary Elizabeth Rose. It was unusual at the time for a woman to maintain her maiden name, but then your mother was an unusual woman. A nuclear physicist of all professions."

"You met her at the university?"

"High school. She and my wife were good friends. We were here often. Your mother had many parties."

Cory couldn't imagine her grandmother allowing strangers into the house. "Parties? Here?"

"She decorated the house with big white lights. Half the town came. Of course, the basketball team. Your mother played. Both in high school and college. She was very good."

"I didn't know." Maybe that was where Sophie got her interest.

"All the neighbors would come. Your mother said they had to be invited so they would not call the police. We danced all night. Your father played the piano. A finer pianist you would never hear."

Cory had no idea he had played the piano.

Dr. White pointed to the window at Pluto. "They had a dog. He looked like your dog. His name was Goofy. Short for Goofus D. Dawg."

Cory blinked and stared at the trees. Goofy and Pluto. Dr. White knew more about her family than she knew. "What happened to him?"

"I do not know. After the accident, your grandmother retreated into the house. She wished to be left alone. She had lost both her children. A son in the war, a daughter in a car crash."

"Did you go to the funeral?"

"Of course. It was held at the campus auditorium. You do not remember? You were there with your grandmother. Your head was still wrapped in a bandage."

"It was? Why?"

"From the car crash."

"Wait. I was in the crash?"

"You were in the backseat."

"I wasn't there."

"You were. I remember it distinctly. It was Christmastime, late at night. You were going to North Carolina. It was snowy, mountainous terrain. There was ice on the road. The car slid on black ice. It was going downhill, and the brakes were of no use. The car went over a cliff and fell two hundred feet. If witnesses hadn't seen the crash, you would have frozen to death. They got you out. The car was crushed. Your parents were dead. There's a newspaper article about it. It was a miracle you lived."

The recurring dream. Her grandmother had said it was nothing, just a nightmare. Mathew had said it was a sign Cory's life was out of control. She thought it was a warning about the crash she'd just had. They were all wrong. It was a memory. It was real.

The contractor was coming down, and the ladder was rattling. Dr. White watched him descend. "Will you come back? Must I beg?"

"To finish my post-doc?"

"And beyond."

"Is that a guarantee?"

"Not in writing, but you have my word that I will do all I can. We will have to advertise the position of course, but I feel it unlikely we will find someone with your ability, or your grant potential."

"What about the university president?"

"This is a departmental matter."

Cory had two conditions. She wanted to choose her own students and would continue to push for Oxylace.

Dr. White watched the contractor lower the ladder. "You are free to run your lab as you see fit. So long as there is no conflict with your work, you may do as you please on your own time. Just remember, actions have consequences."

"As does inaction." Cory offered her hand. "Dr. White, I accept your offer."

"Call me Rupert." They shook heartily. "I will see you tomorrow?"

Cory shook her head. "Workmen are coming."

Rupert sighed heavily. "Let me know when to expect you."

***

That night, Mathew came home past midnight. He crawled into bed quietly, and she scooted toward him. "Dr. White came by."

"You're awake."

"I got my job back."

He moved closer and kissed her lips. "That's good."

"You know that recurring dream? The car that goes off the cliff? It really happened. I was in the car with my parents. Dr. White knew them." Cory felt Mathew's body stiffen. If his mind had been wandering, it was focused now.

"There's the trauma. It's not that your parents died, it was that you were with them when they did. This is what your unconscious has been trying to tell you. What did your grandmother say about the accident?"

"That my parents went away for Christmas and left us. She said it was always me and her. I wondered why they would leave me. Only they didn't. I remember it now. I was in the hospital. My grandmother came and said I had to be strong. I couldn't cry."

"And you stopped crying."

"Yes, Dr. Freud, until I stopped stopping." She leaned into him and kissed him. "I had a dog named Goofy. I think my grandmother gave him away. He looked like Pluto."

"Similar name. The mind is a wonderful thing."

"I want to have a party. My parents had them. They invited the whole street. I'm going to put up the globe lights. You can play the piano. We'll celebrate you becoming a lawyer."

"And you getting your job back."

"The house getting a facelift."

"And the class action suit."

"The summer."

"And us."

"And us," she agreed.

Chapter Fifty-eight

May 3rd

Friday afternoon, at four forty-five p.m., a class action suit was filed by the law firm of Barrow and Craft on behalf of Jane. E. Bartlett and consumers across the country. By five thirty, Mathew was home and watching the stock. Analysts' predictions were still rosy, and according to Tyler, Art Farber had dumped no shares.

It was time to celebrate. Mathew had finished his last exam in the morning and started work at his new job after lunch. Cory found the corkscrew, and Mathew opened the thousand-dollar bottle of Chablis that Art had tossed on the lawn. Mathew poured two glasses, and they toasted each other. The wine had an amber hue, tasted vaguely of apples with a hint of lime, and left a metallic aftertaste that Cory didn't find palatable. She'd had cheaper wine that tasted better. She poured Sophie mango juice and took a sip to clear her throat.

They went out back. Sophie got on her bike and walked it around. Pluto found a stick and began tearing it to shreds. Cory and Mathew swung on the swing. "What happens now?" she asked.

"If the court accepts the complaint, the clerk will draft a summons and officially notify Wellspring of the suit and assign a judge. Wellspring has twenty-one days to respond. Then everyone gets together and decides how to proceed in the discovery process. The judge has fourteen days to sign off on that and then will set a court date."

"What's our chance of winning?" Cory asked.

"Hard to say. It depends on the judge." Which didn't seem to be the way a legal system was supposed to work, but there it was. "If the judge grants a subpoena for Wellspring's computer files, we've got them."

"Won't they delete the Phase 3 files?"

"They'll be in contempt of court, and we'll still get them."

"What about doctors and employees? Have you started talking to them?"

"We will as soon as we agree on discovery. We'll ask the court for carte blanche access to anyone on Wellspring's payroll and anyone they've given money to in the last year. This will include all their political friends and those connected to the government, like the FDA agent."

Pluto brought Cory the stick, and she reached out her hand to play tug-of-war, but he took off with it, bounding across the lawn. "How many people have signed up for the suit?"

"So far, more than nineteen hundred. There will be more. The firm's going all out on advertising, looking for new plaintiffs. After tonight, there'll be a TV and online advertising blitz."

"How much money will Wellspring have to pay if they lose?"

"Could be in the billions. It could bankrupt them."

"Will you be able to bring up Oxylace in court?"

"If they open that door, we'll go through it. Have you heard anything back from the German journal?"

"It's only been a couple of days. It takes a couple of weeks."

Mathew sipped his wine. "We're not in a time crunch. Typically, these cases don't move fast. Wellspring will drag their feet. They'll use every tactic they know to discourage plaintiffs. I wouldn't be surprised if they subpoena you."

"Me?"

"They know you're behind this. They know they were hacked. They suspect it was you and will try to trap you."

"I'm not going to talk to them."

"They can force you. Take a deposition."

"What's that?"

"Their lawyers will meet with you and question you under oath."

"I won't help them with their case."

"They'll do their best to trip you up."

Cory didn't like it. "Art tried to run me off the road. Does he really want me to talk under oath?"

"There's no evidence. You can't say a thing about your crash. The police ruled it an accident."

"What's Tyler been doing?"

"Writing exams. Now they're over, so he'll have time. But he warned me the motor vehicle database is a hard nut to crack." Mathew glanced at his watch. "It's time."

He meant the stock market had closed. The hour of preferential trading was over.

Mathew got out his phone and posted a notice on Facebook that the lawsuit had been filed. A quick online search showed rumors of the suit had already made financial headlines. There was nothing Wellspring could do to protect their stock price over the weekend.

Chapter Fifty-nine

The right of the individual to elect freely the manner of his care in illness must be preserved ... We consider it sheer arrogance to believe that people in government know what's better for the people than they know themselves.

—U.S. President Dwight Eisenhower

May 6th

Art's phone had been off when news of the class action suit rang out around the business world. He was at home with his ladies, Missy and her rapacious friend, Ramone, dining on fine wine, caviar, and escargot, all known to promote sexual vigor. Hank interrupted him. Unable to call, The Fixer came over, finagled a spare elevator key from security, and barged in. That was how Art and the ladies learned about the suit. The bastards had filed just before trading closed for the week. They shot out press releases, and Hank was among the first to hear.

Now, fifty-five hours had passed, and Art was staring out his beloved window watching the sun sink on what looked like his last week in the downtown office. Despite four divorces, Art had never felt so alone. Outside, the city was in the throes of spring and burgeoning with life, while death shrouded Art and his company.

He glanced wretchedly around the room, eyeing the fine polished table, the abstract art, the gleaming marble floors, and the bright skylight. It would all soon be gone. The CFO said they had to tighten their belts. Embrace austerity. As if they were the government! The office had to be sold, leased, or rented. Immediately! Any money owed and not yet paid would not be honored. Every spare dime was needed for employees. Art had to keep his people happy. Especially his physicians. He couldn't have them turn on him now.

Like his women. With Hank's dreadful news, Missy heard the word bankrupt and fled. She would not return his calls. Ramone, who would talk to him, called him a disgusting deviant and never wanted to see him again. His weekend prayer that the stock would weather the news had gone unanswered. In the morning, shares opened at 65.70 and declined all day. In six and a half hours alone, Wellspring shares lost almost twenty-five percent of their value. Analysts unanimously downgraded his stock to a sell. Faced with this bad news, Art had to address the board.

The meeting began at six thirty with every member in attendance. Legal sat in a row of chairs lined up against the wall, with Art at his usual place, standing at the head of the great table. He opened his mouth but was too choked up to speak. Hank rose, but Art waved him down. He took a sip of water and began. "I'm afraid we have to prepare for the worst. As you all no doubt know, the stock closed at 49.38 and will likely keep falling."

"What the hell happened?" shouted Martin Little of Universal Health Insurance. "I've sunk every penny I've got into this place."

"It's a fucking lawsuit," Art said. "A hazard of the game. We got the summons this morning. Nineteen hundred have signed on. So far. No doubt their scumbag lawyers will troll for more."

"Who's behind it?" Martin asked.

"The bitch behind Enough Nasty Drugs who's pushing the Access to Medical Treatment Act. Along with Montclair. She hasn't signed onto the suit, but her fingerprints are all over it. Those cunts want to overturn our health care system and cripple the pharmaceutical industry. They're gunning for us."

There was silence in the room as board members digested the news.

"Is there a case?" Martin asked. His eyes were as icy as his tone.

"You know how chemo works," Art said. "We kill the cancer. Sometimes it kills the patient."

"Can't Alexander do anything?" asked Connor Loy, the ex-congressman from Wisconsin.

He was referring to their man in Washington, now awol. Congressman Harris had stopped taking their calls. Art was so mad at him, he refused to discuss him.

"He won't talk to us," Hank explained. "This morning he returned our nine million Super PAC contribution. He doesn't want any connection to Wellspring, not before the election."

"He's way down in the polls," Loy said. "I'm not sure he'll be much help in the future anyway."

"We've got Kelly Mann," Art said, comforted by Connor's news. "She hasn't returned any money." He liked a politician who could weather a storm. If the company's fortunes improved, he'd jump on her bandwagon. He knew who his friends were, even if Harris the weasel had forgotten.

"How much insurance do we have?" Martin asked.

"Four hundred million," Art said. "We have about half a billion in cash, and a suit this size could cost three to four billion." Just saying the numbers made him feel sick.

"Should we settle?" asked Amet Patel, obviously also discomfited by the numbers. "Cut our losses?"

Art shook his head. He would never stop fighting.

"The FDA will not be able to assist," Amet warned. "Claude has no choice but to convene an independent panel to examine Valurex. He would most like you to voluntarily withdraw the drug from the market."

"He can fucking forget it," Art said. "It saves forty percent of cancer victims. What about the sick?" He would hold on. Even after the best-selling depression medication was shown to be no better than a sugar pill, sales were still half a billion dollars a year. With good marketing, he could weather the tsunami.

The IT manager, sitting with the lawyers, wanted to know if they should delete sensitive files from their server. Art looked at the lead lawyer. It was the easiest solution.

Robert Burns was on his feet. "Absolutely not. You pull a stunt like that and we all go to jail."

Art glared at the man, and Burns sat down. He was a stickler for the books. Burns had forbidden Art to sell any of his stock over the weekend. He was afraid the SEC would pounce.

"Right now, plead ignorance, admit no wrongdoing," Burns advised. "We fight this in court. Your files are proprietary. Trade secrets. Not for public consumption. We'll keep them private. No one will see them. They're as good as shredded."

"I was hacked," Art nearly shrieked. "A crime was committed. I want Mont-fucking-clair's head in a noose. File criminal charges against her."

Burns agreed it was a good strategy. "A crime in the virtual world is no different from a crime in the physical world. We were burglarized. A theft occurred. Hackers go to prison." He would liaise with IT and get the police and FBI on board. "A good judge will send her away for twenty years," Burns said.

"Do we have a good judge?" Art asked. "Can we meet with him discreetly and tell him what Montclair did?"

"Absolutely not," Burns repeated. "That's judicial interference. We depose her. Trap her. She can perjure herself or confess. Either way, she's in trouble."

For the first time in hours, Art smiled.

"We could pressure the plaintiff," Hank said. "Distract Jane E. Bartlett. Get her busy with other things."

Art liked it. "Do what you have to do." Then Art offered the plan he'd been devising and revising since he'd heard the bad news. They would let the corporate headquarters go. They'd pack up, head back to the New Jersey warehouse, and soldier on. Wellspring had tentatively agreed to a Houston court. His opponents wanted Austin, but if it came down to a jury trial, he didn't want to face tree-hugging liberals who thought disease could be cured with meditation and vitamin therapy. He'd already signed a contract with the largest firm in Houston to help with the case. In the meantime, no one would be furloughed. No one would be laid off. On the contrary, raises all around, compliments of Alexander Harris's refund. The good thing about the cocktail was name recognition. He needed his sales force on the ground pushing his drugs. Even an FDA warning wouldn't do much damage. While doctors would see the warning, his people would be there, calling for caution. The truth was, Valurex was the best drug on the market. Nothing even remotely close was FDA approved. Marketing would remind people of that. Their PR team would be on call around the clock to answer negative news, apply positive spin, and monitor all impending video and print publications. They'd pump out fifteen-second TV ads, reminding folks across the country that Wellspring was a name they could trust.

It sounded good to the board, and no one had anything else to add. Amet thought Art should star in the commercials, but no one else seconded the motion, and it was dead in the water. Art closed the meeting and the sad room cleared, save for Hank.

After everyone left, he closed the door. "There is some good news," he said. "Montclair submitted a paper to the *Canadian Journal of Cancer* that compared your cocktail to the Mexican drug. The paper was rejected immediately."

Art sat down. He couldn't believe it. Montclair wasn't making idle threats. She'd written the fucking paper. "Do we have a copy?"

"We'll get it." Hank caught his eye and shrugged feebly. "I'm sorry. This is my fault. I thought the surfer could handle it."

"Is he gone?"

"In Honolulu. Lying low. They'll never find him."

"What do the police know?"

"They ruled the crash an accident. Montclair's a danger to the road."

"She's a danger to civilized society."

"She was poking around the police yard. Snapping photos, taking paint samples. She knows it wasn't an accident. Who knows what she plans to do about it."

"Find out," Art cried. "Depose her. See what she says under oath. Keep that P.I. on her. I'm done with fucking surprises. We get her for hacking. Or for contravening the drug act. I don't care which. I want her in prison."

"She's got money now. Thanks to Congressman Harris."

The scumbag had bought protection for himself, the judge, and his aide—all for a measly one hundred thousand dollars. When Art had offered her three million! And she had her job back. Art stared out the window. She'd blackmailed them. She learned Harris had paid the judge to fix her custody case, and they'd bought her silence. Art ran a hand across his scalp. Montclair had steamrolled all over them. He should have throttled her with the thousand-dollar Chablis when he had the chance. Shoved it up her ass.

Hank left, and Art called Missy. When he was this wound up, there was only one release. Now her phone didn't even ring. She must have turned it off. He flung his phone on the carpet and stomped it to pieces. He'd had enough distractions anyway. He had a war on his hands. It was time to focus.

Chapter Sixty

May 8th

Wednesday night after dinner, Cory got a call from Janie. She was being audited. Cory was in the foyer and sat down on the stairs. It was after eight, light outside, and the roofers were still hard at work, pounding shingles. Cory had a bad headache and could hardly hear. Mathew had taken Sophie to the park to escape the ruckus.

"The IRS wants my last three returns," Janie said. "The only problem is, Greg has them. He couldn't be more obnoxious and unhelpful. I've got to pay the accountant to go through our records and somehow track down hard copies of receipts of charitable donations Greg says he doesn't have." She sighed loudly. "I'm flying to L.A. tomorrow. What's all that noise?"

"Roofers," Cory said, staring at the refinished floors. They had been sanded and varnished and were gleaming. The wainscot on the walls had been cleaned and buffed, and the ceilings were painted. A cleaning agency had gone through the place, and it looked brand new. The only problem was a strong chemical smell that was nearly overpowering.

"Wellspring did this," Janie said. "They want me out of the way. Too busy to find new plaintiffs. Meanwhile, they distract you with a deposition."

Cory couldn't say she hadn't seen it coming. "Anything I can do?"

"We need money. Can you ask the roofers to take a break?"

"They're almost done. I'll write you a check."

"We need lots. There's a new bill in the works. The Good Health Act."

"Sounds promising."

"Except it's legislation to enact the exact opposite of what it says. The act will make it illegal for any citizen to seek any health care option not sanctioned by the FDA."

"I thought that's what we had."

"No. The current law controls physicians. They can only use AMA- and FDA-approved treatments. Up until now, citizens have been exempt. The bill targets people like you. If it passes, you won't have the option to try alternative methods, or refuse treatment. You have to do what the FDA says or you'll violate the law. Expensive, useless, poisonous drugs for everyone."

"And this is called The Good Health Act," Cory said. It came out as a shout, for the banging had stopped abruptly.

"Yes, to protect the people."

"You mean protect the drug companies. Will it pass?"

"It might. It's being pushed as a means to rein in charlatans eager to line their pockets selling worthless snake oil."

Cory watched a line of Mexican roofers descend down the ladder. This was their first day on a three-day job. She rested her forehead in the palm of her hand, reveling in the silence.

"Are you still there?" Janie asked. "They're holding Dr. Arrango up as an example."

Mathew was working with his legal team. He was trying to get him out on bond, so far without success. He thought the comparison paper would help, but Cory had not heard back from the German journal. "I'm here," Cory said. "The roofers are leaving."

"Phew. I'm going to L.A. I won't be able to do any fundraising. When's your party?"

"On the lunar eclipse on June 25th. You still coming?" Cory waved at a worker, who was waving at her though the window.

"We could combine it with a fundraiser."

"What? A fundraiser? No. That's a bad idea. I—"

"It's a great idea. You plan the party, I'll plan the fundraiser. The audit will be done by then, and I'll be free."

"Janie, I've never had a party before."

"Think about it. I'll talk to you after the deposition. Good luck with the lawyers." Janie hung up.

Cory closed her phone. It was the worst idea she'd ever heard. She was nervous enough about having a party.

Chapter Sixty-one

May 10th

On Friday morning, Cory was heading to Houston. Wellspring was moving with unprecedented speed. They responded to the court summons with a request to meet with Mathew's lawyers. Wellspring's first order of business was to slap her with a subpoena. Now she was on her way to a deposition. Declan Craft, senior partner of Barrow and Craft, was representing her, and Mathew was coming along for the ride. He had warned her that Wellspring wanted one thing—to know who had hacked into them. Whatever happened, she had to protect herself and not give Tyler up.

Declan was at the wheel of a late model Cadillac. He was dressed casually, in black slacks with a short-sleeved white shirt and thin red tie. In contrast, Mathew looked stiff in a brand-new brown business suit. He was sitting in the backseat and looked hot. She was dressed in a black suit—her only suit—the one she had planned to wear to Sophie's custody hearing.

"Just tell the truth," Declan advised. "You'll be under oath." He was a nice-looking man with a congenial manner. In his early sixties, he had a shock of white hair, was lean, of average height, and healthy-looking. A man vigorous enough to fight a formidable battle. "The whole case rests on whether the judge will subpoena their files. If he does, we'll win. Wellspring wants to know what you know about their files. They're certain they've been hacked."

"What do I say?" Cory asked.

"You can't incriminate yourself," Declan said. He didn't want to know the answer to the question. "You can plead the Fifth. Refuse to answer. Just don't give them anything they can take to the judge."

Cory looked at Mathew. "They'll try to knock you off guard," he said. "Watch out for abrupt changes in direction."

"They want to get under your skin," Declan said. "It's discovery, so they have wide latitude."

"They'll try to make you mad," Mathew said. "Get you to react from an emotional center so you'll stop censoring yourself."

"Good thing I'm so rational," Cory said, dryly. It couldn't be further from the truth. These days her emotions were percolating near the surface and ready to explode without notice.

Houston had traffic, and they arrived late at the glass building owned by the firm of Chambers, Cruz, York, Ryder, Toscano, Dworkin, Fazzio, Sanchez, Foradori, Rottenberg, and O'Keefe. According to Mathew, it was one of the biggest law firms in the state and the country. The Houston office had three hundred and twenty lawyers practicing all areas of law. Fifty associates had been assigned to the Valurex case. The firm was no stranger to consumer class action suits.

But then Declan Craft was no stranger either. According to Mathew, he had a long history of successful suits against the drug industry. He lived a healthy lifestyle because he'd rather die than see a doctor. The American health system appalled him greatly.

He pulled up to the curb of the blue glass building, dropped Cory and Mathew off, and went to park. Inside, the ambient temperature seemed about sixty degrees, and the sweat on Mathew's brow dried quickly. They passed through security and took a silent elevator up to the forty-first floor. They were shown to a conference room that had glass windows overlooking the south side of the city. Beyond that, in a haze, lay Galveston Bay.

The deposition began thirty minutes late. It was being audiotaped and videotaped, and Cory was instructed to ignore the camera. A court reporter with thick glasses sat at the end of the long table with her laptop, recording everything. There were three Wellspring lawyers led by Helen Shapiro. She was young, Cory's age, and had long blond hair that came to her waist. Helen also wore a black suit, but hers was tight and came way above her knees. Two older gentlemen whose names Cory didn't catch flanked Shapiro on either side. Cory sat between Declan and Mathew, and the two teams faced off across the width of the table. Everyone had water—not bottled—but in fancy crystal glasses, which matched a pitcher on a far table.

Practical information was taken for the record, and then the questioning began.

"You are not a plaintiff in this suit, correct?" Helen asked. "Please answer yes or no."

"No."

"Do you have plans to become a plaintiff?"

"No."

"What is your relationship to Wellspring Pharmaceutical?"

"I don't have a relationship with them. On one occasion my daughter received one course of their chemotherapy cocktail."

"Was it against your will?"

"No. At the time I believed any drug endorsed by the FDA was safe, but I was wrong."

"Please keep your opinions to yourself. Your daughter got MRSA. Do you blame Wellspring?"

"Are you asking for an opinion?" Cory took a sip of water and stared across the table.

"Just answer the question."

"I blame the hospital. Apparently, hospital-acquired infections happen all the time."

"Please refrain from commentary. When your daughter was out of ICU, why did you stop chemo?"

"I saw what it did to her."

"Excuse me. I thought she got MRSA. She was in ICU on account of a staph infection, not a bad reaction to chemo, correct?"

"All right, she wasn't strong enough to handle more chemo after she got the infection."

"Was that the opinion of her doctor?"

"It was my opinion."

"Let the record reflect that Ms. Montclair is not a medical doctor. Now then, you sought alternative treatment."

"I went to Mexico. Sophie got one shot of a drug that—"

"Thank you. Your daughter is currently healthy, is that correct?"

Cory was not going to allow her to gloss over this. "Thanks to Oxylace. It cost one—"

"Please answer the questions that are asked. Do you have proof your daughter is alive today because of alternative treatment?"

"Oxylace works. Forty-four other patients—"

"We are not seeking testimonials. Have any scientific studies shown the treatment you sought was effective?"

"Yes."

"The paper you wrote?" Shapiro lifted a piece of paper. "'A Statistical Comparison of Chemotherapeutic Drugs?'"

"Yes." If Shapiro thought Cory would be surprised Wellspring knew about the paper, she'd be disappointed.

"Where did you get the data?"

Cory heard Mathew gasp. The three opposing lawyers leaned forward. Shapiro lifted her eyebrows. Declan said, "I'd like a five-minute recess."

"Let the witness answer the question," Shapiro said.

The room went silent. The typist stopped tapping. Cory took a gulp of water. "I got the data from a Mexican clinic and the FDA. I filed a FIOA request, and they complied. Not that they had a choice."

"What about Wellspring?"

"Aren't their files the same as the FDA's?"

More silence. Shapiro frowned, Mathew relaxed, and Declan chuckled. Cory wondered if Wellspring thought she was so stupid as to use stolen case files in the paper.

"Is this paper published?" Shapiro asked skeptically.

"Submitted," Cory said, ambiguously. She wondered if Wellspring knew about the German journal.

"So, no," Shapiro said. "Are you aware a scientific paper *was* published by the FDA on this alternative treatment?"

"It was bad science. The—"

"Excuse me. Is this your opinion, or has the paper been discredited?"

"Anyone who has looked at it seriously can see the flaws."

"I'll ask you again, has the paper been discredited?"

"It should be."

"So, no. Do you know computer programming?"

"Some."

"What languages?"

"Java. C. Python."

"So, you're computer literate."

"I wouldn't say that."

"But you could breach a firewall."

"No."

"Do you know anyone who could breach a firewall?"

Mathew stiffened again. "Maybe," Cory said. "I know people at Wellspring know how."

"Are you accusing Wellspring of hacking?"

"Yes."

"Do you have proof?"

"They published private information that could have been acquired only through hacking."

"What information?'

"My personal emails and correspondence ended up in an article in the newspaper that Wellspring wrote."

"You have proof of this?"

"Ask them. Talk to their communications director. He'll tell you."

"You were in a car accident recently, is that correct?"

Shapiro hadn't followed up; she'd changed tack quickly. Was she not going to dwell on the hacking? Cory immediately felt lighter, as if a weight had lifted. She took a sip of water, finishing the glass. "I was in an accident, yes."

"What happened?"

Declan objected. "Relevance?"

Shapiro said, "She's lobbying accusations. Perhaps she's going to blame her accident on Wellspring as well."

"The police ruled it an accident," Cory said.

"Is the case closed?" Shapiro said.

"For now."

"Meaning?"

"As I understand it, cases can always be reopened when new evidence comes to light."

"Is there new evidence?"

"I'm not in contact with the police. You should ask them."

"Do you have evidence the Wellspring cocktail did not contribute to your daughter's recovery?"

Another quick change in direction, and Cory moved with the flow. "Sophie didn't finish chemo. People who do finish usually die."

"Again, I am referring to evidentiary proof."

"My daughter is alive. Most kids under four—that would be about ninety-eight percent—die after taking the Wellspring cocktail."

"Where did you get this figure?"

Shapiro had trapped her. The statistic had come from the Wellspring data. Under oath, disingenuously Cory said, "Facebook."

"This is your evidentiary proof?"

"Broken down by age, what percentage does Wellspring give?"

"I will remind you that we are asking the questions and you are under oath. Did you illegally access proprietary files owned by Wellspring?"

Cory would not be let off so easily. After skirting the issue, Shapiro was tackling it directly. "No," Cory said honestly. Tyler had taken advantage of what he called a security hole.

"Do you know who hacked into Wellspring?"

Cory looked her in the eyes. "No." Tyler didn't work alone. He had help from an anonymous team, and she didn't know their names.

"Do you know Lyle Steele?"

"No."

Shapiro smiled, looking like a shark closing in on her prey. "Maybe a class roster will refresh your memory?" Shapiro passed a piece of paper across the table.

Cory and her lawyers were given a list of the students enrolled in the spring semester's pharmacology class. Lyle Steele's name was underlined. "I remember him now," Cory said. He was the former political science graduate and FDA contractor who was currently doing an MBA. "Can I get some more water?"

One of the lawyers jumped up and refilled Cory's glass. Shapiro waited until he was seated to continue. "Does Lyle Steele know computer engineering? Would he know how to get past a firewall?"

"I don't know. He worked for the FDA. Maybe they taught him."

Declan chuckled again. Cory was beginning to relax. Wellspring had no idea who hacked into them, and the lawyers were fishing. She took another sip of water.

Shapiro changed direction again. "Ms. Montclair, have you ever done drugs?"

"What?"

"Answer the question. Yes or no."

"Not recently."

"I'll take that as a yes. While you were pregnant?"

"No."

"Do you drink?"

"Occasionally."

"While you were pregnant?"

"No."

"Do you smoke cigarettes?"

"No."

"Did you work while you were pregnant?"

"Yes."

"You work with solvents, known carcinogens and toxins. Is it possible your daughter's illness arose from in utero exposure to chemicals from your lab?"

Cory gripped her hands together. "I don't see what that has to do with anything." But it was a question she asked herself endlessly. She handled radioactive DNA bases, known carcinogen solvents, and concentrated aflatoxin. While Cory was pregnant, Evonia had miscarried, and months later, Sophie had gotten leukemia.

"Answer the question," Shapiro said as she stared across the table with sharp focus. "Is it possible?"

"Anything is possible. The whole planet is polluted. Sophie could have been exposed to toxins at day care, riding in the car, shopping in the store, or out in her stroller breathing so-called fresh air. I know she was definitely exposed to toxins when she was in the hospital taking IV drugs that were approved by the FDA."

Shapiro rolled her eyes. "What is the incubation period for cancer?"

"Twenty years."

"Come now, Ms. Montclair."

"It varies."

"Did you cause your daughter's leukemia?"

She looked at Mathew, and he winked at her. What did that mean? Don't get mad? Keep composed? Stay rational? "I assume it was a mutation. A random event."

Shapiro lifted her eyebrows. "Caused by the toxins you work with? After your daughter was born, did you take her to your lab?"

"Infrequently."

"Could she have been exposed to toxins there?"

"Doubtful. No one in the lab has had any problems."

"Yet, one of your own undergraduate students was recently in the hospital."

"That was different."

"Megan Carson went to the hospital as a result of your carelessness."

"Not mine. Her own."

"Are you married?"

"No."

"Can you explain why no father is listed on your daughter's birth certificate?"

"I didn't want to list him."

"Mathew Lang, the man on your left. Are you in a current relationship with him?"

Cory looked at him, and he smiled at her. "Yes."

"A sexual relationship?"

"So what?"

"Last month, did you have a sexual relationship with Drake Mansfield?"

"No."

"I'll remind you, you're under oath."

"No."

"Really?"

Finally, Declan Craft found it necessary to object. "Asked and answered." He looked at Cory. "Right?"

Cory nodded.

"Did the Department of Child Safety try to remove your daughter from your home?"

"No."

Shapiro routed around her file, pulled out a piece of paper, and passed it across the table. Declan glanced at it and then gave it to Cory. It was a photocopy of the offensive article from the *Duane Tribune*. "The allegations are untrue."

"Let the record reflect that, according to the *Duane Tribune*, the DCF was investigating the disgraced scientist for child endangerment."

"It's a lie."

"Has there been a correction?"

"I asked for one. I'm still waiting."

"Why were you cited by the university safety officer for hazardous lab practices?"

"I wasn't."

"Let the record reflect that according to the *Duane Tribune*, Ms. Montclair was cited for hazardous lab practices." Shapiro leaned forward. "Is it possible that your vendetta against Wellspring is a response to your own guilt at endangering your child?"

"Objection," Declan said. "Calling for a conclusion."

"I'll rephrase. You and your daughter have obviously suffered physically and financially from the leukemia. Do you blame yourself for her illness?"

"No. I blame Wellspring for marketing bad medicine. For blocking good medicine."

"So, this is about revenge," Shapiro said triumphantly. "Is that your motivation for this lawsuit?"

Cory sat forward, leaning across the table. "You want to know my motivation? I want people suffering from cancer to have access to a cheap, effective treatment like Oxylace."

"Would you break the law to have that happen?"

"No. But Wellspring would break the law to prevent it from happening."

Shapiro closed her file. "We're done."

One of their lawyers jumped up and turned off the camera. Everyone packed their things. As if it had been a civilized encounter, everyone shook hands. They were all friends now.

Downstairs, Declan went to get the car. Cory and Mathew waited for him on the sidewalk. Cory breathed in the heavy, humid air. "I wasn't expecting that."

Mathew put his arm around her. "You held up pretty well. This is what they do. Look for weak spots. I thought she had you a couple of times."

"Did I give Art any ammunition to use against us?"

"I'd say no if it was anyone else but Art. He's a man who doesn't give up." Mathew pulled her close. "Do you really think you put Sophie in danger? That you caused her illness?"

"I think about it. I'll always wonder. I could have exposed her to something. I'll never know."

"What about when she was born? The tests they gave her. Who knows how safe they were."

He had a point, but that wasn't it. "She was supposed to be born at home. Her placenta was to be buried near a tree. That's the way it's done. It tethers her to the land. Without it, she's hanging on by a thread." A low jet flew by, and the windows in the glass building shook with the roar. When the plane was gone, she added, "I know it sounds irrational, but that doesn't make it less real."

Mathew didn't object. "Hey, we know ten percent of what makes the world tick. Still, your mother died in a car crash and your uncle in a war."

"They didn't get sick."

"Sophie's fine. You saved her."

"For now. But the clinic is closed, the doctor's in jail, and she could get sick again. Then what?"

"That's why we're fighting."

Chapter Sixty-two

May 13th

On Monday, Cory was back at work. She arrived early, parked in the faculty parking lot, and lugged a heavy box to the lab. Still expecting the floor to drop out from under her, she considered waiting a week before moving in but decided against it. She was the only candidate to make the shortlist, and Rupert assured her the university president would exert no undue influence.

Evonia was in the lab making coffee. "Thank God you are back."

Cory dropped the box on the lab bench. "It's good to be here."

"White has been just a nightmare," Evonia complained. "He is dictator. He told me what to wear and what not to wear. Does he think we are in Russia?"

Cory smiled. From the look of her attire, it didn't appear Evonia had taken what he said to heart. She was decked out in black.

"When we hear you are returning, I am surprised you did not hear us from your house crying with joy. We are all seriously dancing. White said there will be none of that at work."

The coffee stopped dripping, and Evonia poured two cups. "How is Sophie?"

"So far, so good."

"And the house repairs?"

"Finished." Cory pulled an invitation from her briefcase. "We're having a party."

Evonia read the invitation. "An unusual combination. View the lunar eclipse and raise money for Enough Nasty Drugs. Hmmm. How will you raise money?"

"I'm not sure. Janie is taking care of that end." And Janie was refusing to discuss it. "You can come dressed like that."

Evonia nodded her head. "I accept."

Cory took a sip of coffee and received an update on the lab.

"Brian graduated. He refused to sign up for the summer until he heard you were returning. He will be here shortly. Megan did not finish. I asked White why she quit, and he said it was not my concern. As if I did not know. What is happening with Joe?"

"He'll retire in August. Rupert's organized a search committee to find a replacement and, confidentially, I'm on the top of the list."

"Rupert now. It is Christmastime in May." They clinked coffee mugs.

Cory went to her office. Joe's name had been removed from the door, and the office was empty and clean. She opened the blinds and unpacked her box. She arranged her favorite textbooks and recent photographs on the shelves. Most were of Sophie. There was one of the family taken at dusk, smiling on the steps of the newly reinsured, revamped house. It looked alive. The lights shining in the windows glowed like eyes in the twilight.

She turned on the desktop computer, wondering if Wellspring still had access. Mathew had warned her not to use it and not to wipe it clean. The installed spyware could be used as evidence in court.

She opened her laptop, logged in, and checked her email. The German journal had replied. In the subject line, Cory read: Thank you for submitting . . . She clicked on the email. It opened quickly, and she scanned it rapidly. They agreed to publish! She leapt up out of her chair and punched the air. She danced around her desk and quietly clapped her hands. Once composed, she sat back down and reread the email. The editors were apologizing for taking so long to respond. It had been all of twelve days! The statistics had been verified, and the paper was accepted "as is." They wished to know her university affiliation and whether a July publication date would be acceptable. She typed a hasty response and sent Mathew a copy. He was finally making headway in arranging bail for Dr. Arrango.

There was more good news. Joe had forwarded her an email from the *Journal of Microbial Science*. The aflatoxin paper was going to be published. Joe was now listed as first author, though he had done nothing but give advice. Unable to convince the *American Journal of Pharmacology and Toxicology* to reverse their decision, they had submitted it to the *Journal of Food Chemistry*, who also rejected it.

At least the breadth of Wellspring's influence didn't extend all the way to Germany. The comparison paper would be a blow. Wellspring was fighting to stay alive. Art was throwing everything he had at the lawsuit. He had fifty lawyers scheduling depositions and browbeating plaintiffs. If any of the sick or deceased ever smoked, drank, was overweight, had a stressful job, was divorced or poor, they were attacked for unhealthy habits that contributed to their own mortality or illness. Their bad health certainly couldn't be blamed on a bad drug. As for the kids, well, if they were in such an environment, it was likely their home or their parents had killed them.

Cory knew firsthand how effective their tactics could be. They made private shame public. It was an effective strategy. Plaintiffs were dropping from the suit at an alarming rate. At one time, over nineteen hundred people had signed on, and now, even with new recruits, they were down to twelve hundred.

Art was on an advertising blitz. He was still promoting his cocktail as if it was the best thing on earth. He accepted no blame and admitted no wrongdoing. The American Medical Association was on his side and fully endorsed the cocktail. In the words of the AMA president, "It's the best treatment for cancer we've got. People would be stupid to refuse it. The lawsuit is a great disservice to the war on cancer."

Wellspring lawyers were trying their best to get the suit dismissed. The Houston judge was still deciding whether to subpoena the Wellspring files and had scheduled a meeting with the lawyers in June to address the issue. The judge publicly declared he was the recent recipient of fifty thousand dollars in campaign donations from the drug lobby. He signed a waiver asserting the donations would not influence any legal decisions. Mathew's firm asked the judge to recuse himself, but so far he had refused.

Meanwhile, Mathew's lawyers had fanned out and were interviewing doctors involved in the clinical trials, as well as current and past Wellspring employees. No one had a bad word to say about the company. Tyler, still in their system, learned everyone had gotten raises. They also got letters threatening dire repercussions if any employee spoke to anyone about the lawsuit without a Wellspring attorney in attendance. So far, employees were toeing the line. As for the Department of Motor Vehicles, he'd hit a wall he couldn't breach. Not that he was giving up.

Cory's phone rang, and Dana was on the line. "Are you back?"

"I'm here."

"I'm coming over. I've got news."

Fifteen minutes later, Dana breezed in carrying a cup of coffee and wearing her standard garb—boots, jeans, and a white button-down shirt. She positioned a chair to her liking beside the desk and sat down. "The proposal passed the vetting process and is approved with medium priority."

"So, no money," Cory said.

"Not yet. We'll keep submitting. We'll get high priority three to four years from now."

"Great."

Cory must have looked disappointed, for Dana quickly added, "It will work out. You'll be on hard money once you get a faculty position. When we get the grant, use it for tenure. Apply the same year, and you're home free. The department will never let the money go."

"Does the university president have to approve every tenured professor?"

"Forget about him," said the everlasting optimist. Then she explained. "Wellspring reneged on their endowment. They can't make their payment. The board is furious. They voted the president out. Edwin Reed is gone in August."

That was unexpected news. Cory tried not to smile. Could she finally let down her guard and accept that life was back to normal?

"How's the lawsuit?" Dana asked.

"Looking better," Cory said. It was turning out to be a happy day. "The Germans are going to publish the Oxylace paper. We'll have a scientifically refereed article to counter the FDA's 1950s paper."

Dana clapped her hands. "Nick said the Access to Medical Treatment Act is coming up for a vote. If that passes, it will be a new day for medical care in America. Doctors can go back to being doctors."

Cory had to tell her about the competing Good Health Act that would give the FDA firm control over the nation's health. "We'll see which bill passes." With the election looming, Janie held little hope. Candidates were loath to piss off their most generous lobby. In the modern democracy, money was everything, and the people's will meant nothing. Which was why Janie said they had to raise money—and lots of it.

"We're having a party," Cory said. She handed Dana an invitation.

Dana read the invitation and raised an eyebrow.

"I know. A lunar eclipse party mixed with an END fundraiser. We need money for advertising. Let people know that the bills are coming up and to pressure their representatives."

"Sounds like a plan."

"Janie is organizing the fundraising part. I'm doing the party. I've never had one before."

"I'll come early and help you. Are the house repairs finished?"

"All done."

"Phew, I don't think I can take any more of that pounding."

"You and me both."

"Who plays the piano?" Dana asked. "I hear it all the time."

"Mathew." Though more played than he. At times, Cory heard it at night when he was lying in bed beside her. He couldn't hear it, but Sophie could. At times it woke her up, and they would listen as Cory rocked her back to sleep. "Moosic nice," Sophie once said. "Maffew downdairs?" But he was fast asleep.

"How is Mathew?" Dana asked, with a gleam in her eye.

"Good."

"You make a nice couple."

"He's good with Sophie."

"And with you. You look happier, more relaxed. I told Nick you'd be together before summer started." Dana raised one eyebrow and smiled a sly smile.

"You knew better than I," Cory said.

Dana finished her coffee and left.

The day passed quickly. There was paperwork to fill out, training videos to watch, and people to see. Cory left just after five. Mathew had picked up Sophie and was making dinner. Cory had a leisurely drive home. The semester was over, many undergraduates were gone, and traffic was light, even in rush hour. It was her favorite time of year. The sun was high, the days were hot, and night came late. She turned on the radio, rolled down the windows, and hummed along to the music. Stopped at a light, she listened to the traffic report unperturbed. In ten short weeks, life had changed. She'd paid off her debt, there was money in the bank, and the house was fixed. The publication of a scientific paper on Oxylace was pending. The university president was on his way out, and Mathew was in. Cory was no longer on her own. She thought it would never happen, but the unimaginable had become real.

She turned down Pecan Lane and pulled into the drive. Mathew, Sophie, and Pluto were waiting on the front steps and rushed out to greet her. Squirrels dashed across the grass and birds sang in the trees. The land felt alive as the sun streamed down, shining brightly on a house built to last.

Chapter Sixty-three

One of the first duties of the physician is to educate the masses not to take medicine.

—*William Osler, Father of Modern Medicine*

May 25

The party-slash-fundraiser was starting at eight, and Cory was nervous all day. She had no idea how the two events would mesh and was apprehensive her first party would be a bust. Mathew advised that she do what she could to prepare and step aside. Whatever happened would happen; it would be out of her hands.

She took Friday off, cleaned the house, and cooked what she could. To Sophie, all parties were birthday parties, and she wanted to know whose birthday it was. Fundraising aside, Cory explained it was just a party, a get-together with people to have fun. But that was too foreign a concept for a toddler who'd spent her life in near isolation. Cory finally said it was a party for the house, and after they strung the white globe lights on the front railings, Sophie got it.

Cory had invited over a hundred guests, but she had no idea how many would show. People wanted to bring friends, and that was no problem. She invited all the neighbors on the street, and that was twenty, not counting kids. She had invited Nancy, though Mathew lobbied hard against it: "She's a stalker!" But Cory held no grudge, nor did Nancy: "I always knew I wasn't his first choice. More like bait." Her initial response was no, but upon hearing there'd be single men and an activist contingent from Hollywood, she decided to think about it.

Janie also invited a hundred people. She was bringing old friends from L.A., including two A-list movie stars, Angelica and Jonathon Pine. A producer from *Sixty Minutes* was a maybe, and a former Texas senator and his wife were confirmed. Move To Amend volunteers were coming from Austin and Dallas, and the END contingent was flying down from D.C.

Cory wanted details about the fund-raising portion, but all she knew was that Janie had planned a game. Everyone would have a ball— as long as there was enough booze. From the looks of the bottles lined up on the sideboard, they would not run out.

Six o'clock came, along with Dana, Nick, and Frankie. While the kids watched cartoons, Mathew fired up the smoker, and Cory and Dana made salads and dip. The garden was in full production, and they were having homegrown lettuce, eggplant, squash, corn on the cob, carrots, and tomatoes. For meat lovers, there was barbecued pork ribs, beef, and Sophie's favorite, chicken. There were chips and dips, salads and casseroles, and cookies and plates of petit fours from the Blé Sucré Patisserie. Cory was full long before the party ever began.

She made drinks. She had found two lunar eclipse drink recipes online and mixed them up. A Baja Luna combined black raspberry liqueur with vanilla liqueur and was served over ice with cherries. A Lune Rouge Sang was blue, not red, and was a mixture of lemon vodka and blueberry Kool-Aid. There was also beer, wine, and an assortment of hard liquor. Anyone who drank too much to drive was welcome to spend the night.

Once the barbecue was smoking, Mathew and Nick rearranged the furniture. They carried the dining room table outside for the food, which made room for dancing. Now that Cory had a dance partner, she was looking forward to it. Sheryl and her three kids appeared, and Cory paid Penny twenty bucks to watch Sophie. Tyler and Layla came with a telescope. They set it up in the backyard, aiming it at the eastern sky where the full moon would soon rise.

But there were clouds on the horizon that seemed to be gathering. Tyler chewed a fingernail and stared pensively at the darkening sky.

"Worried about the weather?" Cory asked. It was on her mind. The last thing she wanted was a thunderstorm to drench the barbecue and muddy the lawn and her rugs.

From behind her, Layla said, "It's his full-moon fretting. Emotions running high like the tide. His parents are coming."

"Actually, I'm thinking about the lawsuit," Tyler said.

"We won't give you up," Cory said. "You invited your parents?"

"Janie made him," Layla said. "They're driving from Austin and should be here soon. Jill and Blaze Madison. He's a former U.S. Senator."

Ah. Cory wondered how Janie had gotten them to come.

"My dad was trying to pass AMTA for years," Tyler said. "Even before my sister got leukemia."

"I can't wait to meet them," Cory said.

Tyler stared at the trees. "Don't tell them you know me. Don't mention the deposition or the lawsuit. They're so suspicious."

"You don't have to worry," Cory said. "Nothing happened at the deposition. The lawyers were fishing. They don't know about you. They think it's someone else."

"Congress is working hard to pass new laws that target hackers," Layla said. "In their view, Tyler's a terrorist. He's a government subversive who poses a grave threat to national security. If they don't manage to catch him, he could be hit by another car or run off the road like you."

Tyler turned and looked at her. "Speaking of which—"

She didn't let him finish. "You found out what kind of car Drake drives."

"A 2010 marshmallow white Chevy Impala."

"If I have paint chips, could they be matched to a white Impala?"

"I don't see why not. Only he sold the car. Dumped it in Lubbock soon after your crash. A few days later he bought a brand-new orange Silverado. It's registered and licensed in Oahu, Hawaii."

"The surfing capital of the world." She patted his arm. "Thanks, Tyler."

He nodded and resumed staring at the sky.

There was a commotion out front. Janie and a crowd were coming up the drive. It was the team from D.C. They were walking billboards with everyone wearing END T-shirts in varying colors. They brought pamphlets, signs, brochures, and sign-up sheets. Janie made introductions, naming too many names to remember. She wanted to move the entrance table out on the porch and grab people as they came in.

"Do whatever you want," Cory said. "Just remember, this is also a party. What's the game?"

"You'll find out."

"How did the audit go?'

"Fine, if you overlook what a pain it was and the number of plaintiffs we lost while I was busy with stupid things. I did manage to see Dr. Arrango. He wanted me to thank you and Mathew for helping him get out."

Cory was glad he was free. But there was a condition—he couldn't reopen his clinic. It had been terrible news. His clinic was the best, and now it was gone. Options for alternative effective treatment even outside the country were dwindling. Elected leaders seemed determined to eliminate good health care. To wipe it off the map.

The Weisses appeared and brought their laptop. Janie's gang cleared the edge of the table to make room for them. If any guests weren't already friends of Danny Weiss or END, Daniel would help them sign up. Anyone who wanted to join the class action suit could sign up.

The house was filling up. Most of the staff from Campus Care came, as did unknown neighbors, and lawyers from Mathew's new firm. Old friends from law school also came, as did the three grad students from Cory's lab. Evonia and her husband arrived on time and suitably dressed in dark clothes.

A limo pulled up, and the Hollywood horde emerged, and Janie went to greet them. Sophie's pediatrician, Haygood Robinson came solo, for yet again his wife was called away for a delivery. Cory ran into him in the kitchen and poured him a glass of non-alcoholic punch because he was also on call. He had seen Sophie in the living room and never doubted that Cory would win custody. She did not enlighten him.

"I wish I could have done more," he said. "As it is, the AMA wrote me, asking for details about Sophie's treatment. An official from the Texas State Medical Board came and photocopied your file. This was after the custody date, so I am not clear what that was about. Routine, I was told, though there was nothing routine about it."

"Did they censure you?"

"I am very careful. I don't like it, but it is necessary. I know very well they are not above sending pseudo patients to assess my bedside manner. Unfortunately, I am bound by professional ethics to recommend and prescribe only AMA- and FDA-approved treatments, many of which I do not approve."

"Can't doctors do anything?"

"The playing field is leveled against us. I don't know what the answer is."

Cory knew. Get money out of politics.

There was a hubbub in the foyer. Cory thought it was the movie stars, but it was Brian the undergraduate, accompanied by Megan Carson and Lyle Steele, the MBA student of interest to the Wellspring lawyers. Brian looked instantly uncomfortable and had to go find Evonia about a matter of extreme importance. After apologizing for crashing the party, Lyle went with him.

Megan had no apology. She was dressed in a stunning black dress with black heels, and looked more relaxed and happy than she ever looked in the lab. "You have a lovely home," she said.

"I hear you dropped your thesis."

"For that, I thank you. You were right. I would never be happy in a lab." Megan scraped the sole of a high heel lightly across the polished oak floor. "I never wanted to do science. I'm no good at it. In fact, I hate it."

"What will you do?"

"I've been accepted into the graduate program at Harvard."

Cory's jaw dropped. Was there nothing money couldn't buy?

"In theatre," Megan said, seeming to enjoy Cory's shock. "All I ever wanted to be was an actress."

"You'd be good at that."

"My parents think it's vulgar. They don't approve. They wanted me to go into business, but I'm no good at math. I scraped by with biology. They wanted me to do a Masters, and I am. Just not in science."

"Congratulations," Cory said, sincerely.

"My parents aren't happy. They refused to help. I did it on my own. I auditioned, was accepted, and applied for a student loan. The committee said I have talent. I've never been so excited in my life."

"That's great news," Cory said. "There are some Hollywood stars out front you should meet."

Megan's eyes brightened, and she went to look for them.

Cory watched her go, thinking Megan had done the hard thing; she fought for the right to be who she was. She stood up to her family and rejected a legacy she couldn't live up to. For Cory, it had been easy. She wanted what she inherited. If she preferred to travel, live in a big city, or work at an Ivy League school, she would have been like Megan, owning something she wanted no part of. But Cory wanted what she had, and like those who came before her, would fight to keep it.

She went to the living room to check on Sophie. There were at least ten kids lounging on the floor, watching the first James Bond movie, and munching microwave popcorn. Sophie was looking important and explaining to a little girl, "Dis my birsday house." Like it or not, Sophie had a legacy too.

Cory didn't disturb her and returned to her guests. Nancy had come after all. She was outside at the entrance table, meeting Janie's friends. She looked animated and eager. Her hair was freshly cut, nicely styled, and she had a new dress, for the tag was hanging down her back. Cory pulled it off.

Lyle Steele had found his people and was excoriating the FDA. "We don't need to regulate them, we don't need to limit their power, we need to exterminate them."

Nancy, eyes gleaming, was hanging on his every word. Janie was applauding.

"People need to ask why we allow this agency to approve toxic drugs. Why we allow it to prevent us from taking harmless drugs," Lyle said.

But he was singing to the choir.

"The only thing we should allow the FDA to do is enforce honest labeling. Use at your own risk. Let people be free to take whatever they want. Why does the FDA get to decide? They should spend their resources tracking harm done by poisons they approve."

Janie grabbed Cory's elbow. "Where did you get him?"

Nancy grabbed Cory's other elbow. "Is he, like, one of the bachelors?"

"I'm not sure," Cory said. "There are some out back. Come on, I'll introduce you."

"Let's do it later." Nancy moved closer to Lyle.

"The FDA has had one success story," he said. "And that was fifty years ago. All we hear about is thalidomide. What about the anti-depressant drugs that make people commit suicide? Sleeping pills that cause sleep-driving. Or high blood pressure pills that cause strokes. Why don't we hear about this?"

Cory waited until he finished his diatribe to talk to him. She wanted to let him know his name came up at her deposition. Nancy wasn't going anywhere, so she got to listen too.

Lyle wasn't surprised. "FBI agents have visited me twice, wanting to 'chat.'" He made quote marks with his fingers. "I'm taking Perl programming, so obviously I'm a cyber threat. Somehow I manage to get my blog back online whenever someone takes it down, therefore I'm a software expert. Which I'm not. They're barking up the wrong tree, but they're too stupid to know it."

Nancy nudged Cory out of the way. "You look kind of stiff," she told Lyle. "Perhaps you'd like a shoulder rub?"

He would. They went to the study for privacy.

Rupert White arrived, and Cory went to the porch to greet her boss. She met his wife, Kamila, who handed Cory the yellowing front page of the defunct *Duane Telegram*. Under the headline: "Christmas Accident Claims Two" was a picture Cory had never seen before. She was sitting with her parents on the front steps of the house along with Goofy. The caption below the photo read: "Mary Elizabeth Rose and Mark Montclair with Cory (3) at the Rose House on Pecan Lane." Then, as now, the railings of the house were adorned with white globe lights. It was summertime, for Cory and her mother wore identical sundresses. Goofy sported a handkerchief.

"The house looks the same," Kamila said, staring through the front door. She looked elegant in a simple gray dress with pumps and a single strand of pearls. She had salt-and-pepper hair arranged in soft curls favored by beauty parlors. She patted Pluto's head. "So does the dog." He leaned against her. She turned her gaze to Cory. "You look like your mother. Different hair, same features." She rubbed Pluto again. "This place brings back many memories. In my younger days, I was here all the time."

If Cory's mother were alive, she would be in her late sixties, which was roughly Kamila's age. "You came to the parties?" Cory said.

"And to lunch, dinner, sleepovers. Your mother and I were good friends."

"My grandmother was okay with that?" Cory was marveling that her mother had a friend who stayed the night.

"Heavens, no. Your grandmother didn't like people. We were all strangers to her. One day, when I was in second grade, I came home with your mother, and your grandmother was waiting. It was winter, and she tossed a bucket of ice water on us from the upper balcony."

Cory was horrified. "My mother put up with that?"

"Oh no. She ran away. Came to my house. Your grandmother had to come to the bad side of town to collect her. Mary refused to leave until your grandmother promised to leave me alone. She agreed, and to her credit, kept her word, up until the car crash. Then she made it plain that she wished to be left alone." Kamila raised her eyes, gazing at the second floor, and lowered her voice. "Is she still alive?"

"She died eleven years ago."

"I didn't see an obituary. Believe me, we old-time residents look."

Which was probably why Anne Catherine hadn't wanted one. "She didn't want a notice or a funeral. She wanted to be cremated."

"I wish I had known. I wondered what happened to you. I assumed you'd moved away."

"Not even over my grandmother's dead body," Cory said, and then winced. That hadn't come out sounding right.

"Yes, yes," Kamila said. "The house, the most important thing. It was, though, even to your mother. When she married, I thought she would move, but she wouldn't consider it. Your father moved in. He loved the house too. It still has a nice feel. The ghosts must be happy." She looked at Cory intently, measuring her response.

"I hope so," Cory said. "I try my best."

Kamila nodded, as if with approval. Rupert concentrated on polishing his glasses.

"Your grandmother changed after your uncle died," Kamila said. "As did your mother. I'd always been involved in the civil rights movement, but your mother held the opinion that public sentiment couldn't change anything. Much like Rupert thinks today." Kamila paused and offered him another appeasing pat. "After your uncle died, your mother caught the anti-war fever. She called it 'reluctant activism.' I suspect it is the same with you and health care. Rupert told me about your daughter. Until we are touched personally, we accept what is. When that is no longer possible, we are forced to act. Your mother and I heard Dr. King speak in Atlanta. He said, 'You do not need the majority acting out to bring change, just five percent.' That is not too much."

Rupert laid his hand on Kamila's arm. "I'm sure Cory does not want to hear about this."

Cory did, but Kamila agreed with her husband. "We'll talk another time."

"Maybe you'll come for lunch," Cory said.

Kamila smiled. "I would like that very much."

The Whites moved on, and Cory ran upstairs and grabbed a handkerchief from Mathew's drawer. It looked like her mother was the exact opposite of her grandmother, and Cory was more like her mother than she ever knew. She was quickly learning that she liked people. Downstairs, she tied the bandana around Pluto's neck. He went to the front door and stood in the entrance, standing tall. He looked proud, like a greeter, as if it were his party.

Tyler's parents arrived, and the movie stars deigned to come in. The level of noise in the house rose. People crowded around the eminent guests, as if trying to soak up their good fortune. The stars took it in stride; it must have happened all the time and was nothing new.

The food was ready, and the dinner began. Ferrying dishes around, Cory began to worry they would run out of food. In the end, empty plates were easily replenished, and there was enough left over for another day. After dinner, Mathew played the piano, and the kids came out from the living room to listen. Sophie sat in his lap and for once didn't bang away. He played a few tunes, and then Janie took the floor.

The noisy buzz quieted down as she explained who she was. She described the Good Health and Access to Medical Treatment acts that were in the pipeline. Enough Nasty Drugs was trying to raise money to raise awareness of the bills. To this end, she'd planned a game. People had to make a donation to play. It was any amount. If you had a penny you could play.

She explained the rules. The game was like twenty questions, only adapted for diseases and their drugs. The guests would split into two groups. There were two sets of cards: one white and one blue. Written on the white cards were symptoms of a disease, while the blue cards held the side effects of the treatment for a disease. Of course, the cards had to be different colors so no one would confuse an ailment with a cure. The goal of the game was to match a disease with its treatment, or vice versa. For example, if the disease was cancer, the white card would have uncontrolled cell growth, weight loss, malaise, death. The matching blue card would be nausea, vomiting, diarrhea, weight loss, malaise, death—the side effects of chemotherapy. People had to select a card at random and get it pinned on their upper back where they couldn't see it. They had to ask questions to determine what was written on the card. You could only ask one question to one person. It had to be a yes or no question. Once you figured out what was on your card, you had to find the person that was your match.

You had to pay every time you made a guess. Janie would let you know if you had it right. If you guessed wrong, there were penalties. These were numbered one to five and randomly selected from a hat. Pull a one and you had to hold your own END fundraiser. Get a two and you had to make a donation to END. A three meant you had to call your representative and advocate an END policy. Get a four and you had to send your representative an email. Pull a five and you had to write a letter to the editor of your newspaper.

The grand winner—the first to guess correctly and find their match—won a prize. This was a trip to L.A. to preview Jonathan Pine's latest movie, compliments of the star. The game would continue until the last pair was matched. When the game was over, the matching partners would dance. Never mind if you were the same sex; for a price, you could switch partners or get out of dancing altogether.

Janie asked if there were any questions—and there were—but she waved these away. "Let's play. You'll figure it out."

The game began. Cory ended up in the line with diseases and Mathew in the line for treatment. She read his card: anti-inflammatory, high blood pressure, swelling, headache, numbness, seizures, stomach pain, vomiting, bloody stools. She could not see her own card, but from the look on his face, she'd never get it.

"Does it affect the heart?" she asked.

"No," he said. And that was the only question she could ask him.

The game not only broke the ice between strangers, it was amusing to see so many side effects of so-called medical cures. There were also unusual alternative treatments. The word written on Nick's blue card was "marriage," which made Cory wonder about the affliction. Another cure was apricots.

Thirty minutes into the game, a winner was declared. Charles, a member of END, correctly figured out from his keyword "asymptomatic" that he was the number two disease affecting Americans—hypertension. His match, the treatment for a disease that had no symptoms, caused increased urination, impotence, fainting, and possible shock.

The game continued. Cory collected three penalties. She had to make a donation, call her rep, and write another letter to the editor. Finally, she figured out she was Lyme disease, which was caused by the bacterium *Borrelia burgdorferi*. Evonia was the treatment—antibiotics and psychiatric therapy. That seemed a strange mix until Cory learned from Lyle that the disease was recurring—it disappeared, came back, disappeared, and came back. But insurance companies refused to accept this. They paid for the first treatment and considered the disease cured. If you still thought you were sick, well, then the sickness was in your head, and you better go see a psychiatrist. But sorry, that's not covered.

She learned from Janie that marriage was a wild card, and a match for five different cancers. After studying three-quarters of a million people with the ten top cancers, oncologists determined which factors helped survivability. It turned out that being married helped more than taking chemo. Apricots, it appeared, also cured cancer.

Mathew figured out he was the treatment for Crohn's disease, and Nancy was his match. She paid a hundred dollars to get out of dancing with him and to fix herself up with Lyle.

It was almost ten and nearing eclipse time when the game came to a close and the matched dance began. The dining room was packed. A Robin Wheeler song was playing, and loud music bounced off the walls. People were bumping into one another. Mathew ended up buying a dance with Sheryl, and Dana arranged to dance with Nick. Somehow, Evonia, who was supposed to be Cory's dance partner, ended up with Brian, and Cory was unfortunately paired with Tyler's mother.

The senator's wife was in her mid-fifties and a teetotaler who refused Cory's multiple offers to get her a Baja Luna or a Lune Rouge Sang. "I don't drink," Jill finally said when the song ended. "I know Tyler is helping you."

Cory looked into her knowing eyes and could not lie. Remembering Tyler's request, she said nothing of relevance. "What about punch? It's non-alcoholic."

"No, thank you. I'm guessing you're in trouble. I wanted to tell you, if you need to, you can always call on us. Blaze may be retired, but he still has contacts." Jill touched Cory's arm and affirmed her words with a nod. "You're doing the right thing," she said before slipping into the crowd. "What passes for health care in this country is abominable."

The iPod went quiet, and the tiny Layla stood up on a chair. "The eclipse is starting."

The gang moved into the backyard. Janie sat down on the piano bench to count the money. She called Cory over. The game had generated over twenty thousand dollars. It turned out the movie stars and the ex-senator had written generous checks. In addition, many guests signed up to hold their own parties and promised to contact elected officials and newspapers. "It's happening," Janie said. "Word will get out. We're going to stop the government from empowering the drug empire. We'll get Oxylace here."

Cory sat down beside her. "Do you think I'm in trouble?"

"With Wellspring?" Janie shrugged her shoulders. "What else can they do to you? They'd have to scrape the bottom of the barrel."

"They haven't taken me to court yet for calling Oxylace a cure."

"You have your paper. That should help."

"Tyler found out Drake drove a white Impala. He ran me off the road."

Janie folded a wad of bills and shoved them into a zippered bag. "That's hardly a surprise. Let Wellspring know you know. If they come after you, you've got dirt on them."

The strategy had worked with Drake. "What about you?"

"I'm careful. I know what they can do."

Mathew came in. "What's going on? You're missing the eclipse." Of course, he had an eclipse story. It seemed Christopher Columbus used his knowledge of one to gain influence over the natives of Jamaica when he was stranded there at the turn of the 16th century. The natives were tired of him and his men eating their food and taking their women, and had cut them off. The starving Christopher had a star map and an ephemeris that predicted the night of an eclipse. On that night, he told the natives if they weren't more helpful, he would take the moon. The eclipse began, the moon disappeared, and the natives begged him for mercy. They would do whatever he wanted if he would only give back the moon. "See, knowledge is power," Mathew said.

Cory didn't agree. "Not as long as we have stupid laws, no representation, and a corrupt court."

"Would you listen to her," Janie said. "She must have drunk the Kool-Aid."

Cory gazed up at the sky. The clouds had cleared, and the moon was up. A big, brilliant, round white ball hovered above the trees. The left edge was blackened, as if by a cover of cloud. Layla zoomed the telescope in on the moon. The shadow looked crimson, the color of blood. It grew slowly, ever covering the moon, as if a curtain was being drawn across its face. It took over an hour to go completely black. Cory stared up at it, thinking it was like her winter. A shadow had fallen upon her life, darkening her days. And then it lifted, like the night gaining light.

Sophie appeared. She came tearing across the grass with Penny in pursuit. Cory grabbed her and swept her up. "Where are you going so fast?"

"Go run." She pointed to the telescope. "What dat?"

"It brings things close that are far away. You want to see?"

Sophie looked through the eyepiece. "See what?"

"The moon. It's moving through the shadow of the earth."

"Down."

"Where are you going?"

"Go play." She took off, with Penny on her heels.

Mathew took Cory's hand. "She's having a ball," he said. "It's great to see her happy. That's what we're fighting for."

"I know," Cory said as Sophie disappeared into the house. Only it wasn't just Sophie she was fighting for.

Chapter Sixty-four

June 20th

On Midsummer's Day, Art and Hank flew to Houston, business class, for a one o'clock meeting with the honorable Judge Laszlo. The jet was up for sale, and they were forced to fly commercial. The CFO wanted them to fly cattle car, but there were some lows below which Art would not go. It was a stressful flight. Art's future rested on the hearing. The enemy wanted all Wellspring computer files. If the judge refused to issue a subpoena, it was game over for their opponent. If allowed, it was game over for him.

He was alone. Missy was long gone, and according to Hank, busy with lawyers of her own. She wanted promissory alimony for the time they'd spent together, which was something Art had never heard of before. He supposedly owed her a ring and a penthouse he'd never de-livered, and she wanted compensation. Well, if he lost, he couldn't pay her, and if he won, he'd fight her. In any case, she was gone. If all went well, there were hundreds out there who'd vie to replace her. If he lost . . . well, he couldn't think about that now.

It all came down to the judge. Luckily, he was sympathetic to busi-ness. He had an eye on a higher court and knew what won elections and appointments. At the moment, Art's bank account didn't support a large donation, and apparently legal rules prohibited it, but in earlier days Laszlo had benefited mightily from Wellspring's largesse. Recent rulings in their favor told Art that Laszlo hadn't forgotten.

They landed in Houston at high noon in the heat of the day. Waiting for a taxi was like standing in a sauna, and Art was soaked with sweat within seconds. Usually when he flew, a limo was waiting by the plane, and here he was at the end of a long line waiting for a taxi. He felt like a pauper in a bread line.

They got to the courthouse and encountered protesters. Climbing the steps, fighting the crowd, Art wondered what the idle unemployed were bitching about now. He saw Access to Medical Treatment Act signs, though the bill never even made it to a vote. In election season, it didn't stand a chance.

In the meantime, the Good Health Act was gaining traction. The lobby was firmly behind it, and elected officials were quickly jumping on board. It was long past time to regulate alternative treatments, to outlaw snake oil, to protect the people. Once supplements were relabeled as drugs, money would be made, and the drug companies were chomping at the bit. Congressman Harris was the bill's biggest supporter, and once more, money was flowing his way. This, despite his own bout with malignant melanoma and his overseas trip to Munich to obtain treatment that he had banned here. He was such a hypocrite. Art wanted him out. When the threat of the class action suit was over, he would leak the story to the press.

Art saw his own photo doctored to look like Hitler and realized the protest was directed against him. Halfway up the steps and out of breath, his hammering heart jumped wildly as he read more signs: *Corporate Health Kills, Valurex is Death,* and *Wellspring Must Go.* The masses had no clue how much he sacrificed for them.

He felt faint and was grateful for Hank's steady hand that cleared the crowd. Art reached the building, fumbling to find his ID. The door swung open. Art went inside and passed through security. Struck with a blast of arctic air, he wondered if he was getting sick. His heart wasn't up to this. His back was cramping, and he had trouble swallowing. Noting his distress, Hank pressed a handkerchief into his hand. Art mopped his forehead and his scalp. He had lost so much hair, he was shaving his head.

He stuck the handkerchief in his pocket and bid Hank good-bye. It was a closed hearing. Hank would have to wait in the lobby. The public had wanted to come, but Art's lawyers successfully fought to keep them out. Art took that as another good sign.

The informal meeting was held in the judge's conference room, and Claude Smite was waiting. The enemy wanted him banned, but the judge said no; the FDA agent could attend. Art was limited to only two of his fifty lawyers, and Robert Burns from the New York office was lead council. Burns had all but moved down to Houston and was guiding the local team. He was assisted today by Helen Shapiro, a sexy fox from the Texas firm. Art had specifically requested her. She did a good job on Montclair's deposition. It was clear the bitch was lying and guilty as hell. Shapiro wanted to go after her, and Art had to tell her to stand down. Mont-fucking-clair knew too much. She'd sent a threatening message to his private email account: *Drake hidden but not lost. Impala sold but not gone. Incriminating evidence remains. Aloha.* Obviously, she was the one who hacked into his server. Unfortunately, he could do nothing about it, not without calling attention to his own misdeeds. All he could do was fortify his firewall, which he had done. He was leaving her for the FDA.

But the FDA was in hot water too. An investigative committee, with the power to pass judgment on his drug, was reviewing the Valurex trials. The committee was awaiting the decision of the judge. If Valurex was banned, it was the end. Their three other drugs complemented the DNA synthesis inhibitor. Lose Valurex and he'd lose everything. Likely go bankrupt. It was too heartbreaking to imagine.

Art shook hands with his team. He ignored his opponents while studying them covertly. Montclair's diabolical boyfriend was here. Mathew Lang, a green lawyer fresh out of law school had come with Declan Craft, Barrow and Craft's heavy-hitter. Claude would eat them for lunch.

Everyone took their seats. There was a long table with the four lawyers positioned in the middle. Claude and Art were relegated to one side, and he took the end chair. He sunk down beside Claude, reassured by his presence. The man carried the weight of the federal government on his shoulders. Claude leaned toward him and whispered behind a hand, "The committee assessed your data. There's nothing to fear. It passes muster. This is a witch hunt. The case should be tossed."

That brought more comfort than words could say. Art hated to admit it, but he was scared. He felt like the kid on the playground watching the bully advance. Or, a sick man waiting to learn if the disease was terminal or benign. "What happened with the attorney general?" he asked. "Did you meet with him?"

Claude looked pained. "I did. Unfortunately, there are no grounds for arrest. The AG said Montclair wasn't advocating using the drug, she was advocating it be tested. Apparently, there's a difference. I'll keep looking, but—" He shrugged his shoulders apologetically.

A back door opened, and the judge strode in. Everyone stood. Laszlo waved them down. He wore jeans, a polo shirt, cowboy boots, and looked as relaxed as he could be. He sat in the lone chair across the table. He was Art's age, and, like him, looked like he'd been around the block.

The hearing commenced, the lawyers went at it, and the judge let them argue without interruption. At one point the judge peered at Art and looked quickly away. Art tried to read the meaning in his gaze. The judge looked sympathetic. Was the ruling about to go against him, or did the judge understand Art's unenviable plight? After all he had done to advance chemotherapy, all the risk he had taken, and the effort he had made, only to end up here.

Finally the judge stopped the babble. "The plaintiffs would like to subpoena the Wellspring data. Does the defense object?"

Of course it would fucking object. Both Robert Burns and Helen Shapiro were on their feet. "The files are proprietary," Helen said. "The FDA has already relinquished the relevant data."

Claude stood up and introduced himself. "An independent panel has reviewed the submitted records. The panel is of the opinion there is no evidence of wrongdoing. No justification for a lawsuit."

Mathew Lang shot up. He wore a cheap brown suit that looked too big for him. "That is the reason for the subpoena. We need to verify this claim. No children were included in the Valurex trials, yet we spoke with two pediatric oncologists who were involved with the trial. Why weren't their patients included?"

Burns objected. "Your Honor, some patients died during the trial, others moved, and some dropped out. It's standard practice to exclude these from the final tally."

The judge looked to the expert, and Claude concurred that this was so.

The enemy disagreed with the long-standing protocol. "This is preferential exclusion," Lang declared. "Wellspring willfully and deliberately submitted data to make their drug look better than it was. They submitted no data from children at all."

Burns shook his head and sighed audibly. "Children don't have to be tested. It is up to the FDA to decide who uses a drug. It is not the purview of the company."

Again, Claude agreed. "Your Honor, cancer is a complex and multifaceted disease. It is notoriously difficult to treat and can never be considered cured. At this time, the Wellspring cocktail is the best available antidote for the disease."

The enemy objected stridently. "That's simply not true. We will show in court there is a drug far superior to the cocktail, and that this drug was been willfully and deliberately withheld from the American public by the machinations of the FDA."

Burns raised his hands, beseeching the judge. "Is the FDA on trial now too?"

Disturbingly, the judge ignored him. "What is this drug?"

The enemy handed a folder to the judge and another to Helen. "For the record, this is a scientific paper that will be published next month in the *German Journal of Cancer Research*. The article compares the Wellspring cocktail with a drug called Oxylace." Mathew Lang turned around and looked Art in the eye.

Goddamn it! Art's chest squeezed tight. His heart felt like it was about to explode. The Canadians turning down the paper had been no deterrent.

Claude was already on his feet, objecting. "The FDA looked at the drug in the fifties and concluded it was worthless. This is a German journal. It's common knowledge that American medicine is exceptional."

"Hardly," Lang declared. "But the paper was written by an American."

"Doing junk science," Claude said. "In this country, only double-blind, placebo-controlled studies are acceptable in scientific journals. Let us never forget it was Europe who gave us thalidomide."

Burns was up too. "Motion to exclude. This paper is extraneous. At issue is whether or not Wellspring willfully marketed a harmful drug. All labels are determined by the FDA and not the industry. This paper has no relevance."

The judge looked to the expert. "It's true," Claude said. "We examine the data and determine how a drug can be used. It is not up to the drug company."

"Motion sustained," said the judge.

Poof! With two words, the article Mont-fucking-clair fought so hard to publish was banished from court. The paper would not be admissible in trial! She could run all the statistics she liked. No one of consequence would see it.

Burns went on. "Furthermore, the fact remains, industry files are proprietary. There is precedent."

Art calmed down, paying rapt attention. Here was the argument that would determine whether or not he had to release his files.

"A patent negates proprietary material since it is already protected by law," Lang said. "We would like access to the raw data. See for ourselves what cases Wellspring decided to exclude."

"They're fishing," Burns cried. "There's no proof of wrongdoing. The doctors in the clinical trials have been subpoenaed. There's no cover-up. No smoking gun."

Lang objected. "There's no valid reason the files are confidential. Unless they have something to hide."

The judge stroked his chin. Art was on the edge of his seat. The whole ruling came down to this. His heart was hammering. He heard the beat in his ear like a death knell. The judge banged his gavel. His next words shaped Art's future.

"Subpoena denied."

The lawyers continued haggling, but Art heard no more. He gasped, his heart stopped seizing, blood began to flow, and he could swallow once more. His cramping back relaxed. He wanted to clap his hands, jump up, and dance a jig. His sentence was commuted. The bully was defeated. He would live. He wanted to yell in jubilation. He had to stop himself from punching the air in triumph.

Lang looked small and petty as he argued minor points. Art was laughing silently. He was still facing the class action suit, but his files were safe. As good as shredded. The enemy had no case. They couldn't prove anything against him. He would win, Montclair would lose. It sent a strong message to greedy lawyers and thankless plaintiffs. Screw you. They wouldn't take a cent of his money.

The hearing was over. Everyone stood as the judge left. The enemy grabbed their briefcases and skulked away. Art hugged Claude and the two men thumped backs. He shook Burns's hand heartily and hugged

Helen Shapiro provocatively. Everyone would return to New York and plan the next phase. Art smiled at Helen. He could not wait.

He knew as soon as word got out that stock price would soar. Right now it was trading under twenty dollars a share and that would soon change. Art pulled out his phone and sent Hank a text: *Get taxi.* It was code for *buy.* Call the broker immediately, and start the rally. With luck, stock price would rebound to what it was in April—almost ninety dollars a share. He would buy his stock on the cheap. In retrospect, the lawsuit could turn out to be a financial boon.

He bid good-bye to Claude, who thought it best they leave separately. Cameras were rolling, and Claude preferred to keep a respectful distance from the industry that was under his oversight. It was prudent to avoid the appearance of conflict of interest, etcetera, etcetera. Though Art publicly complained bitterly about the FDA and the hoops they threw at him, privately, he needed them. They were protection; the fall guy. They took the heat if something went wrong. The government could never be sued.

Nearly weeping with joy, Art went to the lobby and found Hank. In an untypical show of emotion, The Fixer squeezed Art in a death lock. "You did it."

Yes, Art was back in business. Take that, Montclair, you stupid, slanderous, hacking whore. Winning was the best revenge. He would reopen the corporate office and take back his jet. Fuck Helen Shapiro to kingdom come. Thank God for a functioning legal system.

Art left the building. As he pushed his way through the pack, jeers from the horde rose in intensity. He did his best to ignore the cameras and the taunts: *Get government off drugs; Fire the FDA; Regulate drug companies, not people.* He reached the steps. Hank was down on the curb, flagging a cab. The crowd roared. Art turned and raised two fingers, flashing the universal sign of victory. The hateful losers rushed him. He scampered down the stairs. Hank flung open the taxi door. Art paused before getting in. He faced the feckless mob and thrust his middle finger at the sky.

The End